SHADOW AND ICE

GENA SHOWALTER

SHADOW AND ICE

HQN™

ISBN-13: 978-1-335-08094-3

Shadow and Ice

Printed in U.S.A.

CONTENTS

SHADOW AND ICE   7

LIST OF COMBATANTS   433

KILL TALLY (contains spoilers)   441

To Jill Monroe, brainstorming champion of the world!
Thank you for all the amazing things you do.
But mostly, thank you for being the best friend a girl could have.

SHADOW AND ICE

1026 AA (After Alliance)

To: Members of the All War Alliance

Welcome to the 103rd All War.

We are pleased to announce a new realm has been discovered, known by its citizens as Terra, Midgard or Earth. The next battle is set to begin.

You don't want to miss this one!

You'll find: Inhabited and uninhabited territories teeming with resources. A climate and terrain for every preference. Massive bodies of water—both salt and fresh. Mountains. Flatlands. Swamps. Forests. Ice lands and deserts. Whether you prefer animal or plant, there's an unending supply of food.

This world is a prize among prizes, but only one among you will earn the right to rule it.

In one week, a fight to the death will commence, winner takes Terra.

Currently, there are ~~thirty-eight~~ thirty-nine battle-ready realms recognized in our alliance. A single representative from each location must portal to Terra. (Date and coordinates enclosed, Addendum A.) Choose wisely, for your warrior must go head-to-head with every other.

Your combatant is allowed to bring one item from home. ONLY ONE. No exceptions.

*Supernatural abilities inherent to genetics/race/breed do not count as a weapon.

*A "matching pair" is acceptable.

The rules are simple:

(1) Once they enter Terra, the combatants may not exit the realm until the war ends.

*Time isn't a factor.

(2) A monthly Assembly of Combatants is mandatory. (Addendum B.)

(3) Warriors may choose to withdraw by carving the Mark of Disgrace on their forehead and contacting the assigned Enforcer for transport home.

*Kings and queens of each participating realm are responsible for punishing the disgraced.

*The disgraced cannot reenter the war, or participate in any other battle.

(4) After making a kill, your combatant will be granted the power needed to activate and use the victim's chosen weapon.

*A kill is rendered through decapitation, removal of the heart, and/or burning the body to ash.

(5) You may not send anyone or anything else to Terra. However, you may communicate with your combatant to (a) learn the status of the war and (b) offer instruction.

Those who violate these rules will be hunted, captured and punished by Enforcers.

May the best realm win.

Happy warring!
High Council of the All War Alliance.

PROLOGUE

AD 701, human timeline
103rd All War, Month 5
Terra

Twenty-five combatants stood between Knox of Iviland and victory.

He waited on a mountain plateau, a dagger clutched in each hand. Shadows bathed him, frigid wind battering his bare chest. One of his myriad trainers once told him he was as cold and treacherous as the icy world now surrounding him.

The trainer wasn't wrong.

Over the centuries, other Iviland soldiers had called Knox sadistic, barbaric and pitiless. They weren't wrong, either. Or alive. They had died painfully, by his hand. *As practice.*

Live a violent life, suffer a violent end. Sow seeds of suffering, reap a harvest of the same. One day, Knox would meet the same end as his victims, could not avoid his dreaded fate.

He might meet his end *tonight*—assembly night.

In eleven minutes, forty-three seconds, green and purple lights would set the night sky ablaze, and the next Assembly of Combatants would begin. A time mockingly dubbed "check-in."

You check in, and help others check out.

Acid coated the inside of his chest, scalding him, but not by word or deed did he reveal his discomfort. With combatants, perception was vital. Reveal a weakness, become the day's target.

An assembly lasted an hour, occurred once a month, and helped hurry the war along. Attendance was mandatory, forcing every participant in the Terran All War to visit this icy tundra, even the cowards and hiders.

Stroll in one second late, and you would be disqualified. A fate worse than death. You were hunted by an Enforcer who had the means to track you and disable any special abilities—your own, and those of your weapon. All because of a mystical tattoo.

Before the war, every combatant was permanently marked. The ink permitted the Enforcer to link with you anywhere, anytime. Supposedly this allowed the High Council to facilitate a fair war. Knox had his doubts, and suspected the ink did so much more. Considering he bore the mark on his left shoulder—a tree inside a circle—there was nothing he could do about it. He was as vulnerable as everyone else.

Removing the tattoo wouldn't help. The ink got in your blood. Running from the Enforcer wouldn't help, either. When he caught you—and he always caught you—he would chop off your limbs, and nail what remained of your body to a wall of ice that was within sight of the assembly. While you were still alive.

You were to serve as a cautionary tale.

If your limbs regenerated, the Enforcer removed them again. However many times were necessary. You were executed only after a winner was declared.

Sometimes combatants set traps before an assembly to encourage others' tardiness without actually breaking the rules. The very reason Knox had yet to move from this spot high on a cliff, hidden by boulders and trees. Last month, Zion of Tavery managed to trap him in an ice pit; by some miracle Knox had climbed out and crossed the threshold with eight seconds to spare.

Most of his opponents congregated in a clearing below him, imprisoned by walls of energy. However, the warriors themselves remained visible. They were loaded down with weapons, and trash-talking.

"Hope you enjoyed your last day on Terra."

"Your severed head will look amazing on my mantel. Note to self. Get a mantel."

"I need a new workout song—your screams should do the trick."

The Terran All War had kicked off five months ago, and hostilities had blazed hotter every day since. The combatants had only one thing in common—their hatred for Knox, Zion and Bane of Adwaeweth.

Understandable. Knox was ruthless beyond compare, a four-time champion who'd already eliminated three men. Both Zion and Bane had taken out three, as well. A handful of others had made a single kill.

How many warriors will attack me when the assembly ends?

Last month, he'd had to fend off twelve at once, nearly losing an arm in the process. He dreaded assembly day...and greatly anticipated it.

For one hour, the Enforcer would telepathically communicate with the High Council, letting them know who lived and who had died, and bloodshed would be prohibited. Powers and weapons with any kind of supernatural capability were deactivated. Knox wouldn't have to look over his shoulder, expecting an ambush. He could scheme, even nap, or silently rage about High Council members who were luxuriating in opulent homes while honorable men and women were forced to commit terrible acts in order to win new territories for a king or queen just as despicable as the High Council members.

Hate the High Council. They governed those kings and queens, while supposedly remaining unbiased about each All War's outcome. Knox suspected they'd cheated a time or twenty, but voicing such an accusation would get him killed sooner rather than later. He'd seen it happen time and time again, good soldiers taken out under mysterious conditions after daring to speak the truth.

A worry for another day. *Survive now, thrive later.*

When the assembly ended, the ban on fighting would lift. Between one blink and the next, everyone's powers would reactivate, and warriors would spring into action. There would be casualties.

Eight minutes, twenty-eight seconds until check-in.

Knox scanned the battlefield, not yet catching sight of his prey. He rolled his head left, right, popping bones and stretching his muscles, preparing. *I won't hesitate. I'll do what's needed, when needed.*

His gaze snagged on the Enforcer who'd been assigned to Terra. He was known as Seven. Every Enforcer had an identification number rather than a name. One through ten. The higher the number, the more vicious the individual. There were hundreds of thousands of men and women who bore each number.

Seven wore a hooded black robe, his face obscured by darkness. Like a grim reaper of legend, he carried a scythe.

Knox sympathized with the death dealers, knew they were slaves, just like him, their pasts as fraught with violence as his, but he'd never met one willing to go against orders, even for the safety of another living being. They were brainwashed as children, and grew up to serve as the arm of the High Council, a seemingly undefeatable force that ensured every realm obeyed every edict, no matter how big or small.

Some Enforcers possessed special powers, some didn't. You could win against one, even twenty, but overcoming the force as a whole was impossible. There were simply too many, unshakably loyal to each other and their leaders, and they couldn't be reasoned with or swayed from a chosen task.

Six minutes, fourteen seconds.

Behind Knox, ice crunched. His muscles knotted, his body preparing to strike. Someone approached.

He used his ability to control shadows, forcing darkness to rise from the ground and surround him in thick waves, until he blended into the landscape. This particular skill had saved him over and over again.

He could even make the shadows spin, creating a vortex that flung opponents hundreds of yards away.

He was on alert... Waiting, ready...

Finally, Shiloh of Asnanthaleigh appeared.

{*No malice or threat detected.*}

During Knox's second All War, he'd developed an *eyaer,* or hard-core battle instinct with one purpose, and one purpose only: to ensure he lived. To the *eyaer,* he didn't even have to live well.

Despite the instinct's reassurance, Knox trusted no one, ever, and kept his guard up.

Shiloh stopped at Knox's side, radiating wariness as he studied the clearing.

Knox maintained a mental file about every combatant and constantly added details, tallied who had killed whom, who possessed what weapons and supernatural abilities, preferred climates, lovers, potential lovers, and who had formed alliances or vowed vengeance.

Different facts about the six-foot-eleven male raced through his mind. *Comes from a heavily forested realm. Good with swords and daggers. Avoids battle if innocents are nearby. Sensitive to the plight of others.*

For his home-weapon, the Asnanthaleighling selected special eye lenses that allowed him to see through *anything,* even Knox's shadows.

I want. I take.

Patience.

"Hello, my friend." Though Shiloh spoke a language Knox had never learned, the device surgically attached to the inside of his ear translated each word. Thanks to technological advancements gained every time a new realm was discovered, every combatant had a similar device, and it updated automatically.

"I'm not your friend," Knox replied. "If you trust me, even for a moment, you'll regret it." That wasn't a threat, but a fact.

Before the war, their kings had come to an agreement— Knox and Shiloh would work together to reach the final two. An unprecedented development. Most other-realmers despised Ivilandians, often referring to them as "gutter rats." The insult wasn't unearned. To evade a deadly topside environment, the citizens had flocked underground, where they'd lived ever since. They were led by Ansel, the king of gutter rats. He kept his word only when it suited him.

Just before Knox had left for Terra, Ansel had told him, *Slay Shiloh as soon as you feel it's necessary.*

When the time came, Knox *would* strike, and he would strike hard, compelled by a force greater than himself.

But here was the kicker. No matter Ansel's order, Knox would do *anything* to advance his personal agenda.

Some men had moral lines they wouldn't cross. Knox found the concept of moral lines confusing. Not do everything possible to win? Foolish.

"Yesterday, I beheaded Ammarie," Shiloh said, continuing on, ignoring Knox's warning. "She attacked me. I merely defended myself but…"

Knox updated his tally. Twenty-four combatants stood between him and victory. "Guilt is pointless. You survived." Shiloh had also gained custody of a mystical bow and arrow known as The Bloodthirsty. That arrow chased its victims like a heat-seeking missile, increasing in speed and ferocity with every kill it made.

I want. I take.

Soon…

Shiloh's shoulders slumped. "She had a daughter."

Knox's hands curled into fists. *Ignore the heartache.* "Learning about her family was your second mistake. You cannot allow another warrior's loved ones to mean more than yours." Bitterness laced his tone, icing every word.

"If that was my second mistake, what was my first?" Shiloh asked.

"Having loved ones at all. Family and friends are one of two things. Anchors that weigh you down with worry, distracting you, or they are leverage that others can use against you."

Knox had firsthand knowledge of the latter. Once, *he'd* had a daughter.

Oh, yes. Once.

Blessed and cursed.

A sharp pang of sorrow and grief tore through him, leaving a trail of destruction in its wake. One day, Knox would avenge her and slay the king of Iviland—and he would make it hurt. Ansel was the one who'd forced him to fight. The one who'd allowed his baby girl to die while he performed his "duty."

Now, Ansel used freedom to motivate Knox. *Win five All Wars in my name, and I'll free you from your slave bands.*

Those bands ringed his neck, wrists, and ankles. Upon each vertebra of his spine, he bore an X. But whether rings or Xs, each mark had been made with mystical ink similar to what the High Council used to create the tree of life. This particular ink compelled Knox to do everything Ansel demanded, zero exceptions.

Knox had no choice but to continue on, as if the king had spoken true. What else could he do?

If Ansel had lied… He bit his tongue until he tasted blood. If Knox won a fifth war—*this* war—and wasn't freed…

A sharper pang tore through him, cutting so deep he doubted he would ever recover. *I'll just have to find another way to gain my freedom.*

The moment he succeeded, Ansel would die. Badly. People would hear stories for centuries to come and marvel at Knox's cruelty.

He almost smiled, anticipation dancing with fury.

Focus. Emotion of any kind would only distract him; distraction would get him killed.

"How can you be so callous about the death of another?" Shiloh asked.

"Because I want to live, and mind-set is everything. While you will hesitate to end a friend, you will eagerly take out an enemy. These people are our enemies."

Wearier by the second, Shiloh scrubbed a hand down his face. "This is my first All War. I knew it would be tough, but I am my home's strongest competitor, and I believed I could do… anything. I was wrong."

"You sound as if you're eager to die. Good news. I'm happy to help."

"I'm sure you are, but I don't want to die. I don't want to kill, either."

"Ah, I see. You'd rather make your people suffer."

Shiloh glowered.

For the "privilege" of participating in an All War, a realm's sovereign had to give the High Council thousands of children. The exact number depended on a combatant's order of elimination. The faster you were eliminated, the more your realm had to pay. But in order to forfeit a war entirely, sovereigns had to hand over even more children.

From infancy to the age of eighteen, boy or girl, children were chattel, commodities raised to be Enforcers.

Only the winning realm was exempt.

"My people already suffer," Shiloh said. "Our realm is over-crowded."

Iviland was overcrowded as well, more and more immortals born or created every day. New realms were desperately needed.

In the beginning, whenever a new one was discovered, multiple armies invaded at once. Battles raged, the trespassers hoping to seize control. Violence spread far and wide, ultimately destroying *everything*, leaving the lands uninhabitable.

Under the guise of saving future domains, ruling factions created the High Council and All War—an ongoing battle between a single representative from each otherworld, the new realm acting as the arena.

In the past few months, the people of Terra had begun fighting back and setting traps. Not a first, but definitely a problem on days like today. The citizens weren't bound by assembly rules. But then, they had no supernatural abilities and were no match for immortals.

Knox had seen no sign of a human army today. Maybe they'd fled in fear? To them, combatants were gods.

Knox, they'd nicknamed Loki, the "evil trickster." A moniker he bore with pride.

"When I killed a woman I respected, a part of my soul died," Shiloh said, pulling him from his thoughts. "Why can't the realms reach terms without bloodshed?"

"Greed." Why else?

Movement at the side of a mountain. Knox slid his gaze across the ice—at last. Zion. A man of six and a half feet, like Knox, with dark hair, wide shoulders and a body honed on the most savage battlefields with no hint of softness. Also like Knox.

But unlike Knox, he refused to use the weapons he won. Reasons unknown. The choice angered Knox, even though it aided his cause. Such a waste.

He tightened his grip on his most prized possessions—the

daggers he'd taken from his first victim. The blades were serrated, hooked at the tip, and had brass knuckle hilts. With a single blow, he could slice, dice and pulverize.

Zion reached the check-in point and spread his arms, all *Here I am, come and get me.* Embedded in his arms were jewels, each one set in specific patterns, as bold as the man himself. On his hands, a pair of spiked metal gloves able to punch through *anything.*

I want. I take.

Locked on tonight's target.

Anticipation resurged and redoubled, burning inside Knox, and growing hotter by the second. Zion was a warrior he would gladly slay.

"Come." Knox jumped from his perch, falling down, down, landing a few yards away from the check-in point. Though the impact jarred him, he walked forward without a hitch in his step, boots crunching in the snow.

Shiloh jumped, as well, and hurried to catch up.

As they passed the invisible wall that sealed them inside the clearing, Knox experienced a familiar and abhorrent vibration from the top of his head to the soles of his feet. His ability to control shadows had just been neutralized.

"So nice of you to join us," Bane said, his tone as smug and condescending as ever.

Like most Adwaewethians, he had pale hair, golden eyes— and a beast trapped within. When the creature took control of his body, his appearance changed. He became a monster, hideous beyond compare, *strong* beyond compare, and developed an appetite for blood. No one and nothing was safe.

Bane's greatest vulnerability was light. Adwaeweth was a dark realm, shrouded in gloom and without a sun. The very reason he'd brought a pair of goggles as his weapon of choice. Like Shiloh's lenses, those goggles allowed him to see *everything.*

Knox tipped an invisible hat. "Glad to see you left your balls at home."

As Bane cupped the balls in question and made a lewd expression, a chorus of insults erupted from the others.

"May you die bloody today, Knox."

"I won't just remove your heart. I'll eat it."

"Hope you're ready for some internal body bling, murk."

"Murk" was another derogatory term used for Ivilandians, but only those like Knox, who commanded shadows. He'd been called worse, but insults of any kind tended to burn like acid in his ears.

Ignore.

"Where are Major and Cannon?" Emberelle of Loandria waved a deceptively delicate hand to indicate the group, the rings on her fingers glittering in the moonlight. With hair like snowflakes, skin a pale shade of blue, eyes the same green and purple as the glowing skylights, and delicately pointed ears, she looked as fragile as glass. A deception. Of the females, she was the deadliest.

"I took out Major," Ronan of Soloria replied, not exactly proud, but not exactly remorseful, either.

Knox added a notation to his mental file. Now, twenty-three combatants stood between him and victory.

"What of Cannon?" Ronan asked. "Is he dead?"

Silence reigned, no one taking credit for a kill.

A clock continued to count down in Knox's head. Thirty-two seconds until Cannon of Dellize missed today's check-in.

Thirty...twenty...ten...five...

Still no sign of the male. Three...two...

The ground shook. The Assembly of Combatants had just begun.

Only twenty-two warriors stand in my way.

From his position outside the circle, Seven slammed the end of his scythe into the ice. The ground shook harder, shafts of light spraying from the curved blade to shower over the combatants.

"Would anyone like to volunteer for a merciful death?" Zion

asked conversationally. He couldn't bring himself to fight the fairer sex, and constantly looked for ways to prevent an all-out battle. "My offer will expire when the meeting ends."

Prickles erupted on the back of Knox's neck. He scanned... Celeste of Occisor gave him a come-hither smile.

He scowled. *Trying to curry favor?* Impossible!

Despite the fact that she'd won an All War, he'd never considered her a threat. He'd seen no evidence of combat skill, only a knack for seduction. To his knowledge, three males had succumbed to her allure, and each had possessed a supernatural ability the female had exploited for her own gain. Of the three, only one still lived—Ranger of Jetha.

Zion and Bane had killed the others, and Knox had often wondered if Celeste had helped.

Another warrior—Gunnar of Trodaire—glared daggers at him and inched closer to Celeste's side. A fourth conquest? Who had time for such drama?

Emberelle shifted into Knox's line of sight to flash her pearly whites in a parody of a smile. "You trolling for a date, *murk*? Because my sword is interested in getting to know your insides. Care to arrange an intro?"

Teeth, grinding.

Darkness slithered across the ice, catching his notice. He'd left shadows stationed throughout the mountains to act as scouts. This one entered the clearing and ghosted through him, leaving an image branded in his mind. He stiffened. Hundreds of humans had crossed the northern border. They were running, running, closer and closer, their swords raised.

"Vikings," he shouted. A word meaning "native dwellers" in the All language.

The other combatants quieted, a stampede of footsteps echoing through the mountains. War cries erupted.

"They've come to avenge their fallen," Bane said, practically foaming at the mouth with eagerness.

"End the assembly," Zion commanded Seven. "If the energy wall comes down, our powers will be activated, body and weapon. If not, the mortals will have an advantage."

Wind blew back the Enforcer's hood, just an inch, but enough. Knox caught sight of a flawless face *seething* with hatred. For combatants?

Seven remained silent, sparks still shooting from his scythe. The wall of energy endured.

"We must work together, then." Guess he had a temporary alliance, after all. Knox squared his shoulders. "Form four lines of five, each one facing a different direction."

"So a square?" Emberelle asked, her tone suggesting he was an idiot.

"Do it," he snapped. "As close to the Enforcer as possible."

Warriors raced into position, armaments at the ready. Knox stood between Zion and Bane and scrutinized the approaching enemy. Mostly males who topped out at five-nine or -ten. All had mud smeared on their faces, fury in their eyes, and fur draped over bodies built for combat. Some wore helmets made of iron.

Knox couldn't help but respect the army. These soldiers defended their homeland and protected their people. But they threatened the All War, therefore they couldn't be spared.

"Twenty seconds," he shouted.

"Females, move to the center of our—"

The females in question interrupted Zion with threats to remove his testicles.

"If you want to know how I'm going to kill you, Knox," Bane said with a cold smile, "watch me kill the vikings."

"How adorable," he replied, his tone dry. "You think you're going to survive the night." Addressing everyone, he counted down. "Five seconds until impact. Four. Three. Two." He braced—

Vikings breached the circle.

Knox ducked, avoiding a sword swipe to the throat, then spun and straightened—and punched a dagger into the offender's side. His daggers had no special powers and worked the same as always.

When the weapon exited the man's body, pieces of liver dangled from the hook. A pained grunt blended with a macabre chorus of groans, wails and curses.

He spun once again, stabbing two more mortals. As warm blood sprayed over him, he lost track of everything but battle. Adrenaline revved him up, taking his heart for an impromptu joyride, the world around him seemed to slow to a crawl. He stabbed, head-butted, elbowed and kicked, bodies quickly piling up around his feet. More blood sprayed. More internal organs shredded as they met his daggers.

Any viking who dared approach Seven immediately fell unconscious without ever making contact. Neat trick.

Laughing, Bane picked up a discarded sword and cut through two men with a single swing.

With one metal-gloved hand, Zion lifted a viking by the throat. With the other, he punched, his fist coming out the male's other side.

Another viking sneaked up behind the Taverian, a mere blink away from landing a blow. Lunging, swiping out, Knox hacked through his wrist, the sword and hand plopping to the ground.

"I won't thank you," Zion told him while cutting through an opponent's neck.

"I wouldn't accept, anyway," Knox replied. Jab, jab. He ended another challenger with a double-tap to the heart.

No match for me, even when I'm unable to summon shadows.

One shout drowned out all the others, causing vikings to rush from the circle to form a wider ring around the combatants. Then a male splattered with blood stalked forward. He stopped just short of the invisible walls. He was the tallest of his brethren and the only one wearing a horned helmet. Scars littered one side of his face, and a thick black beard covered his jaw. He'd paired a fur-lined tunic with sheepskin pants, neither of which protected vital organs.

He held the Rod of Clima, Cannon's weapon.

Knox tensed. If the viking had killed Cannon after check-in, he had entered the All War, gained immortality and the ability to activate the rod *without* being placed on Seven's kill list. And since he wasn't within the check-in circle, the rod remained active.

Timing was everything in an All War.

The sea of vikings split down the middle, allowing two males to drag a headless, bleeding body closer. A fresh kill. They dropped their cargo, and someone else threw the head, pitching inside the circle. Cannon's lifeless eyes stared at nothing, his features frozen in an expression of horror.

Curses and threats spewed from the combatants, some even throwing themselves against the invisible wall, only to bounce back.

"You invaded our land and killed our men because you did not fear us." The one with the horned helmet raised his chin, pride and strength in his bearing. "I am Erik the Widow Maker, and I will *teach* you to fear us."

Erik of Terra. A new name to add to Knox's list of combatants. *Twenty-three warriors stand in my way.*

The leader lifted the rod high in the air, then slammed the end into the ice. The ground juddered so violently, hunks of snow tumbled from the mountaintops. In seconds, an arctic blizzard blew in, howling wind seeming to bristle with thousands of nails and glass shards.

Next, a hill of ice grew beneath Knox's feet—then *swallowed* his feet. He kicked…*tried* to kick, but couldn't. Wasn't long before his boots were fully concealed.

Panic stole his breath as the ice spread up, up, winding around his calves, slithering past his knees, and there was no stopping it. Ice spread up *every* combatant's legs, even the Enforcer's.

Knox fought harder, fought with all his might. His torso— covered. His shoulders…neck. Shock set in. Defeated? By a much weaker Terran? No!

Grunts and groans filled his ears, the other combatants fighting the horrifying entombment just as fervently.

When the ice reached his chin, he lost the ability to move.

This is a minor setback, nothing more. I will overcome, and I will repay. Then the ice grew over his face, entombing him, leaving him aware but powerless.

CHAPTER ONE

Present Day
Somewhere in the Arctic Circle

"Heads are going to roll."

Sore, tired and chilled to the bone, Vale London dropped her ten-thousand-pound backpack, leaned against a wall of ice and scanned her surroundings—a sea of snow broken up by mountains and seracs that looked like ocean waves had flash-frozen just before they'd come crashing down. Subzero wind blustered, screams of pain and helplessness seemingly echoing within.

"Are we talking literally or figuratively?" Her beloved foster sister Magnolia "Nola" Lee dropped her pack as well, sat atop it and drew a thick flannel blanket around her shoulders. "With you I never know. You aren't known as a street-tough scrapper for nothing."

Vale savored the flavor of sweetened brown butter that coated her tongue. At some point in her childhood development, wires had gotten crossed in her brain, leaving her with a severe case of synesthesia. She heard sounds, just like everyone else, but she tasted them, too. Letters also registered as colors, and numbers appeared as a three-dimensional map inside her head.

The more nuanced the sound, the richer the flavor.

"Figuratively…maybe," she replied, then sighed. "The next time I see our guide, he'll be lucky to walk away. Or even crawl." The POS had ruined what was supposed to be the vacation of a lifetime.

Dang it, Nola hadn't needed this kind of stress. The girl worked two full-time jobs. If she wasn't baking and selling the goods at local offices, she was writing How To copy for a dating column on the *Oklahoma Love Match* website.

Vale had hoped to enjoy one last hoorah—or maybe a *first* hoorah—before she and Nola settled down and opened a fancy-schmancy gourmet doughnut shop slash catering center slash speed dating and bachelorette party hub, with Vale on paperwork duty and Nola behind the oven and the counter.

And okay, okay. She supposed some of the blame for this situation rested on her shoulders rather than their absentee guide's. She'd booked each of their excursions with the cheapest companies available, hoping to do more stuff on a very limited budget.

Well, quality beat quantity every time. She understood that now. *So how about a break, world?*

If only time travel were possible…

Three weeks ago, she and Nola arrived in Jukkasjärvi, Sweden. For five days, adventures abounded. Then they'd road-tripped into Russia and hiked through the Khibiny Mountains with a thirtysomething guide who'd promised a kick-A experience. Temperatures had proved frosty, but there'd been very little snow, and no ice. A plethora of trees had thawed, their leaves plush and green enough to rival freshly polished emeralds, seemingly dusted with diamond powder. Here and there, rivers had babbled happily, and breathtaking waterfalls had cascaded into crystal pools.

Somehow, their little trio had veered off path between one blink and the next, and ended up in this icy wasteland.

Backtracking hadn't helped, the ice stretching on. Eventually, a single set of footprints had led them to a cozy cabin, where Vale and her sister had spent the past two weeks. Day one, the guide had gone off to scout the perimeter and never returned.

This morning, they were forced to make a difficult choice: remain in the warmth of their lodgings and slowly starve to death, or set out to find help, and possibly (quickly) freeze to death.

As their foster momma used to say, *If you want to experience the miracle of walking on water, you gotta get out of the boat.*

A pang of homesickness cut through her. The world was a sadder place without Carrie, aka Care Bear.

In extreme need of one of those water-walking miracles, Vale and Nola had strapped on snow gear they'd unearthed in a trunk only a few days before. Oddly enough, the garments had fit perfectly, as if tailor-made for them. The coincidence had roused her suspicions, sure, but in the end she hadn't cared about how or why, only the end result. She and Nola had set out bright and early this morning, and trudged through mile after mile of snow.

Now sunset approached. So far, they'd found no hint of life, and Vale was getting worried.

Getting? Please. She'd been worried every second of every day since the nightmare had started.

I'm not ready to die.

She'd put her life on hold for years, working various jobs while going to school full-time. Just when she'd completed a business degree from the University of Oklahoma—*Go Sooners!*—with zero student debt, she was going to kick the bucket? No! Unacceptable.

And die knowing she'd caused her sister's demise? *Never.*

"I'm sorry," she said, guilt overtaking her. Despite a top-of-the-line face mask, her nose and lungs burned when she breathed.

"The blame is mine, and I never share. You know that." Nola's breath no longer misted the air. A bad sign. Very bad. "I was feeling so good, I kept bugging you to add more stops to our itinerary."

Her sister suffered from fibromyalgia. On any given day, Nola's overactive nerves could cause extreme fatigue, total body aches, and swell her joints. A cocktail of medication helped alleviate the symptoms, but couldn't cure the disease.

"Sorry, sis, but the hike was my idea." Apparently, relaxing wasn't her thing. Anytime she'd had a quiet reprieve, she'd considered the avalanche of responsibility headed her way and panicked. Which made zero sense. She'd dreamed of opening the donut shop for years. And yes, okay, her dreams had revolved around Nola's happiness rather than her own, but come on! Making Nola happy should make *Vale* happy. Still, in an effort to hide her panic, she'd made sure she had no quiet moments. "The blame is mine, and that's final."

"Fine. We'll go halvsies." Nola pretended to fluff her hair. "If we die, we die, but at least we look cute."

"Dude. We *do* look cute." They wore sleek coats, downy jackets, thermals, fleece tights, goggles, face masks, hats and gloves, multiple pairs of wool socks and hiking boots with ice cleats. "We could charm the flannel off a snow-biker gang."

"Or win the heart of a yeti with a Southern girl fetish."

"If he doesn't want to eat *our* hearts first...battered and deep-fried, with melted butter on the side." Her mouth watered. "I wonder what sautéed yeti tastes like."

"If you start licking your chompers when you look at me... I won't feel so guilty for debating whether your liver would pair better with a nice red or a six-pack of cheap beer."

"You've seen my hangovers. Avoid my liver and go for the rump roast." She gave her butt a little slap.

Nola chuckled, only to lapse into silence when a bitter wind nearly knocked them both off their feet. "D-distract me f-from the cold, and I'll l-l-love you forever." Her lips were tinted blue, her teeth chattering with more force.

"You already love me forever." Just as Vale loved Nola, the greatest person in the world, living or dead, real or fake. *Would move heaven and earth for her.* "But I'm awesome, probably the awesomest, so I'll take on this herculean task. Tell me your favorite part of the trip."

"Only e-everything." Nola shifted atop her bag, unable to stifle a whimper of pain. Then she continued as if all was well. "Except f-for the abandonment, starvation and h-hypothermia, of course."

"Such trifling matters." Helplessness pelted Vale's insides. *Tamp down, move on.* "We did everything on our BA lists." BA—before adulting. "We marveled over the northern lights."

The teeth chattering slowed, and Nola said, "We went on an overnight dog sled expedition that made me want to adopt a rescue pet as soon as I get home."

"We ice sculpted. FYI, my blob was better than your blob."

"It's true. Oh! We also hot-tubbed while drinking champagne."

"Lastly, we hiked through the Arctic Circle."

"Only one item remains unchecked."

"Fall for a handsome local," they said in unison.

Nola grinned and added, "I thought I had a connection with our guide, until he left us to die and all. But even then, he was better than my most recent online dates. Would you please explain why so many modern guys like to send complete strangers unsolicited pictures of their genitals, and why they do it with such pride?"

"Because *of course* women are catapulted into a foaming-at-the-mouth sexual frenzy the instant we catch sight of some rando's man-junk. Duh."

"You're right! That's it. And of course, it's *soooo* flattering when the creeper doubles down and asks for a tit pic in return. I'm all, yeah, sure, let me reward you for making me vomit in my mouth."

They snickered.

"But," Nola added.

"Oh, no. No buts." Her sis was a hopeless romantic and optimistic. Nola believed everyone deserved a second, third and fourth chance—which was why she wrote such an excellent How-To column. How to intrigue your crush blah, blah. Vale, however, was a realist.

She wasn't closed off to relationships, per se, but she wasn't open, either. People were intrinsically flawed. At some point, they were going to disappoint you—and they were going to leave you. So she lived by a code. *Always be the leaver, never be the leavee.* And yes, she knew the code had roots in childhood abandonment issues. So what? Issues were issues for a reason. Intrinsically flawed, remember? Most people sucked a nut.

Nola and Carrie were exceptions. Her mom, too…until she'd died of a brain aneurysm, forever altering the course of Vale's life.

Once, her dad had been an exception. But soon after her mother's funeral, he'd taken off, leaving Vale to bounce from home to home. He'd never written, or called or visited, leaving her to wonder what was wrong with her, why no one ever wanted to stick around.

Danger. Avoid! That particular thought train had one station—Depressionville.

Moving on. Vale had a low tolerance for BS, and believed happily-ever-afters were merely an illusion. The longer families, friends or couples stayed together, the more they got to know each other, the more they glimpsed the garbage heap piled inside their loved one's heart. In relationships, someone always got hurt.

Get in, get out.

Vale had dated around, but she'd never allowed herself to get serious with a guy. And really, no guy had ever wanted to get serious with her. She had to spend an enormous amount of energy pretending to be sweet and gentle, and it stressed her out, which had made her even more prickly, blunt and abrasive.

There wasn't a man alive who was willing to put in the work and fight to be with her, and she couldn't blame them. She wasn't willing to fight for a guy, either.

"Lately, my love life has been *exactly* like a private jet," Nola said.

"Oh, yeah? How so?"

"I don't have a private jet."

She laughed. Funny girl. "Come on. Let's travel a little farther before we settle in for the night." Their bodies needed heat, and movement would add logs to the fire.

Nola lumbered to her feet, and they helped each other strap on a pack before marching forward. Vale hauled the bulk of supplies while her sis had blankets and medications, but even still, guilt robbed her of breath every time Nola grunted or groaned from exertion.

Okay. Another distraction, coming up. "I miss Carrie," she said.

At thirteen years old, both Vale and Nola were assigned to the woman who handled "difficult" cases—young girls with a disability of some sort. Carrie had done more than open her home and heart; she'd taught her charges how to love themselves, and how to thrive.

Vale, honey, do you think a twenty-dollar bill is worth any less if it's dirty and wrinkled? No way in heck! You might be a little rough around the edges, but you are still priceless.

Carrie and her words of wisdom. She'd loved the adage about the potato, egg and coffee bean most of all.

In boiling water, the potato softens, the egg hardens, but the mighty coffee bean changes the water. Don't let difficult times weaken or harden you, girls. Get up and change the situation!

Eyes gleaming with fondness, Nola nodded. "If she were here, she'd cook up a feast. Snowcakes. Slush omelets. Ice bacon. Hail biscuits and blizzard gravy."

Vale grinned, even as hunger gnawed her empty stomach. But the grin was quickly shaken off by a trembling chin. Last year, Carrie had suffered a massive heart attack and never recovered.

Her death left a hole in *Vale's* heart. "I vividly remember the day I moved in. Back then, I lived by prison rules. You know, show them who's boss on day one. So *of course* I destroyed Carrie's living room, toppling furniture and breaking anything glass."

"Of course."

"When I finished, she calmly asked if I'd like my sweet tea iced or steaming."

Mimicking the prim and proper Carrie, Nola said, "Always be a lady, until you need to be a land mine."

Carrie had only ever exploded when it came to the protection of her girls.

Another pang of homesickness. Great! Now she needed a distraction from the distraction.

As they motored on, she asked, "What are we going to call our donut shop, anyway?"

They'd toyed with The Donut Bar and Drunkin' Donuts, since their sweet treats paid homage to alcoholic beverages, but both names were taken.

"What about Happy Hour Donuts?" Nola asked.

"Cute, but it doesn't say gourmet."

"Well, frick."

Frick—Carrie's favorite "curse" word. "We could simplify and go with Lee and London," Vale said.

"I love it, but no one will know what we're selling."

"Maybe not at first but select ad campaigns can help spread the word."

"Well, if we're going in that direction, why not something like… I don't know… Lady Carrie's?"

"Duuuude. I know we're high-end and all, but you just gave me a girl-boner. Lady Carrie's is *perfect*."

"Well, sprinkle sugar on my tush and call me a donut. Did we just name our shop?"

Vale was just about to reply—when she spotted an ice hill up ahead. There was something about it... Something odd. But what, exactly? Nothing seemed to be out of place.

"I'm going to scout ahead." Heart and legs picking up speed in unison, she crossed the distance. A perfect six-foot hole had been carved into the side of the hill, leading to a tunnel with an upward tilt. Definitely man-made. What was inside? Or better yet, *who* was inside?

Anticipation shook her. If the tunnel led to a cavern—occupied or unoccupied, it didn't matter—she could get Nola out of the elements sooner rather than later.

"Wait here," she said when her sister reached the hill. "I'll go inside and—"

"Nope, sorry. We go in together."

"What if there's a wild animal just waiting for a meal on legs to show up?" *Mmm. Meal.*

"You'll be the main course, and I'll be dessert."

Stubborn girl. "Fine." Vale withdrew a long coil of rope from her pack, knotted one end around her sister's waist and the other around her own. No way Nola would fall to her death on her watch. Next, she withdrew ice axes. Two for each of them. "We'll find a cavern or drop. Whichever comes first."

After adjusting her bag, she swung an ax, inched her spiked boots up several jagged steps, then swung the other ax, and inched up a few more steps. Rinse, repeat, slow and steady. Nola did the same.

The higher they climbed, the darker the enclosure became, and the more her muscles protested.

Drip, drip. Drip, drip.

Ironically, the steady chorus of water drops tasted like melted

vanilla ice cream on a hot summer day. Like hope. Hope gave
her strength. Up, up. Higher still.

"I'm not sure… I can go…much farther," Nola said, heaving from exertion.

When a soft, warm—well, warmer—breeze caressed a patch
of exposed skin, she gasped. "You can. You will. Now move
that little sugar tush of yours."

The tunnel curved to the right and—

Revealed a small pinprick of light. "There's something ahead!"
She climbed faster, closing in.

The light expanded as the tunnel leveled out…and opened
into a cavern. Into salvation! Massive ice pillars propped up a
domed ceiling at least eight feet high. There was enough space
between each pillar to stretch out and get comfortable.

Trembling, Vale dropped her tools and bag, then helped her
sister over the ledge.

As Nola sank to the ground, panting, Vale pulled the logs and
kindling from her pack, and used a match to start a fire. Instant
heat. Oh, such glorious heat. Smoke billowed, curling upward,
and she removed her goggles and face mask.

"Thank you, thank you, a thousand times thank you." Nola
followed suit, ditching the headgear, revealing a face so perfect
she looked airbrushed. Dark eyes, delicate nose and model-
plump lips, all surrounded by flawless brown skin and a fall of
straight black hair.

The best part, she was just as beautiful on the inside as she
was on the outside. She deserved better than the tragedy and
adversity she'd been dealt. Her parents had died in a car crash
when she was a baby. With no other living relatives in her family tree, she'd been placed in the system.

Using the axes and rope, Vale made a hanging line to dry
her hat and coat.

After hanging her items, Nola frowned and pointed to one
of the walls. "Is that…ice graffiti?"

"Let's take a look." She approached the wall.

Well, hello there, beautiful. Images had been carved throughout, like ancient hieroglyphs or something, depicting some kind of battle. Twenty men and four women holding various types of weapons. A cloaked figure clutching a scythe stood nearby. The grim reaper, maybe?

A headless body sprawled on the ground, separating the warriors from a crowd of shorter men. She shuddered. A man—beast?—with horns, had a staff lifted high.

Drip, drip, drip.

The taste of melted vanilla ice cream intensified, aggravating her hunger. "Someone has to live here, or at least visit upon occasion. We could be close to civilization. I'm going to have a look around for clues."

"Be careful."

"How about I be armed and ready for anything instead." She grabbed an ax before following the artwork around the farthest column...and entering another chamber.

No one waited within, but she did find more carvings. Impressed by the intricate details, she walked forward—only to draw up short. *No way!* More pillars littered the new enclosure, forming a perfect square, only these pillars were unlike the others. They glistened, in the process of melting, and they had... They...

I can't possibly be seeing what I think I'm seeing.

Her pulse points thundered, and a cold, clammy sweat slicked over the back of her neck. Each pillar contained a human being. Twenty males, four females.

At five foot ten, she was used to towering over people. These guys towered over *her.* They were a range of ethnicities—and species? One of the women had pretty blue skin and pointed ears. One of the men had wings. Another maybe kinda sorta had *gills* that flared on each side of his neck.

This was fake, absolutely, positively. It *couldn't* be real. Maybe she'd stumbled upon some kind of frozen wax museum intended for people like Vale who read sci-fi and fantasy voraciously and watched any movie or TV show featuring *anything* magical, futuristic or dystopian.

Whatever the reason, she'd been right; civilization—and salvation!—were nearby. And gold seal of approval to the company responsible for this masterpiece. Never had Vale encountered such lifelike figurines—and those bodies! Each guy could star in a porno. Not that she ever watched those, cough, cough.

When tourists came through, they'd definitely get their money's worth. *Come one, come all, see barbarians and their concubines on ice.* To be fair, though, the women appeared just as vicious as the men.

As Vale moved deeper into the cave, different sets of eyes seemed to track her. So creepy. Just beyond the columns, she spotted what looked to be the staff depicted in the carvings. The one the horned man had held.

Unlike everything else, the rod wasn't obscured by ice. It stood on its own, no sign of the horned man.

Intrigued, she reached out...

A powerful blast of wind knocked her backward, and she slammed into a pillar. Electric pulses danced over her skin, stars winked through her vision, and air gushed from her lungs.

Crack, crack. Lines appeared in a handful of pillars.

Frick! This had better not be a you-break-it-you-buy-it situation.

All right, forget the staff. She straightened on unsteady legs and returned her attention to the soldiers. Yeah, definitely soldiers. They stood in assorted battle poses, clutched weapons and wore varying expressions of absolute, utter fury.

Her gaze skimmed over a black-haired man, only to zoom back. He exuded enough power to crush...anyone. And he was heart-stoppingly gorgeous. The kind of gorgeous that stole your breath *and* your thoughts *and* incinerated your panties.

One look at him, and she was certain she'd ovulated.

He was sex, rough and raw, primal and animalistic, his masculinity a palpable caress against her skin.

No one, real or fiction, was sexier. Not even Legolas, the standard by which she measured every man.

This statue had the sinister aura of a pitiless conqueror, radiating both icy cold and boiling heat, his hard expression promising both earth-shattering orgasms and a torturous death. His eyes outshone the bluest, rarest sapphires; they were framed by long, curling lashes reminiscent of black velvet, somehow both pretty and primeval.

So many contradictions. So intriguing.

His cheekbones appeared to be carved from granite, and his lips...*glory hallelujah*. His lips were plump, scarlet, and made for kissing. His chin was square, his jaw slanted and shadowed by stubble.

Her gaze returned to his lips, drawn like a magnet, and her fingers followed, tracing a swirling pattern over the ice—not just any pattern.

Ugh. She'd drawn a heart. "I believe every life is a book in progress, and my story just got a lot more interesting," she told him.

He was shirtless, revealing a ring of black tattoos around his neck and wrists. Taking up prime real estate on one of his muscle-cut shoulders was a tree of life, set inside a circle. In fact, all of the frozen men and women bore a tree of life tattoo somewhere on their gorgeous bodies.

Her attention returned to the sex god. Or war commander. He held two daggers with brass knuckle handles. Pants made of a black leathery material covered his lower half, and a silver belt buckle rested atop his snack basket—a modern gadget when everything else about him screamed ancient warrior.

"A shame you aren't naked." He—

Vale jolted. *Plot twist*. He'd just blinked.

No way. Just…no way. While some part of her had always be-lieved ancient myths were based in fact, aliens and ghosts walked among humans, and magic truly existed, she had trouble accept-ing what she'd seen. What she *thought* she'd seen.

She wasn't crazy—most of the time; she just hadn't found any evidence to support her suspicions. Therefore, he *couldn't* have blinked. And those ocean-water blues couldn't be staring at her, intent with challenge, daring her to come closer.

He wasn't *aware* of her. He wasn't aware of *anything*. Because he wasn't alive.

He *couldn't* be alive.

Could he?

CHAPTER TWO

Knox fought the ice with all his might, doing his best to ram his body forward, then backward, then forward again. Since his confinement, he'd never stopped fighting and, because of the fervent and constant strain, his bones had been broken repeatedly, his muscles torn. Pain seared him every second of every day.

He should be used to forced incarceration. Before coming to Terra, he'd spent more than eleven hundred years under Ansel's control.

Here, now, a problem persisted. Knox was surrounded by enemy soldiers. If he failed to gain his freedom first, he would die. No doubt about it.

Every fiber of his being rejected the possibility of defeat. *Kill the competition, win the war.*

He *had* to win, had to return to Iviland. If Ansel kept his word and freed Knox from the slave bands, even for a second, the entire royal family would die screaming. *By my hand.*

Finally, Knox would know peace. True peace. His fellow slaves would be freed. No longer would they be mocked, ridiculed and treated as if they deserved such a dreadful fate, told they should be grateful the All Wars had given them a purpose.

If not...

He would just have to find another way.

The slave bands posed the biggest problem. Once, as a young boy, he'd flayed off the tattoos. But the ink had already tainted his blood, and the marks had grown back. But he would try again, and again, using a different weapon each time; he would try until he found something that worked, or died.

He already had his next weapon in mind.

As the centuries had passed, he'd had time to think this through—*despite* the lack of air that had left him in a perpetual haze. Carrick of Infernia was a well-known prince of his fire realm. A prince by might, not by birth. He obeyed no dictates but his own.

Carrick had tattoos similar to Knox's. However, the other man's markings aided rather than hindered, somehow causing a strange force field to spread around him. He owned a special dagger capable of burning a victim from the inside out, turning the veined blood into lava.

Knox planned to win the dagger and use it on himself. As long as he had the power to activate it, not even he—the wielder—would be immune to its powers. Perhaps the lava would burn away the poison that tethered him to Ansel. Then, Knox could use another weapon to turn his blood back to normal.

In theory, he would heal. In reality, he might die.

Worth the risk. A dark entity seemed to live and breathe inside him—the puppet master who pulled his strings. This entity had a single purpose, a task it couldn't be swayed from: avenging Knox's daughter.

Her name was Minka, and she was conceived after Knox had won his first All War.

As a reward for his victory, Ansel had released him from service, though he'd refused to remove the slave bands. On some level, Knox had always known the king would demand a return to battle. He just hadn't known the bastard was biding his time, waiting for Knox to develop an attachment to someone, anyone, so that he could be better managed.

Back then, Knox hadn't cared. For once, he'd gotten to eat, sleep and fight whenever he'd wished. And, though he'd never dropped his guard, his suspicious nature ingrained, every day had been a gift, every night a revelation. He'd bedded more women than he could remember.

What he hadn't suspected? His lovers had been paid to get pregnant with his child.

He'd been careful, but one woman managed to succeed. Or maybe she'd lied, and another man had fathered Minka. Either way, Knox had planned to forsake the pair. Then the mother left the little girl in his custody and walked away without looking back.

The moment, the very second, he'd held the beautiful newborn in his arms, her tiny fingers squeezing one of his, his heart had swelled with more love than he'd ever thought possible. Minka had been perfect in every way, so soft, so delicate, and he'd vowed to forever cherish the miracle he'd been given.

She had been his greatest treasure—and she had been taken from him.

Soon after her second birthday, Ansel decided to reenlist his "ace." *Do this, or the girl dies.*

Knox did everything in his power to win a second All War. To this day, tales of his savagery were talked about in hushed voices.

The war lasted sixteen years. While he'd fought, earning another kingdom for Iviland, a family chosen by Ansel had raised his precious Minka. Upper-class snobs who'd treated the innocent child as less than nothing.

Upon Knox's return home, he'd learned his daughter had run away a few months before, and no one had been able to find her.

But I did. I found my sweet angel.

She'd ventured topside, where others feared to tread, where

lawless criminals lived with abandon, torturing the desperate, their minds slowly corrupted by toxins. A place where Ansel dared not send his soldiers.

The things that were done to her before she took her last breath...

I hugged and kissed a smiling toddler goodbye, and returned to a dead teenager.

Rage and sorrow seared him. Tears welled in his eyes and frosted, obscuring his vision. *Focus.* Emotions wouldn't aid him. He needed to see to escape. More accurately, he needed to see to escape *first.*

Inhale, exhale. He blinked until the frost thinned, melted. Then he attempted to ram his shoulders into the ice. Ram, ram. Snarls rumbled in his chest, his level of pain increasing exponentially. So what. Nothing compared to the horrors he'd already suffered.

Then, suddenly, a stunningly beautiful female stepped into his path, shocking him into immobility.

She wasn't part of the war, but she was here. *How was she here? Why* was she here? Who was she? Thousand other questions raced through his mind, and he reeled.

She was the second person to enter the ice prison in...ever. Erik of Terra, once a viking king—*still* a viking king?—must have taken measures to keep intruders at bay.

For centuries, Erik had visited once a month. He'd never missed an assembly. Did he know why he felt compelled to return so often, or that doing so had kept him from disqualification? He definitely didn't know he was part of a war, everyone in this cave determined to win his homeland, or that he needed to slay the other combatants. Otherwise he would have done so already.

In the beginning, Knox had expected an army of Enforcers to portal in and liberate the frozen warriors, allowing the war to resume. After a few decades, he'd realized the High Council *couldn't* interfere, or losing realms would have the right to question the eligibility of the winner.

At long last, the ice had begun to melt. Cracks branched through 60 percent of the pillars. Had the Rod of Clima weakened after near-constant use, or had weather conditions changed drastically? Perhaps both.

Now, a human walked among them. Why?

"I'm losing my ever-loving mind," she muttered, his translator interpreting the words.

Such a low, raspy voice. His muscles clenched, an involuntary—and intolerable—reaction.

Through agonizing conditioning, he'd trained his body to overlook desirable females during times of war. Too many males had met their demise in the bed of a temptress. A combatant never knew who to trust, or who had been paid to distract him.

If ever Knox's conditioning failed, he simply obliterated the distraction. No mercy, no problems.

{*Protect the girl. She is necessary…for now.*}

Denial echoed inside his head. No. No! The *eyaer* could not consider this woman necessary for his survival. *Her?* She was a tiny fluff of nothing, not even big enough to act as a human shield.

Besides, Knox needed nothing and no one. *Wanted* nothing and no one. Except…

As the female looked him over with languid fascination, the clenching intensified. His blood heated. Could he really be blamed, though? She was unlike any woman he'd ever seen, with an exquisite, fine-boned face and fascinating hair. Silken waves, the top half snow-white, the bottom half raven black. And her skin…pale and flawless, made for a man's caress.

How soft was she? How warm?

Would she flush when he touched her?

He pressed his tongue to the roof of his mouth. *When* he touched her? Like it was a done deal?

Her eyes were a startling mix of amber and emerald, rimmed with thick slashes of kohl and mile-long lashes of the purest jet. Scarlet lips boasted the perfect heart shape and silently offered the sweetest temptation.

Her clothes…so different from the styles worn by everyone he'd come across before the freeze. Just how vastly had the world and its citizens changed?

Her fingernails were painted the deepest shade of black, and strange symbols were tattooed around each of her knuckles, giving her rings of ink.

Was she owned by a Terran king?

Knox tensed, angered on her behalf and confused by his growing awareness of her.

Between wars, he'd gravitated to women who were quiet, gentle, reserved. Or at least the ones who'd pretended to be. The "high class." The supposed best of the best. *Ladies.* His preferred bed partners had represented everything he'd lacked as a child, everything supposedly too good for him.

What perplexed him most—those high-class women had never really satisfied him. He'd been too afraid of losing control and accidentally hurting them, or frightening their delicate sensibilities.

Then again, he'd never wanted to be satisfied. Losing track of his surroundings, even while at peace, could cost him *everything.*

"If we were in a book or movie, you would be a warrior frozen in time, and this would be the start of our passionate love affair," the Terran said. "Too bad you're man-made. Although there are story possibilities there, too. If you're based on a real person, I want his number, because you, baby doll, are a total smoke show." Her hazel gaze looked him over more leisurely, taking his measure.

She walked around him, every step a revelation of grace and carnality.

"But those blue, blue eyes," she said, sounding awed. "I swear they're following me."

His heart thudded against his ribs, harder and harder. A snarl rumbled deep in his chest.

If she affected him despite his training, she had to die. She had to die *before* another combatant decided to use her against him.

{*Protect. Necessary.*}

He bellowed an obscenity, the sound muffled by the ice.

"Whoa. Did you just *shout* at me?" She licked those red, red lips. "I taste whiskey and honey, with a dash of cream, so I definitely heard something. But you can't make sounds because you aren't alive. I must have heard something else. Yeah, yeah. Something else."

She heard a shout and tasted whiskey and honey? Knox failed to make a connection.

Forget her oddities. He formulated a plan.

He would break free—today—even if he had to lose limbs to succeed. This wasn't an assembly day, the invisible wall down, all weapons activated.

Knox would seize the Rod of Clima, ensuring the viking couldn't use it a second time, and then he would kill Carrick. Once those objectives were met, he would slay as many warriors as possible...taking out pillars in the process. It couldn't be helped. At some point, the cavern would collapse. At the first sign of trouble, he would whisk the female with the odd white and black hair to safety and find out why she was "necessary" to him.

Yes. Perfect plan, no flaws.

Next, he ordered his kills. After Carrick—Zion, Bane, Ronan and Ranger. The others could die in random order, their weapons and the threats they posed a lower priority. Perhaps, though, Knox would take out Shiloh last, as dictated by the truce.

Come on, come on. First, he had to get free. Snarling, Knox fought… Fought so hard, harder…but the ice continued to hold steady.

Footsteps echoed as a second female entered the corridor. A dark-haired beauty with the aura of delicacy Knox had always preferred, and yet his gaze returned to the other female. The *wild* one.

"Vale!" The newcomer pressed a hand over her heart. "Are *people* trapped in here?"

Vale? He hailed from a realm with three *vales*, or suns. Valina, the sun that warmed. Valtorro, the sun that lit. And Valeique, the sun that guided. Which was his necessary female supposed to be? His warmth, his light or his guide?

"These freaky things?" Vale propped a hand on her hip. "Nah. They're statues. Some kind of tourist attraction, I think. Men and women will come from all over the world to view these frozen sexcakes."

Her jacket—thin though it was—prevented him from making out the size of her breasts. Skintight black pants hugged her lower body, revealing toned legs he would like to—

Blank your mind. Ignore the yearning.

"Statues? Yeah, that makes more sense. But sexcakes?" The brunette chuckled.

"Why, my sweet Nola Lee, you'd rather I call them life-size lady boner figurines, wouldn't you? Well, you're right, I like that description better. Take a gander at this one." She hiked her thumb in Knox's direction. "Grade A beef."

Vale and Nola. Noted. Their affection for each other was obvious. He'd seen similar bonds in others but had never experienced one firsthand. Had never *wanted* to experience one firsthand. Attachments weakened you, made you vulnerable.

Nola approached Zion and gasped. "Okay, yes. Sexcakes is absolutely right. I just made eye contact with this one, and I'm pretty sure I'm pregnant. With twins."

As Vale joined her, Knox jammed his shoulder into the ice

with more force. He wanted his female farther away from the brute, not closer. If the other man—

Cracks appeared in front of Knox's face, distorting his vision. He stilled, shocked. Triumphant. Finally, blessedly, a development in his favor.

Cracks meant liberty awaited.

CHAPTER THREE

Overcome by violent fervor, Knox fought harder, harder still. *Can't stop, can't stop.*

"You were right, Vale." The brunette traced a heart over Zion's icy chest. "We did it. We survived. We're close to civilization. Rescue is more than a dream. It's a probability."

Rescue. Had the two gotten lost in the mountains, and merely stumbled upon the prison?

The cracks prevented Knox from seeing Vale's expression, and he desperately wanted to see her expression.

"Are you thinking what I'm thinking?" she said, sounding more worried than relieved. "Celebration dinner of the year!"

"Let's be all lavish and crap and fold our napkin—aka scarves—into swans."

"How about fists with a middle finger extended instead?" As the other woman laughed, she said, "So what's on tonight's menu, chef?"

"You're in for a real treat. Tonight only we're offering a can of fermented herring, paired with a side of vomit, probably. For a vegetarian option, we've got the most delectable handful of snow."

"Mmm. What's for dessert? Air cookies?"

When the two females vanished around a corner, Knox swallowed a roar of denial. *Let her go.* No matter where she went, he could find her.

Ram, ram. The cracks…lengthened. Suddenly, he could move his hands an inch, maybe two.

An inch was all he needed.

Knox—utterly—unleashed. Head-butting, shoulder bumping. Kicking. Grip tightening on the daggers, he chip, chip, chipped away at the ice. New waves of pain washed over him, but so what. Victory was within his grasp!

Minutes passed, perhaps hours. Thin shards of ice began to fall, granting him more room. More still. He redoubled his efforts, new cracks forming, old cracks expanding, creating a beautiful labyrinth—until the slab in front of his face gave way and tumbled to the ground.

For the first time in centuries, a soft breeze kissed his face. He closed his eyes, basking in the sweetness of the sensation, and breathed in a long, deep breath. Oxygen flowed into his lungs, stinging like needles.

Another slab of ice fell, then another. Soon, he was rolling his shoulders and moaning with pleasure. Oh, the glory of uninhibited movement.

Nerve endings tingled as they blazed back to life, his blood rushing with new purpose. He scanned the remaining pillars. No one else had gained their freedom—yet.

The pitter-patter of footsteps caught his attention. The women entered the chamber and stopped abruptly when they noticed him, their jaws dropping. The aroma of jasmine and honeysuckle permeated his senses, toying with his self-control—Vale's scent?

He pointed to her, the action part ecstasy, part agony. "You will stay put." The words rubbed against his unused throat like sandpaper, raw tissues burning. Like all the other combatants, he was immortal and healed too quickly for any sustained damage, but that didn't mean he felt his injuries any less. "Do not run."

"You're talking." Her mouth floundered open and closed. Shock glimmered in her eyes, the gold flecks molten. "You're talking, and you're alive. You're alive, and you're real."

Up close, without the ice between them, she was even more stunning. A beauty without equal.

"How is this possible?" Hysteria tinged Nola's tone. "You can't be real. You just…can't." She reached out to grab Vale's hand. "He can't be real. Hypothermia causes hallucinations, right?"

Muscles screaming in protest, Knox kicked away the final piece of ice and crossed to the Rod of Clima. *Destroy it and kill Carrick of Infernia.* Except, the moment he passed Carrick, instinct stopped him. He backtracked. *Kill him. Kill him now. Can't waste this opportunity.* And, after watching the protective shield around the rod nearly incapacitate Vale, he wasn't sure he would fare any better.

Vale tugged Nola toward the exit, saying, "We need to leave. Now."

Abandon him, after he'd ordered her to stay put?

He reordered his tasks yet again and closed in on her. The other woman stood petrified. Despite the palpable dismay that enveloped Vale, she took a step in his direction. To challenge him?

{*Protect. Necessary.*}

The lush scent of jasmine and honeysuckle strengthened, fuzzing his thoughts, reminding him of long-ago summers, and dark, sultry nights.

What if she was nothing but a dream?

Touch. Gently. After shifting both daggers to one hand, he reached out to trace his fingertips across her cheekbone. Solid. Soft as silk. Warmer than expected. Hot.

He groaned. She was real, and this was his first contact with another living being in centuries…

Was she equally befuddled by bliss? Her lips formed a perfect O, her irises glittering and crazed as she blinked up at him. "You aren't a hallucination."

"No. Nor are you."

"You aren't a hallucination," she repeated, and began to wheeze. "I'm *freaking out* right now. Like, I'm seriously hyperventilating. I just... I can't..."

Hyperventilating—breathing at an abnormally rapid rate. He could press his mouth against hers, give her the air she so desperately needed... Taste her...

Enough!

"How long have you been trapped here?" she asked. "*How* were you trapped here? Who are you? *What* are you?"

"I am Knox of Iviland."

She smacked her lips, as if she'd just enjoyed something delicious, and his body responded without his permission, hardening.

"How are you—" The other girl tensed and quieted as more ice cracked.

Reality zoomed back into focus. Zion was breaking free. Ranger, too.

No, *every* combatant was breaking free.

Knox hissed and shoved Vale out of the way.

"Nola," she shouted, and he pushed the other female in her direction.

Just in time. Ice shards flew through the air, combatants with centuries of pent-up aggression emerging from their cocoons. Their movements were slower than usual, stiffer too, but it took only seconds for a savage brawl to break out. Roars, groans and grunts blended with the sound of shattering ice, creating an inharmonic and truly wretched chorus.

Knox kicked a large frozen hunk in front of the humans, then summoned shadows to cloak them.

"What happened?" Vale rasped, her gaze darting this way and

that. No one could see her, but she couldn't see anyone else, either. "Too dark…"

"Stay put and you'll survive," he said, his voice gruff.

He blocked a swinging sword. Close-quarters combat required a very particular skill set and absolute focus.

Mind on the fray, Knox sliced his attacker's throat. Went in for the kill, only to lose the male in the crowd.

He charged toward Carrick, his main target—

Ronan crashed into him, tossing him onto his back. Precious oxygen, gone. As they grappled, a head rolled past them, no body. Orion of Sieg was dead, and someone in the cavern had just acquired his motorized axes.

Twenty-two combatants stood between Knox and victory. Would have been twenty-one, if Erik hadn't joined the war.

Ronan rose to his knees, straddling Knox's torso, and punched, punched, punched. His nose broke. Capillaries burst in his eyes, clouding his vision. His teeth shredded his gums, blood filling his mouth, choking him. Only then, when his sight was compromised, and his lungs were emptied, did the other warrior risk swinging the Sword of Light.

Knox ignored the flare of pain and rolled to his side—*without* looking at the sword. A single glance at the glowing metal could blind him for hours. Perfect timing. The blade hacked into the ice and stuck. Using the unintentional pause to his advantage, he returned to his back, then worked his legs around Ronan's neck, hooking his ankles together.

Applying pressure, Knox jolted upright to jab the male's eye with a dagger, removing it as well as a piece of his brain. An agonized bellow joined the chorus.

Knox rolled to the side a second time, and Ronan gave his sword a wild swing. A sharp pain slicked across his biceps, skin and muscle tearing, blood pouring. No time to retaliate. Fingers tangled in his hair and jerked him backward, toward a blazing blue fire.

He was dragged past Colt of Orfet, who was crawling away from the melee. With good reason. His weapon of choice was a metal ring comprised of hundreds of microbots. Those microbots could separate, burrow under a person's skin and shred their organs. And yes, it hurt. It hurt badly. But immortals healed too swiftly to be stopped in such a way.

Rolling, kicking his legs overhead, Knox punted his captor in the sternum—Petra of Etalind.

Different facts buzzed across his mind. *Hails from a heavily treed mountain realm, possesses a sword that can grow towers of ice, mud or rock in seconds, allies with Ronan, might be his lover.*

Unprepared for the action, she stumbled back, taking hanks of Knox's hair with her.

Keep them with my compliments.

She tripped over Orion's body, landing in the firepit. The flames licked over her, and she screamed.

Crouched, Knox surrounded himself with shadows and scanned the cavern. Seven watched from the sidelines, the hood draped over his face, the scythe in hand. He was as free as everyone else but forbidden from joining the fight, lest he affect the outcome of the war.

Once again, a bright light shone in Knox's periphery, courtesy of Ronan's sword. *Ignore its allure.*

Where was Carrick?

Still scanning... One combatant lashed out with a glowing whip, the end coiling around another combatant's neck, sending electric pulses streaming down his spinal cord. A warrior came upon the whip wielder—Thorn of D'Elia—and struck with a hammer, shattering every bone in his body.

Despite the deluge of sounds, Knox's ears picked up a soft feminine whimper. He glanced over his shoulder. His shadows were in place, but there was no sign of the female. If someone had hurt her...

He bit out an oath.

{*Find her. She's necessary.*}

I know! Scanning with more fervor, still avoiding the blinding glow produced by Ronan's sword... There! Slade of Undlan had backed Nola into a corner, and Vale had plastered herself over his back to pummel his face. The Undlanian reached up and over to grab a handful of her hair. With a single swipe of his arm, he flung her next to Nola.

Knox sprinted across the cavern, ducking, diving, menace in every action. Undlan was an underwater realm, and with his trident, Slade could flood the area in seconds. Right now, he had to fear freezing again. Understandable. Everyone had individual strengths and weaknesses, but they all shared the same vulnerability.

Halfway there, Knox dropped to his knees. Momentum propelled him forward, allowing him to slick his blades through someone's femoral artery...a kneecap...a gut.

Just before reaching Slade, Knox exchanged his daggers for a sword. There! With a single swing, he sliced through the other man's wrist. The trident dropped to the ground—and so did the hand.

Vale and Nola shouted with fear and dismay as blood spurted from the severed artery.

Focus. Knox raised the sword, ready to deliver a death blow. But Slade dove out of the way, popped to his feet, and ran.

No retaliation attempt?

Disappointed, Knox jumped up, lifting Vale in the process. "Come."

"Get your hands off me!"

He yanked her closer, out of harm's way.

She beat at his chest, the blows barely registering. "Get your hands off me *now!*"

He kept his attention fixed on the battle...where was the Infernian? "I'm getting you out of here, female. Help me help you."

"What? Okay, yes. I will." She took his hand and tugged him in the direction he didn't want to go. "Let's get my sister and go."

Sister, not just friend or loved one.

No sign of the prince. Disappointment flooded him. No matter. He would go hunting later.

Knox homed in on Cannon's rod, intending to destroy it as planned—gone. Someone else had snagged it. More disappointment joined the deluge.

He adjusted the position of Vale's hand and led her in the other direction.

She dug in her heels, saying, "What are you doing? Stop! I won't leave without my sister."

"Wrong. You don't *want* to leave without your sister. There's a difference." Someone must have escaped with the other girl. There was no sign of her, and he wasn't going to waste time looking.

He motored forward—

A hard weight slammed into him. As he fell, he maintained his hold on Vale and pulled her beneath him, letting his body act as a buffer against any oncoming attacks. Instead, the culprit—Zion—held on to Nola with a gloved hand and reached for Vale with the other.

Trying to take my prize? Knox kicked his hand away and leaped up, leaving Vale sprawled on the ground and swinging his sword at the other male.

Zion blocked with his glove, metal clinking against metal. Vibrations rode the length of Knox's arm but he didn't hesitate to swing a second time. A louder clink, a more intense vibration.

This time, Ronan's sword had blocked the blow. *Avert your gaze!* Too late. A bomb of too-bright light erupted from the blade, blinding him—but not before he caught sight of Vale and Nola racing around the far corner.

Frustration and fury mounting, Knox dropped and slid across the ice backward, summoning shadows along the way to hide his body from everyone else. A familiar gloom settled around him, more welcome than a lover's embrace.

"This way, my friend." Shiloh's voice. A hard hand rested on Knox's shoulder. "I'll lead you out."

It's him or me. I choose me. Always.

Do it! Compulsion kicked in a split second later. He did it; he struck. His dagger cut through Shiloh's throat, the other man's body jerking against his.

As Shiloh fought for breath, Knox hacked, again and again, until the man's head detached. A brutal act, yes. Savage and utterly merciless, too.

"I warned you. Never trust me," he said. Now, twenty-one combatants stood between Knox and victory.

He hardened his heart against a torrent of guilt and remorse, and claimed Shiloh's lenses. The male had to die at some point; only one winner could be crowned. It was imperative that Knox see now, before the effects of Ronan's sword had worn off. He had to find Vale—his necessity—and whisk her to safety, no matter the cost.

Lenses in place, he blinked rapidly to adjust. The world whooshed back into focus. The cavern. Soldiers clashing. Blood everywhere, even splattered over the ceiling, raining down. Different body parts were strewn across the ground.

His gaze locked on Zion, who had just finished punching a hole in Ronan's throat. Without a trachea, the Sword of Light owner didn't have the strength to move. There was no better time to take him out.

Zion went in for the kill. The removal of the heart.

He punched through one of Petra's towers instead. Her sword could only create towers from the substance on the ground, so this one was made of ice.

The Taverian could have punched a third time, but he surprised Knox by pivoting and slamming his fist into a cavern wall. Cracks spread swiftly.

The structure would collapse sooner rather than later.

Go! Knox followed the path Vale had taken, entering a less spacious antechamber where a small fire blazed. An empty can rolled across the ground, bumping into a pair of large, oddly shaped spectacles.

The females were gone.

The exit... Where was the exit?

There! He dove into a tunnel, letting gravity pull him down, down. Cracks had spread here, too, slowing his momentum. No matter. A wealth of black-and-white hair came into view.

Arms tucked to his sides, gaining speed... He purposely slammed into Vale, who'd gotten snagged by one of the cracks. They soared into motion, her back pressed against his chest, her soft, floral scent filling his head.

In a world of ice, blood and battle, she was a hothouse flower.

"Not you!" She threw an elbow, nailing his chin with so much force he saw sparks. "Anyone but you."

A hothouse flower with *bite*.

"Yes, me." He caught her arm, halting a second attack, and grated, "You should stay on my good side, female, considering I'm the one who will decide whether or not you survive the night."

CHAPTER FOUR

Shudders racked Vale. Knox had caught up to her. Knox, whose eye sockets had turned black just before a cloud of darkness had risen from the ground to surround her. A man who exuded blatant masculinity, primal aggression and sent shivers down her spine with a single glance. Whose glittering blue gaze pierced her defenses and promised untold sensual delights. Who wielded his daggers with lethal accuracy, moved with inhuman grace—who had stabbed a man right in front of her.

Dangerous in more ways than one…in *all* ways.

"What, are you going to stab me, too?" she demanded as they slid down the tunnel she'd been so happy to find only hours ago. Every time her clothing snagged on jagged ice, she jerked to a stop until Knox pushed her free.

"Vale?" Nola called, a few paces in front of her, stopping and starting again.

Must keep Knox's attention on me.

"Go for it, then. Stab me," Vale told him, continuing as if her sister hadn't spoken. *Please don't stab me.*

"I'm not yet sure what I'm going to do to you, female," he

said, his tone eerily casual. "If you aren't careful, pain will be involved."

Why did she have to taste honeyed whiskey even now, when he issued a threat? A taste both intoxicating and sweet, made all the sweeter as it blended with the ruggedness of his masculine scent, making it the perfect combination of exotic spices and whatever the heck aroused a woman's most primitive lust. Even better, he somehow overpowered the disgusting clash of flavors caused by myriad noises.

Death noises, mercenaries doing their best to murder each other.

In her younger years, she'd run away from a few foster homes, and spent some time on the streets. She'd seen terrible things. Beatings, crimes. Assaults of every kind. Each one had scarred her.

Some nights she woke up screaming and drenched in sweat, terrifying memories clinging to her subconscious. This—what she'd witnessed tonight—would haunt her worse. An ocean of blood...a bodiless head pitching past her feet...a sword amputating a hand.

Hysteria and panic burned through her, her stomach knotting, threatening to spew out the few bites of canned fish she'd managed to choke down. *If you aren't careful, pain will be involved.*

As Knox's words echoed in her mind, she got snagged by another crack and stopped abruptly. She erupted, then, wiggling free of his hold, threw another elbow. Contact. He grunted, blood pouring from his nose.

"Enough," he snapped. "Be still."

And accept her fate like a good little victim? Never! "I'm just getting started." She bucked, slamming the back of her head against his chin. Another elbow, then another, his breath gushing out.

When he snaked an arm around her neck and squeezed, the hysteria and panic conquered more ground. She dug her nails in his forearm and clawed, but he merely squeezed harder, cutting off her airway.

"Bastard," she rasped. "Let...go...now!"

"Are you ready to behave?"

I'm ready to peel off your face!

The tunnel began to quake, the cracks burrowing deeper, stretching farther. As the entire structure neared collapse, stars winked through her vision.

"I mean it. Calm down, female," Knox said.

Must escape. Fight...harder!

"I can't get unstuck," Nola cried.

He moved his grip to Vale's waist, allowing her to breathe. Sucking in a mouthful of air, she faced him. It was too dark to make out his features, or the position of his body, but she did her best to ram her fist into his goodie bags. Success!

He grunted, then snarled. She braced for retaliation, even as she attempted to ram his goodie bags again. But...

He never struck back, only blocked the second blow before hurling himself against her. The abrupt motion pushed her into Nola, and their group of three began sliding once again.

"What's happening?" Her sister's petrified voice ricocheted through the tunnel.

"You will not harm the females," another male snarled.

Vale tasted the citrusy tang of orange. Zion. He'd made a hasty introduction during the battle royal. He was as tall and muscled as Knox, with dark hair, black eyes, pale skin that appeared to have actual jewels embedded in select places, and a pair of spiked metal gloves. He too exuded untold savagery and a seemingly inexhaustible supply of carnality. More than once, he'd used his body to protect both Vale and Nola, taking blows meant for them.

What if he had saved them in the cave just so he could hurt them later?

Better question: How were these once-frozen guys alive?

Knox and Zion threatened each other. She *knew* they threatened each other in a foreign language. The menace and aggression they were throwing off gave them away.

As the two wrestled, she wiggled free of Knox's hold. Never had freedom been so sweet. Up ahead, she caught sight of a glimmering green light. The exit neared. Relieved, she leaned into Nola to increase their speed, and put more distance between her and the brutes.

When they spilled out of the tunnel, Vale landed on top of her sister with a thud. Nola had grabbed the backpack filled with blankets and medicine, and it cushioned the blow somewhat.

"Sorry, sorry," she said when the girl hissed in pain. No time to waste. Grabbing Nola by the coat, Vale rolled her out of the way just as Knox and Zion exited with even less grace than she had displayed.

As quickly as possible, she took stock. Night had arrived, northern lights streaking the sky with brilliant bursts of emerald and amethyst. So vivid. So cold! She lumbered to her feet, the whole world shaking, cracks spreading across the cavern walls.

Zion crouched, then slammed a gloved fist into the ground. More shaking. Massive crevices branched from the spot he'd punched.

Vale watched, horrified, as Knox fell through the widest opening, disappearing from view. Only, he must have grabbed hold of a groove on the way down because he swung his body up, up, legs first. And there must have been blades hidden in the toe of his boots; with a swipe of his leg, he disemboweled Zion.

She gasped, nearly vomited.

Little whimpers rose from Nola. "We have to stop them. They're going to kill each other."

"If we stick around, they're going to kill *us*. Come on!" Heart banging against her ribs, Vale jerked her sister upright and claimed the backpack.

As she ran, arms pumping, feet surely winged, northern lights highlighted a smooth path, but icy wind burned her eyes. Frick! She'd left her goggles behind. And her scarf. Nola was missing a glove.

At this rate, subzero temperatures would kill them before the men had a chance. Men who were…what? Ancient barbarians? How long had they been frozen? *Why* had they been frozen?

Had she and Nola somehow unleashed a horde of evil?

And how were the warriors frozen in the first place, without suffering any permanent damage?

Don't look back. The perfect slogan for today's adventures.

Vale swallowed a maniacal laugh. A business slogan, here and now? Well, why not? The habit had developed in college, when a professor had walked into the room and said, "Have a new motto or slogan ready to go each morning. Sell me on the reason you deserve an A, or fail the entire course." In times of stress, she reverted to her old ways.

Possible slogan for Knox: *Him fatale.*

Or maybe: *Ready to lay, eager to slay.*

"Don't understand…what's happening," Nola said between huffing breaths.

"Hide first, answers second," Vale replied. "Tell me you're feeling okay."

"Hurting, tired, cold. Heartbeat…warped."

Fury crackled, an undeniable fire in her veins, and yet it failed to heat her up. Or her sister, apparently. Nola's teeth chattered, and she shivered so violently she nearly tripped.

A hard weight suddenly collided with Vale, two intractable bands wrapping around her waist. With a gasp, she careened forward, losing her grip on Nola. Warm breath on her nape, a face-plant imminent. At the last second, her captor switched their positions, absorbing the bulk of impact himself.

He grunted, imbuing her mouth with the taste of honeyed whiskey. Knox!

Despite his actions, impact jarred her, air exploding from her burning lungs, bones almost shattering. Her brain rattled against her skull and opened a floodgate, allowing dizziness to rush in.

She groaned as Knox hauled her up, tossed her over his shoulder and took off in a mad sprint.

Those intractable arms held her in a vise-grip, squeezing tight enough to bruise. "Let me go!" Where was Nola? "You have to let me go."

"Vale!" her sister shouted. Then, at a lower volume, she cried, "Wh-what are you d-doing? S-stop, please."

"Be quiet, girl. You'll give our position away." Zion's voice boomed through the mountains—giving their position away.

He had Nola. Must have recovered from his disembowelment, then.

Desperate times, desperate measures. Vale kicked and squirmed with no regard for her own well-being, and finally managed to throw herself from Knox's shoulder. After everything she'd already endured, landing hurt. Landing hurt *bad*. Ignoring the avalanche of pain, she crawled to her feet and darted in the opposite direction.

When she spotted Nola trapped within Zion's arms as he raced away, she quickened her pace to give chase.

"Stop! Please! You don't understand. She's sick. She needs her medicine."

A few years ago, when Nola's fibromyalgia had flared, she'd become too weak to crawl out of bed. Her doctor prescribed opioid pain pills. Those little white pills had been a blessing and a curse, offering her a somewhat normal life while also making her dependent on each new dose. She could go twelve hours before withdrawal symptoms started. Profuse sweating. Full body aches. Thunderous heartbeat. And they only worsened, until she prayed for death. Vale couldn't, wouldn't, let her go through that kind of agony.

"Come get Knox," she shouted at Zion. "I'll help you kill him, if that's what you want, honest."

The guy never even slowed. Argh! Why abscond with Nola at all? Unless he wanted a woman for a very specific reason…?

"No!" The ice invaded Vale's soul. "Please, take me instead."

Nola flailed, tears freezing and glistening on her cheeks. Though she reached over his shoulder, desperate to make contact with Vale, the merciless Zion continued on.

"I'm coming…for you." Running, running. Every breath a painful chore, the frigid air stinging her nostrils and chilling her lungs. "Right behind…won't let him—*umph*!"

A hard weight slammed into her, throwing her down. Not again! Knox rotated faster, cursing her when they landed.

He flipped her over, restrained her with his muscled strength, and scowled at her with the kind of malevolence that would send an entire army fleeing.

"Enough, female."

Their gazes met, something hot and electric arching between them. She went still. *He* went still. For a moment, the clock seemed to stop, the rest of the world fading from her awareness. All she saw? His eyes. They weren't just bluer than any ocean, they were deeper, too. A woman could cannonball into those babies and drown—with a smile.

Knox's warmth enveloped her, until she was shockingly close to overheating. Beads of sweat even popped up on her brow.

"Let. Me. Go," she repeated, the breathlessness of her tone embarrassing her.

He shifted, every point of contact coming alive, rousing the most delicious prickles. Her breasts ached, and the apex of her thighs began to throb.

Her mind didn't like the man, but her body loved him. Her body *needed* him. No, no. Ridiculous! Her wrongly wired senses had confused dismay with desire, that was all.

His scowl grew darker. "Stop running from me. You're only making things worse for yourself."

"Wrong. *You're* making things worse for me." She tried to

ignore the fresh infusion of honeyed whiskey in her mouth...
and failed. Mmm. So good.

Would he taste just as good? Or better?

Whoa. Wake-up call! She wanted to kiss a *murderer*? No!

The world-fade reversed, everything coming back into focus.
Darkness, light. Chaos. The heat evaporated, making her feel
battered by frigid wind. Her mind replayed the brawl, the plethora of severed body parts. The chase. Her sister— Vale sucked
in a breath.

Save Nola, whatever the cost.

Without cataloging her intent, she punched Knox once, twice.
Dang it. He had a face like concrete, and her knuckles quickly
cracked and swelled. But he leaned back, out of striking distance, allowing her to wiggle free, like before.

She popped to her feet and glared at him. "I'm going after
my sister. Help me or get out of the way."

"Going to try to trade my life for hers again?"

"If that's what it takes, yes. I love her. I don't even like you."
Go!

One step around him, that was as far as she got. From his position on the ground, he was able to grab her ankle and sweep
her off her feet. Literally! And, because he didn't absorb the
worst of the impact, she cut her tongue on her teeth. A copper
tang eclipsed the honeyed whiskey.

As fast as lightning, he loomed over her. Black lines branched
from his eyelids, quickly shadowing both of his sockets. The
transformation like something out of a horror movie.

"Zion will protect her," he said. "Probably."

Probably? Not good enough. "He's a killer, just like you." The
second Vale's head stopped spinning, she tried to knee Knox's
testicles into his throat.

He caught her ankle and held on tight, a dark god lovingly
stroked by the glow of the northern lights. "Attack my manhood
a third time, female, and I'll assume you work with vikings."

His timbre smoldered with barely suppressed rage, and yet, it was also as cold and hard as steel. "I yearn to *torture* vikings."

He couldn't mean the ancient warriors...could he? No, of course not. Judging by his odd accent, English wasn't his first language. He'd meant something else, surely.

Even still, tendrils of fear slipped down her spine. "Stop calling me female." She wrenched free and vaulted up. "And stop stopping me! My sister needs her medicine, okay, which means I need to rescue her."

"I was able to observe Zion for five months as we fought in this All War. She'll be safe with him."

All War?

"I've never seen him harm a female," Knox continued. "Even an other-realm assassin with every intention of killing him."

Other-realm? "How can I get this through your thick skull? Nola. Needs. Her. Medicine." Unwilling to wait for his response, she faked left, darted right.

Knox caught her; of course he caught her. In a blink, he had her draped over his shoulder, clearly his favorite position, and carted her off.

She fought him until the cold turned her blood to sludge and sapped her strength. Soon, she couldn't move, could only shiver.

"So cold..." Too cold. "Please...follow... Zion."

"I'm taking *you* to safety. *Female.* You're welcome."

She gnashed her teeth. *Pretend to be reasonable.* "Win my sister...from Zion...safety...wealthy family pay...millions." Translation: Vale would write him a hot check. "Will do anything... you want."

"You'll do anything I want, anyway."

Okay, she clearly wasn't getting anywhere with him. She needed to think this through. If Zion truly was a good guy and wouldn't hurt a woman—a sentiment Knox didn't share, obviously—Nola *was* better off with him. Could Vale trust Knox's gold stamp of approval, though? He was a murderer, so lying wasn't too far outside his wheelhouse.

"Don't care about...your realms or All War," she finally said. "Only care about...sister."

Knox thought for a moment, then nodded as if he'd just made a monumental decision. "I have questions about Terra, you have answers. Give me the information I seek. In exchange, I'll let you go—maybe—and you can hunt for your sister on your own."

Maybe? Maybe wasn't good enough. Until she ditched him, though, she had to play along, and buy herself a little time. T-minus eleven hours before Nola became desperate for another dose of her pills. In the meantime...

Be the coffee bean. Change the water.

"All right. Yes," she said. "I'll tell you anything you want to know about, um, Terra. Yep. Good ole Terra." It was the Latin word for "earth," but might—probably—mean something else to him. "My favorite..." Person? Place? Thing?

"Realm," he offered with a frown.

"Yep. Realm. Of course." Her next full-body shiver nearly knocked Knox off his feet. "Too cold to think."

"Be careful, female." His deep baritone held a low, seductive growl of menace that was more potent than—

Whoa! Seductive menace? *Who am I?* Menace was *never* sexy.

"If you lie to me," he said, "or betray me in any way, you will become my enemy. My enemies die painfully—and always."

CHAPTER FIVE

As Knox sprinted across the frozen tundra, he summoned a thick cover of shadows. In seconds, total blackness shrouded him, hiding him—and Vale—from the view of others.

"Can't see," she said, her teeth chattering. "So dark."

"You don't need to see." The urge to return to the prison and pick off survivors besieged him, but somehow his desire to save the little Terran proved stronger.

One second ticked into a minute, more and more of her strength draining, until she stopped fighting entirely. She even lost her grip on her bag.

Earlier she'd mentioned medicine contained inside it. He doubled back, grabbed the pack and hefted a strap over his shoulder. She offered him no thanks. The feisty mortal had grown quiet. Too quiet. At this rate, she would freeze to death before he got her to safety.

Rifters at the ready? He glanced at his right hand. Three rings made of a crystal-metal hybrid adorned his first, second and third fingers, stretching from nail bed to middle knuckle.

A single clink caused the Rifters to vibrate. Then, when you waved them through the air, they mystically cut a doorway to somewhere else on Terra. You had to imagine where you wanted to go, so you could only visit places you'd been before, or seen in pictures.

On his left hand he wore a bejeweled ring that acted as a type of projector for the rice-sized device injected in his knuckle—the key to communicating with Ansel.

Every combatant owned a transmitter and a set of Rifters just like his.

Though Knox was too close to the combat zone for comfort, he pictured the bunker, his safe house. Then he picked a spot with his gaze about a hundred yards ahead, clinked the Rifters together, and waved the vibrating pieces through the air. In the spot he'd selected, two layers of air peeled away from each other, as if they'd ruptured, and an entrance to the underground paradise appeared.

The rift would remain open for sixty seconds. No more, no less. To prevent others from seeing inside the home—and rifting inside later—he summoned shadows, the darkness rising to shield the doorway.

The bunker was a masterpiece of technology earned from one of his previous All War victories, able to update automatically, self-clean, self-sustain and produce what he needed, when he needed it. The very reason he'd chosen the bunker as his weapon for this war. He'd known he could steal swords, daggers and guns from other warriors. Could—and had.

Minutes after arriving on Terra, he'd beheaded Legend of Honoria and claimed possession of his brass knuckle daggers. Mere minutes after that, he'd removed Jagger of Leiddiad's heart and won a revolver. Holster the gun, and it would mystically reload. An alcove and closet were filled with other weapons he'd taken from vikings and villagers. Shadows kept everything hidden and safe.

Vale groaned, and he quickened his stride. Almost there...

Knox entered the bunker, pleased to find everything intact, as expected. To the right, a small table with different maps, just as he'd left it. To the left, a waterfall cascaded into a large, stone-rimmed tub that resembled a natural cenote. Just ahead, a soft bed positioned underneath a canopy of fruit trees.

If the other warriors ever discovered the riches here, he would become even more of a target.

Knox tossed Vale and the bag onto the bed and spun, facing the rift, positioned to kill anyone who dared follow him through. Five seconds. Ten. Vale muttered incoherently about coffee beans. He needed to tend to her, and soon, but didn't allow himself to look at her. Fifteen seconds. Twenty.

The rift wove back together at last.

Knox sheathed his daggers and rushed to the bed to examine his guest. Her lips were tinted blue, her cheeks were chapped and too pink, and the rest of her was too pale. Once vibrant hazel irises had dulled and were now glazed with pain; her movements had become uncoordinated.

When mortals were exposed to cold for a long period, their bodies sacrificed their extremities to care for their internal organs. Vale had reached that stage, and was no longer able to shiver.

"Tired," she managed to whisper.

"Stay awake—that's an order."

"Trying…"

"We need to warm you up."

"Warm…yessss," she breathed.

"We must do it slowly." Too quickly, and her heart could burst from the strain created by uninhibited blood flow.

But how? The bunker had no fireplace.

The bath was controlled by a mix of magic and technology. With simple vocal commands, he could heat the water to his specifications. He could even heat different areas to different temperatures.

Very well. "I need to remove your clothing, Vale. All right? A bath is the best way to get you warm."

"Yes, anything. Hurry."

Motions strong and sure, he removed her jacket, thermals and tights, leaving her in a bra and panties. While some of the garments were strange to him, his translator supplied the proper words—until his brain short-circuited, and his jaw went slack. *Her body*. All feminine curves, ripe sensuality and wicked temptation.

Desire delivered a hard one-two punch to his gut—desire he couldn't control or override. He rubbed a hand over his mouth. *Ignore her appeal. Do not stare.*

She was curvier than he'd expected, with plump breasts, a trim waist and delightfully rounded hips. On the flat plane of her belly and thigh were multiple tattoos of flowers. Some petals appeared raised—to cover scars?

Yes, oh, yes. Someone had hurt her.

Ignore the rage!

Knox slid his arms underneath Vale's exquisite frame, then lifted her against his chest. Light as air. Though she hadn't succumbed to sleep, her limbs remained lax, her head lolling back and forth.

For a moment he missed her indomitable spirit. Which was foolish. Her indomitable spirit would cause him nothing but problems.

Knox carried her to the tub, and he plucked a piece of fruit from a tree along the way. After kicking off his boots, he stepped into the cool water, stopping when the surface reached his navel. He was shirtless, but still wearing pants for the sake of the girl—mostly.

"Gauge the female's core temperature, and heat gradually to prevent complications from hypothermia," he commanded, ensuring her face remained above the surface of water.

As they soaked, he ate the fruit, his stomach grateful for nour-

ishment after being empty for so long. At the same time, the grit
and grime from battle washed from his skin, and the antisep-
tic qualities of the self-cleaning water disinfected any lingering
wounds, speeding up the healing process.

In the ensuing fifteen...thirty...forty-five minutes, the water
warmed to an Iviland summer of old. Hot, but not stifling. Finally, Vale's coloring brightened.

Relief suffused him. Allowing her to float on her back, he
kept one hand under her head and moved behind her, her luscious little body stretching out before him, a buffet of sensual
delights.

His muscles clenched all over again, his blood growing hotter than the water. He wanted to see all of her, every nuance. If
he activated Shiloh's lenses, he could. Shouldn't he study every
inch of his enemy in great detail? Shouldn't he look...touch...
or even seduce her to his side? One kiss and—

He recoiled. One kiss would ruin centuries of hard work.

During training, instructors had repeatedly warned their
charges never to kiss a woman. *You'll find your downfall in her
lips.* Knox had understood the reason why the moment he'd
witnessed a couple locking lips. The two had lost sight of the
world, no one and nothing able to gain their notice. The absolute worst thing that could happen during war. Or ever. Even
when you were free, you had to remain ready for battle.

One day, though, all of that would change for Knox.

When Ansel and the entire royal family were dead, and the
High Council and its army of Enforcers had been eradicated...
then, and only then, would Knox discover the rich pleasures derived from devouring every inch of a woman. Maybe he would
even consider starting a family.

Never again would someone have the power to take a child
away from him.

Vale moaned and blinked rapidly. Appearing dazed, she swept
her gaze over him—

And gasped. She wrenched upright and scurried to the other side of the tub, shock and horror glittering in her kohl-rimmed eyes. Long locks of hair clung to the lace that shielded her breasts. In the light, multiple silver piercings glinted along the shell of her ear.

"You." Somehow, she turned the lone word into a thousand accusations. "The murderer."

"Yes. Me. An immortal made for war. Killing is what I do, what I'm good at. I do not live by societies' rules, and I'm abhorrent to those who do—those who've never had to fight to retain their liberties, those who are content to let others do the fighting for them, only to scoff at the results."

Her eyes widened. "You're immortal."

"I am. And I apologize for not bathing naked—the way you prefer me."

A blush spread like wildfire over her cheeks. "You heard me in the cave."

"I did." And he'd enjoyed every proclamation.

"Well, the list of things I know about you is growing. An immortal soldier who enjoys disemboweling his victims, teasing strange women about full frontal, and just all-around sucks."

His translator was supposed to update automatically, like the bunker, but he had trouble deciphering her meaning. He sucked—on what? It was supposed to be an insult, he was sure... but how?

He wouldn't ask. Her opinion meant nothing to him, because *she* meant nothing.

As she cast her gaze over her body, tremors rocked her, sending ripples through the water. When she caught sight of her undergarments, the roses in her cheeks deepened.

Rather than draping an arm over her breasts, she jutted her chin and glared at him, all *look your fill but never touch*, stunning and impressing him. Delighting him.

"Where are we?" she asked. "Wait. I remember. The air...

you created some sort of door." She blanched. *"How did you create a door?"*

"I will ask questions, female, and you will answer."

Now she flinched, as any intelligent person would when he used such a harsh tone, but this one bowed up a second later, as if gearing for a fight. "I have a name, you know. I'm—"

"Don't care."

"—Valerina Shaylynn London," she said, then acted as if he'd begged for more information about her. "My friends call me Vale. And I know what you're thinking. Valerina is a ludicrous name. I agree. And also, if my name is Valerina, why does my nickname rhyme with *hail* rather than *pal*? Funny story. As a child, I couldn't pronounce—"

"Enough!" Knox had no friends and wanted none. "What were you doing in the ice prison, *Valerina*?"

She humphed. "You didn't let me finish. *You* may call me Miss London. My sister and I— You remember her, yeah? The sick girl who needs her medicine? We were lost and looking for shelter. And I *knew* you belonged in prison. *I knew it!* What crimes did you commit, besides cold-blooded murder? Only all of them?"

Ignoring her questions, he barked, "Tell me everything. How you found the cave, and why you were lost in the area. Leave out no detail."

"No, thanks. I've seen this movie. Once you learn what you want to know, you'll have no more use for me, so you'll slice and dice me, then call it a day. Why don't we switch things up? *You* tell *me* everything, then *I* slice and dice *you*."

Knox crossed his arms over his chest. Usually, when someone threatened him, they died. So why did he admire this female for her bravery?

"Slicing and dicing won't kill me," he said. "I can regenerate organs and limbs."

"So, how *do* I kill you, then?" She batted her lashes at him, all innocence. "Asking for a friend."

Enough. "Back to a subject that matters. Before we arrived in my bunker, you agreed to answer my questions. You will hold up your end of the bargain. What you will not do—issue another threat. Because I won't ignore the next one. I'll make you regret it."

Paling, she scrambled up the pool's rocky ledge. Where did she intend to go? Knox swam the distance and dragged her back into the water.

As she struggled for freedom, her feminine softness rubbed against his masculine hardness, and he hissed in a breath. "Be still, Valerina."

"Rape wasn't part of our deal." Despite his threats, she nailed him with an elbow to the chin, her patented move. "You know what? Screw our deal. I refuse to answer your questions until my sister is at my side. Alive!"

He tightened his hold. *Do not let her continue to rub against you.*

He didn't try to stop her.

Resist the urge to rub back.

He rubbed back.

She wiggled with more force—rub, rub, rubbing, so wet, so warm—his resistance crumbling...

Will grind against her so hard I'll wring—

With a growl, he tossed her away from him, lest he do something they would both regret. She slipped under the surface, then came up sputtering. When she opened her mouth to most likely deliver a stinging retort, he realized and accepted he couldn't intimidate her. She wasn't like other people, which meant he shouldn't treat her the same as everyone else.

"Do not elbow me again, and do not run," he snapped. "And do not make me warn you again."

Another flinch, sheer terror radiating from her. But the terror didn't last long. She sneered and saluted him, saying, "Sir, yes, sir. Anything you say, Commander Douche."

Well, well. Her prickly exterior was a type of armor. He recognized the signs. After losing Minka, he'd been a walking, talking wound, predisposed to roar at anyone nearby. Anything to hide the hurt. If he'd let his emotions overtake him, Ansel would have exploited his vulnerability, and made everything worse.

He felt a wrench of sympathy for Vale—and a pang of connection. "How did you receive your scars?" he asked, giving voice to his earlier curiosity.

"A brute just like you didn't appreciate my finer qualities," she said.

His hands fisted. "Was he punished?"

"Oh, yes. I cut up his face. For the rest of his life, he'll see a reminder of me every time he looks in the mirror."

"I'm glad." Now, to figure out how to proceed with her. Interrogation had never been his greatest strength; he tended to rely on aggression, and pain. But the thought of crushing this female held no appeal.

Perhaps if he pretended to be reasonable, she would respond in kind and actually *be* reasonable.

Worth a shot. Water rippled as he softened his stance. "Give me ten minutes of your time, and absolute honesty. That's all I'm asking... Vale. In return—"

"You'll take me back to the mountain, so we can search for my sister," she interjected with a nod. "Yes. Okay. Agreed."

No. In return, he wouldn't take harsher measures against her. Let her assume whatever she wished, though. He couldn't be blamed.

"Tell me how you reached the prison," he prompted.

"I was on vacation with Nola. We went for a hike in the Khibiny Mountains. One second we were surrounded by grass and trees, the next we were surrounded by ice. We stumbled upon a cabin, and our guide left us to die. Two weeks later, we were running out of food and decided to venture out to find help. That's when we came upon the…prison."

"What do you know about the All War?"

"Nothing." She arched a dark brow. "What do *you* know about the All War?"

And he'd missed her spirit?

Again, he crossed his arms over his chest. "What do you know about vikings?"

"The basket…foot…base…*sports* team? Or the ancient, uh, barbarians?"

"Barbarians. Do you know where they reside, or what they are doing?"

"I think they're busy feeding worms. Underground. Because they're extinct."

"Are you asking me or telling me?"

"Telling?"

He pursed his lips. Exactly how much time had passed since Erik had used the Rod of Clima?

"Wait." Vale jolted, as if excited and dismayed all at once. "Were you frozen in Viking times?"

"Yes." They'd died out? "What year is this?"

She told him, and he jolted. He should have been prepared for the answer, since he'd known centuries had passed. He just hadn't realized he'd gone thirteen hundred years without speaking with Ansel…or that Seven had gone just as long without making contact with the High Council.

To Knox's knowledge, no All War had ever lasted more than five centuries.

He should contact Ansel now. The king had requested countless meetings throughout Knox's confinement, but he'd been unable to respond.

No, he decided. He would wait. The king would want answers he couldn't give, might even command him to do things he wasn't ready to do. He would hold out and make the king open communication with *him*.

"The news is stunning to us both, I see," Vale said. "I mean, you're walking, talking proof that sci-fi is real. I shouldn't fangirl, right, because you're a killer and all."

"Fangirl?"

"How were you imprisoned? A curse? Magic? It was magic, wasn't it? I *knew* myths were steeped in truth. How did you survive the ice? Your immortality?"

Her excitement drew him, a force too strong to deny. Slowly, every motion measured, he swam toward her. As she clocked his every movement, some of her excitement ebbed. She became wary, but also...fascinated?

He stopped directly in front of her and straightened to his full height. The scent of jasmine and honeysuckle hit his awareness, more delicious than before, and he was grateful he still wore pants.

But any second, his erection might break the fly.

Focus. Resist her appeal.

Can't. "Tell me, female. Do you have a clan? Better yet, do you have a man?"

A strange mix of panic, exhilaration and astonishment provoked the edges of Vale's mind, and she fought to maintain her composure.

Revealing your emotions gave others power over you. No, thanks. But come on! Myths were real, and Knox was part of one. She'd always secretly suspected fiction was more than fiction.

Once, she'd admitted her thoughts online. Within days, internet trolls had utterly annihilated her with comments about "conspiracy theories," telling her she was a nutjob and shouldn't procreate, and the world would be better off without her.

Go screw yourselves!

Hogwarts might actually exist, and mutants could be hiding in society. Maybe he was cursed. Or an incubus—a male demon who had sex with sleeping women. He was looking at her as if he was starved, and she was an all-you-can-eat buffet. The change in him stole her breath.

Did he look at every woman that way?

I'm not disappointed. I'm not.

Fight his appeal. Murderer, remember?

Dang it, maybe *she* was the one who'd gotten cursed. She'd stepped into that cave, and everything had changed. Her senses had heightened, and her body had developed an instant crush on the most inappropriate man on the planet.

Who was this man, really? *What* was he, exactly? Why did his eye sockets sometimes turn black? What powers did he possess? Besides creating invisible doorways and surviving an ice prison without physical injury for over a thousand years, of course. And how was he more beautiful with every minute that ticked by?

Maybe she could—and should—leverage his horniness to aid her escape. No other reason.

Or maybe she should just skip the crap altogether and engage prison rules, showing him who was boss.

Truth was, Vale would do horrible, depraved things to help her sister. Nola was still out there, withdrawal symptoms soon to hit, unless she or Zion found new pills.

Where had he taken her? Somewhere like this? Whatever *this* was. The rocky walls, stone floor and cenote told her they were in a cave of some sort, but that made no sense. Trees couldn't grow underground without sunlight, yet four fruit trees flourished amid zero rays.

"Vale?" he prompted.

Right. He'd asked her a question. "By *clan*, I assume you mean family. Yes. My sister, who still needs my help. *Our* help. And by *man*, I assume you mean husband. Yes," she said. A lie, sure, but only technically. Sometime in the future, she would get married, and the claim would be true. "I'm his moon and stars, and he'll pay a *huge* ransom for my safe return. He'll pay even more for my sister's safe return."

A muscle beneath Knox's eye ticked like a bomb about to detonate. "There will be no ransom. The male can do without you for a short time."

His voice...so rough and raspy, still so intoxicating. Once again, she got drunk on the sweet taste of whiskey and honey.

Wait. He'd just implied he had no plans to keep her long-term or chop her up into little pieces and eat her.

Let's get this Q and A wrapped up.

"Why am I here, Knox?" She used his name, hoping to spur him into using hers. The more he saw her as a living being with hopes and dreams, the kinder he would be, probably. "What is it you really want to know? And what is this place?"

He stared at her, exuding menace, but Vale refused to back down.

"There is only one thing you need to know," he said. "As long as you are necessary to my cause, as long as you do not seek my downfall, I will protect you."

I'm necessary? Excitement bloomed, but she quickly tamped it down. *Doesn't matter.*

See Vale pretend not to seek his downfall.

"All right." She checked a wristwatch she wasn't wearing. "You've got five minutes left. Come on. Dig deep and tell me what else you want to know."

"I want to know about Terra." He swam around her, once, twice, as if he wanted to see and savor every inch of her. "Your world."

Terra...world. Yep, just like sci-fi. "You mean Earth." *His nearness doesn't affect me. Nope. Not even a little.*

He stopped behind her and straightened.

She spun—realized he was *closer*. His crystalline eyes instantly mesmerized her, the massive size of his body thrilling her most feminine desires. How would his thick black stubble feel against her skin? Then there was his tree of life tattoo. It gave a girl lots of naughty ideas.

And it wasn't her fault. He was made up of all these sexy pieces that fit together and formed an even sexier picture, wreaking havoc on her heartbeat, causing her nipples to pucker, and igniting an ache much lower...

Dang it, what did his appearance matter? She wasn't going to date him. Knox wasn't a viable candidate for her love life. After her wild high school days, she'd asked herself the same three questions anytime a guy had expressed interest in her—which hadn't been often, since word had spread that Vale London no longer put out.

Those questions? How likely was he to (1) lie to her, (2) cheat on her, or (3) steal from her? If she'd answered 80 percent or more to even one, she'd declined the invite.

"Earth, yes." Knox stepped forward, only the barest whisper away. "I have also heard citizens refer to this realm as Gaia."

"Realm" again. She breathed him in, the exotic spices...the insatiable lust. "Why do you need me to tell you about Earth?" *Will pay zero attention to my shivers, and the ever-intensifying aches.* "Shouldn't you know about your own planet? Or—" *gulp* "—are you an alien?"

"My translator ascribes the most probable meaning to each word you utter. I'm currently picturing a little green man with big black eyes."

His translator? "Are you from another planet or not?"

"Yes and no. The most accurate description is 'another realm.'"

Argh! "What is a realm, then? I think *my* translator is on the fritz."

He frowned but said, "A realm is another plane, dimension, world or kingdom connected to other planes, dimensions, worlds or kingdoms through a system of portals."

Portals, à la *Stargate*?

"Upon our arrival," he added, "your people called the portals Bifröst."

Beef-roast? What the— *Forehead slap.* Bifröst, not beef-roast. The rainbow bridge in Norse mythology. The way people in one world traveled to another.

"Did you create a portal earlier, to enter this home?" she asked. Oh, frick. Was she on another world?

"No, I created a rift. Portals take you from one plane, dimension, world or kingdom to another. Rifts take you to other locations within the same plane, dimension, world or kingdom."

Okay, then. She was still on Earth, which was kind of a letdown. "What's the difference between planes, dimensions, worlds and kingdoms?"

"Planes are stacked on top of each other. Dimensions exist within the same space without interacting, and worlds play host to kingdoms."

Okay, she kind of wished she hadn't asked. *Information overload.* Deep breath in, out. Mistake! As close as he was, as decadent as his scent, she was growing dizzy with desires she couldn't fight.

Great! Now she needed a distraction from (1) the overload and (2) her attraction to Knox, which meant she needed to seek more information. "If you aren't an alien, what are you?"

"I'm an immortal warrior sent here to fight in the Terran All War, and win, whatever the cost."

"I know there are different types of immortals. Like, say, vampires and werewolves. What are you?"

"You mean the fanged blood drinkers of Leiddiad, and the beasts of Adwaeweth—though the latter are more like dragons than wolves."

Excitement restored, and she nodded.

"I'm not one of them, no," he said. "I'm more like a god."

He was joking, right? "A god of what?"

"Darkness."

In other words…the devil. Peachy. "And what is an All War?"

He ignored the question, and said, "Earth still has armies, I assume. They fight wars of their own." He reached out to sift a lock of her hair between his fingers. The jet-black strands looked like ribbons of silk against his damp skin, and the sight momentarily stole her breath.

Then his gaze met hers, his pupils spilling over his irises, and frozen oceans became infernos of arousal.

"Yes," she rasped. She didn't like the sight...because she liked it far too much. Yank. "Why do you want to know about our armies? Because *your* armies are planning a wide scale invasion? Well, you should watch a little *documentary* called *Independence Day* to find out what happens when our planet is threatened."

"If these military forces try to stop our war, the High Council will send in a contingent of Enforcers. Trust me when I say you do not want a contingent of Enforcers sent in."

High Council. Enforcers. All War. Too much!

As if sensing her rising tension, he reached out once again, and gently traced his knuckles along her jaw. She leaned into his touch, seeking comfort and more warmth.

What are you doing? Stop! She straightened with a jolt. Only one thing mattered right now. "Tell the truth. Will there be an invasion?"

He paused just long enough to ratchet up her stress level. "As long as your governments behave, no one from the other realms will step foot on your Earth until the war ends...and I'm crowned the victor."

CHAPTER SIX

The longer Knox peered at Vale, inhaling her lush sweetness, the more unhinged he felt. He was hard, his erection forged from titanium. Surely. Masculine awareness clawed at his insides, the need to taste his captive nigh overwhelming him, the desire to experience a kiss, his first kiss, a tantalizing temptation.

I see... I take.

Must resist! Men lost their heads around women—in more ways than one. And Knox didn't need to know whether or not Vale tasted as delectable as he imagined. He could guess the answer: She tasted *better.*

Victory depended on his ability to resist the urge to kiss her. But he could do other things with her...

He *needed* to do other things with her. But every time he gave in to the urge to touch her, she would accept him one minute, and reject him the next. The white-hot and ice-cold treatment was maddening.

"I'm going to touch you," he told her, announcing his intent, hoping to prepare her. No surprise, no ice-cold reaction. Probably.

"Why?" she croaked, even as she trembled. With anticipation?

"Because I want to." *Because I must.* "Because I can't not."

She gulped, her defenses…moldering? Slowly he reached out, giving her an opportunity to move out of range…

Contact.

He sucked in a breath. She moaned, the pulse at the base of her neck quickening.

Still white-hot.

Emboldened, Knox conquered more ground. He smoothed a lock of her hair from her forehead and cheek and hooked the strands behind her ear. The feel of her velvet soft skin… His erection throbbed. Any moment his pants might split.

Where was *his* ice-cold calculation?

He shouldn't have started this. And he definitely shouldn't do more. He had combatants to kill, a war to win, a royal family to execute and a home-realm to save. Distractions wouldn't be tolerated.

Although, if he *were* to indulge, there was no better location. No one could rift into the bunker, because no one had ever seen inside it.

Voice hoarse, he asked, "Do you desire me, Vale?"

Her mouth floundered open and closed, then her expression darkened. She lifted her chin. "Desire you? Please! I fear you. How many men did you murder today?"

"Only one." Unfortunately. "I also protected you."

"*Only* one." Her dry tone mocked him. "You sound disappointed."

"I am. If you hadn't noticed, they tried to murder me, too."

She ran her bottom lip between her teeth, making him wild for her. *He* wanted to nibble that bottom lip. "My point is that I do *not* sleep with killers," she said.

"Even killers who are trying to save themselves?"

"I get that you were in the middle of a combat zone," she said, brow crinkling, "but come on. You liked what you were doing."

"I like winning."

"You like bragging rights."

He hiked a shoulder. His vengeance depended on his victory, but he wasn't going to explain his reasons to her, or anyone. "I notice you make no mention of resisting me because of your husband."

Anger sparked at the reminder of her marriage, his grip on her hair tightening.

Why such a strong reaction? The husband wasn't here and wasn't a concern. Their bond bore no significance to the situation at hand. If Knox decided to keep her, he would keep her.

I'm considering forever now?

"You're the one hitting on a married woman," she said. "Does commitment mean nothing to you?"

"Commitment means *everything* to me." But only his commitment to victory. "And I'm definitely not hitting you."

"Hitting *on* means *flirting with*. Anyway." She rolled her eyes. "Your ten-minute inquisition is almost over. Do you really want to waste time debating whether I might or might not have the hots for you?"

Yes! Her attraction to him had somehow become a matter of great importance. "Have you *tried* sleeping with a killer?" He glided a fingertip under her smoky, I-want-you-to-remove-my-panties-with-your-teeth eyes, the gold molten, the green blazing. "You might like it."

Awareness sizzled between them.

"No. I haven't tried sleeping with a killer," she replied, her tone the vocal incarnation of an eye roll. "The liars and cheaters were bad enough."

Was any woman sexier than this one? She was so unlike the shy, reserved women he'd bedded in the past. She was forthright and confident, with a hard edge. Did she demand absolute satisfaction from her lovers?

Knox swallowed a moan of arousal. "The women in my realm wear makeup, but it smudges. Yours doesn't. Why?"

"Because it's tattooed." Her lids narrowed, her lashes nearly fusing together. "Now, enough about me and my sexual partners."

"How *many* partners?"

She stiffened. "Not that it's any of your business, but more than a horde, less than legion. Does that make me used goods in your exalted opinion? Huh? You wouldn't touch me with a ten-foot pole, right?"

He thought he might...envy those men. Either that, or he had indigestion. "Is that what you hope? Well, you're right. I would never touch you with a pole. I'd rather use my hands."

"I... You... Well. I don't know what to say."

"Did the males please you?" *I will make it my mission to please her.*

No. Enough!

"Like I said," she said, and cleared her throat, "we're done chatting about me and my sexual partners."

Not enough. Not done. "Shall we talk about me and mine instead?" he asked silkily.

"No, thanks."

"Do you want to know *anything* about my romantic history?"

"No need. I can guess. You've never had a serious girlfriend, and your favorite thing to make for dinner is a reservation for one. Long story short, girls want nothing to do with you. Because whoever told you underground lockup was a good first date lied."

He pursed his lips.

"Don't man-pout," she said, and sighed. "Lookit. I think you're sexy, okay. All right? There, I admitted it. You know my biggest secret. But news flash. You're only sexy to people with eyes."

Somehow, she had turned the compliment into a grave insult. Not that it mattered. His shaft throbbed harder. *She thinks I'm sexy.*

Doesn't matter. Blunt the need. Forge ahead. "Tell me why my *eyaer*—my instinct—would tell me you are necessary to me, something it has never done in the past."

Her gaze widened, and he caught a glint of excitement. *"Eyaer?"*

"Translated literally, it means *to see.*"

"And it sees that I'm necessary? Never mind. Haven't you realized I'm clueless about what's going on here? I don't have answers, only more questions. And now your time is up, so back to the ice mountains we go. We'll search for my sister—"

"I never agreed to find the girl."

"No, no, no. You did agree! A ten-minute Q and A followed by a hunt for Nola. Don't add no-good pretender to your long list of faults."

"I didn't lie. You assumed I agreed to your terms but think back. I requested ten minutes, with no promise of anything in return."

Frustration radiated from her, and she breathed in and out. "I'm approaching land mine level. Proceed with caution."

"Female—"

"Stop calling me female!" With a screech, she dove at him, water splashing. Again and again, she pummeled her fists into his chest. "You knew what I thought, so you had better take me to Nola or...or..."

Knox tossed her across the pool, sending her underwater for a cool down. As she came up sputtering, he climbed out, putting distance between them at last, lest the *eyaer* decide she was more of a threat than a necessity.

Drawing on the icy reserve that had served him well through every All War, he plucked and ate a second piece of fruit, then stalked to his closet, a small walk-in on the other side of the bed.

As he peeled away his pants, the drenched material caught on things—important, throbbing things—but he emerged with his appendage intact, so he'd consider it a win. He donned a black

T-shirt and a fresh pair of multipocketed, leathery camo pants. Both items were made from cloth he'd acquired on another realm; they shrank or expanded according to size and acted as a type of armor. They wouldn't stop a sword, but they could prevent minor scrapes. Next, he strapped on his preferred daggers and boots, then a belt and buckle.

He'd made the buckle himself, a required skill for victory. If he couldn't earn or steal a weapon, he had to create one. The buckle hid a small blade. A just-in-case precaution.

Though he listened intently, he heard no movement to indicate Vale had left the pool. Did she think the water offered a measure of protection against him?

Silly female.

However, she was right about one thing. Returning to the mountains wasn't a bad idea. Not to search for her sister, of course, but to find Carrick's trail, and kill any combatants who hadn't yet fought their way free of the rubble.

Knox would leave Vale in the bunker. She was warm and healthy, his weapons were hidden, and she had no way to escape. The only way in or out was a rift, and without Rifters, she couldn't create one.

When he emerged from the closet, Vale still hadn't left the pool. She watched him warily, and he realized he liked having her gaze on him. As he strode to the small alcove in back, he purposely flexed.

Inside the alcove, a funnel of shadows mimicked a tornado, hiding his arsenal within. If anyone other than Knox were to enter, the shadow winds would knock the offenders away—but only after the weapons did a little damage, metal slicing, hilts and gun barrel banging and battering.

"Avoid her," he commanded quietly. "Do her no harm." Berating himself for such a foolish allowance, he returned to the pool to glare down at her. "I'm leaving."

"Is this the part where I'm supposed to shed a tear?" she asked, and mockingly waved. "Bye-bye."

He gnashed his molars. "There is fruit on the trees. Eat it."

"Fruit." She grimaced, as if the word left a foul taste in her mouth. "Don't you have donuts? I'm pretty sure my blood type is sugar, vegetable oil positive, and it's time for a transfusion."

Whatever that meant. "I know you're starved. Why pretend otherwise?"

She lifted her chin—an action he now recognized as the donning of her armor. In that moment, he thought he understood. She wanted the fruit, but she would never admit it and risk revealing a weakness.

As much a warrior as I am.

"The fruit contains all the nutrients your body needs," he said, showing mercy. A first for him. "Also, there are clothes in the closet. Dress. There's a bed. Rest. Do nothing else. Anything you destroy, you'll pay for. And under no circumstances are you to enter the darkened alcove in back. You do, I'll know, and I'll be…displeased. Bad things happen when I'm displeased."

A shudder rocked her—a shudder she tried to hide with a yawn. "Where are you going?"

"Back to the mountain."

She perked up. "How long will you be gone?"

"As long as it takes."

"As long as it takes to what?"

He offered no response.

"Fine. Don't tell me. But will you pretty please with a cherry on top search for Nola while you're there?" Clad in only her lacy black undergarments, she finally climbed out of the pool. Water droplets sluiced over her curves as she rushed to the bed.

The sight of her…

Blood pumped through his heart valves faster, harder. So much harder.

Why did he react so strongly to this woman? Why was she

necessary to him? "If I come across your sister, and I'm not doing anything else," he added in an effort to prove he couldn't be manipulated by lust, "I'll kill Zion and bring her here."

She sighed, as if disappointed in him. "Is killing the man a must in this deal?"

"It is."

"Well." She thought for a moment, cleared her throat, then nodded. "If you see Nola, but you can't...uh, take care of Zion, please, I'm begging you, give her this backpack, anyway."

A favor, then. "I will do this...but you will owe me." Tit for tat.

"Yes, yes," she said without hesitation, surprising him. "I'll owe you."

"Don't you want to know what I'll demand as payment?"

"Don't need to know. I'll do *anything* to ensure my sister is as healthy as possible."

Such loyalty was admirable, and Knox envied the girl. He'd never had a brother, sister or friend in his corner, never had anyone willing to so much as spit on him if he were on fire, much less aid him. Only Minka had loved—

Blank your mind. Forge ahead. Motions clipped, he accepted the bag and hooked the strap over his shoulder.

Needing space from his captive, he peered about twenty feet away from Vale, clinked the Rifters together and waved his hand through the air, at the same time summoning a veil of shadows. Air peeled back, revealing the ice mountains, but only to him. Vale couldn't see past the gloom.

Frigid winds blustered inside the bunker, snowflakes dancing with dust motes.

She gaped and shivered from the sudden cold. Feeling oddly protective, he picked her up and carried her back to the bed, then draped the covers over her wet body.

"I have working legs, was just about to run for cover," she

grumbled, scrambling to her knees. Armor still in place. "I'm not a doll."

"You are whatever I say you are." She was a vision of loveliness.

"So...did you just open a rift?" she asked, scrutinizing the array of shadows.

"I did. And now I must go."

Without another word, he unsheathed his favorite daggers and entered the subzero terrain. A swift visual sweep revealed no one lurked nearby, and night still reigned, though the parade of skylights had faded.

Knox waited for the rift to close, ensuring no one sneaked into the bunker and harmed Vale while he was away.

No one harms my mortal.

Determined to get this done and return to her—because he had more questions—he marched across the ice, his gaze scanning, scanning.

Clang. Whoosh. Clang. His ears twitched as the telltale sounds of battle registered. At least two combatants were in the middle of a brutal sword fight.

With shadows concealing Knox's body, he trekked up a ridge. The only thing that gave him away was the snow crunching under his boots.

Careful. He had to remember. The moment he had an enemy in range, that enemy had *him* in range.

At the top of the ridge, he took stock of the fallen prison. Large hunks of ice had piled up, forming towers. There was no movement underneath to indicate life. Four ice towers had sprouted, each with jagged icicles protruding from their sides. Petra's doing.

Three combatants sparred: Bane, Celeste and Gunnar.

The female and Gunnar worked together, attempting to corner Bane. The male was too skilled and repeatedly dodged their blows. Even the ones he couldn't see. His goggles rested on the crown of his head, allowing him to track the pair with his beast-like senses rather than sight.

A startling new development—Celeste had abilities Knox hadn't suspected. She could disappear from view, then whisk to a new location. Because of Knox's eye lenses, he was the only one who could see her when she vanished. But he only detected a hazy outline.

The more he watched her, the more determined he became to end her. Celeste became intangible, too, ghosting through her opponents.

Yes, she had to die. And soon. Before she gained more weapons from her kills.

No mercy.

His gaze returned to Gunnar. *No real threat.* There was nothing special about his sword—wait. There was something about it. Something had changed since the last battle. Now the *eyaer* suddenly shouted {*Must have it.*}

Very well.

Even though Gunnar hadn't spoken to Celeste in more than thirteen hundred years, he fought to protect her, as if he loved her, using his power to move objects with his mind, exposing himself to injury in order to shield her. A mistake. When he used his power, his body freeze-framed for a split second.

A split second could be the difference between life and death.

Knox made his way down, quiet, quiet, nothing but a creeping shadow.

When Celeste reappeared behind Bane, the warrior sensed her and tried to spin out of the way, but Gunnar blocked one side and an ice tower blocked the other.

A triumphant Celeste took advantage, ghosting through to drive her sword into Bane's sternum. The blade came out his back, stopped only by the hilt.

Before she could render a death blow, he kicked her in the gut, sending her stumbling back—without her sword.

Roaring, he yanked the weapon free. Blood rushed out, and he smiled coldly. Smiled *viciously* when he lifted his blood-soaked prize. Then his body began to turn, bones elongating and sharpening, muscles plumping, skin glimmering as if sheened with iridescent scales.

He took one step toward Celeste, only one, before his knees buckled, the sword falling from his grip. Head thrown back, he unleashed a second beastly roar.

Knox came to an abrupt halt. Celeste and Gunnar tensed, preparing to flee. Like him, they knew they would need help if Bane fully turned. The *world* would need help.

Waiting...

The transformation ceased, the male batting at the gash in his chest.

Interesting. Rumors suggested Celeste's sword leaked a poison capable of nullifying innate abilities. Knox had wondered, but she'd used it so infrequently it had been difficult to tell. He made a note in his mental file: *the rumors are true.*

Want that sword!

Celeste dove and rolled across the ice, picked up the discarded weapon to stab the thrashing Bane in the back.

Gunnar rushed over, his own sword raised and ready.

He'll kill Bane. As he celebrates, I'll strike. Still unseen, still quiet, Knox rushed forward.

With one hand, Bane blocked the blow; with the other, he backhanded Gunnar so forcefully he flew into Petra's thickest tower and slid to his ass. The pop of breaking bones rang out, his head hanging at an odd angle.

He'd damaged his spine, then. For the next few minutes, he would be paralyzed. All right. Knox adjusted his game plan. He would take out Gunnar, the one closest to him, then Bane.

Closing in on his target... The male remained awake and aware, radiating panic as he tracked the approaching cloud of shadows. He knew. He knew death had come for him.

On guard just in case Gunnar sought to lure him into a false sense of security, Knox stepped on the sword, holding it down. No lure. Gunnar remained unmoving.

Without a moment's hesitation, Knox thrust a dagger through the warrior's throat. Once, twice, again and again, hacking, hacking until Gunnar's head detached from his body.

Twenty combatants stood between Knox and victory.

Suddenly, crackling power surged through Knox, the ability to activate the sword taking root. Whatever the sword could do. Until he knew, he wouldn't be using it.

Kill Bane, then Celeste. Search for Nola—maybe. Return to Vale.

"No!" Celeste screamed.

Knox expected to find her ripped apart by Bane. Instead, the male was on the ground, still writhing in pain. Celeste stood between them, staring at Gunnar with horror, shock and anguish.

Won't feel guilty. It was him or me. I chose me, always.

Win the war, gain my freedom.

"There cannot be two winners." Knox sheathed Gunnar's sword, letting the blade rest against his back, and approached his next target. "I did you a favor."

"You did *yourself* a favor. You are nothing but a gutter rat, just like everyone says. You killed him. You killed the best person I've ever known."

"I killed him easily—and I enjoyed it," he lied, deciding to razz her and use her emotions against her.

A wise move. With a howl of rage, she advanced on him. Knowing he had to be swift if he had any hope of superseding her ability to ghost through him, he met her halfway. She swung her sword wildly, but he blocked, trapping the metal between his daggers. He kicked her in the stomach, just as Bane had, sending her stumbling backward, gasping for breath.

Knox followed her down, pinned her shoulders with his knees and lifted the daggers.

Sudden, crippling pain shot through his collarbone, spreading through every muscle in his body in seconds, making him feel as if he'd been roasted on an open flame.

He'd been fast, but Celeste had proved faster. And despite the distractibility of her rage, she'd had the presence of mind to ghost, glide an arm up, up and stab him with her poisonous sword.

As the sensation of roasting became more exaggerated, the shadows surrounding him dissipated without his permission.

I'm weakening? His thoughts fragmented, black dots winking in front of his gaze.

Going to pass out? Here, now?

I'm defeated?

No! Not tonight, not ever.

Even as the dots expanded and bled together, Shiloh's lenses prevented full-on blindness. *Hurry.* Knox readjusted his position and jabbed a dagger into—the ground. She ghosted and rolled. Not missing a beat, Knox rolled with her—over her. When she solidified, he worked to repin her shoulders. She bucked, nearly unseating him, but still he managed to nick her carotid.

As her movements slowed, he wrapped his hands around her bloody throat and squeezed. But her skin was too slippery to clasp for extended periods of time, and his grip was too weak to do any harm. *Growing feebler by the second.*

"Gunnar was a good man," she screamed, clawing at his arms. "He had family, people who loved him."

"Bane has people who love him, and yet you planned—plan—to kill him." *Bane. Can't forget he's nearby.* "To win the war, Gunnar had to die. You know this."

"No! We would have found another way."

This always happened. A group of combatants would band together, hoping to live in peace. As long as an All War winner wasn't declared, the High Council couldn't claim the new realm. In theory. But alliances never lasted. And trust between individuals tasked with killing each other could never be sustained.

"There *isn't* another way." *Feebler...* Probably her intention all along. Waste time with conversation—distraction—then strike when he could no longer fight back.

He had to face facts. He wasn't going to prevail against her. Not tonight, not like this. He needed to run.

Run? From an enemy? Oh, how the thought chafed.

"You're wrong, murk." Celeste pounded her fists into his chest, and her knees into his back. "We would never hurt each other. We would have spent the rest of eternity here. If the All War doesn't end, the High Council cannot invade. The rules—"

"The rules mean nothing. The corrupt High Council controls Enforcers—the true power. They'll get their hooks in this realm one way or another, no matter the outcome of the war."

Knox believed the High Council could use the Enforcers to overthrow every leader in every realm, all at once. He believed they continued to build their armies, intending to do just that. One day...

A worry for another day. Today, now, he had to run or he was going to die. There were no other options.

He lumbered to his feet and jumped back. Just in time. Celeste swung the sword, the blade slicking across his chest. More poison, more pain.

With a hiss, he leaped into motion. Running, running, knowing his life depended on it.

CHAPTER SEVEN

A reprieve from her captor! Time to think up a way out of this mess and get her mind off the awesome awesomeness of "fiction" coming to life right before her eyes, and her body's unprecedented, wanton reaction to Knox.

Or not. Her mind wanted what it wanted—more time to dissect thousands of thoughts about Knox.

At least she'd worked up the perfect rationale for her shocking desire for him. Trapped in the mountains, she'd been in survival mode, thinking she and Nola were going to die. It would have been weird if her body *hadn't* reacted when a gorgeous dark knight entered the picture. Relief was a powerful aphrodisiac, probably the greatest aphrodisiac in the history of ever. She hadn't read a scientific study about it or anything, but then, she didn't really need to. She was living proof.

And Knox *had* saved her life, whisking her away from the elements. He'd never actually harmed her. He'd even carried her away from the big, bad wind after opening a rift, and gently settled her on the bed, as if she were a treasure in need of protection. He'd ordered her to eat and offered her clean clothing.

There was a wrench in her argument, though. While the big

bruiser had saved her, he'd condemned her sister—maybe—the only person Vale loved. On the other hand, Knox believed Zion would take extra special care of her sis.

Was Knox searching for Nola even now?

The man was a puzzle Vale had no idea how to solve.

Ugh. Wrong analogy. Puzzles had always intrigued her. As a teen, she'd spent hours with Carrie, putting together the most complex mechanical puzzles, while challenging each other with riddles.

The more you take, the more you leave behind. What am I?

Come on, Care Bear. Give me a tough one. You are footsteps. *Duh!* No way Vale was hanging around to try to piece together the intricacies of Knox of Iviland, though. If escape was possible, she was going to escape. Obvi.

Mind set on a plan of action, she clambered from the bed, balanced on unsteady legs. She would dress, as requested, and pray her undergarments dried fast; at least the pool had cleaned them. Then she would search the entire enclosure for weapons and eat her weight in fruit.

If she discovered a way out, she couldn't use it until Knox Her Socks Off returned. Just in case he'd captured Nola. So, she'd also have to find somewhere to hide as she awaited his return. After he fell asleep, she could free her sister—if he'd tied her up—and get the heck out of Dodge.

In the closet, she performed a quick inventory. Four racks, two on each side, overflowing with black shirts, pants and fur vests, each garment made of a fabric she couldn't identify. Buttery soft, incredibly stretchy, seemingly more durable than leather, but made of natural fibers—natural *alien* fibers? She shuddered. Between the racks were five drawers, one stacked on top of the other.

Vale selected a shirt and a pair of pants at random. When the two settled over her body—

"What the—" She nearly jumped out of her skin as the shirt and pants shrank, conforming to her smaller shape and size.

Suddenly they were a perfect fit. Not too tight, and zero sagging. Advanced technology, or resources or whatever it was rocked the house.

In one of the drawers were folded socks. Like the other garments, they shrank to fit. The same thing happened with a pair of steel-toed boots.

Dude. A girl could get used to this. Vale kicked out a leg, liked how powerful it made her feel, then kicked again.

Okay, enough thrilling over her new out-of-this-world outfit. Time was a-ticking, and she had a lot of crap to do.

She made her way to the bed and plucked a piece of purple fruit. Squishy like a peach, smooth like an apple. Scentless. If this thing tasted like burnt hair on a donkey's behind, there would be hell to pay, and Knox would be the one to get the bill.

Tentative, she took a bite...and moaned. *Oh, glory hallelujah.* If cotton candy had married chocolate dipped strawberries, this fruit would be their sugar baby.

Oh, the possibilities! If she and Nola made donuts out of the fruit...talk about life-changing! And, even better, if the fruit was truly healthy, as Knox had claimed, sales would double—no, triple.

Considering she experienced a new torrent of strength with every bite, she believed him.

The shop isn't a priority right now. Get your butt in gear. Right.

Vale moved on to her next task: investigating every inch of the home, on the lookout for doors and windows...*frick!* Where were the doors and windows? Considering the immense height of the ceilings and the space needed for those trees, the enclosure was smaller than she'd assumed. And those trees...they were indeed thriving without sunlight. The only source of light came from the glowing—limestone?—walls, and the only source of water came from the waterfall that fed into the gorgeous cenote.

Furniturewise, there was a bed and a table with a couple chairs. The bathroom had a sink and a mirror, but no toilet. Did he not have the same needs as humans?

But, but… What if she had to go? Hopefully the toilet was just hidden. Lastly, she approached the alcove Knox had forbidden her to enter.

Don't want me messing with your stuff, don't kidnap me.

She peeked inside. Good size, but empty. Dull walls, no glow. So dark, in fact, it looked like an endless abyss. The same kind of darkness she'd experienced inside the ice cavern, and on the trek through the rift, when she'd watched shadows rise from the ground and encompass her. She'd been horrified but also fascinated, yet Knox had continued on, unaffected.

Now she wondered if he could *manipulate* shadows. Ancient humans had considered him the god of darkness for a reason.

Concentrate! Had he hidden weapons in here?

Opportunity Knox.

He might know if she entered, he might not. A visual search revealed no hint of a motion detector or sealing tape. Maybe he'd only wanted to scare her. Anything to keep her out of his inner sanctum, right?

Cautious, unsure, she stepped inside. The thickest shadows darted away from her, as if pushed by a strong wind. Weird. She felt around but encountered no shelves. Several times she thought she caught a glint of metal in the center of the gloom…a dark tornado that remained in the alcove, even as it maintained a strict distance from her, as if programmed to avoid anything human.

Excitement sparked. Weapons could be hidden in here, the tornado-thing swirling them around and around, keeping them steady in the eye of the storm.

Curious to know what would happen, she roundhouse kicked the shadows an-n-nd they whipped toward her face to avoid her foot, brushing against her cheek before switching directions.

Sharp pain. Warm blood. She reached up, felt a cut, and grinned. There *was* something sharp hidden in there.

Her body, her *movements*, were a catalyst to the relocation of the shadows.

What if she could be in two places at once?

Vale returned to the bed to steal a tree branch. Except, she tugged on one—no luck. She kicked another—no luck. Finally, she wrapped her arms and legs around the longest, thinnest branch and hung from it, letting her weight and gravity do the work.

Success! She raced back to the alcove, branch in hand. For the first time in her life, her ballet classes were going to pay off.

Before her mom died of a brain aneurysm, Vale had taken lessons. In fact, Bethany London had named her daughter after her dream job—ballerina—and *her* mother, Valerie. And oh, crap, thinking about the family she'd loved and lost caused an invisible knife to stab Vale's chest. Her eyes burned; because dust had thickened the air or something, and she was super allergic, probably.

Forget the past. Concentrate on the present.

She lifted her arm, extending the stick she'd liberated. Just like before, the shadows darted to the other side of the little room in a bid to escape her. Keeping the stick in position, she leaned over and kicked out her leg. The shadows darted away, whizzing toward her face.

She was ready—nope. She wasn't. Something sliced her palm, but she'd failed to catch it.

Trying again. She performed a pirouette, gaining momentum, moving, always moving. *Now!* Extended branch. Darting shadows. Kicked leg. Darkness zoomed toward her face to avoid her foot—

Yes! Her fingers wrapped around something cold, hard and sharp. Pain lanced her palm, blood dripping from a new wound. Other objects banged into her neck and shoulder before whisking away. Despite the terrible onslaught, she held on tight to her prize.

She grinned. A dagger. And what a pretty dagger it was. The crystal handle reflected countless rainbow shards.

A sudden, arctic gale caused the temperature to drop a few thousand degrees. Dread skittered down her spine, because she knew. Knox had just opened a rift.

Clutching the blade, she raced into the living room. Her mind whirled. There was no time to hide. She would have to face him head-on.

Through a new doorway, she spied mountains, moonlight and yes, her captor. He sprinted closer, without his usual grace, and finally stumbled into the bunker. Crimson soaked his shirt. His features were pinched with strain, his skin ashen.

Her first reaction disturbed her. Fear—for his life.

He dropped Nola's backpack, saying, "Get away from the rift."

Had he even searched for her sister? Yes, he was injured and might have been waylaid, but fury overrode any hint of sympathy. Her new tasks took shape: *Injure and weaken him further, tie him up. Interrogate him, escape the bunker without freezing to death.*

No mercy. She couldn't hesitate, would act. Now!

As Knox reached out—to push her aside?—Vale struck. The dagger sliced his powerful shoulder. The sight of blood coupled with the knowledge that she had been the one to hurt another living being nearly emptied her stomach.

A bomb of rage detonated in his crystalline eyes, and he roared, eradicating any sense of safety she'd had. Fear turned her feet into concrete blocks, leaving her defenseless as he grabbed her and flung her toward the bed. Upon landing, her lungs deflated, her head spun, but she never lost her hold on the dagger.

A glaring Knox took a step in her direction, radiating pure menace, only to crumple to the floor.

How bad were his injuries? And why did she care?

Doesn't matter. Determined, she leaped up and raced to the

closet, where she filched another shirt. She would use it to bind
Knox's wrists.

Halfway back, she paused. A woman had just stepped through
the veil of shadows—the rift—entering the bunker. Dark hair,
tall, slender. Even in profile, Vale recognized her. The dead-
woman-walking who'd tried to decapitate Nola. DWW still
held a sword.

Incapacitate the brunette, then *tie up Knox.* No way she would
allow Nola's would-be murderer to go free and try again. Plus,
the brunette was too focused on Knox to notice her. This was
the best time to strike.

Brunette swung at Knox, who hadn't moved from the floor.
As he blocked, then rolled, and Brunette followed him, Vale
sprinted over, unnoticed.

Now! She struck, the dagger sinking into Brunette's shoulder,
metal anchoring to bone. The ensuing scream of shock and pain
left a lemony taste in Vale's mouth.

Frantic, Brunette dropped her sword, reached back to wrap
her fingers around the dagger's hilt and yank the blade free. A
river of blood gushed out.

Weaponless now, Vale dove for the discarded sword. By the
time she straightened, however, Brunette was gone.

"Where is she?" Vale demanded.

"Behind you," Knox rasped, the taste of whiskey and honey
overshadowing the lemon.

Vale spun, just in time. Brunette reappeared and slashed at
her, but she managed to jump out of range.

Their gazes met, held, fury to fury.

"Stay back," Vale commanded, wildly swinging the weapon,
an action meant as a warning.

But Brunette stepped toward her at the same time, so the
blade slicked over her throat. Also at the same time, Brunette
swung *her* sword. And oh, frick! A sharp pain erupted in Vale's
collarbone, warm blood pouring down her torso.

Vision flickering in and out, she stumbled backward, dropping the steel.

Brunette dropped her weapon, as well, and clutched her bleeding throat, starlight eyes wide with alarm, shock and anguish. Her mouth opened and closed, but she never made a peep. Then her head just…slipped off her body.

The sight paralyzed Vale. Acid flowed through her veins, and nausea stirred in her stomach.

The headless body thumped to the floor, spurting an ocean of crimson. She had…she had killed…she had killed a woman… she had killed a woman so awfully.

But…she should have felt more resistance. So much more. Unless the sword was super mega sharp, like one of those ninja type kitchen knives you bought after watching an infomercial.

Order now! Our blade removes a human head so smoothly you'll swear you're only cutting a tomato!

A hysterical laugh escaped, maniacal even to Vale. This was an accident, only an accident, but it was also a heinous, unforgivable crime.

She couldn't cope…needed…what? *Nothing* would help. She—

Was driven to her knees by a wave of unfettered energy, a thousand scenes suddenly playing like movies inside her mind, each one filled with people she'd never met, places she'd never visited and training she'd never received.

Crying out, she pressed her palms against her temples, her fingers tangling in her hair. Too much!

Faces, so many faces. A queen and her harem of male concubines. Field after field of flowers. A family of five girls. Vale was the oldest. No, no. Not Vale. One of the girls called her Celeste.

The name opened a mental door to a thousand other voices, all screaming, desperate to be heard.

Win Terra, or I'll make pelts of your sisters' skins.

Whatever you must do, come home to us, dear sister.

Chanting. *All hail the Savior of Occisor.*

Occisor. Home of all those flower fields, to potions and pheromones, where females ruled society, and men were merely procreation chattel.

During the Occisorian All War, women had feared loss of control more than anything. Bow to males? Never! Celeste had seduced a combatant for information, killed him to ensure he couldn't win her world, and inadvertently entered the war... then purposely and methodically did everything in her power to win it.

The High Council congratulated her. Twelve men and women whose smiles never reached their eyes. *Evil...*

Later, one of her sisters said, *I'm going to infiltrate the High Council. I must. They cannot build a vast army of Enforcers merely to keep the peace as they claim. Someday, they'll attack us, and we must be prepared.*

Eyes squeezed tightly closed, Vale gave a violent shake of her head. *Enough!* But the scenes played on, one man battling his way to the forefront. A hot black man named Gunnar. He looked at her with such longing, such devotion, and she felt the same for him.

We'll work together, my love. We'll lie and cheat if we must, to ensure you are Terra's winner and the savior of your family.

What of you? Celeste had asked. *How can you forfeit victory on my behalf?*

I am the seventh son of Trodaire's king. If I win this realm, I will rule it, a sovereign in my own right. But what good is a king without his queen?

The same man later said, *I've studied past victors. We must take out Bane, Knox and Zion as soon as possible, or they'll continue to kill, gaining more and more weapons, and we'll lose.*

Any second now, Vale expected her skull to crack open and the bombardment of thoughts and emotions to spill out. She was uncomfortable in her skin, her body no longer her own; she was like a house filled to the brim with uninvited guests.

"Help me," she pleaded, opening her eyes.

Knox had climbed to his feet. The tendons in his neck strained as he snapped, *"Little fool."*

He stretched out his hand and—she gasped. His eye sockets had turned black again as dark mist rose from his fingertips, drifting to the dead woman, removing her jewelry, then picking her up and tossing her through the rift. Disposing of her, as if she were garbage. The severed head received the same treatment.

Then the rift closed.

Doing her best to ignore the mental onslaught jumbling around inside her head, Vale lumbered to her feet, hissed. The pain was worse, but at least the blood loss was less severe.

Then her gaze landed on the discarded jewelry. A sense of possessiveness eclipsed everything else. Three crystal rings. *Mine!*

With a groan, she stumbled toward them. Knox swooped in, beating her to the punch. The jerk confiscated the jewelry and the weapons.

"Give me," she commanded.

He flashed perfect white teeth somehow more menacing than fangs. "You have no idea what you've done, female."

"Yes, I do. I saved your life…*killed* a woman." Earlier she'd felt an invisible knife stab into her chest; now the blade returned and twisted. "I—I didn't mean to do it, just wanted to injure her, to stop her from going after Nola."

Knox closed in, gripped her forearms tight enough to bruise and shook her. "You've guaranteed your death, Vale. And now, you'll leave my bunker."

Leave? Something strange was happening to her, and the thought of being on her own suddenly terrified her. "I'm necessary to you, remember?"

Or had she misunderstood during the Q and A? Right now, Celeste's memories were screwing with her own.

"I don't care. You must go. I won't allow a combatant to stay in my home."

Men never wanted to keep Vale around. She should be used to it. And what did he mean "combatant"? Celeste had used the same description. "You're wrong about me, okay?"

"You *are* a combatant," he said, intractable, merciless. "A member of the All War. No more stalling. Out you go."

Tears welled, but she blinked until they were gone. No way she'd cry in front of him or anyone.

She forced a sneer. "Fine! I wasn't a fan of Hard Knox University, anyway. Be a lamb and take me to Zion, would you? Unless you're too scared of him?"

His upper lids dipped low. "You don't want to be around another combatant right now." Radiating menace, he clinked his crystal rings together—rings just like the ones Celeste had dropped—and waved his hand through the air. "I'll take you to the other side of the realm."

A rift opened, air splitting down the center, the two sides peeling away from each other—

Cool, clear water poured into the bunker, soaking them both, and he spewed curses.

"One last dunking for old times' sake, eh?" she said, offering another sneer.

"The landscape has changed since last I rifted to that particular location."

Small, circular sections of the floor opened up, revealing drains. As soon as the rift closed, the water gone, the drains did a Transformers-type modification, becoming fans, blowing air through the entire bunker.

Fatigue settled on her shoulders, weighing her down. "Just… take me home."

"To your husband?" Humanity vanished from his countenance, leaving an expression of such cruelty, she wished she'd found somewhere to hide—forever. "No. I've changed my mind. You'll stay here."

Do not cave. "Too bad, so sad—for you. I haven't changed *my* mind. I want to leave."

Knox tilted his head to the side and glared at her. "You're staying here, and that's final. But hear me well, Vale. If you make one move against me, I will kill you without a qualm."

Caving...

No! "Save your threats," she said. "I'm sick of them."

"You mistake me. I never threaten. I vow."

CHAPTER EIGHT

The effects of the poison ebbed more with every minute that passed, until Knox was steady-ish on his feet, the pain in his shoulder nothing but a dull ache. His mind remained in turmoil.

He could barely comprehend the things he'd just witnessed.

Celeste had followed him through the rift. Vale—his necessary—had killed her, becoming immortal and entering the All War. Between one second and the next, her hair had shimmered as if dusted with diamond powder, her skin had deepened in tone, appearing dipped in a startling mix of gold and bronze, and her eyes had brightened.

Immortality looked good on her. Understatement. Immortality looked *incredible* on her.

With Celeste dead, there were now nineteen combatants—

Wrong. Vale had replaced Celeste. There were still twenty combatants standing between Knox and victory.

Vale had no idea she'd entered a battle to the death, or that she'd just become his enemy and a major target for *all* combatants.

She gave him one of her mocking salutes. "Since I'm not currently making a move against you, why don't you tell me why I'm seeing Celeste's entire life inside my head?"

Her memories? No. An impossibility. "You're mistaken. You can't—"

"Occisor, Celeste's home-realm. Gunnar, her lover. Her *love*," she amended. "You lopped off his head."

She *had* taken Celeste's memories. How? Why?

The answer hit him in an instant. Vale had a supernatural ability of her own. Did she only absorb memories alone, or everything that had made up the person? Like preternatural powers?

If so... Vale could now render her body invisible and intangible.

He stroked his jaw. Either way, she was doing something no other combatant could do, and she had the potential to be the most dangerous competitor in All War history.

Forget the downside for a moment. If she could siphon the memories of Knox's foes, she could share their secrets with him, perhaps even find a foolproof way to cut ties with Ansel. That. That could be the reason she was necessary to Knox. Perhaps Vale wasn't necessary for his survival on Terra, but for his survival *after* the war.

But there was still a problem. As soon as she learned the ramifications of the war, her word would be garbage to him. She'd want him to fail.

A trainer's voice whispered a warning from the past. *Your enemies will only attack at two times. When you are ready, and when you aren't. You alone decide which it will be.*

Forget what Vale could do for him. Knox should end her here and now. Such a dangerous competitor couldn't be allowed to live. And in this environment, he could make the kill as humane as possible, even painless.

He tightened his grip on his dagger...

{*Protect her. For now. She's needed.*}

There was the qualifier—"for now." He could spare her a few days, even a week. Or two.

Very well. He would grant her a stay of execution.

"We're going to spend some time together," he said.

"Roomies. Yay."

He frowned. "For your safety, you need to remember I'm not a forgiving man, and I despise threats."

"Really? So, why'd I think you loved them? Oh, yeah. Because you're constantly dishing them," she quipped, and raised her chin.

He disregarded her comment and the accompanying flare of guilt. "When it comes to my safety, I act first and question later."

"That's great, wonderful. But instead of vowing to harm me again—which is getting super old, by the way—why don't you let me go, as originally suggested?" The more she spoke, the less substance her voice possessed.

He looked her over. The shirt she'd borrowed from him was soaked with blood and gaped at the collar. At least the gash from Celeste's sword was in the process of healing, thanks to Vale's immortality.

She swayed, in spite of her recovery, and he said, "You must have an internal injury. You're hemorrhaging strength."

"Must I? Am I? Thanks, Captain Obvious, I hadn't noticed." She sighed and seemed to wither. "Sorry. I don't mean to snap. I've just never been stabbed, so I'm unsure about proper after-care etiquette. That's a good excuse, right? You're buying it?"

"I don't think you're supposed to announce the methods you're using to manipulate me." But it was kind of adorable.

Adorable? The frown returned.

"I wasn't trying to kill you earlier," she said. "I only wanted to wound you."

"And then what, hmm?" He patted her down, checking for weapons.

She leaned into his touch, as if desperate for his warmth. "I was going to tie you up, then figure out how to escape."

"Tie up an enemy. Excellent idea." He scooped her into his arms.

No protests. She rested her head on his shoulder.

Either she was in shock, too weak to fight, or some part of her liked some part of him...

His chest clenched. He laid her on the bed and gently bound her wrists with tree vines. He had chains hidden in the closet, thin metal links she couldn't cut through or break, hands down the better choice, but he couldn't bring himself to use them and mar her skin.

"Is this truly necessary?" she asked. "I learned my lesson, honest. Swords are dangerous, and we shouldn't play with them."

He tilted his head and narrowed his gaze, giving her the same look he'd often given his targets. An expression known as "the death stare." "You can remain tied, or I can kill you. Lady's choice."

Silence, the wheels in her head clearly turning. She actually needed to think about this?

Then she sighed. "Tied it is. For now. But I reserve the right to revisit my decision at a later date."

"Too bad, so sad," he said, using her own words against her. "While we're together, I reserve the right to make your decisions for you."

"Oh, good. I'm so glad you understand," she continued as if he hadn't spoken. "Because of the time you spent trapped in ice, you know the horrors of forced confinement, and you don't want me to suffer the same fate. That's so kind and sensitive of you. Thank you."

Trying to kindle his sympathies? She needed to accept the truth: he had no sympathies.

To prove it, he tightened the vines. When she flinched, he

experienced another clench in his chest, but he didn't loosen the bonds.

"This is probably for the best, anyway. There's a war raging inside my head." The skin around her siren's mouth pulled taut as she squeezed her eyes closed. Sweat beaded on her brow, trickled down her temples.

"Tell me what you see and feel, courtesy of Celeste."

"Hatred...determination...must kill...don't want to kill."

He debated the wisdom of explaining what he thought had happened versus letting her figure things out on her own.

Would ignorance make her less of a threat, or more of one?

"You were right," he said. "Celeste and Gunnar were lovers. Did he happen to tell her about his sword? Any special powers it possessed." He tried to sound nonchalant, but he failed miserably.

"Sword...no. Sorry."

Truth or lie? He popped his jaw but said, "All right, let's get you patched up." The clenching in his chest only worsened as he gathered medical supplies. By the time he returned to the bed, he was surprised his heart hadn't exploded.

He wasn't the only one who'd deteriorated. Vale watched him, her hazel eyes glazed with agony.

"Are you just going to stand there?" she snapped. Anyone else would have cursed his existence or begged for clemency. Not his Vale. "You said you'd patch me up, so fricking patch me up."

"When in pain, you put the beasts of Adwaeweth to shame. Noted."

If she had a prim and proper side, Knox had seen no real evidence of it. And he was glad.

Why did her waspishness appeal to him? Why did *anything* about her appeal to him? He had no use for her, or anyone. Necessary? Hardly. She was baggage he didn't want to carry. Beautiful baggage, yes, but a burden all the same.

She was going to be a major target. Killing her here would be a mercy.

{*Protect.*}

Fine. Twist my arm. You've convinced me.

Perched at Vale's side, Knox got to work. He cut away her shirt and studied her wound more closely. It wasn't as healed as he'd thought, the center cut so deep he could see bone. Only the edges had scabbed over. Blood smeared the rest of her torso and stained the lovely roses tattooed on her stomach.

Motions stiff, he cleaned her up and applied a numbing salve.

"Do I need stitches?" she asked.

"Probably," he said, but wrapped a bandage around her shoulder, anyway. "Your skin would only grow over the threads, and I'd have to cut them out."

"No stitches. Good call." She batted her lashes at him, all innocence. "Gift me with another shirt?"

"You can have a second one when we're certain you won't bleed through it."

"Another good call. I just wish—" She gasped. Groaned. "Make it stop, Knox, *pleeease* make it stop."

He gripped her chin. "Focus on me, *valina.*" The endearment slipped out unbidden, confusing him, but the reasons weren't worth dissecting right now. "Despite your turmoil and pain, you have much to celebrate. When you killed Celeste, you gained more than her memories. You are now immortal."

At "killed Celeste," she flinched. Her moral compass had taken a major hit, and it would soon take another, and another, until it shattered beyond repair. "I'm immortal, just like you?"

"Exactly. You can die only by the removal of your head or heart, or the burning of your body to ash."

"Immortal," she repeated hollowly.

"Memory transfer isn't something that happens when we make kills. That's specific to you. Tell me what you see and leave out no details."

"Sisters...family, love. Maybe I can save them? There has to be a way."

"There isn't."

"Maybe—"

"You think the rest of us haven't tried to save the people we love?"

Vale sniffled, the sound both pitiful and gut wrenching.

Harden your heart.

Knox had done terrible things to save his daughter. Ultimately, only one of those things had mattered—winning.

Every millisecond of All War #2, three "if's" had run through his head.

—If he died.

—If Minka was under the age eighteen when he died.

—If she was considered an adult when he died.

As a child, she would have been handed over to the High Council to train as an Enforcer. As an adult, she would have been rebranded as a candidate for death—if she hadn't run away from her temporary family.

But in the end, she'd suffered and died, anyway.

I should have returned to a happy adult, delighted to see me again. Instead—

Inhale, exhale. Good, that was good. He was breathing. *Blank your mind. Feel nothing.*

"Uh-oh. You're dealing with *emotion sickness* right now. I can tell." Vale gave a crazed laugh, as if amused, disgusted, and ready to sob all at once. "Just…forget about yourself for a sec. I don't understand any of this. Break it down for me toddler-style. Please and thank you."

He massaged the back of his neck. "When a new realm is discovered, leaders of thirty-nine established realms hope to claim it as their own. More land means more resources, and more citizens to use as slaves or payment. To prevent a large-scale war and thereby the destruction of these newly discovered territories, the High Council was created. They organize the All Wars, in which a king or queen sends a single representative to fight on their behalf. Winner gets the realm. Losers die. Sometimes, multiple All Wars rage at once, in different realms. Sometimes, centuries pass before a new realm is discovered."

"All War. High Council," she echoed, her voice seeming hollowed out by a blade. "You're here to fight for control of Earth. Not with an army, but with a contest."

"Yes."

"You're war whores." Her frown deepened. "This is…this is my origin story. Since the hero of every tale saves the day, I'm guaranteed victory. Unless I'm the villain."

Her nonsense was adorable.

Inner slap. There was that word again.

Paling, she added, "I beheaded someone. I *must* be a villain."

"You are a survivor, Vale. Just like the rest of us."

He doubted his words penetrated her dark haze, so he tried again. "Kings and queens mark a representative's loved ones to use as incentive. If the combatant wins, their loved ones are saved. If the combatant loses, their loved ones are killed or given to the High Council, depending on their age. The moment Celeste died, her queen knew. We all have transmitters." He held up his hand, tapped his index finger, then pointed to the tree of life on his shoulder. "One is for our ruler, one is for the High Council. Both are active and die with us. If Celeste's queen is like my king, every member of her family was executed within minutes of her death. It's a common practice to prove to future combatants that failure has consequences. No mercy, ever."

Tears wet Vale's lashes, then spilled down her cheeks. "When I killed Celeste, I condemned her sisters. Meaning my death tally now stands at five."

The sight of her unchecked vulnerability ripped Knox's insides to shreds.

"Will *my* loved ones be marked for death?" she croaked.

"Your leaders know nothing about the war. Yet."

"Yes or no?" she insisted.

"No."

A measure of her tension evaporated. "How many loved ones await your victory?"

Now those shreds caught fire. "None." He shoved the word past a barbed lump in his throat. "I had a single loved one, but she died soon after I was forced to leave my home to fight for ownership of another."

Her features softened, and she said, "I'm sorry, Knox."

Compassion for the man who'd abducted her and tied her up? A trick, surely.

"I know how it feels to lose family," she said, her voice as soft as her expression.

"Yes, but you've always had your sister to—"

"Not always. We aren't blood related. I was alone for years before I met her. She's my only friend, my saving grace. My SWAT. Special Wingwoman And Therapist."

And he had separated the two. *Rip, burn.*

Her brows knit together, a crease forming above her nose. "If you aren't fighting to save family, why *are* you fighting?"

Admit he was a slave, compelled to obey his king's every command? No. Pride demanded he hold on to that gem a little while longer. "What other memories do you see?"

She allowed the subject change without complaint. "Mostly I see the brutal way you killed Gunnar, my protector." Gasp. "You were going to kill me, too."

"You mean *Celeste's* protector. I was going to kill *Celeste.*" Did the distinction really matter? One day, he would kill Vale, too.

Her eyes glimmered with revulsion. "You tried to stab her in the throat. When that failed, you tried to choke her."

"I did." And he wouldn't feel guilty about it. Victory equaled freedom.

She gave a violent shake of her head and mumbled, "So many memories and feelings. I'm losing track of what's real and what isn't."

"Here is what's real. When you decapitated Celeste, you

joined the All War. You are a combatant now. A Terran representative." The second one, in fact. "You must fight twenty other warriors to the death."

Blink, blink. "Joined the… No. Nope. Absolutely not. Not me. I refuse."

"Refusal doesn't negate reality, Vale. It's done. Anyone who kills a combatant is automatically added to the roster."

"No."

"There are few rules, and there will be only one survivor. He will gain control of Earth on behalf of his sovereign."

"No," she repeated, shaking her head. "I wish you guys all the best with your homicides, but I forfeit. I'm returning to my old life."

He went still. "There *is* a way to forfeit."

"Tell me!"

"You must carve the Mark of Disgrace in your forehead, present yourself to the Terran Enforcer named Seven, and forever live with the knowledge that you failed your people."

Any hope she'd garnered now withered. Still, she said, "I don't care about failing my people. Everyone sucks. We've turned this world into a steaming trash factory."

"Take the mark, then. Allow another realm to win your trash factory, placing your sister's fate in the hands of another species." *What are you doing? Cease!* If she wanted to exit the war, he should encourage her, not talk her out of it.

"First of all, we might be better off in the hands of another species. What do I know? And second, we have a kick-A military squad. Good luck taking us over."

"Your people will bow to the new king, this I promise you. They'll have no choice. As part of the victor's reward package, Enforcers portal in, slay the current leaders and brand every citizen as a slave. You'll see." Actually, no. She wouldn't. By then, she would be dead.

Do not roar a denial. A good warrior cared about nothing and no one; he exhibited control in all things. *Remember that.*

A teardrop glistened at the edge of Vale's lashes. *Walk away. Do not reach—*

He reached out—*can't stop*—and gently wiped the moisture away. "If you return to your sister while the war rages, you'll put her in the crosshairs of very dangerous warriors who won't hesitate to use her against you."

"But…she's sick," she gasped out.

"Think, Vale. Think back to the soldiers you encountered at the prison. Do you believe they'll hesitate to harm a sick girl if the act puts them a step closer to victory?"

"Will *Zion* use her against me?"

"He is the sole exception. As I told you before, he doesn't hurt women, even the ones who actively attempt to kill him. I believe he will guard her."

She shuddered with relief, rattling the vines. "So where are these other realms located? How many have been won like this?"

"There is an All War Alliance comprised of the thirty-nine realms I mentioned. Long ago, they banded together to share their advanced technologies. The High Council uses those technologies to seek out other worlds."

"Keep going," she said.

"At last count, there were one hundred and seventeen wars. I'm sure the number has increased since my imprisonment. However, the number of territories mostly remains the same. When a new one is won, it takes the name of the winning realm."

"Like when a woman takes the last name of her husband."

Nod. "Only when the territory wins its own All War is it added to the tally. So, the number could have increased during the past thirteen hundred years. Some of the realms are beloved universally, some are despised. Some are violent, some peaceful."

"I still don't understand. Why go to so much trouble?"

"In the past, whenever a new realm was discovered, the others invaded, determined to claim it. Battles ensued and destruction reigned. To preserve the prize, a new system was created."

That was the propaganda spewed by the High Council, anyway. Knox believed the High Council preserved resources, lands and people for themselves, and only themselves. *One worry at a time.*

Vale's chest rose and fell in quick succession. "A game," she said. "All of this...it's just a game. A game with living, breathing players."

"In a sense, yes, though it has very real consequences and rewards."

"So does *Jumanji.*" She laughed, crazed. "How long does this particular game last?"

"As long as needed. There's no time limit." He would bet the High Council regretted *that* decision.

"The game should have stopped when you guys morphed into frozen sex puppets. Or do you prefer the term *meat* puppets?" she said. "How did you finally break free?"

"Meat puppets? Explain." The images his mind conjured...

A lovely blush stained her cheeks. "Blood loss, amirite? Let's move on."

Very well. "The Rod of Clima has the power to control weather. Either it malfunctioned or a chance in outside temperatures superseded its range."

"Global warming." The blush faded, leaving her pale. "I studied it, the greenhouse effect and melting permafrost in one of my classes."

"Explain."

"Over the years, humans have used so many fossil fuels and razed so many trees that the amount of carbon dioxide in the air has increased, causing a gradual increase in the planet's overall temperature."

"Ah. I understand now. Iviland was headed down the same path. During a war that predates my birth, we passed a point of no return—our world becoming toxic, driving the citizens underground."

"I don't want the same thing to happen to Earth."

"Then you'll have to win it and fix it."

"Is that even possible? Be honest."

"Like you, Celeste killed a combatant to enter the war for her realm. Because she won, her queen retained her role as leader."

Vale expelled a breath, and he decided not to mention the difference in her circumstances. Celeste hadn't been pitted against Knox.

"How did she win, exactly?" Vale asked.

"You have her memories. You should know."

Before coming to Terra, he'd studied the chronicles written about every war. Details collected by royal scribes. There were two different theories about Celeste, and both demonstrated ruthlessness that rivaled his own. Either she'd seduced combatants and used them as shields, or she'd seduced combatants and used them as bait.

After watching her face off with Bane, after feeling the sting of her sword, Knox suspected she'd done her fair share of killing. She had been trained, clearly, but had wisely hidden her skills. Surprise was as much a weapon as a sword.

Now, through her memories, Vale would receive a crash course in combat, making her even more of a threat.

While other men had made fools of themselves over Celeste, Knox would not be so gullible. He would never trust Vale. Trust equaled betrayal, without exception.

Do not *forget.* "When Terra—"

"Earth."

"When *Earth* was discovered, the queen of Occisor sent Celeste here, betting she would be the one to win it."

"Survive being hunted by assassins, keep my home," Vale muttered. "Got it."

There it is. The moment a reluctant combatant began to hope, to plan.

Knox wouldn't tell her about the other Terran representative—Erik the Widow Maker—because he didn't yet know what it meant. To his knowledge, two mortals from the same realm had never joined a war.

"If I win," she said and licked her lips, "everything will stay the same?"

"Nothing will ever be the same again." He softened his tone. "Since you did not enter on behalf of a king or queen, you will be crowned queen, answerable only to the High Council." They were entering dangerous waters here, the topic beginning to point to his enslavement to Ansel. These details didn't pertain to her, anyway; there was no way she'd win. He would take steps... *Ignore the guilt!* "I've shared knowledge with you. Time for you to share knowledge with me."

"One, I've been sharing knowledge with you since we met. Second, I'm still processing everything you told me. And everything I'm learning from Celeste. But all right, shoot. I'll tell you what I can."

"How did you obtain my dagger while I was gone?"

She winced. "Of course you'd start there. Considering you're currently vibrating with anger, I think I'll keep that bit of info to myself."

He could torture it out of her, he supposed. But—

{*For now, do her no harm.*}

He ground his teeth. *But.* The thought of marring her pretty flesh sickened him. She'd been hurt enough. Too much.

"I'll figure it out on my own, then," he grated.

Knox stalked to the alcove. Spotting a tree limb on the floor, he ground his teeth *harder.* His shadows were obedient, not sentient; they would have reacted to Vale's movements in a bid to avoid her, as ordered.

If she'd gotten too close, too fast...if she'd stood in one spot and waved the limb in another, she would have seemed to be in two places at once.

Clever female. He ignored a flicker of respect, the flare of dismay. Before the last check-in, he'd told Shiloh not to fall in like with another combatant. *Exactly what I'm doing now.*

Knox blanked his expression and returned to Vale's side.

Her gaze remained steady on his, the gold a brilliant star-burst rimmed by the green. "Oh, goodie. I'm pretty sure we've reached my favorite part of the conversation. The moment you threaten me."

She mocked him?

No, he realized. The barest hint of fear wafted from her. She was afraid of his reaction but determined to hide it.

A clench in his chest, a sensation he was coming to loathe. "For now, I'll keep you alive. Do not make me regret it."

CHAPTER NINE

Can't process. Vale was smack-dab in the middle of another information overload. Any second, she expected her mind to break. So, she pushed out thoughts of wars and high councils and forced assassinations committed by herself or others, and focused on the only puzzle piece she had the power to reshape. Knox.

As he stalked through his evil overlord lair, doing whatever evil overlords did, she remained splayed on the bed, watching him, bound by those stupid vines, her mouth imbued with the taste of whiskey and honey. Since she'd stabbed him, killed an unwanted guest inside his home and joined a too-legit-to-quit turf war, she supposed she shouldn't complain about a little light bondage. Plus, she suspected her captor would seize any opportunity to lop off her head.

Not that a man like him needed an excuse.

He could don a particular look that said, *There's no line I won't cross.* He tilted his head to the right, his gaze becoming as sharp and hot as lasers, but also as cruel and merciless as ice.

She'd been the extra-special recipient of that look more times than she cared to count.

One day, he *would* make a play for her head, and she doubted he would feel the teensiest bit of guilt.

One sure way to save herself? Captivate him with her feminine charms.

Well, not a sure way. But a *possible* way. All of her past dates would certainly get a kick out of Vale London attempting to captivate with her feminine *un*charms.

Fine. Forget the captivating thing. She'd have to make herself useful. Make him *want* to keep her around, no matter how great the temptation to harm her. Already he considered her *necessary*. Which just happened to be her new favorite word in the English language.

New favorite? Ha! She'd dreamed of being necessary to a man… Had fantasized about it repeatedly, hoped and prayed, before finally giving up and deciding the world could suck it, she was better off on her own, anyway.

Knox had more than proved his claim. He hadn't killed her when she'd inadvertently joined his war, or when she'd been too weak to fight back. Also, he hadn't ditched her, even though he'd really, really wanted to ditch her.

Allegedly, he had no idea know why she was necessary to him, so she couldn't capitalize on the skill, or info or whatever it was. But she *could* test the boundaries of his "instinct," find out how far she could push him—and then never ever cross that line.

Bulletproof logic. On the right track.

She also needed to lay groundwork for an escape. Which she could totally do now that she had Celeste's memories.

Vale remembered more about Celeste's past than she'd admitted to her captor. How to contort to undo knots. How to sneak up on a man and use his weapons against him. Most important, how to steal Celeste's Rifters, the crystal rings Knox had pocketed.

The pretties would open a doorway to her apartment in

Strawberry Valley, Oklahoma, or allow her to travel to one of Celeste's safe houses. Places the other woman had set traps.

The ones Vale saw with absolute clarity—an underground hideaway in the UK and a cave in the Amazon.

But first and foremost, she needed to heal and regain her strength. If something went wrong, she'd have to start fighting.

Face it, she was going to have to fight one way or another.

"How was I able to absorb Celeste's memories? Any theories?" she asked, only to jolt when the answer clicked. Her screwed up senses. Of course!

Knox emerged from the closet, surprising her. Dude. She'd lost track of him, a dangerous development; she needed to remain aware.

He wore a clean T-shirt and a pair of those leather-like pants. In one hand, he carried a large tool box, his biceps bulging. His hair was damp and slicked back. He'd taken another bath and she'd missed it.

Wait, had she just whimpered?

"Save your questions for another time." Never glancing her way, he plucked a piece of fruit with his free hand, then sat at the table. He unloaded weapons and tools, placing them end to end. "I have no interest in listening to your chatter."

Oookay. Since he'd returned from the alcove looking shell-shocked, something had changed for him. He'd worn the same expression as Vale during the three worst experiences of her life. The day her mother died, the day her father had taken off, and the day she'd said goodbye to Carrie. What had caused such a staggering reaction in Knox?

"No worries, big guy," she said now. "I already figured out the answer. And to be honest, I have, like, zero interest in listening to you mansplain. Silence suits me well."

He frowned, as if disappointed in her, as if she should *want* to speak with him, even if he didn't want to speak with her. As if she should move heaven and earth to win him over.

Men! Half the time they sucked donkey balls. The other half, they sucked regular balls.

But still, how was Vale supposed to kill Knox? Technically, she had a home court advantage but she also had, like, zero urge to behead him. Could she even go through with it? Celeste had been an accident. Purposely seeking the death of another combatant would be cold-blooded murder. No, thanks.

Why risk her life, and her sanity, for a world filled with terrorists, rapists and school shooters? And yeah, okay, those craptastic individuals were a minority. But what about internet trolls who spewed venom? And how could she forget the everyday liars, cheaters and thieves?

Ugh. Earth really was a steaming trash factory. Maybe another species could clean things up.

Or make things worse.

Oh, the dilemma! On a search for more information about the different species, she retreated into her mind to poke at Celeste's memories...she got stuck on all things Occisor instead.

There, certain women emitted a powerful pheromone that filled anyone within sniffing distance with an all-consuming, insatiable lust. An ability Vale had inherited from Celeste. Even now, the pheromone was heating inside her, preparing to lure Knox to his doom.

Must use it sparingly, and only as necessary. Never seduce more than one target at a time...the danger...

She jolted. Danger? Why? The reason teased her, the memory fragmenting, rotating, connecting to others in an odd way, her mind quickly becoming chaotic.

No, no. *Concentrate!* The pheromone was dangerous because— why? *Fragmenting, rotating.*

Invisibility, intangibility...a sword that leaked venom...

Vale grabbed hold of the thought with every ounce of her might. The sword. *Mine!* She couldn't rely on people, but she could rely on her weapon—

Fragmenting, rotating.

Finally, something other than Occisor. She saw a corrupt High Council…saw different men in the brunette's bed, worshipping her body. But only one man had ever wormed his way into her heart…

Fragmenting. Suddenly Vale could feel Celeste's desire to kill Knox. He'd murdered her love.

Stomach cramp. Knox had taken away the woman's lover, but Vale had taken away everything else.

She blinked back a hot sting of tears. *Can't break down. Must carry on.*

A ragged laugh devoid of humor lodged in her throat. Had she really just thought *carry on*? About a homicide?

I'm the egg. I've already hardened…

No, no, no. She hadn't. She wouldn't. And she wouldn't kill anyone else, either. There had to be another way to stop the war and protect Nola's future.

Yes. That. That was what Vale wanted to do more than anything. To stop the war and protect Nola. And maybe she could find a way to make her sister immortal, too, *without* having to kill a combatant. Immortal Nola wouldn't need pain pills, wouldn't have to go through withdrawal and wouldn't have to deal with stupid fibromyalgia.

But what if there *wasn't* a way to end the war? Celeste had wanted to end it, too…until she was killed.

A sob of helplessness bubbled up, only to get snared by a humorless laugh. Good! *Show no weakness. Keep it together now, break down later.*

"Female."

Knox's craggy voice pulled her into the present, and she blinked rapidly, focused. He towered beside the bed. Uh-oh. *The look.* His head was tilted, his eyes both fiery and icy. Worse, the weapons he'd sharpened were strapped to his body.

"Tell me how you think you acquired Celeste's memories," he commanded.

She luxuriated in the taste of honeyed whiskey, and the sweet intoxication and momentary oblivion. A sensation only he could elicit, one she enjoyed immensely, and another reason she needed to remain here, with Knox, where she could taste individual sounds rather than a bombardment.

Even still, she snapped, "Read the room. I'm obviously done talking to you."

Frowning, he eased beside her, his hip brushing against hers. *Will not gasp. Nope. Not me.*

"Do you care nothing about your fate, then?" he asked.

"Another threat? How original."

"Vale...please," he grated.

Astonished, she stared up at him. The gruff warrior had just asked nicely. Well, nicely for him. How could she deny him?

"Only because you spared my life," she said.

"Deal."

"Three of my five senses are miswired. Or four of six, if you consider the memory absorption thing." Should she tell him about Celeste's pheromone? Nah. A girl needed *some* surprises. "It's called synesthesia. Usually people only have to deal with one oddity, but I'm an overachiever. I taste sounds, see letters as colors, and picture numbers inside a map."

Intrigue lit his gaze. "You taste whiskey and honey whenever I speak...and you like it."

"How did you—never mind. I keep forgetting I let info slip when I thought you were a statue."

"You called me a *sexcake, smoke show* and most recently a sex puppet." Satisfaction joined the intrigue. "You absorbed memories...and abilities?"

Well, frick. He already suspected the truth. No reason to confirm it, though. She shrugged, and tried to play it cool, even as a blush burned her cheeks.

He stroked two fingers over the dark stubble on his jaw. "What else is different about you, I wonder."

I'm not looking forward to finding out, bud. "How many foes have you killed?"

"In this war? Only five."

"Only," she parroted softly. So, he'd gained five different weapons.

Better to kill you with, my dear…

At least he'd answered. She'd expected resistance. "I'm your competition. Why are you helping me?" *Why am I necessary?*

He arched a brow, as if to say, *Competition, female? Dream on.* "I doubt I'll tell you, even if I figure out the answer."

What *did* he know? "Any tips or tricks to impart so I can help myself?"

A pause, crackling with tension. Then, "Trust no one. Suspect everyone of deceit. Soldiers will lie to you, use you and hire mortals to trap you. Paranoia is your best friend."

"Ha! That's just business as usual, then."

His eyes did the narrowing thing. "We will rest now."

Did he have to make *everything* a command? "You think you're going to rest with those weapons strapped to your body?"

"I never rest any other way. I'm ready for battle, always. You'd do well to follow my lead."

"I'd love to, thanks." She motioned to a dagger with a tilt of her chin. *Do not request Celeste's sword. Not yet.* "I'll take that one. No? Too soon?"

"You'll remain unarmed, for both our sakes. We've both suffered injuries and must recharge. Before you protest, don't. You'll remain bound." He stood, so darkly, perfectly, intensely masculine, so danged sensual, he was the personification of carnality.

The times she'd lived on the streets, she'd yearned for a protector. Someone who couldn't be intimidated or scared away. As a teenager, she'd chosen bad boys, the ones *she* couldn't scare away. Knox was something else entirely.

Only a crazy person would be tempted by his sinister hotness, right? Or maybe just anyone with a pulse. Those eyes. So blue, so deep. Those lashes. So long, the color of a raven's wings. That jaw. So strong and chiseled. That body. So ripped with muscles, yet also sleek and as lethal as a panther.

Who am *I?* Vale never waxed poetic about anything but donuts.

Now, as she drank in everything Knox, he seemed to drink in everything Vale. Her blood warmed and fizzed. Pleasure fluttered in her belly while heat pooled between her thighs. Her limbs trembled and her nipples beaded, as if desperate to gain his attention.

Resist!

A tantalizing mix of jasmine and dark spices wafted to her nose, and she breathed deep, all but purring her approval. Where was the fragrance coming from, and why was desire fogging her mind?

Want Knox. Neeeed him.

He sniffed the air, tension pulling the skin around his mouth taut, bunching the muscles in his shoulders. One step, two, he backed up, widening the distance between them.

The sweet scent only intensified.

"Why do you suddenly smell like you're wearing perfume?" he croaked.

The truth crystalized in an instant. The scent came from *her.* Somehow, she'd unwittingly unleashed Celeste's pheromone.

How was she supposed to make it stop? And how could she keep the information from him now?

"Some perfumes are, um, heat activated," she said. Maybe it was true.

"You will wash it off." He returned to yank the vines from her wrists, then wrenched back yet again. "Now. Or I'll *make* you do it."

As panic chilled her to the bone, the flames of desire cooled, the sweet scent faded, and she offered up a prayer of thanks. But even still, she hastened to the pool, thrilled to splash water onto her overheated skin. Let him assume the water had done its job.

With her movements, blood hustled back into her shoulders, making her feel as if she were being pricked with a thousand needles.

"Back to the bed," he called. "Now."

"Can you be any more demanding?"

"Yes."

"I don't want to go back to bed."

Eyes glittering with a mix of danger and desire, Knox crooked his finger at her. "Then come to me."

Gulping, she obeyed—why, why? Shivers cascaded down her spine as soon as she stood in front of him. "What do you want?"

"Confirmation." He leaned over to sniff her neck, and the tip of his nose tickled her skin.

Do not moan with bliss. Don't you dare!

Voice hoarse, he said, "Better." Before she could protest, he picked her up, carried her to the bed, maneuvered her flat on her back, and retied the vines.

This time, she fought him. Not that it did any good. He avoided her blows with expert skill.

"Why are you fighting now?" he asked. "I'm not going to harm you."

He didn't say it, but she heard it. *Yet.*

She shuddered with dread. "Excuse me for not wanting to be tied up with a homicidal maniac nearby."

"Excuse me for not wanting to be stabbed while I sleep. Guess who wins this argument?" As she glared at him, he added, "Hear me well, Vale. When it comes to my safety, I take no chances. If you obey my rules and remain honest with me, we'll get along fine."

She had to choke back a wheeze of dismay. She'd *already* lied to him about having an adoring husband. Well. There was no way she could cop to being single now. Or, you know, *ever.*

Knox traced a fingertip along her jaw, something he'd done a few times before. Each time, shivers cascaded through her—and they were only growing stronger.

"How about you keep your hands to yourself, hmm?" she said, no real heat in her tone. *Because I like your touch far too much.*

"I want to. I should…" He sounded drugged and looked entranced. "Your skin is *incredible.*"

It was? He was the first man to say so. And dang it! The praise further addled her mind, part of her really, really wanting to preen for him.

He shook his head and scowled, ruining the moment, acting as if she was a galactic spy and she'd just tricked him into spilling confidential secrets.

"No more conversation." He tossed her a final glare, as if she were to blame for *his* presence and *his* words, and stretched out in a spot within sight of the bed but completely out of her reach.

"Good riddance," she muttered.

Vale womaned up, pushed every noncritical thought out of her mind and attempted to cobble together a new plan of action—or POA. Every successful venture had one. As her professor once said, "The best POAs are fluid, adjustable as needed."

First, she would stick with Knox until she'd obtained Celeste's sword and Rifters; they called to her. Once she had the items, she would make her escape. No telling when Knox would turn on her. Then, she would hide out in Celeste's digs until she'd figured out her next move—a way to stop the All War and make Nola immortal.

Also, Vale needed to learn as much as possible about the war and its many players. And she absolutely positively had to stay away from Nola in the meantime, just as Knox had suggested.

He was right. As long as Earth was a full-on gladiator arena, she was a danger to her sister. And though Vale wanted to sob her eyes out, she consoled herself with the knowledge that Nola had a special power of her own. One Vale had always envied. Her sister could charm a jerk into a prince; Zion wouldn't stand a chance. The sweet, sassy Southern belle would convince the metal-glove-wearing warrior to obtain pain pills for her, and all would be well.

Please, let all be well.

CHAPTER TEN

Dreams plagued Knox the entire night. *Erotic* dreams, with Vale London cast in the starring role. His hands and mouth wandered over every inch of her extraordinary body, and he felt like a conqueror who'd just discovered a new kingdom to plunder. When she rolled him over to return like for like, sensual torment for sensual torment, he nearly came undone. They writhed against each other, male to female, hardness to softness, until he could stand it no more, positioned her flat on her back, spread her legs and plunged into her hot, wet depths. Excruciating pleasure, eternal bliss. Her cries of abandon and surrender were a symphony of forbidden indulgence.

How perfectly she gloved him. And the scent of her... In the endless eons of his life, he'd never encountered a lusher, more feminine fragrance than Vale's. With a single inhalation, he'd had to contend with a wildfire of lust, his control torched.

In his reverie, they finished round one, and began round two. She licked her way down his chest. Plump red lips hovered over his throbbing shaft, arousal sparkling in her luminous hazel eyes. No one had ever sucked him off. He wanted this, wanted it desperately, madly.

"I'll give myself to you, body and soul," dream Vale whispered, "but first, you must lay the world at my feet... Do you agree?"

Cede victory to another, accepting defeat, dying a slave?

"No!" He came awake with a roar, jolting upright.

He was panting, shallow breaths not nearly enough for his starved lungs. Sweat drenched him, his clothes sticking to his skin. Despite his emotional upheaval, he was rock hard and aching.

Ready to stroke himself off, Knox gripped the base of his erection. He imagined kissing and licking every inch of Vale's body. How eager she was—

A soft moan drifted from her, and he frowned. That moan had sounded real.

"Mmmm."

That moan *was* real. He stood in a rush, palming a dagger, and stalked to her bedside.

A blistering wave of arousal nearly burned him alive. Shadows clung to her, a beautiful adornment that hid her from the rest of the world... *from everyone but me.*

"Leave us," he rasped, and the shadows scattered.

Vale tossed and turned, her color high. On her nose was a smattering of freckles he'd somehow missed before; perhaps he'd been too enraptured with her eyes. Her lips—those plump red lips Dream Vale had used to tempt him—remained parted, and she panted in time with Knox.

Did she dream of him?

As gently as possible, he removed the cloth that covered her wound. Excellent. She was completely healed. And a deep sleeper. His ministrations failed to rouse her.

He glowered when he noticed the condition of the vines; they'd twisted, pulling taut, applying added pressure to her wrists. Ignoring a spark of guilt, he untied the vines, massaged blood back into her hands, then ghosted his fingers over her bruises and abrasions. The guilt sparked hotter as he tied her back up.

Still too tight. He loosened the shackles…a little more…until she could free herself with a single tug. Perfect.

What is wrong with me?

"Yes," she whispered, shifting and arching her back, lifting her breasts in supplication. Her nipples were hard, beckoning his tongue. *Explore here…*

Resist the want. Look away. Knox would never act on his lust for her. And not just because she was a combatant. She continued to exasperate and confound him. Continued to say and do adorable things.

Hate that word.

Reminder: He wasn't going to make the same mistakes as Celeste's protectors, wasn't going to sacrifice his life for another.

Tenser by the second, he stalked to the bathroom, washed his face and brushed his teeth. He had a war to win and, rather than stroke himself off here, in private, he would use the restless energy to his advantage, and channel it on the battlefield.

Like him, none of the other combatants comprehended the modern world. How many safe houses and base camps had been destroyed over the years? How many warriors returned to the ice mountains, the only location that remained familiar?

Knox could pick them off, as hoped.

First, he would visit Shiloh's hideout to search for Ammarie's bow and arrow. Knox had seen the heavily wooded site through a rift the second month of the war. Once was enough. He could visit anytime, from anywhere. Maybe the area had been compromised, maybe it hadn't. He would find out.

Already weaponed-up and dressed in a T-shirt and leathers, he pictured the camp and clinked the Rifters together. Vibration. A wave of his hand. As a rift opened up, a wealth of shadows hiding his bunker from anyone who might be waiting on the other side, he braced, part of him expecting an onslaught of water, fire or, worse, mortals.

A spacious, well-lit room appeared. No furniture other than display cases that contained weapons. Weapons also hung on the walls, things Shiloh had taken from vikings.

Was this a museum of some sort?

In Iviland, Ansel always cherry-picked, keeping the best weapons for the representatives who would compete in future All Wars and displaying what remained in museums dedicated to teaching the masses about his great feats.

Yes, he took credit for every victory won in his name, as if he had personally done the fighting.

Knox spotted Ammarie's bow and arrow—*my* bow, *my* arrow—locked in one of the cases at the far end of the room.

Leaving Vale asleep in bed, he palmed two daggers and, on alert, stepped through the rift.

Half the shadows moved with him, concealing him as his long legs ate up the distance.

In front of the case, he wasted no time, using the hilt of a dagger to punch once, twice. The glass cracked, then shattered, and an alarm screeched to life, nearly bursting his eardrums.

Beneath the high-pitched wail, he detected a barrage of footsteps. An army approached.

Knox grabbed the weapon, made a mad dash to the still-open rift and dove through, rolling to a stop inside the bunker and leaping up. He left the bow and daggers on the floor, aimed his revolver and cocked the hammer. Until he'd inspected the bow, he wouldn't risk using it.

The door burst open and Erik rushed inside the room. Well, well. Interesting development. Erik had invaded Shiloh's hideaway and created...what? Not a museum. Some sort of trap?

What other hideaways had the viking found?

Questions for another day. Mortal soldiers wearing thick black vests spilled in behind Erik.

Knox's shadows remained firmly in place. Only he knew the rift was there, his bunker on the other side of it. *Advantage: me.*

Unseen, he hammered at the revolver's trigger—

Several mortals dove in front of Erik, taking the bullets for him. Then the rift closed, and Knox lowered his arm, cursing as his mind whirled. Should he return and make another play for Erik, or turn his sights elsewhere?

Elsewhere. Definitely. Until he learned more about this modern world, he had best avoid the viking, a man who knew *everything* about it. While everyone else had been trapped in ice, Erik had roamed free.

Better to concentrate on building of his own arsenal. Carrick's dagger... Zion's gloves... Ronan's sword... Domino "Dom" of Rhagan had a shield able to withstand *anything*, including the gloves and sword.

Knox didn't have a bead on Carrick yet. *Want that dagger!* Returning to the fallen prison to retrace the prince's steps was an option, but was it a good one? The man preferred hotter climates and would avoid the mountains, even if his base camp lay in ruins.

Same deal with Zion or Dom. No bead.

Before the last check-in, Knox had glimpsed one of Ronan's hideouts. What's more, Ronan had admitted to killing Major of Etheran, which meant he'd acquired Major's spyglass. A piece of equipment capable of spying on competitors, wherever they happened to be.

If Knox could spy on Carrick, he would have a better chance of finding out where the male resided. Assuming the location wasn't mystically protected, of course.

Ronan it is.

Knox would take Vale with him. She would be his guide and—

Vale! Despite the high-pitched alarm, she hadn't roused. Fearing something was wrong with her, he stalked to the bed to give her a hard shake. No reaction.

"Wake, female." Shake, shake. "Now."

Again, nothing. Perhaps Celeste's memories had damaged her once-mortal mind. Desperate, Knox decided to shock her system. He leaned down and pressed his lips against hers. A kiss. His first, and a total shock to *his* system.

Her lips were softer than he'd imagined. Sweeter. Hotter. His heart raced, and he longed for another kiss. Now. Now! A deeper one. With their mouths open, their tongues dueling.

Treading on dangerous ground. He swallowed a moan of need as he straightened. *Control.*

Hazel eyes blinked open, and he heaved a sigh of relief, even as his mind got caught up in another storm.

No more kissing.

Ignore the disappointment. Would she become dead to the world for a short period of time anytime she made a kill? Did a victim's age and experience matter?

He would have to teach her how to—

No! He would teach her nothing. An attraction to her would not dictate his actions. Gunnar, Hunter of Klioway, and Malaki of Highgard had died protecting Celeste, and it was the last mistake any of them ever made.

And what about Ranger, a warrior known as the god of fire, who owned a pair of boots with wings, granting him the ability to fly? He was another of the men Celeste had seduced pre-Gunnar. Ranger still lived. If Vale had memories of sleeping with him, she might crave his body, might help him launch a sneak attack against Knox. And what of Vale's husband? What dark deeds would she commit to return to the man?

Ignore the flare of jealousy.

Gaze catching on Knox, she unveiled a slow, welcoming smile. "Hey."

Ignore the ripples of astonishment and the new currents of arousal.

"You." Her smile vanished. She jerked upright, multi-colored hair tumbling around her arms. "You look more constipated than usual. What's wrong?"

"Your laziness. We have errands." He unfastened the vines around her wrists for good, pleased to note the abrasions had faded. "Come. It's time to go."

"We're leaving? Together?" Moaning, she rolled her shoulders. How they must ache.

Guilt pricked him all over again. "You would rather I leave you behind?"

"Yes. No. Maybe?" Next, she rubbed the sleep from her eyes. "I should probably use the bathroom first. Even though I don't feel like I need to use the bathroom."

"You're immortal now, remember? You process foods differently."

"Immortal. Right." Determination hardened her features. "I'd still like a moment to freshen up."

Impressed by her quick resolve, he said, "By all means. I hope you also remember my previous warning. Do not make a play against me."

"Yeah, yeah, yeah." She rose to shaky legs and lumbered into the bathroom. As he waited, he stuffed a bag full of things they might need.

When she returned, the top half of her hair was plaited, her face scrubbed pink and her teeth brushed. She'd commandeered a dark T-shirt and leathery pants, and he derived a strange mix of satisfaction and possessiveness in knowing his garments hugged her curves.

"By the way," she said, shifting from one booted foot to the other. "I'm usually a much better dresser."

"You look good just as you are." Too good. His gaze lingered on her, his blood heating.

"Apparently I do," she muttered, motioning to his straining fly. "So where are we going?"

Brazen female. Going to act nonchalant? Very well. He would do the same. "We're going hunting. After I ensure you aren't smuggling a weapon under your clothes." He moved behind her to perform a pat down.

"Is this how you get your thrills?" she asked, suddenly breathless.

Breasts. Stomach. Thighs. His temperature jacked up a few thousand degrees.

Wait. She'd said something. Respond! "You assume I want to be thrilled."

He should double check her breasts...and her stomach...and her thighs... Her feminine softness beseeched him: *linger, savor... give me more pleasure than I've ever known.*

Wishful thinking. Lethal *thinking. Resist!*

"Don't you?" she asked.

"Want? No." Need? Oh, yes. But only here. Only now. With her.

Voice filled with smoke and promise, she said, "Why don't you do something to thrill yourself? See if you like it."

A dare. A taunt. Perhaps even a play to beguile him so that she could make her escape.

Did it matter? Silent, he settled his hands on her waist, clasped her tightly...and drew her closer. When her back pressed against his chest, she *purred* her approval.

"What are you going to do next?" she whispered.

I should stop. He grazed his cheek over hers, imagined pushing his hands down her pants and shoving his fingers into her feminine sheath. Would he find her wet?

"What do you want me to do?" he rasped.

"Surprise me." She arched her back, rubbing her ass against his erection, thrilling him.

Sweat beaded on his forehead. *Take her. All of her.*

He trembled as he cupped and kneaded her breasts. *I. Am.*

Dead. She was plump and perfect here, her nipples hard little pinpoints against his palms.

"Excellent choice." She lifted her arms and reached back to comb her fingers through his hair, wrenching a ragged groan from deep inside him.

The pulse at the base of her neck drummed erratically, mesmerizing him, a seductive provocation to desires he no longer wanted to resist. One lick, only one. Yes… He lowered his head.

One lick—and then what?

From white-hot to ice-cold in less than a second. Whatever the answer, it wouldn't end well for him.

Inwardly cursing, he dropped his arms to his sides and stepped back, severing each point of contact.

Vale, the irresistible temptress, turned and offered him a smug grin. And yet, it wasn't smugness glimmering in her eyes, but undeniable vulnerability.

"I think you do want to be thrilled," she said. "I think you are more than thrilled right now."

She'd rubbed against him simply to prove a point? Teeth gritted, he said, "If you're implying you didn't enjoy yourself—"

"Oh, I enjoyed myself," she stated baldly.

"—then you—" He blinked. Would this female always amaze him with her ready admissions and frank speech? "You won't make me a slave to my desires, Vale. You won't use me as Celeste used so many others."

The color in her cheeks deepened, and she bristled, as if he'd poked at her internal armor. "Let's forget what just happened—only a momentary bout of insanity—and go about our day. Okay?"

He would *never* forget the feel of her. "We're going after Ronan of Soloria. He has a spyglass. I want, I take."

"Uh, you know what I just heard? *I am Gollum, and victory is my precious. Riiing.*"

Whatever that meant. "During our expedition, you will explain anything I don't understand. That is your only job."

"Sir, yes, sir." She performed her customary salute, only to deflate. "I'm the rottenest piece of trash in the factory. Yesterday I killed a woman. Today I'm acting like nothing happened."

Factory? He gently chucked her under the chin. "If you aren't careful, guilt will immobilize you. And really, you have no reason to feel guilty. Celeste would have killed you. You stopped her. Do not mourn. Celebrate."

"I guess," she muttered. "What if someone else attacks me? You should probably give me a weapon. And before you turn on the paranoia—yeah, like that—I'm not currently plotting against you, just trying to stay alive, which you totally need me to do. I'm *necessary*. I mean, I'll have to ditch you at some point, of course. We both know it. But good news! That point isn't now. You're the only player who isn't going to off me immediately."

She placed a hand over her heart and fluttered her lashes. "My hero!" Then she added, "You and I have formed a temporary alliance. I will help you...by letting you help me. We're a team. Equal partners, and all that jazz. Now how about that weapon?"

Hardly. "What would your husband say about such a partnership?"

"He'd probably agree that I'm doing you a *huge* favor by sticking around," she said.

Let it go. Move on.

Can't. He grated, "You're immortal now. He's not. Like your sister, he's become a liability." Did Vale enjoy rubbing up against her husband? Did her divine scent drive him wild? Did he appreciate her uninhibited sensuality?

Hate the male! Today Vale becomes a widow.

Cruel to be kind.

"Forget him and give me a fricking sword already." She stomped her foot, the picture of pique. "I need to protect myself. Give me a fighting chance, at least."

"Fighting chance?" He laughed without humor. "You still don't understand. You *can't* protect yourself. You don't have the skill."

She glowered and might have maybe possibly appeared ferocious if not for those eyes, like sunlit emeralds. "You're afraid of me," she said. "Admit it."

Afraid? She wasn't wrong. The things she made him feel... The way she shredded his control. "If you were to strike at me, I could confiscate the weapon and kill you with it before you could apologize. I'm doing you a favor by keeping you unarmed."

Some secret part of Knox rebelled at the thought of harming her for any reason, at any time. He'd never met anyone like her. So loyal to her sister she would risk a warrior's wrath in order to find the girl. So loving she would walk away from the only people who mattered to her, shattering her heart, as a simple matter of protection. Did Nola understand how lucky she was?

"It's clear you're crushing on me hard." The glower melted away, and she wiggled her brows. "Here's a pro tip, free of charge. When you do a favor for a girl, actually do a favor."

Now she dared to tease him? "Considering I'm the one keeping us alive, you should be nicer to me."

She scratched her head, as if confused. "You mean I should show my gratitude by pretending to desire you again?"

Pretend? Hardly. After every All War, women had thrown themselves at Knox. He'd had his pick of society's darlings. Yes, Ansel had paid them. But Vale could do no better. Unless Knox wasn't her type?

What did her husband look like? What talents did he possess? *Doesn't matter. Survive. Gain your freedom, win the war. Forget the girl.*

If Ansel were to learn about Vale, he would order Knox to slay her.

He swiped up the bag he'd packed and hooked the strap over

his shoulder, his limbs as heavy as cinder blocks. Vale released a soft sigh of relief. Because he hadn't touched her again? Perhaps she was afraid of the intensity of her reaction to him.

Perhaps he was deluding himself.

Time to hunt. "If I'm right about Ronan's general location, he'll be with a woman named Petra." If the two were lovers, as he suspected, they had probably fallen straight into bed the moment they'd escaped the mountains. "Are you able to access Celeste's memories of the pair?"

"Let's find out." Vale closed her eyes and, as seconds passed, scrunched up her features. "She definitely interacted with them. I'm detecting admiration, regret, determination. Problem is, there's a lot of fog."

"Fog disappears with heat." Knox brushed a fingertip along her jaw, the action springing from his subconscious. Her skin was as soft as silk and as deliciously fevered.

She leaned into his touch, only to open her eyes and stiffen. Spine ramrod straight, she jumped away from him, looking anywhere but his direction. "I think I can easily access what was most important to Celeste, but I have to work for everything else."

"Or maybe you don't *want* to learn more."

"It's possible," she admitted. "You plan to murder the pair." She nibbled on her bottom lip. "Here's a thought. We lock them up rather than kill them. Dead is dead and can't be undone. What if you need them for something later on?"

"Combatants are taught to escape any prison."

One of her black brows winged up. "Except one made of ice, eh?"

"And yet, we escaped even that, eventually." To make certain she understood the gravity of his next words, he pinned her with a hard stare. "A word of warning, female."

She groaned. "Great! Another one."

"There's an added danger to working with another combatant. Alone, you can sense when your enemies approach. There's a crackle of energy in the air. When two combatants are together, the crackle is already present, and you sense nothing."

The color in her cheeks dulled, leaving her ashen. "Got it. I won't sense anyone, so I have to remain on alert at all times."

"If a fight breaks out, stay out of my way, but stay close. I can protect you better if I can see you. Just don't expect me to jump in front of a sword for you."

"Trust me, I don't expect anything but the worst from you." She licked her bloodred lips. A nervous tell, but erotic all the same.

Want those lips wrapped around my shaft.

He tensed. If this kept up, he might eschew the war and move into Vale's bed.

Tone harder, he said, "Enough chatter. I'll summon shadows and we'll go."

CHAPTER ELEVEN

As Knox "summoned shadows," his eye sockets did the blackening thing, the darkness spreading from just beneath his brows to the rise of his cheekbones, creating circles about the size of her fists.

Before, Vale had been creeped out by the horror-movie visual. Now she was kinda sorta soothed by it, because she knew his shadows would shield her from the men and women determined to end her.

Without further ado, he clinked his Rifters together, then waved his hand through the air—exactly as Celeste had done a thousand times in Vale's new memories. The shadows prevented her from observing the doorway as it opened between two different locations, but a warm breeze caressed her skin, letting her know it *had* opened.

What would she find on the other side?

As different answers played Whac-A-Mole with her mind, her stomach shriveled, and she wrapped her arms around her middle.

Knox glanced at her, frowned, and took her hand. The shriveling stopped...and fluttering began. Little tremors cascaded through her as he led her into the veil of gloom.

The bunker surrounded her one moment, pure darkness the next. "I can't see." Her heart rate hit warp speed. "Where are we?"

"The language… French. Mountains surround the area, and homes are nearby."

The French Alps?

"Everyone leaves a trace of energy, light and shadow everywhere they go. Ronan's trace leads to another rift, and I'm attempting to follow the trail." Knox released her.

Blinded, she reached out, rested a hand against his biceps. He was moving his arms while standing in place, his muscles flexing and unflexing. If she had to guess, she'd say he was clinking his Rifters and waving his hand again and again, opening and discarding rifts.

"What if an innocent person stumbles through one of your rifts?" she asked.

"I never leave a rift until it has closed." Minutes passed before he added, "Let's go."

He retrieved her hand and led her forward once again. From darkness to a sundrenched playground. The light stung her eyes, and she kind of wanted to hiss like a vampire.

"The site is much changed," Knox said.

Kids laughed as they played on monkey bars. Adults jogged and biked on nearby dirt trails. Next to the trails were paved roads and zooming cars. Mountains peppered the horizon in every direction. So many people, so many spots to lie in wait, and take out a newly minted immortal…

For two long, miserable weeks, Vale had dreamed of returning to civilization. Now, the dream was a reality and part of her longed to rush back into the bunker, where she was safe. Well, *safer.*

Stick to your POA. Right. If she hung back, she'd never learn more about the war, and she desperately needed to learn more.

Multiple conversations rang out, most spoken in familiar, American English. Well, all right, then. They were somewhere in the United States. But which state, exactly? If she narrowed down the mountains—the Rockies, Ozarks, Smokies, Appalachians, or one she couldn't remember?—she could pare down her choices. Maybe. Geography had never been her thing.

As she searched for clues, the cornucopia of sounds left a terrible taste in her mouth, too many flavors at once, all melding together, and she cringed.

"Why do you wear this expression?" Knox asked before scanning the terrain. He gave her hand a comforting squeeze.

He'd noticed such a minute detail about her? "I told you about my screwed-up senses. I'm tasting every giggle, shout, bark and roaring engine."

"Learn to ignore it. Distraction is your enemy."

"Yeah, yeah, yeah." Easy for him to say. "By the way. You do know your eye sockets turn black when you summon shadows, right? If anyone sees you like that, they'll freak—" No. No, they wouldn't. They would assume he wore contacts and makeup or played a trick. People were so suspicious these days. Still, the transformation presented a problem. "It's distinctive, and people will talk, allowing other players to track you through social media."

He thought for a moment, nodded. "I'll be more careful."

So. He could be reasonable. "Also, I have a word of warning for *you*. I know this world, you don't. When I give an order, you need to obey it. But only *if* you want to live." She enjoyed the glint of affront in his eyes. Enjoyed the way the sun highlighted his golden sun. "First order of the day. Flee the scene of the crime."

She tugged him forward. Or rather, she *tried*. He dug in his heels, ensuring they went nowhere fast.

"A rift remains open for sixty seconds, and you are to remain nearby until it closes," he said. "Forget innocents. A combatant could sneak in, hide in your safe house, and ambush you upon your return."

See! This was the kind of info she required. "Rifts must close. Got it. But we're in modern society now. Someone could be filming us." She looked around. All right. Okay. No one seemed to care about them. Well, except for a little boy in the process of picking his nose. He caught sight of Knox and froze.

"And you," she continued, "you're loaded down with weapons. You aren't exactly inconspicuous. If you *are* photographed, the posts and pictures will go viral, guaranteed, and you'll become infamous. You'll be arrested."

"Your ability to speak gibberish and wisdom at the same time amazes me. For once, I think I understood the gist. I'll cloak my weapons with shadows. And I can assure you that no one noticed our abrupt appearance. I made the shadows fade gradually. No one can see the rift, either."

She turned, a black hole greeting her. Until her mind filled in the dark space, showing her the other side of the park. A wild process. Then, shadows began to rise from the ground like ghostly apparitions, tucking around Knox to conceal his weapons while also causing the darkness to blend into the background. Incredible!

"Distraction kills, remember?" he said.

Right. She faced the playground and performed another visual scan. Nothing had changed. The little boy hadn't stopped staring at Knox with wide-eyed fascination.

I know the feeling, kid.

The warrior was a walking contradiction, and she still hadn't figured him out. He was a killer who hadn't killed her. A soldier determined to win the war at all cost, who was keeping her—an enemy—safe. He was ruthless enough to tie Vale to a bed, but kind enough to hold her hand in an effort to keep her calm.

He was a beast on the inside and a storybook prince on the outside, hot enough to send her hormones into overdrive.

Ugh. This attraction to him had to end. Wasn't like she could rehab a murderer or anything.

Celeste had a crush on him, guaranteed. Well, before he'd murdered her lover and all. That was why Vale kept reacting to him on such a visceral, sexual level. That was why, when he'd patted her down, she'd wanted his hands to slip under her clothes...his lips to press against hers...his resistance to crumble—just as hers had done.

News flash. Your logic is flawed and doesn't check out. You reacted to him before you got hit with another woman's memories.

A whoosh of wind brushed her backside, and she squeaked with surprise.

"You should have known when the rift closed, should have counted down the seconds in your head." Knox ushered her forward, the black faded from around his eyes. "Remain aware. Don't lose track again."

Hello, new contradiction. His tone was total bastard, but his intention was total saint.

"Don't worry," she said, squaring her shoulders. "This Valerina ain't messing around."

When they came upon a jam-packed parking lot, Knox looked ready to torch the entire world and call it a day. "What are these things?" He motioned to a car.

Compassion slithered through her. To be stuck on a strange world with unknown technology, surrounded by foreigners—while being hunted by assassins—had to suck a nut.

She'd felt compassion for him once before, yes, when he'd admitted he had no family waiting at home. The raw pain she'd glimpsed in his eyes...she would bet he'd loved and lost someone. Poor Knox.

Whoa. Poor *Knox? Screw your head on straight, girlie.*

"They're vehicles, used for travel," she said. "People sit inside and zoom to a new location."

On the back of a minivan, someone had written in shoe polish: Breckenridge or Bust! Almost all the other cars had Colorado plates.

She reeled. She'd traveled overseas, gone underground, then stepped into the States without ever getting in a plane or driving in a car.

A sedan motored past them. Interest lit Knox's expression.

Vale almost laughed. Apparently "boys and their toys" was universal. Or rather, realmiversal. Whatever.

"You will acquire us a vehicle. That one." He pointed to a cherry-red sports car worth more than she made in...ever.

Of course *that* one. "I'll have to steal it. Well, not that one. There are too many anti-theft devices. But I can steal an older, cheaper model, no problem." Vale hadn't used this particular skill in a long time. When you spent time on the streets, you adapted or you died. "But theft is a crime, and we'll be hunted by police. Lawmen and -women. The authorities. Cops."

"Enforcers," he said, and judging by the harshness of his tone, he wasn't a fan.

Through Celeste, Vale had memories of an Enforcer named Seven. He would kill you if you broke a rule...but only after he played with you a bit.

"If you rift me home to Oklahoma," she said, "I'll drive my car through it. Or get some identification and money so we can *rent* a car here. A perfectly legal transaction."

He stared past the lot, the street, and examined a small shopping center. "Legal, but also trackable, I assume." He motioned to a license plate. "And you cannot go home. Ever. An ambush could be waiting for you, even now. Just...steal the car. I'll hide your actions and handle any fallout."

Cannot go home...

Keep it together. "Why don't we rift into Ronan's base camp?"

"Never rift directly into someone else's base camp. You cannot plan for every eventuality or trap, and the odds of being maimed or killed are vast."

Perfect segue. "What's going to happen if we're forcibly separated, and I need to rift somewhere else in a hurry?" *Don't act too eager. Play it cool.* "I should maybe probably have Celeste's Rifters. I guess."

He stiffened, the cords in his neck popping out. "You could escape danger with Rifters, yes. You could also steal my weapons while I'm away from the bunker, and escort enemies to my home."

"So, for now, that's a soft maybe. Got it."

He pushed out a breath. "Does nothing faze you? Never mind. Don't answer that." Eyes narrowed, he said, "Steal the car, and I'll handle the fallout as promised."

Ugh. "That's kind of what I fear most. A rising death toll—of humans." She might not be the biggest fan of people, but there *were* some good ones out there. Like the parents who actually cared enough about their kids to bring them to a park…the kids themselves, so innocent… Good Samaritans like Carrie, trying to make a difference.

Carrie would expect her to fight, to protect the world and all the people in it. Her foster momma would also want her to find a way to save the combatants.

Could she?

Could she even save herself?

CHAPTER TWELVE

Knox enjoyed cars—metal animals capable of great speeds. In Iviland, everyone traveled on foot, or in carts that ran on tracks. But there was something he enjoyed *more* than cars. Observing Vale. She sat in the seat next to his, in profile, the piercings in her ear glinting in the waning sunlight. Her tattooed, black-tipped fingers were wrapped around the "wheel," fascinating him with their elegance. Even though the wheel didn't belong to the car he'd wanted.

Vale had said they needed something "inconspicuous" in order to "blend in," and he'd reluctantly agreed. Then she'd said, "Do not, I repeat, *do not* cloak the car with shadows. Other drivers need to see us, or they'll crash into us."

She'd also insisted he "buckle up," willingly restricting his movements. When he'd flat-out refused, she'd said, "I'm going to give you a hands-on demonstration about car safety, and when I'm done, you'll want to curse me, but you're going to thank me instead."

She'd then sped up only to slam on the brakes. After his forehead had introduced itself to the dashboard, he'd decided the seat belt buckle wasn't so bad, after all. And yes, he *had* thanked her.

Vale could have launched him through the windshield, injuring and weakening him, but she hadn't. The woman confused him, defying his understanding of an opponent and wrecking his infamous control.

All his life, the words most often used to describe him had been *sadistic, barbaric,* and *emotionless.* Somehow, she was peeling away *his* armor, layer by layer, allowing guilt, regret and sorrow to surface.

He should be studying the world around him, learning *everything.* Instead, he continued to examine her, the sight of her fraying more and more of his calm.

Maybe *barbaric* still applied.

Knox wanted to touch her silken skin again, to fist her hair, blending the white strands with the black, wanted to angle her face and claim her lips in a hard, punishing kiss—no more soft and gentle. He wanted to thrust his tongue against hers and discover her taste. He wanted to cup her breasts harder, wanted to knead the giving flesh and roll her nipples between his fingers.

In that moment, desire ruled him—*Vale* ruled him, for whoever tempted you enslaved you.

Never give another person power over you.

Knox blamed her scent, despite the fact that he'd wanted her *before* he'd noticed the exotic perfume that lingered on her skin. One inhalation, and he'd frothed with undiluted arousal.

You froth with undiluted arousal, anyway. He had only to glance at her. As he was doing now...

Look away. He'd castigated her for being easily distracted, and yet his own concentration was shot.

It took every ounce of his willpower—*victory means freedom*—but he finally forced his attention to the terrain. He was instantly transfixed.

The difference between past and present astounded him. Paved streets had supplanted wild lands filled with trees and bush. There were buildings of every shape and size, towering poles and wires...everywhere.

On Terra, you weren't pinned in from every side. There were wide-open spaces, fresh air yours for the taking, and an incomparable caress of warmth from a single sun. Crowds of people strolled along sidewalks, unhampered by the fear of being hunted, unafraid to turn a corner because they were certain someone lay in wait, ready to strike. Vale had once been this carefree, he would bet. But she would never be this way again. Her life had been forever altered, her future set—her death imminent.

"Question," she said, and he wondered if she'd noticed his upset and now hoped to redirect his thoughts. "Do we have the power to turn everyday average mortals into immortals?"

"There are only a handful of ways to impart immortality, and your realm currently offers only one of them. A mortal must slay a combatant."

Disappointment caused her shoulders to roll in, and he could guess why. The sick girl, Nola. *Ignore the clench in your chest.*

He was becoming used to that clench. "You had better not try to sacrifice your life for hers," he said.

"If I thought for a second she'd go for it, I'd do more than try. But she would never hurt me. Not ever, for any reason."

Oh, to have such unwavering trust in another person.

Thoughtful, she asked, "In AW history, has anyone successfully stopped a war?"

AW... All War. "Never, though many have tried. The High Council is too greedy to forfeit a new world. This one in particular, where resources are abundant. They'll receive hundreds of thousands of slaves from participating realms as payment. They'll also receive a tax from Terra. Earth."

"What kind of tax?"

"It's different for every realm, and depends on what the High Council needs at the time."

"Peachy." She rested an elbow on the driver's door. "You fight on behalf of your realm. I assume your government—"

"King."

"Well, well. A *bad* king, judging by the sharpness of your tone. If you win, *he'll* rule Earth, not you. So what do you get? What do the other warriors get?"

"They will save their families, as I mentioned, and save children from enslavement. Perhaps they'll acquire the respect of their peers."

"Child enslavement? Are you kidding? Tell me you're kidding."

"I'm not kidding."

When he said no more, she grumbled, "You left out *your* prize."

"I hope to receive my heart's greatest desire." Again he said no more.

"I used to love mysterious. Now?" She shook her head. "Not so much. But okay, sure, I get the gist. You want something so badly, something I can't give you, so you can't be lured to my side."

"No. I can't." His gaze roved over her, and a stray thought caught him off guard. *If anything could change my mind, it's you.*

His gut churned. *Foolish* thought. And wrong. So wrong.

He decided to warn her, just as he'd warned Shiloh—a good man who deserved better than he'd got. *Ignore the prickle of guilt.* "Have no doubt that I'll do everything in my power to win this war, Vale. No deed is too despicable."

"I believe you," she said, her tone grave. "Any idea why Ronan came to Colorado? Don't get me wrong, I love it here, but it hardly seems like a hot spot for alien warriors."

"Petra hails from a mountain realm, and most combatants seek out locales that best match what they know. She built a camp here, and Ronan followed her."

Her gaze darted to him, darted away. "So, you come from an underground society?"

"Yes. The surface of Iviland was destroyed centuries before my birth, during an other-realm invasion."

"There wasn't an All War back then?"

"No." Knox only knew what he'd been taught. "Iviland was invaded by other realms. We won, driving out their armies, but it took years. But then the surface of my world was destroyed, the suns rendered toxic."

"Suns...plural?"

"Three." He'd seen pictures, each sun a study of magnificence. "The surface of Iviland is still uninhabitable, the underground cities massively overcrowded."

"What do you guys eat? Those trees in your bunker are somehow thriving without light, but I can't imagine there's enough fruit to feed everyone," she said.

"Technological advances gained through All War victories help provide sustainable meals. Also, denizens are selected to move to new realms when they're won, while still remaining under our king's rule."

"Your king, a man you so clearly despise. How was he selected?"

"A right of birth."

"So there's no getting rid of him after a term of service. Sucks!"

Very much so.

"How many wars have you won?" she asked.

"Four." If he gained his freedom before this one ended, the fifth would be his last. If not, and Ansel had lied to him... His hands fisted.

"Wow! That's incredible, Knox."

Her awe struck him as *appropriate*. "I'm not the only Ivilandian to win. We've given Ansel twenty-two realms in total."

"I don't think I want to know the number of people you and the others had to kill, or the weapons you've acquired."

Bitterness turned his heart to stone. "After each war, the king confiscated everything. And if not the king, the High Council."

"That's gotta sting." Vale gave an exaggerated wince. "You do the work, and the king takes the credit and the prizes."

"Tsk, tsk. You're trying to lure me to your side, despite my assurance that it can't be done. If you continue down this path, female, your manipulations will only infuriate me."

"Female again." She pretended to gag. "Look. All I'm saying is the High Council sounds like a real suck fest, and I'm pretty sure your king won't go down in our history books as a dream leader."

"None of which affects my determination to win."

"How can you be so cruel, condemning another world to such a terrible fate?" Her voice rose, rage dripping from every syllable. "How can you fight to enslave an entire planet?"

"How can I not? I am but a tool." A tool wielded by another man. "If I wasn't here, you'd be facing a different Iviland. He might not be as nice as me."

"I. Can't. Imagine."

Again he debated the humiliation of admitting his own enslavement to this beautiful creature. How he was purposely conceived to create "the next great champion," forced to train from suns rise to suns set in the worst possible conditions, every meal selected for him, meant to strengthen his body and sharpen his mind, every action scrutinized and judged in order to hone his battle skills. How he was only rewarded after he won.

As a child, he'd been forced to kill other slaves with histories similar to his own. Forced to kill friends—actually *compelled* to do it, unable to stop himself. The mystical ink in his tattooed bands guaranteed absolute obedience to Ansel, always. It was the same for the other slaves. Many had been commanded to kill *him*, and when they'd failed, Knox had to make a decision:

end their lives before they'd ever tasted the joys of freedom, or let them live, so they could be used as leverage against him later.

He'd killed, soon becoming little more than an animal, until he was unable—or maybe unwilling—to care about others. Until Minka. His baby girl had changed *everything*.

Soon, I'll avenge her death. Ansel and his horrible family will be dead, and I'll be free. The citizens of Iviland and Earth will be liberated.

"After I win, I'll return," he said. "I'll—" No. He couldn't tell Vale about his plan, shouldn't give her any leverage to use against him, and wouldn't risk the High Council learning of his intentions.

"If you win and come back, don't bother looking me up. I'll be dead, remember?" She inhaled deeply, exhaled heavily, reminding him of the times his own emotions had gotten the best of him, before muttering to herself. "I'm a lady, not a land mine. I won't explode."

"Vale—"

"Nope. You're done talking." She reached over to pat his knee, the way he'd sometimes seen mothers to do with their children, only Vale offered no comfort or encouragement, only anger. "You want me dead, so your thoughts are worthless to me."

The touch electrified him, causing lightning strikes to zing from the point of contact. It must have electrified her, too. Posture going rigid, she jerked her hand back to the wheel. A hint of her jasmine and dark spice perfume thickened the air, making every breath a test of his strength. Tension overwhelmed him.

Want her…need her.

"To survive, you'll have to slay the other combatants," he said. "Even the other player from this land. A viking named Erik the Widow Maker. He joined the war the day he created the ice prison."

"Like, a real-life ancient Viking?" Fascination saturated her voice, irritating Knox.

"He's your enemy. I think. To my knowledge, this is the first time two representatives have fought for a realm. Though it's possible your entry voided his." Except, as of this morning, Erik still lived. If he'd been disqualified, Seven would have killed him already, yes? "We'll find out during the next assembly."

The assembly. Knox's gut churned anew as he imagined Vale participating in the bloodbath that always followed.

She frowned and rubbed her temple. New memories from Celeste making themselves known?

"We'll talk about it another day." Before he shredded the car into millions of metal ribbons. "Distract me. Tell me about your childhood."

"Um, aren't you the one who repeatedly reminded me that distraction kills?"

"Enthrall me, then. Take a page from Celeste's war manual. Try to win me to your side."

"Ha! That's a trick request, and I'm not falling for it. One, you *just* told me I would never ever lure you to my side, and I would only infuriate you if I tried."

Still true—probably. And yet... "I'd like to know about you, Vale. Indulge me."

Tremors rocked her. "You want to know about my childhood? Fine. I'll tell you." Except, she paused and swallowed, as if she regretted her agreement already. Then she said, "My mom died of a brain aneurysm when I was six." Her voice began to tremble. "The loss devastated my dad and me. He used to love me, had even doted on me, but suddenly he could barely look at me. I think I reminded him of what he'd lost. He finally took off, leaving me behind."

"He *abandoned* you." Knox hadn't left Minka's side without a fight. A contingent of armed guards had to beat him within an inch of life and drag him away. As soon as he'd revived, he'd done everything in his power to return to his baby.

"I tracked my father down when I turned eighteen but…"
She shrugged, a casual action that belied the hurt she projected.

"Where is he now? Who cared for you during his absence?"

Board-stiff, she said, "All right, now *I* want a subject change."

A new clench in his chest, stronger than all the others. What
kind of life had this spirited beauty led? One of loneliness and
abuse? No wonder she loved and protected Nola so fiercely;
she'd become a ray of light in a world of darkness.

Knox understood. Minka had been *his* light.

Though he wanted to demand answers and barrage Vale with
more questions, he held his tongue and ignored the compassion
she'd roused in him. Ignored the shocking urge to take her into
his arms, hold her close and promise all would be well, and he
would protect her, always. A lie.

She was right. He'd issued a trick request. No matter how
much he liked her, no matter how much he might wish otherwise, he would kill her the moment she ceased being necessary to his cause. When she killed Celeste, she'd signed her
own death warrant.

"Frick." The car swerved, and Vale yanked the wheel. "My
eyes were watering—because of dust—and I veered a little too
far to the left. Sorry."

"You're crying. Because of dust," he echoed, wishing she
would admit the truth, and hating the thought of her unhap-
piness.

"Wrong! I don't cry, like, ever. This girl is made of glass
shards, nails and dragon scales."

Stubborn female. *Strong* female.

"What about your husband?" Knox asked. "When and how
did you meet him?" What was his name? Where did he live?
What did she like about him? Did she want Knox to kill him
with a sword or bare-handed?

In lieu of answers, she reached out to turn a dial on the dashboard. Fast-paced music spilled through the vehicle, the sound grating his ears.

For a moment, only a moment, he wished he possessed the ability to read minds, like Emberelle, something he'd never before wanted to do. To be plagued by other people's thoughts when he could barely handle his own? He would rather be gutted. But he believed he would do just about anything to discover Vale's secrets.

Svaney of Frostland possessed a crown that allowed her to see the past, present or future of anyone around her—except herself. Knox might just target her next, and study Vale's future. And if the wild thrum of music persisted, he was going to ram his fist into the dash.

He turned the same dial in the opposite direction, and the volume decreased. Better. "We were discussing your husband."

"From now on," Vale said, "Khal Drogo London is a taboo topic, because anytime you mention him, you put on your murder face. You can answer more of my questions instead. What happens if a realm doesn't want to participate in a war?"

Khal Drogo London. *Hate him.* "Realms must pay the High Council an exclusion fee."

"Could *Earth* pay an exclusion fee before a winner is declared and keep our leaders in power?"

Smart girl. "No. The war had a beginning, and it will have an end. Otherwise, combatants who met their deaths will have fought for nothing." Not that the High Council cared about combatants. Only the protests from the sovereigns...occasionally.

"Well, dang."

He stroked his jaw and said, "You have a surprisingly cunning mind, Valerina London."

"You don't have to sound so shocked about it, but thank you." She fluffed her hair, all sass and sweetness. "Hey, maybe I can use my surprisingly cunning mind to get what seems to be the best gig in the galaxy—High Councilwoman."

The thought of Vale seated with the other council members disturbed him greatly.

Steering the car to the right, she said, "I know certain competitors have intrinsic supernatural abilities, while others have supernatural abilities tied to specific weapons. How does your shadow thing work?"

"I was born with it." His parents possessed the gift, as well. The very reason they were chosen to spawn him.

"Can everyone in your world control shadows, then?"

"Some, but only a rare few can create shadows from nothing and use them to create a whirlwind." And if those people weren't already enslaved, they were tattooed with slave bands as soon as they were found out.

"Because of Celeste, I know each player came to Earth with a single weapon. She chose a sword that leaks poison, but what about you?"

"The bunker."

"Wow. And you've actually *won* wars?"

The corners of his mouth twitched, as if he wanted to smile. Odd.

"The others don't have bunkers of their own?" she asked.

"What they have, they had to build upon arrival here. I merely had to pick a spot and have the bunker portaled in. Their safe houses, way stations or whatever they want to call their homes on Terra are not equipped with advanced technology like mine. And I knew I could win weapons the first day of battle. Which I did." He paused, his next words poised at the end of his tongue, ready to escape. *Do not appear too eager.* "Have you recalled anything about Gunnar's sword?"

Her brow furrowed. "I'm picking up thoughts about liquefying and bonding, but nothing else."

What liquefied? The people he cut? But Knox had seen no evidence of that. Bonding—to whom, or what?

Had she told the truth? Did she know more? *Never trust a combatant.*

Perhaps *he* would have to take a page from Celeste's war manual and seduce information out of *Vale*.

His body reacted swiftly, intensely, his shaft going rock hard and straining against his fly.

Control. He shifted in his seat, peered out the window. The sun had begun its descent, turning the sky into a maze of brilliant colors.

"Are vehicles able to travel at night?" he asked.

"Yep. Thanks to headlights." She messed with a knob beside the wheel, and lights glowed in front of the car. "Why are you guys given Rifters? Transporting to a new location in seconds only prolongs the war, giving everyone an escape hatch."

"The kings and queens insisted. They wouldn't send their warriors to fight without assuring they had every available advantage, and an even playing field. Also, I suspect they are easily bored. As immortals, they live a long time, and need new amusements. I think tales of our exploits, and the uncertainty of the wars, excites them." He pointed to a corner up ahead. "Turn there." Once she obeyed, he instructed her to take another turn, then another, until they reached a dead end. He frowned. "We're close but not close enough."

"Do you have the safe house's coordinates?"

He rattled off the latitude and longitude, and she punched buttons on a screen in the center of the dashboard. An automated voice offered direction—and almost died a quick death when Knox unsheathed a dagger.

"Calm down, Mr. Overreact. Navigation isn't out for your blood." Vale steered down different roads, following the correct path, passing other cars.

As they approached one of the larger buildings, he thought he spied Rush of Nolita. The pale-haired male with eyes as dark and fathomless as Knox's shadows owned a crossbow capable of

shooting three arrows at once, at three different targets. He usually stuck to swampy areas, so what was he doing here?

Kill him, claim the crossbow. "Stop the vehicle," Knox demanded.

"Let me find a spot to—"

"Here," he snapped.

"If I stop here," Vale snapped back, "I'll cause a wreck and
people will get hurt. Including us!" She snaked another corner
before coming to an abrupt halt at the curb. "All right. Now
what?"

"Now we hunt."

CHAPTER THIRTEEN

Knox slid his gaze over the sea of mortals striding along the sidewalks. If Rush had another combatant with him, he wouldn't sense the arrival of others. If Rush rolled solo, it would be a completely different story; the moment they stood within range of each other, he would sense Knox, but Knox wouldn't sense him, not with Vale at his side.

Wait. Had he just thought the words *rolled solo*? What hellish update to his translator was *this*?

"I spotted a combatant named Rush," he explained.

"Rush," Vale echoed with a frown. "Comes from a swamp kingdom…handsome, seemingly seducible, tricky, volatile temper, noncommittal."

"Swamp, yes. Handsome and seducible, no. Not for you." Knox was the only male Vale would be seducing.

He cursed. In a perfect world, no one would have the power to seduce him, ever.

"If we remain together," he added, shoving the words past gritted teeth, "I won't sense him in the crowd." He would have to remain alert, undistracted and rely on sight and instinct.

"Hint taken," she replied. "I'll stay in the car and keep the motor running in case we need to make a fast getaway when local PD chases you down for sword fighting in public."

Leave her behind, outside his bunker? Every muscle in his body rebelled. "You'll come with me." He grabbed the duffel bag, reached for the door. "Let's go."

{*Wait.*}

The *eyaer's* command stopped him cold. What was wrong?

Extreme patience was a skill he possessed...usually. However, he'd spent the past thirteen centuries in stasis, and he was primed and ready for the next battle. The next win. Also, a part of him liked the idea of eradicating one of Vale's enemies.

{*Danger lurks nearby.*}

So what? Danger *always* lurked nearby.

"My first official hunt," she said with a tremor. "Warning. I'm going to slow you down out there. I won't mean to, but it's bound to happen."

He latched onto her wrist. Scanning, scanning, he said, "We must wait."

"Sure, but just so you know, the mental pep talk I'm giving myself has an expiration minute." Paling, she wiped down the interior of the car and said, "Or do you just mean we need to destroy our prints first?"

Scanning... "According to my instincts, we will be placed in unnecessary danger if we leave the car right now. I have no desire to put you—either of us—at risk." No other signs of Rush. Had the male already rifted out of the area?

Vale settled back in her seat with a soft puff of breath. "Those instincts ever steer you wrong?"

"No. People are liars and cheats, but my instincts remain a faithful companion."

"People are the worst," she agreed. "Most people, anyway. There are exceptions."

"Agreed." *Ignore the heartache.* "I had a daughter. Before she died, there was no one better."

He gnashed his molars. Why had he shared such a personal fragment of his life?

"Oh, Knox." Vale pressed a hand against her heart. "I'm so sorry for your loss."

That was the second time she'd expressed remorse for the great tragedy he'd suffered, and it made him feel as if up was down and down was up, and he'd gotten flayed alive in the process.

"What happened to her mother?" she asked softly.

"Don't know. She left after Minka's birth, wanted nothing to do with me or the babe."

"I'm so sorry," Vale repeated. "Minka is a beautiful name."

"In my language, the word *minka* refers to an infinite amount of time."

Tears welled in her eyes, and she pressed a hand over her heart. "You took one look at her and knew you would love her forever."

Yes, exactly. Vale understood. He'd known he would be forever transformed.

She sniffled and said, "Stupid dust. Allergies, amirite?"

"Dust sucks," he said, mimicking her sassiest tone.

A laugh burst from her, genuine and sweet, lighting up her delicate features, giving him the same thrilling high usually only achieved with victory.

Focus!

"FYI, we need to abandon the car ASAP," Vale said. "Before a cop runs the plates. And I'm pretty sure we're currently fish in a barrel to other players."

FYI. ASAP. Run the plates. Would he ever understand the Terran vernacular?

Sensing his confusion, she said, "Acronyms. FYI—for your information. ASAP—a super amazing penis. I kid, I kid. As soon as possible." She tapped her chin. "You know, if I can steal a cell phone, I can search for reported sightings of other warriors.

Considering you guys appear out of nowhere whenever you walk
through an invisible doorway, I'm *sure* people are taking note."

Cell phone?

"Although, it might be smarter to steal money and *buy* a
phone since there are so many security measures on preowned
devices—dude. I can't believe I'm falling back into a life of
crime so easily." Moaning, she rested her face in her upraised
hands. "Carrie is looking down and shaking her head with disappointment."

"Who is Carrie?"

"Another exception." She looked up and offered him a soft
smile. "She was my favorite foster mom."

As she explained different aspects about the foster system—
moving from one strange home to another, some nice, some not
so nice, some bad enough she'd had to run away and live on
the streets just to survive—he had to fight to listen. So beautiful. So kind.

Stronger than he'd realized.

"The word *favorite* indicates you had more than one foster
mom," he said.

"Yes." She nodded. "I had many. Carrie is the only one I
stayed in touch with after I was declared an adult, but she died
a few years ago."

"I'm sorry your father let this happen to you," he said. He
hated the thought of Vale rejected by the man who was supposed to love her, without a family of her own…cared for by
others, like Minka…suffering as Minka had, suffering so much
she'd felt she had no recourse but to run away.

Oh, how he'd enjoyed killing Minka's foster family.

The need to exact vengeance on Vale's behalf consumed him,
to lay the heads of her tormentors at her feet. *Forget the war, if
only for a little while. What will one personal errand hurt?*

Only everything! "Let's not share other personal details with each other," he croaked. As he'd warned Shiloh, making friends during wartime was foolish.

Hurt flashed over her features, but she bucked up fast, donning a blank mask.

He hated the hurt, and he hated the blank mask, too.

Knox needed out of this car. He needed fresh air and action, and he needed to get Vale's sweet scent out of his nose before he ruined his life simply to make her happy.

Desperation gnawed at him as he reached for the door handle. "Let's go. I think the danger has passed." His instinct had gone quiet.

"Yeah. Good call," she said, her prickly tone making a resurgence. "As the old adage goes, sharing is erring."

If he managed to get through the day without ripping out his heart and handing it to her, he'd consider it a win.

He exited the car and draped the duffel bag over his shoulder, breathing deeply. Varying scents were mingled together, blessedly obscuring Vale's perfume.

As soon as she stood at his side, he took her hand—*ignore the rightness of it*—tucked shadows around his weapons and led her down the sidewalk. Men jumped out of his way while women stopped to stare.

"Hey, look it. We match," Vale said. "Black shirts and leatherish pants seem like our uniform. Team Knale. No, Team Valox."

"We are not a team," he said out of habit. In Iviland, he was used to being an object of both fascination and ridicule. Unbothered, he focused solely on his mission. Nothing would distract him from his—

Had a mortal just stripped Vale with his gaze?

Something dark and hot blazed inside Knox. Something akin to rage. Over something so trivial? And did Vale have to roll her hips so sensually?

She bumped into one man after another, as if physical contact with strangers was her greatest ambition.

"If your walk wasn't a living example of a mating call," he grated, "you wouldn't fall into gawking males quite so often."

"Um, you're welcome." She held out her hands to reveal four miniature leather pouches. "I distracted the guys so I could filch their wallets. I think I got enough to buy a phone." Free of Knox's grip, she withdrew sheets of green paper from each of the pouches. "Yep. Plenty."

She'd been picking pockets, and he'd had no idea. He ran his tongue over his teeth.

Do better. Be more aware.

After she'd tossed the wallets into a metal bin marked United States Postal Service, her stomach gave a loud rumble.

A new prickle of guilt had him barking, "I told you to eat a piece of fruit."

"And I did. But I've gone two weeks with very little food, so my body is demanding more, more, more."

He relaxed but only slightly. "Very well. I will provide for you." He shouldn't enjoy the thought. No, he shouldn't.

Scenting meat and bread, he reclaimed her hand and led her in front of a short, squat man with silver hair who was holding a small brown bag. The food must be inside.

Silver paused, looked up and paled. "C-can I help you?"

"Your food. I want it. Give it to me."

Without a beat of hesitation, Silver extended the bag.

Vale yanked Knox away before he could claim his prize. "Sorry, he's usually an indoor dog," she called over her shoulder. Then, glaring at Knox, she said, "You're going to get yourself arrested, and I will *not* post bail."

Whatever that meant.

"You can't just take things from people," she said.

"Why not? You took a car and multiple wallets." Might equaled right.

"I took in secret, out of necessity. And I'm eaten up with guilt about it!"

The fact...didn't settle well. "We'll visit Ronan's safe house, buy our phone, then purchase food. If her highness is amenable?"

"Her highness is," she said with a mocking curtsy.

His internal navigation sent him around two more corners, until he came upon a large brownstone. "This is it."

Tone as dry as sand, she said, "I should have guessed some-one's ancient safe house would end up being a coffee shop."

Knox entered, cool air chased away by warmth, weapons still hidden by shadows. Vale remained behind him. The aroma of... He wasn't sure what it was, but he liked it.

"I'm going to order a couple drinks," Vale muttered.

"Do what you must." As he moved around the building, studying walls, tables and chairs, even the floor, she stood in line and spoke with someone standing behind a wooden counter.

Beneath a new bouquet of scents, he detected Ronan's tell-tale fragrance; something that made him think of a desert oasis bathed in sunlight. The male had visited recently, but hadn't stayed long.

Knox decided not to bother questioning the Terrans. He wouldn't trust anything they said.

Would Ronan return here?

If Knox waited and Ronan *did* return, their brawl would catch the notice of the authorities. Witnesses equaled trouble.

Involving mortals wasn't forbidden, but complications would follow. He'd have to whisk the warrior to a secondary location, an act with just as many problems.

Thinking to examine the back of the shop, Knox moved be-hind the counter. A frowning mortal tripped over, calling, "Sir! Sir! You can't come back here."

"Why?" he demanded. "What are you hiding?"

"My apologies," Vale said, sidling up to Knox. "He's from, uh, somewhere else, and doesn't yet understand our customs."

His *eyaer* was dormant, which had to mean no danger lurked

in back. Therefore, he allowed her to draw him outside into the fresh air.

"Going behind a counter, any counter, is prohibited," she said, handing him a hot paper cup. "In other words, a big fat no-no."

"Drinking something you picked up in Ronan's territory is also a no-no—*my* no-no, which is the only one that matters." He dumped both cups in the nearest trash can. "He could have paid the servers to poison our drinks."

"First, modern people wouldn't— Never mind. For profit, they totally would. Second, we're immortal, remember? If Ronan poisoned the coffee, and that's a big if, we wouldn't die. Would we?"

"No, but we could be incapacitated. Then combatants would attack. *Then* we would die."

"Thanks for ruining every meal I'm ever going to eat." She sighed. "Let's go purchase our phone." She took his hand and tugged him in the opposite direction. "I saw a store with burners back this way."

"We are going to burn our phone?"

"No, no. Burners are a *type* of phone. They're untraceable, and we won't have to sign a contract or pay monthly fees to access data."

More nonsense. Just how technologically advanced had this world become? What new dangers awaited him?

When a male whistled at Vale, Knox spun and glared. The man withered before racing away.

"My hero," Vale muttered, and though her tone was mocking, she peered up at him, her hazel eyes wide, her sexy red lips parted, as if waiting to be kissed.

His body responded, all systems go. His heartbeat sped up, his core temperature rising. Muscles tensed, but not in preparation for combat. A stray thought left him reeling: *I want to be her hero in truth.*

He ground to a halt right there in the middle of the sidewalk.

Vale halted just as abruptly. They stood there, staring at each other, panting, snared by a force greater than ambition, deeper than need, more electric than awareness. Inside him, barriers seemed to fall.

The world around him faded, the erotic scent of her perfume thickening the air, heating his blood... *Boiling* his blood. He'd thought he'd escaped that scent when they'd exited the car, thought he'd eluded the sensual assault.

He'd only delayed the inevitable.

His shaft hardened painfully. His vision hazed, Vale becoming his sole focal point. The things he wanted to do to her... The things he *would* do.

She was a fantasy come to life, temptation made flesh, and the essence of all three of Iviland's *vales*. A ray of sunlight in his very dark world, a source of irresistible heat...and a force that guided him straight to his doom.

Doom. Exactly right. At no point in Knox's life had he ever stood out in the open like this, all but daring an enemy to take a shot.

"What are we doing, Knox?" she asked softly.

Hating the war, hating *himself*, he said, "We're buying a burner. Lead the way."

A blank mask covered her features, but not before he caught a glimmer of disappointment and perhaps even an accusation—*coward*.

He couldn't deny it. Put a gun in his face, and he would not falter. When Vale neared, he crumbled.

"Try to keep up," she said, blazing onward.

Knox remained close to her heels, scanning once again. Soon, he'd have to reevaluate Vale's necessity to him. He'd known her a short amount of time, but already he liked her and anticipated the next time he could make her smile or laugh...or touch her.

What the hell is happening to me?

Just in case his control shattered and he put her well-being before the war, he should make arrangements, find a way to undo any mistakes. Rumors suggested Lennox of Winslet had a pair of wrist cuffs with the ability to reverse time. But because Emberelle had killed the warrior after the fourth check-in, she now had possession of the cuffs.

Should Knox hunt Ronan, as planned, or go after Emberelle?

Easy. Ronan's spyglass was the key to finding the others. Therefore, the spyglass remained his top priority.

And Vale? What would he do with her in the meantime?

He'd never before had a problem walking away from a woman, his iron control unbreakable.

He roved his gaze over her black-and-white hair, the elegant line of her back, the beautiful curve of her ass and the long length of her legs, and his pulse jumped with anticipation, all *welcome to your new addiction.*

If he bedded her, perhaps he could finally, blessedly, end his strange, too-strong desire for her.

Worth a shot. Had any other man ever considered such a genius plan?

He straightened his shoulders and lifted his chin. He would face this sexual need—no, this sexual curiosity with Vale, and soon. Before, he'd worried that experiencing her feminine wiles would only make him want more of her, whatever she offered. Now he knew the truth. He *couldn't* want her more—lust already consumed him.

Afterward, he would regain his focus, and his fascination with her would be eradicated. He was sure of it.

There was only one wrench in his plan. Vale had to *agree* to share his bed.

Would she?

He would find a way to win her over. Victory was his specialty, after all.

Excitement raced through him, determination not far behind. It was decided, then. If she wanted him, she would have him. Her marriage…didn't matter. The husband couldn't defeat Knox. Who could? Therefore, the husband didn't deserve her.

So why are your hands fisting?

The answer didn't matter, either. Knox intended to kill the male, anyway, so he was as good as dead.

Knox wouldn't allow himself to get caught up in passion's throes or lose his head over Vale—figuratively or literally. He would sleep with her, but he wouldn't trust her, and he would take measures to ensure she couldn't harm him in any way.

Then, once he'd spent himself inside her, life would return to normal, and he would concentrate on the war, just as the future winner should.

CHAPTER FOURTEEN

Tension sharpened Vale's nerves to razor points as she hustled into a small motel room. She'd wanted to return to the safety of Knox's bunker, but he'd wanted to people watch on TV, hoping to learn more about modern times.

Something had changed over the past few hours.

It started with the almost-kiss, when they'd stared at each other on the sidewalk. For the thousandth time, her mind replayed what happened afterward.

They'd visited the electronics store, where she'd procured two burner phones—one in secret. Then they'd gone shopping for toiletries and clothes, using the money she'd stolen. Money she still felt guilty for taking.

Although, the men could consider it tax for saving Earth from evil overlords.

All the while, Knox had watched her intently, almost obsessively, as if she'd become the center of his world rather than a part of the game. And she'd liked it.

Despite his distraction, he'd managed to mask their tracks everywhere they'd gone. He'd also picked out a change of clothes for her.

She'd taught him how to order takeout—outside of Ronan's "territory" of course—and showed him how to secure lodging without ID. Through it all, anticipation had rolled off him in great, sweeping waves, and she'd gotten caught up.

She'd tried so hard to remain unaffected, but come on! The pheromone had been on constant simmer, arousing her to an unbearable degree. And if the pheromone wasn't to blame, well, Vale had a ready store of excuses. (1) She'd almost died and needed to celebrate life. (2) She could die at any moment, and had to live while she had the chance. (3) Every second alive was a miracle. Never waste a miracle. (4) Knox was sex incarnate, and she was shallow. (5) The human body wasn't concerned about morals. Oh, and she couldn't forget (6), provided by Celeste's memory: she could seduce him, and win him over. He might volunteer to act as her shield. Also, (7) Vale could be herself around Knox. She didn't have to pretend to be a nice, sweet girl with a pure heart. When he wasn't snipping and snarling about enemies and distrust, he seemed to like her just as she was. And finally (8) Knox was one of a kind. She had to enjoy him while she could.

He entered the room behind her, shut the door and engaged the lock with an ominous *click*. She trembled as she faced him, gulped. The way he was looking at her…as if she was already naked and ready for his possession.

I want to be possessed by him.

His anticipation had sharpened, becoming a sensual blade that stroked over her skin, dangerous to her resistance. Would he make a move on her?

The barest hint of pheromone seeped from her, so very little, but so rich with sweet spices, Vale had to press her weight into her heels to stop herself from launching at Knox.

Careful. If he scented the "perfume," he might shut down, like last time, or let passion morph into rage. But the *real* kicker? Vale didn't want him to desire her because of her cohost's stupid ability, but because of her own personality. *I'm good enough, promise.*

He paused, his blue, blue gaze hotter than a furnace, and making her sweat. If he made a move, she'd have to say no. In spite of her myriad reasons to say yes. She would not cheat on her imaginary husband. And did she really want to get intimate with a man who had no problem sleeping with a married woman?

"Do you have any other questions about…anything?" he asked, his voice as soft as silk.

Something about his tone sent a red alert to every hormone in her body. Or maybe a green alert. Her hormones said: *Go for it!* Did he hope she would ask about something specific? Like something *sexual*?

"I, uh, do." About the AW. Only the AW. Because she hadn't changed her mind. She had to—would—find a way to stop it. "How did you win those four All Wars?"

He arched a brow, projecting a trace of disappointment. "You ask because you wish to defeat me. You think you will have an advantage knowing my secrets. But you cannot beat me, Vale, even with this knowledge."

Oh, that burned. "Prove it, then. Tell me. How did you win?"

"Besides my skill with weapons and strategy, you mean?"

"Obviously."

"I decided the realm was mine even before I arrived, and the other combatants were uninvited guests." Knox strode closer to her… "Uninvited guests must be punished."

Anticipation slithered through *her*. "Well, too bad so sad. This realm is mine. You are the uninvited guest."

"No, female. The realm is mine, just as you are mine. And I always keep what's mine." Closer… Gaze crackling with an entire romance novel's worth of seduction…

But he bypassed her completely, making zero contact with her.

Uh, maybe she'd misread him? Which was good. Yep. Definitely good. Only a dumb-dumb got wet thinking about her former captor/current mentor/future killer pressing his naked body against hers, and slowly grinding to orgasm. Their already complicated relationship didn't need sex added into the mix.

"How very possessive of you," she finally said. Was he possessive of, say, his lovers? Or rather, a former captive turned protégée? No guy had ever wanted Vale as his very own.

"When you have nothing, you guard everything." He dropped their purchases and his duffel bag at the foot of the king-size bed.

She'd requested two doubles, but Knox had insisted on the biggest one available, and he was bigger and badder, so here they were.

She observed the way his biceps flexed as he dug through the duffel's contents. Clothes, toiletries, weapons—Celeste's sword! *Do not make grabby hands.*

"Unless our enemies find some kind of guide," she said, desperate to fill the silence, "they have no idea how to thrive in this modern world."

"Everyone will find a guide soon enough."

As he organized small, circular objects in a line, she eased onto the mattress, near the headboard, and pulled the non-secret cell phone out of its box.

He shuffled through the room, placing two of the circle thingies at every window and the exit. Then he summoned shadows.

Darkness rose from the floor to cover the glass panes, and even the walls.

So creepy!

He continued to work, his every action methodical. Rather than drool over the way his muscles rippled with each movement—and sigh dreamily—she surfed the web for news about Colorado, hoping she could find Ronan. Currently the biggest story on tap featured a large group of people with no noticeable ties had walked away from jobs, homes, stores and cars last night, for no discernible reason, and disappeared in the mountains.

Though she did a search for "men and women trapped in

ice for centuries"; "hot warriors on ice"; "ancient killers on the loose"; "weird muscle men from other realms"; "all war" and "men and women appearing out of thin air", she came across no useful information.

When the words began to blur, she decided to shower and rest. She was tired, dirty, sore and stressed. And still turned on.

With the goodies they'd purchased in hand, she headed for the bathroom. "I'm going to take care of some personal needs. Do *not* enter the bathroom."

"Do not try to escape, and you may have as much privacy as you wish." He kept his back to her. "If you leave, I'll find you, and you won't like what happens next."

"Another vow masquerading as a threat. Yippee. I'll add it to my collection, maybe regift them later." But then, she suspected "vow/threat" was Knox's default language. "Second, I've had plenty of opportunities to ditch you, but here I am, resisting temptation. You could trust me just a little."

He merely said, "Leave the cell phone with me."

"Well, we can't say you didn't give the trust thing your all." She rolled her eyes and tossed the device his way. "Good luck surfing the web without my help, big boy."

No response. Whatever. She sealed herself in the bathroom and locked the door, not that a cheap, flimsy bolt would keep out a guy like Knox. If he wanted inside, he would shoulder his way inside.

She waited one minute…two. When he remained outside the small enclosure, she relaxed a little.

After brushing her teeth, she fiddled with the knobs to turn on the shower. Water sprayed from the faucet, and steam thickened the air as she slid the second phone from her back pocket. Who to call, who to call? Considering how busy she'd been with school and work the past few years, she had no friends other than Nola. And dang if she knew anyone else's number by memory.

Why not *try* her sister at least? A single phone call wouldn't put the girl in danger. Especially a quickie—boom, in and out, over before anyone remembered Vale had a loved one to exploit.

Nola had been in possession of her phone when they'd fled the ice cavern; the device had all of her doctors on speed dial, so it was never far from her side. Maybe Zion hadn't filched it. Maybe he hadn't known what it was and had let her keep it.

It was worth a shot, anyway. Trembling, she poked at the keypad…ringing…twice, three times, four…

"Hello?" her sister said, sounding pained, reedy.

Vale's heart thundered with love and relief as she tasted sweet brown butter, and tears welled in her eyes. "You're alive," she whispered, her knees buckling. *Careful, careful.* If Knox came barreling inside…

"Vale? My gorgeous ballbreaker! *You're* alive." A sob burst over the line. "I've been so worried."

"Nola." Deep male voice, soft tone. The taste of citrus. Zion must be right next to Nola. "The caller upsets you?"

"No, no, I'm happy," her sister said, and sniffled.

Still whispering, Vale said, "Where are you? *How* are you? He's treating you well?"

"I don't know where we are. Zion told me it's better if I don't know, and I agree," Nola replied. "He's protecting me from one of the warriors, a blonde trying to abduct me, reasons unknown. And I'm…surviving minute by minute, and some are tougher than others."

They would talk about the blonde in a second. Right now, Vale had to stuff a fist in her mouth to silence a cry of despair. Her sister was in agony, and there was nothing she could do to help. "Tell Zion to steal pills for you."

"He did. Got me a whole bucket full. I've taken one or two, and have been tempted to take more, but I'm determined to get clean. I'm tired of my life revolving around a little white pill. But enough about me. How are *you*?"

"No changing the subject, sis. You know you can't go cold

turkey." The last time Nola attempted it, she'd ended up in the hospital. "You have to taper, or the strain on your heart—"

"Someone comes." Zion again. Static. "We must go, Nola."

"I love you, Vale. I love you so—"

At the same time, Vale said, "I love you, sis, and I will do—"

The phone went silent. Hardly mattered. Nola was alive, being protected and cared for by Zion, as Knox had promised. Well, well. He wasn't as much of a POS as she'd originally thought.

Once Vale had her breathing under control, she powered down the phone and stored it behind the toilet, then stripped and entered the shower stall. A thicker cloud of steam enveloped her before she maneuvered under the hot spray of water. Feeling as if a weight had lifted from her shoulders, she washed her hair and scrubbed her body.

Then her mind returned to Knox.

She'd learned a lot about him today. First and foremost, he was jealous to the max. Anytime a guy had expressed any kind of interest in her, Knox had stepped in front of her and growled. Growled! As if he coveted her affections. A true and unexpected anomaly.

She kind of liked Knox, too. He was smart, adapting to this new world with ease. After they'd made their purchases, *he'd* stolen a car, repeating what he'd seen her do. But the real shocker? He'd driven like a pro. And dang it, he'd looked so sexy behind the wheel.

He'd ignored humans unless they'd had something he'd wanted. *Give it to me.* A phrase she'd heard countless times.

If someone had asked him a question, he'd glared until that someone beat feet. He'd never relaxed, but he'd never hurried, either. He'd expected absolute obedience anytime he'd issued a command, and he'd mowed down anyone who had dared resist.

He'd shared a painful part of his past with Vale, revealing a softer side. Anguish had filled his eyes when he'd spoken of his daughter, and maybe tears, too, but he'd quickly blinked away any moisture, leaving her to wonder if she'd imagined it.

Vale had wanted to hug him so badly. How would Knox react to a show of affection? And what kept him forging ahead in the game, determined to win a kingdom for a man he clearly despised? What was the *something* he wanted more than anything?

Whatever the answer, Vale was kinda sorta glad to be stuck with him…but not so glad to be stuck in the midst of a savage war.

Life as she knew it was over. So much had changed in so little time. A vacation meant to reenergize her had ultimately broken her.

Legs instantly weak, Vale sank to the floor of the shower stall and drew her knees up to her chest. Now that she'd reached a safe-ish place, adrenaline no longer drove her to push on and on and on, and her strength just…evaporated.

Somehow shock had kept her relatively sane. No longer. Without strength or shock, she shattered. Sorrow, grief and regret consumed her, big fat tears pouring down her cheeks, scalding her skin.

This was the first time she'd cried—really, truly cried, with her entire body involved—since her mother's funeral and her father's *see you later, alligator.* Her dream of partnering with Nola to open Lady Carrie's had crashed and burned. The business degree she'd worked so hard to achieve? Worthless. Only survival mattered. Unless she could make Nola immortal—and end the war, of course—Vale would have to watch her beloved sister die, and spend an eternity without her best friend. No more laughs over breakfast. No more pep talks before bed. One day, Nola would be a distant memory from a previous life.

Or, Vale could die first. It wasn't just possible, it was probable.

Before the start of her vacation, she hadn't been too interested in meeting a man, falling in love, and starting a family. Now she shouldn't *want* to meet a man or start a family, not when her life plan was supposed to involve killing other people and/ or dying horribly. And yet, suddenly what she yearned for was the husband she'd invented, a couple of snot-nosed kids to raise, a dog named Groucho Barks and a cat named Poopsy Meow.

Vale London had been taken off the market for good. As Knox had said, who could she trust?

Her tears became great, heaving sobs.

While hiding weapons throughout the motel room, Knox perceived the faint sound of crying. He stilled, his heart sharpened, scraping his chest raw with every beat.

He knew what had happened. The weight of Vale's circumstances had crystalized at last and realization had set in. This was a positive development. So why was he moving toward the bathroom door, determined to wrap his arms around her, hold her close, and coo words of comfort to her?

Him, offer comfort?

How could he give someone else what he'd never received?

Except, he had received comfort. From *Vale.* In the car, she'd expressed sympathy for the loss of his daughter. More important, she'd *understood* the depths of his pain. But…

His steps slowed, ceased. He shouldn't *want* to comfort her. The uncharacteristic desire pointed to an unacceptable development. Namely, he was growing to care for her.

Sex was permitted; emotion wasn't.

Could he keep the two separated? Vale was the sexiest piece of femininity he'd ever seen, the strength of her spirit staggered him, and her loyalty to her sister continued to amaze him. But at the end of the day, she remained Knox's enemy. So yes. Yes, he could—he would—separate the two.

A truly wise man might have walked away, rather than risking everything for a night of passion. But Knox would risk everything if he *didn't* get her into bed. Here, now, he was distracted. Needy.

That would change tonight. For the first time in his life, his enemy would become his lover. Afterward, the wanting and needing would end.

Could he kill her then? *Thanks for the orgasm, my sweet, now hold still while I remove your head.*

Knox rubbed his chest. Forget the sharper beats. He felt as if his heart had been ripped out and stomped on.

He wouldn't kill Vale tonight, even if his instinct demanded otherwise. He would make sure she understood sex wouldn't alter the course of their relationship. One day, they *would* be pitted against each other, and only one of them would walk away. One day, he would fail her as he'd failed Minka.

Stomp, stomp. What woman in her right mind would accept such a proposal? He could think of only three reasons. To use him for protection, to betray him while he was distracted, or because she was as crazed with lust as Knox.

Every time she'd glanced in his direction, her pupils had expanded, her tantalizing flesh had flushed a lovely shade of rose and the pulse at the base of her neck had quickened.

She *did* lust for him. But did she want him gentle or rough? Which did *he* prefer? He'd never gotten rough with a woman. As sheltered, delicate and easily intimidated as his Iviland lovers had been, he'd feared they would run screaming if ever he'd displayed a modicum of aggression. But Vale was tougher, braver, bolder, and he wanted her more than he'd ever wanted another.

A vibration in his hand. The hand with the rice-sized comm injected in one of his knuckles. He cursed.

King Ansel had just requested a meeting.

Hatred seethed inside him, but not by word or deed did he reveal it as he lifted his hand and grazed his thumb over the ring.

A beam of light shot from the jewel, an image appearing in the center.

Most royals opted to enjoy the spoils they stole from their representatives, but King Ansel had never ceased his combat training, his muscle mass as bulky as Knox's. He had shoulder-length violet hair, and eyes the color of a winter forest. He'd spent centuries underground, sheltered from Iviland's ruined suns, before moving to another realm—one Knox had won—choosing to rule the citizens of Iviland from afar. His skin was pearly white, nearly translucent.

Speaking in Ivish, Ansel demanded, "Are you in a safe location?"

"I am," he replied in the same language. He wouldn't have answered the call otherwise. If ever a meeting would endanger his life, or he wasn't physically capable of responding, he had permission to ignore a request.

He pressed his tongue to the roof of his mouth. One day he wouldn't need permission for *anything*.

Ansel smiled coolly. "Tell me again, properly this time. You are addressing your king. Kneel."

With every fiber of his being, Knox fought the compulsion to obey. *I bow to no one.* His slave bands sizzled, sweat pouring from him, and his limbs shook. He was fighting a losing battle, and he knew it.

"Kneel!"

His knees buckled, and he dropped. "I am in a safe location."

Ansel's cool smile acquired a smug undertone. *Going to make his death hurt. Soon…*

"Much better," the king said. "Thirteen hundred years have passed with no word from you, the Enforcer or any other combatant. An All War first. Measures had to be taken and new rules established in case something like that ever happened again."

Something about the king's tone…

"What measures?" Knox asked.

"All you need to know is that I'm meeting with the other rulers and the High Council, and we will decide what to do about your war. Until then…" Ansel waved a hand, a silent command to let the subject drop. "Tell me why communication ended the day of a check-in only to suddenly begin again centuries later."

Words spilled from his throat, in a hurry to greet the king's ears. He detailed the viking attack, the part Cannon's rod had played and the eventual collapse of the prison, making no mention of Vale.

If she exited the bathroom before the conference ended…

"You've made new kills since gaining your freedom," Ansel said, expectant.

"Yes. Shiloh and Gunnar."

A cold laugh. "Shiloh, our ally. Interesting."

Guilt spiked. *Ignore it.* "His death saved my life."

"Then you did the right thing. If the Asnanthaleigh king protests, I'll handle it."

A cruelty disguised as a kindness. Ansel would arrange for the king's murder, or the kidnapping and impregnation of one of his daughters, so that he could use the child as leverage. *His specialty.* Knox's hands balled into fists.

Say nothing.

"You have a plan, I'm sure." Ansel gave another royal wave, a silent command to share the details.

"I do have a plan, and I'm keen to return to it." Before the male came face-to-face with Vale.

Ansel narrowed his eyes. "There isn't another realm like Terra, and I *will* rule it. I've waited long enough. Too long. Win this war as quickly as possible. Have you forgotten what you'll gain when you emerge victorious?"

"I have not," he grated. *Freedom. Vengeance.*

Peace.

For a moment, one startling moment, a part of him *wanted* to lose. To die so that the toxic cycle would end, and the misery would cease. He would no longer have to deny the raw, agonizing guilt that accompanied the destruction of other combatants who were stuck in a similar situation, who had *families.*

The strain and shame of being considered *less than*, a sub-being...the consequences of a loss—Ansel delighting in his life and the victories other people won on his behalf, never made to pay for his crimes, while billions of other people suffered under his oppressive rule. The burden of it all... *Too much for me to bear.* Too much for *anyone* to bear.

But Knox wouldn't lose. Hate wouldn't let him.

Knox knew Ansel wished he'd sired more children. Knew the king longed to threaten someone he valued. The very reason he'd decided there would be no more children until Ansel and the High Council were eradicated, not even by accident. But abstinence hadn't been an option for Knox; he could be ordered to bed a fertile woman. He'd known of only one sure way to save himself the heartbreak of losing another child. Temporary sterilization.

His third All War, he'd won a magical realm populated by witches, warlocks and other mystical beings. Ansel had no idea he'd procured a potion while there or that, until Knox returned and procured an antidote, he would remain sterile.

No other child will suffer as you did, darling Minka.

Ansel's voice whisked him back to the present. "My spies have picked up chatter among other sovereigns. Adonis of Callum has used the Horn of Summoning to create an army of mindless mortals willing to die to protect him. If the opportunity presents itself, you will kill him."

"Yes, I will." At least the king hadn't ordered Knox to kill Adonis *now*, and stop at nothing to see the deed done. But then, the king knew better than to screw with a combatant's battle plan; he'd gotten others killed that way.

The knob on the bathroom door turned.

"Someone comes," Knox said. Truth, without revealing any details. He was forbidden to speak a lie to his king. "I must go." He pressed his thumb against the ring, the light fading, a scowling Ansel vanishing.

Hinges squeaked. A cloud of steam ushered Vale out of the bathroom, making her appear to step from a dream. Though her eyes were red and puffy from crying, she was still the most beautiful female he'd ever seen.

"Did we have a guest?" Her brow furrowed as she looked around. "I thought I heard two voices."

"I was contacted by my king," he said, rising to his feet.

She'd changed into a white T-shirt and miniscule pink shorts he'd picked out during their shopping extravaganza, her flawless legs exposed, the sight playing havoc with his concentration. The material was thin enough to reveal glimpses of the bra and panties underneath. Black lace embroidered with crimson roses.

The ends of her hair dripped, the white locks plaited over her crown, the black locks hanging down her back.

He didn't just want her. He wanted her more than he'd ever wanted another woman. Every sensation she'd ever aroused in him surged anew, his body aching, *throbbing*.

Tone as sharp as a dagger, he said, "We are going to discuss your husband."

She paled. "What about him?"

"Tell me true. Do you love him?" If she did…

Do not tear this room apart.

"Um." Shifting from one bare foot to another, she whispered, "No. Why?"

The response hit him like Zion's punch. "Good. He no longer exists for you. Consider yourself single."

She narrowed her eyes, but not before he caught a glimpse of intrigue and relief. Why relief? "So I'm single? Just like that?" She snapped her fingers.

"Just like that." Knox stepped toward her, stopped. Stepped. Stopped. How to handle this? He motioned to the bed with a trembling hand. "Sit down."

"No, thanks. It's easier to run away if I'm standing."

"Please sit," he said, molars grinding. "I've already explained the foolishness of running from me."

"You're right. I'll happily pop a squat." She lifted her chin. "*After* you tell me what's going on."

Frustrating woman! How did he explain his intention to bed her and what he expected to happen afterward without enraging her?

Do you desire me the way I desire you? Will you risk everything to spend a single night in my bed?

None of that left his mouth. "Your vocation," he said. "What do you do for income?"

She regarded him with suspicion, but said, "For the past few years, I've been a professional student working as a waitress and barista, dreaming of the day I open a sweet treat shop with my sister. What about you?"

"Professional killer," he muttered, and paced back and forth, back and forth. He could scent her—soap, jasmine and spices, with a hint of honeysuckle. A fragrance as luscious as the woman herself. His head fogged, arousal a ravenous fire in his blood, torching one reservation after another, until none remained.

"I know you're a killer," she said. "But what do you *want* to be?"

The answer slipped from him, unbidden. "Free."

"You aren't free now?" A beat of silence before understanding dawned in those exquisite hazel eyes. "I'm sorry, Knox."

"You will not pity me," he snapped. "I'm strong. A victor!"

"I know you're strong, and a victor. But you don't strike me as the type to laze about, so I'll ask again. What do you want to be when you're free?"

"I…don't know." *Do it. Tell her.* "I only know I want every inch of my shaft buried inside you."

CHAPTER FIFTEEN

Vale reeled. Knox wanted her. Wanted *inside* her. Knox, with his heavy-lidded eyes and desire-flushed skin, wanted inside her *bad*, and now her skin was overheating, her limbs shaking, the knowledge battering any defenses she'd managed to reerect after the crying bout in the shower had left her wrung out and vulnerable.

"How deep do your desires go?" she croaked. Deep enough to give her a vow of protection, rather than of harm?

His eyelids hooded as he said, "Strip, spread your legs, and we'll find out exactly how deep my desires go."

A half moan, half chuckle escaped her. Surprise, surprise. Knoxie had a sense of humor. Unfortunately, it only made her want him more.

"I desire you, too," she said, and primal satisfaction glowed in his irises. "But I don't know why. I don't know you." Or did she? Because of the circumstances surrounding their introduction and subsequent interactions, she'd already seen the best and worst of Knox. The kinds of things most couples didn't usually learn about each other until they'd dated for months. "You've killed."

"And I'll kill again."

A point in his favor—he hadn't reminded her of the murder *she'd* committed.

He took a step toward her, peering at her with such raw desire, his beauty acquired an aura of cruelty, as if no deed was too dark as long as he got what he wanted.

"You'll kill *me*," she said between panting breaths.

"Yes." Another step closer. "One day."

He looked…anguished.

A startling truth hit her. Before this moment, he'd always worn a mask when they were together. Now the mask was gone, his true nature on display. She saw pain and hopelessness far beyond anything she'd ever known, making him tragic, haunting and haunted all at once.

To win four All Wars, he'd had to do unspeakable things, and he hadn't emerged unscathed. He might deny it, but deep down he hurt.

"If you win Earth," she said, "you'll be set free?" Before, he'd mentioned the enslavement of her people. Only when he'd expressed his own hope to be free had she connected the dots.

Knox was *already* enslaved.

"That is what I've been promised, yes. Then, and only then, will I be able to avenge my daughter's death, liberate the slaves still trapped in Iviland, and go after—" He sealed his mouth shut, narrowed his eyes.

But that was okay. She got the gist and comprehended he truly could not be lured to her side. What he did, he did for a higher purpose—for others.

This man was so much more complicated than she'd ever expected.

Respect for him skyrocketed, right alongside compassion. What a solitary life he must have led, afraid to trust or love after his daughter's death, expecting betrayal at every turn. How many times had he gotten knocked down, only to force himself to rise and march on?

For the first time in their association, she looked at him and thought, *He has significant other potential.*

And he clearly thought the same about her. He'd commanded her to forget her husband. The bond—fake though it was—bothered him.

The questions she'd used to ask herself before agreeing to go on a date whirled inside her head. *Will this man lie to me?* Probably. *Cheat on me?* No. He was too honest, too in-your-face. *Will he steal from me?* Most definitely. He planned to steal her life.

And yet, the negatives weren't going to stop her. She wanted him still—wanted him *more.*

Aching, desperate, Vale jumped on him, winding her arms around his neck and her legs around his waist, leaning down to feed him a scorching kiss.

Just before their lips met, he wrenched his face away from hers. "Sex, yes." The huskiness of his voice was as potent as a caress. Didn't help that he was staring at her lips with dark possessiveness. "Kissing, no."

What! "Why?" Visions of *Pretty Woman* danced in her head. Was she not good enough for mouth-to-mouth?

Never worthy of affection.

Rigid, she climbed off him. Or tried. He held firm.

"I want a kiss, or nothing," she snapped.

"I've seen what kissing does to other men. They close their eyes, and become lost to the world. With sex, I can remain aware."

The hottest flames of her anger cooled. Would he remain aware with her, or would she push him past the boundaries of his control?

"You don't want to be distracted, got it. But," she added, grazing the tip of her nose against his, "you mentioned other men, not yourself. Why?"

"I've never kissed, or been kissed." The words were as thick as molasses, and just as sweet.

No way. Just no way. "You mean *never*, as in *never*?"

"The word *never* has a second meaning?" He arched a brow, then confirmed with a nod. "Never." Then he grumbled, "Not in a way that counts, anyway."

She kinda sorta…believed him. His body tenser by the second, he stared at her mouth as if it was an exotic animal he wanted to pet but feared he'd get bitten.

Knox of Iviland feared nothing. *Until me.* Feminine power was a fine wine, and Vale quickly got drunk on it. How had he lived so long without his defenses crumbling, or at least cracking?

Ripples of desire agonized Vale. *I want to be his first kiss.*

Let the seduction begin.

Time to engage his mind. "I have a riddle for you," she said. "I am light as a feather, but no one can hold me for long. You cannot live without me. And the faster you run, the harder I am to catch. What am I?"

He frowned, and his brow furrowed. "You are… breath?"

"Correct." Now it was time to (figuratively) go in for the kill. Voice low and raspy, she said, "Give me your breath, Knox. Feed it to me. I *crave* it. I crave you."

"Crave…yes." But still he resisted, his iron resolve seemingly unshakable. "No." A snarl. "We will have sex. Only sex."

She inhaled deeply, exhaled sharply, her nipples rubbing against him. As friction sparked fires in her blood, exotic masculine musk filled her nose, and honeyed whiskey and a dollop of cream teased her tongue. Combined, the sensations were more than any woman could resist.

If Vale had sex with Knox—

No! She'd traveled that road with others—pleasure without emotion—and she'd ended up depressed, lonely and straight up pitiful. Repeating the mistakes of her past would just make everything worse.

The past… Ugh. In high school, she'd desperately wanted boys to like her. And they had, but only in the weeks or months before they'd gotten her into bed. Mere minutes after they'd busted a nut, they'd rushed off. A few had even called her terrible names, as if she was less of a person and they were more of one.

As tough as she'd pretended to be, every desertion had hurt. Sure, she was stronger now. But old fears whispered poison in her ear. *Once he's had you, he'll leave you in his dust. Or worse!*

"Okay, listen. About my marriage," she said, and sighed. He deserved the truth. "Drogo and I...we're in the middle of a divorce. Yep. A legal separation." *Why are you doubling down on your lie?* In her defense, it was difficult to get past Knox's threat to murder her if she fibbed. "I *am* a single woman."

"Single." Tremors shook him.

"The truth is, I haven't been out with a guy in a really long time, and I kind of need to be eased into this kind of relationship drama. Especially with my former captor! So all I'm offering is a kiss."

"Kiss..." He sounded drugged.

"You want to taste me, and I need you to. Imagine it. Your mouth pressed against mine...our tongues thrusting together..."

"Together..."

"I'm so hungry for you," she whispered. *"Ravenous."*

"I want to kiss you but won't. I *need* to be inside you." One of his big hands slid up to cup her nape and squeeze, while the other slid down to settle on her ass. He spread his fingers to cover more of her flesh. "Say yes, and I'll have you screaming my name in a matter of minutes. Your pleasure will be my top priority."

Yes!

No, no. Not ready to lose him.

He stalked forward, keeping Vale in the circle of his arms, every step grinding his erection against her core. Little fires sparked in her bloodstream, and she groaned.

The wall met her back. Cold behind her, heat in front of her. He trembled, and the grinding got worse—better. Argh! If he

didn't acquiesce to her kiss soon, she would accept the scraps
he was willing to give.

She had to up her game.

"I'll make a deal with you." She leaned down and slowly drew
his lower lip between her teeth. He stiffened, but allowed the
action without protest. "We'll kiss for one minute. Only one. If
you aren't a fan, we'll stop, and I'll never ask again."

An eternity passed in silence, his inhalations growing more
and more ragged. "How you tempt me."

Strike while the iron in his pants is hot! Vale threaded her fingers
through his hair and toyed with the ends. "Only one," she repeated softly. *"Please."*

More tremors. *Stronger* tremors. "A kiss will change nothing," he rasped.

Pay the blip of sadness no heed. "I know."

He worked his jaw back and forth. "If you make a play against
me while I'm distracted—"

"I won't. And you had better not make a play against me,
either." Maybe he was right to resist. Maybe they should cut
their losses while they could. "You were right. This is a mistake. We should—"

"One kiss, *valina*. Only one." The words rushed from him.

Then he claimed her mouth in a fierce kiss.

Yes, yes. Their tongues rolled together, again and again, and
oh, he learned quickly, reaching an expert skill level in seconds.
Brain cells melting...

He didn't explore, he conquered. Every lick and suck, thrust
and parry swept her up in a tempest of sensation, maddening
her, reducing her to a creature concerned with pleasure, and
how to get more.

How to get everything.

He was like a starving man who'd been offered a feast, a king
invading a new country, a warrior who would kill anyone who
tried to take away his prize. She could not get enough, emotion

seeming to pour from him. Pain, hate, guilt, sorrow—things he must have buried long ago rising to the surface in this moment of vulnerability. She took the darkness into herself, willing to carry the burden for him.

Groaning, he angled her head just the way he wanted it, granting himself better, deeper, *perfect* access. He arched his hips and gyrated against her, wringing a strangled cry from her—a cry he swallowed.

As tightly as he squeezed her, she suspected she would feel his possession for weeks. *Not nearly long enough.*

"Think...your minute...is up," she managed to say between flicks of his tongue.

"Not done. Want more. *Give me more, everything.*"

"Yes, yes. Everything."

The most delicious sex noises left him as he spun, marched across the room and lowered her onto the bed. His weight settled over her, and oh! The size of him! He engulfed her with heat and power, muscle and man.

"What are you doing to me, *valina*?" He plunged a hand under her shirt to knead an aching breast. "Tell me."

"Same thing...you're doing...to me." With every wicked caress, the ache intensified, her nipple rock hard. The contact electrified her, the bra an unwanted barrier.

As he plucked the distended crest, her desires flamed hotter, sensual smoke blowing through her, filling her, drawing her body as taut as a bow. She undulated her hips; his erection was like rigid steel—so big, so wonderfully hard—and it tormented her feminine heat.

Desperation liquefied her bones, her legs falling open in invitation, pleasure skidding through her. Pressure built, so much pressure, and it was agonizingly sweet, until the pheromone began to churn inside her, demanding release.

Vale thrashed, fighting the pheromone while seeking a release of her own. Never had she reacted so intensely to a man.

Formerly neglected nerves became overly, deliciously sensitized. Every movement he made, every breath, every movement a wealth of incomparable stimulation.

Then it happened. The pheromone escaped, wafting from her to create a perfumed cloud around them. One reminiscent of midnight fantasies and boundless passion. Knox didn't seem to notice, not consciously. Or perhaps he was too far gone to care. He deepened the kiss, increased the pace of his seeking tongue and continued grinding his massive erection against her.

Pressure building...

Need more!

Growing crazed with desire, Vale planted her feet on the edge of the mattress, and met the next thrust of his hips with one of her own. Heating...heating... Still building...

"You smell so good," Knox murmured.

If he ended this, she would kill him, or she would die. Maybe both. She'd gone too long without this blissful sense of connection, and required more. Actually, she'd *never* known this sense of connection.

"Can't get enough." A fine mist of sweat glistened on his forehead as he lifted his head. He was panting, still moving against her. "I'm losing control."

"Yes. Lose control with me."

"Never want to stop." He was snarling now, his pupils enlarged. "Whatever you're doing to me...*do more.*"

More. Yes, yes. "Clothes off. Now." They would be skin to heated skin. Male to female. Hardness to wetness.

A hidden corner of her mind whispered, *Going to give him what he wants, so he can walk away, then?*

Yes. No. Maybe?

Maybe *she* would take what she wanted and walk away from *him.* She just... She needed some part of him inside her. Once they were naked, she would figure out—

The window shattered, a man diving into the room.

Vale's mind processed his entrance at warp speed, real time seeming to slow. He held a crossbow, three arrows nocked. *Whoosh.* Those arrows soared.

She screamed in shock, momentarily frozen, her head emptied of all thought. Knox had no such problems. Without missing a beat, he rolled to his side, creating an immortal barrier around her, taking an arrow in the shoulder, back and thigh.

He protects me, even though he said he wouldn't?

In spite of his injuries, he leaped to his feet. He yanked out the projectiles, palmed a revolver and a dagger with a brass knuckle handle, then closed in. He was vengeance incarnate, capable of any dark deed.

By the time the intruder landed, he was jerking and shaking, as if he was in the midst of a grand mal seizure. Courtesy of the safety measures Knox had stationed around the window? Shadows remained with Arrow-man, encompassing his face and upper body, clearly blinding him.

Celeste's memories recognized him as Rush.

What should she do? Fight or flee?

While she debated her options, Knox unloaded the entire cylinder of rounds into the newcomer. Rush bellowed with pain, blood pouring down his legs as both his kneecaps splintered into countless bone shards.

The sheer violence of the action left her cringing. And Knox wasn't done. *Stab, stab.* The first blow sliced through Rush's throat. Or maybe his arm. Vale couldn't see past the shadows, either, only knew his hands were raised protectively. The second blow cut into his chest, the blade exiting with tissue attached.

Breathe. Decide!

Maddened, Rush kicked out a leg. A metal spike glinted from the toe of his boot, and it was clear he planned to realign Knox's throat chakra. Knox reached up to block, and the spike slashed his wrist. He dropped the revolver and stumbled back, a scarlet river streaming from the wound.

Neurons in Vale's brain began to rapid-fire suggestions. The loudest one—*Grab the weapon, protect your man.*

He's not my man. Still she lunged—

Dang it! The guys crashed together in a tangle of limbs, blocking it. Blood spurted as the warring pair snipped and snarled at each other.

Ding, ding. Motel cage fight, round two.

Knox tossed shadows like daggers. Rush dodged with inhuman speed.

More of Celeste's memories tore through Vale's mind, and she cried out. Everything centered around the newcomer. He had a wife awaiting his return home. Since he could only return if he won the All War, he would stop at *nothing* to ensure victory.

Must stop him. Vale sprinted to Knox's bag and dug inside. *Come on, come on.* No sign of Celeste's sword or Rifters. Argh!

Go! Run. Let Knox deal with him.

Should she?

In a pro/con situation, aiding Knox might not be the wisest move right now. Before their kiss, he'd said, *This changes nothing.* When the time came, he would kill her. Yes, he'd granted her a temporary stay. Yes, he'd protected her. Yes, she wanted to learn more about the war and get her hands on Celeste's stuff. None of that mattered if she died tonight.

At the end of the day, he would look out for number one. She had to do the same.

Thump, thump.

She gasped and whipped around. Two other males had just climbed through the broken window. A bearded man who held a rod—the rod she'd seen in the ice cave—and a guy with a multicolored mohawk, strange symbols shaved into the sides of his head, and a black horn hanging from his neck.

Again, Celeste's memories filled in the blanks. The bearded man was Erik, and the mohawked one was Adonis.

Dread flash-froze the blood in her veins, momentarily immobilizing her. Then adrenaline surged, melting the ice. Not that it did any good. Where could she go? Erik and Adonis had blocked the exit. And what were the odds she could overcome two skilled warriors with supernatural abilities who'd once been known as gods?

Zero to none.

Erik and Adonis sniffed the air and pivoted to face her, eyeing her up and down as if she were slab of barbecue ribs. Her heart hammered against her ribs. She had no weapons, no escape route, no training and no shield.

No hope.

Left with no other recourse, she sprinted for the bathroom. *Shut and lock the door. Break the window, scramble through. Run.*

Strong arms snaked around her waist. Her world spun as her captor tossed her atop the bed. As she bounced on the mattress, yelping, he leaped on her, pinning her down.

Adonis, she realized with a flare of panic.

They tussled. She managed to slam the heel of her palm into his nose. Score! Cartilage snapped. Blood poured, dripping onto her neck and chest.

He didn't notice or care. "Want you...*need* you." His heavily accented voice tasted like cinnamon and cloves, filling her mouth as he peered at her with blatant masculine appreciation. "Accept me as your man."

Always be a lady, until you're forced to be a land mine.

Vale—utterly—exploded.

She clawed at his eyes, bit his chin and rammed her knee between his legs. His only reaction? A grunt.

Tougher times, tougher measures.

Punch, punch. She put every ounce of her strength into the blows. Bone met bone—and hers cracked. Again, he didn't notice, just leaned down to sniff her hair.

Frick! Thanks to the pheromone, sexual lust had overshadowed his battle lust.

With an animalistic snarl, Erik ripped Adonis away from her. Not to offer aid, but to take his place. Before she could buck him off, he'd dropped the rod and cupped her face.

"Let me go," she commanded.

"Never." His softer accent tasted of salted caramel. He stared down at her, navy blue eyes glazed with hunger. "You're mine now."

She grappled with him, but was only managing to tire herself. Not sure…how much longer…she could…

A blade flew from the nightstand drawer, riding a wave of darkness, and plunged into Erik's eye.

The sounds he made would forever haunt Vale.

Freed at last, frantic, she scrambled up. Knox and Rush still fought. They'd disarmed each other, and yet the clash was just as lethal. They punched and kicked, breaking bones that quickly reset. Skin tore, but soon wove back together.

Erik latched onto her arm before she could run. With his free hand, he jerked out the blade—and removed his eyeball in the process.

Vale hunched over to retch on the bedcovers, her thoughts swirling. Despite his own dilemma, Knox had used his shadows to toss the knife at Erik.

Maybe things *had* changed between them.

Only fooling myself. Everything Knox did, he did to ensure victory. Nothing more.

From the corner of her eye, she saw him roll across the floor, pick up a dagger and swipe Rush from hip to hip. The other man's intestines spilled out of his body.

Another retch. Too much violence, real and in her face, not on the other side of a screen or in the pages of a book.

Rush gathered his organs and reclaimed his sword.

Ding, ding. Round three.

One-eyed Erik picked her up and darted away from the bed, and she was too weak to stop him.

"Mine." Adonis latched onto her other arm, preventing her from going any farther.

"Run," Knox shouted to her. "I'll find you."

Yes. Run! But how? She had become the rope in a tug-of-war between Erik and Adonis. What was more, Knox and Rush blocked the window and door. If they inadvertently landed a mighty blow on her, she'd be out for the count.

"Hear me well, viking. I won't be giving her up." With no other warning, Adonis stabbed Erik in the gut.

Blood, so much blood. Another retch geared up.

"I will die before I part with her." Erik brandished the rod like a baton, nailing Adonis in the side of the head, the tip slicing his cheek.

Such a savage display of unwarranted jealousy. Then, shockingly, the two stopped fighting. One frowned, and the other scowled. They spun in a circle, scanning the room.

Erik: "Where did she go?"

Adonis: "Is Knox hiding her in his shadows?"

They couldn't see her? But…how? Knox hadn't used his shadows, that much she knew, because she wasn't blinded.

The answer hit her like a baseball bat twined with barbed wire: Celeste's ability. Of course! She had the power to render herself invisible.

Guilt hit her *harder* than a baseball bat. *Can't afford to wallow.* She had no idea how she had accessed the power, or how to sustain it—or if she would be able to reappear—but she wasn't going to stick around to ponder.

"We must find her." Adonis reached out, patting the air.

Go, go, go! Vale raced to the window, intending to shove Rush out of the way. She passed through him instead, her entire body tingling. So weird!

Don't slow. Broken glass sliced her bare feet, the sharp stings dulled by a fresh rush of adrenaline. As she climbed outside, she cast a final glance at Knox, and their gazes met. Could he see her?

Could she help him, now that she was invisible, or would she only make things worse for him?

Rush landed a punishing blow to Knox's jaw. As he fell, he shouted, "Run!"

Definitely worse. She obeyed him, sprinting away as fast as her feet would carry her.

Knox struggled to center his thoughts. *Invaders. Enemy. Kill them, kiss Vale.*

One moment he'd been frantic with lust, starved for the woman beneath him, lost in the throes of his first kiss, unaware of anything but his female, the next he'd been fighting for his life—and hers.

When Rush had burst into the motel room, Knox had reacted without thought, taking the two arrows meant for him, and the one meant for Vale. The foolish move had cost him, damaging his arm, momentarily affecting his aim. She was immortal now, and an injury to the skull wouldn't have killed her. Hurt her, yes, and would have made her helpless for a time, but she would have survived, and he would have maintained proper use of his arm.

What's done is done. Focus on the present.

The *eyaer* screamed an angry command. {*Kill everyone!*}

Yes. *They threatened my female. They die bloody.*

Knox picked up the sword he'd dropped, blocked Rush's next blow, advanced. Retreated. Advanced again, while tossing shadows at Erik and Adonis. He holstered and unholstered the revolver, reloading.

When the viking and Adonis shed the darkness and flew outside, Knox was ready. He peppered the pair with bullets, then gave chase. Three pains cut through his back before he could clear the window, throwing him off course, momentarily paralyzing him.

Rush and his cursed arrows!

Knox smacked into the wall. On the plus side, impact shoved the arrows out the other side of his body.

He wasn't going to reach Vale before the viking and Adonis. He told himself Vale would be okay.

She had better be okay.

Before leaving the room, she'd winked in and out of view. An ability Celeste had possessed before she was killed, which meant Vale *had* inherited the Occisorian's abilities, on top of her memories. He'd suspected, but he hadn't really believed it possible. No other combatant possessed such a skill.

Erik and Adonis wouldn't sense her power if they caught her, as long as they stayed together. And if they couldn't sense her power, they wouldn't suspect she'd killed Celeste and joined the war. If they didn't suspect her participation, they wouldn't kill her. They would keep her alive to use as bait. Considering she was the first—the only—woman Knox had expressed interest in since the start of the war, she was *valuable* bait.

If she happened to use Celeste's ability again, the males would simply assume Knox had concealed her with shadows despite the distance between them.

Still, the urge to go after her was strong. He wanted to be her shield.

Think this through like a combatant determined to win, not a boyfriend willing to lose.

Truth: At the moment, Vale wasn't in danger of dying.

Truth: If Knox gave chase, Rush would follow him and pelt him with more arrows.

Truth: Rush's crossbow would come in handy in battle.

Decision: *Kill Rush first, and fast, then find Vale.*

With a roar, he rotated. Rush had already swung a sword. One of Knox's that he'd picked up from the floor.

Target—Knox's head.

There was no time for finesse. Knox hit his knees, and the sharp metal whizzed over him, then he used shadows to shove Rush away.

As the other man wheeled, Knox crashed into him like a freight train, whaling all the way down. Bones crunched beneath his pounding fists. Impact. Unaffected, Rush rolled backward and, with his boots pressed against Knox's stomach, kicked him overhead.

In one fluid motion, Knox landed, stood and unleashed a torrent of shadows, blinding Rush while hurling a chair, mirror and lamp at his body.

While he was busy trying to dodge, Knox used the same power to free Celeste's sword from under the mattress.

Whoosh. The blade sank into Rush's heart—

The warrior had turned at the last second, the blade piercing his shoulder. A smear of poison must have remained active on the metal, because Rush's knees gave out and he collapsed, his sword and crossbow thudding beside him.

The dried poison must not be as strong. Though trembling, the male was able to pull a dagger from his boot, lumber to his feet and attack.

Knox blocked with one arm and used the other to slice Rush's throat, just not as deeply as he'd hoped.

They dove at each other, trundled over the ground, then came up with their swords extended. The bastard gathered his strength and made a play for Knox's head.

Dodge. "Working with the viking and Adonis...or just pretending? Either way, you're a dead man walking. They'll betray you without a moment's hesitation."

Rush parried, then lunged. "Unlike you, murk, not everyone is willing to murder an ally to progress their cause."

Ignore the guilt. "You are more like me than you want to admit. You'll do anything to return to your wife. And Erik and Adonis have *already* betrayed you. They left you behind to deal with me while chasing after a puny mortal."

The taunt missed its mark, Rush swinging and dodging without missing a beat. "Erik plans to stop the war and hinder the High Council with their own rules, and Adonis believes he can do it."

"Adonis is a fool." Metal clinked and clanged against metal. "But not you."

For slaves like Knox, Rush and Adonis, the prospect of continued freedom appealed greatly. Doing what they wanted, when they wanted. Living in the terrain of their choosing. Bedding as many women as they wished, whenever they wished.

"You're pretending," Knox continued. "Waiting until the viking convinces others to lay down their weapons in the name of peace. The moment they are unarmed, you'll strike."

"You don't know—"

"I do. You will never choose an illusion of freedom over your wife."

What would I do for my *wife, if I had one?*

"Anyone who opposes Erik will be killed," Rush said. "Anyone he feels he cannot trust, too. Your name is at the top of the list. And Knox, you won't be able to defeat him. He's spent more than a thousand years preparing for our escape from the ice."

Knox evaded another swing, caught the male's wrist and punched his forearm. Rush lost his grip, the sword clattering to the floor. A swift kick to the ankles sent him crashing to his knees.

A kick to the head followed. Rush blocked and retaliated, but Knox dodged and came up beside him to elbow his temple. As he floundered, Knox delivered an uppercut to the nose, snapping cartilage. More blood, but not enough.

Rush wasn't yet out for the count; he wound an arm around Knox's neck in an intractable choke hold and a leg around his waist, then pulled himself up so that they were eye to eye. Air snagged in Knox's throat, starving his lungs.

Stars winked through his vision. Dizziness rushed through his head.

Focus. Steady. Becoming panicky would herald his demise. He kneed Rush in the stomach, his leg like a wrecking ball. Then, as the other man gasped, he withdrew the small blade hidden in his belt buckle and jab, jab, jabbed. The first cut was between two of Rush's ribs, deflating *his* lung. The second, through a kidney. The third, the femoral artery.

Suddenly free, Knox stumbled backward. He prepared to charge like a bull, but Rush seized his crossbow and raced out the window.

No time to waste.

Knox gathered his weapons and supplies, knowing he'd need them if he was going to save Vale. He wanted her back. He wanted her back *now*.

The only thing he'd ever relished was victory. And now… Vale? Her kiss…

I will get her back, and I will get her into my bed.

Once he'd collected his bounty, he shot into the night, ready to tear the world apart.

CHAPTER SIXTEEN

Moonlight glowed. Buildings stretched on both sides of Vale, dark inside, their resident businesses all closed, no witnesses nearby. Good. There was no need to endanger innocent people.

As she charged this way and that, her thoughts jumbled up. Where should she go? She wasn't familiar with the area, and wasn't sure how to evade experienced hunters.

Run. I'll find you.

Did she *want* Knox to find her?

No, she realized. No, she didn't. She just wanted out of this stupid war.

Only Knox and Zion knew her name. Hopefully. Maybe she could hitch a ride with a trucker, go home to Oklahoma, get a new ID, empty her savings and…what? The same problem would plague her. Where would she go afterward? What could she do?

What about Nola?

Thunder cracked, startling her. Lightning flashed. Though there'd been no signs of a coming storm, the sky began to cry, to sob, rain soaking her in seconds.

Cold invaded every inch of her, down to her marrow, and

the power of invisibility ebbed. Vale trembled, her steps slowing. No, no, no! Discernable, she had no advantage.

"Not so fast." Once again, strong arms banded around her, stopping her in her tracks.

She opened her mouth to scream, but her hijacker—Adonis—muffled the sound with his hand.

Nooooo! She hadn't gotten far, only a few blocks.

Was *this* the end of her game?

A few yards ahead, a van's tires squealed. The passenger door was already open. Adonis dragged her over, tossed her onto a ripped seat, then climbed in beside her and closed the door. Erik perched behind the wheel, and if she hadn't known he was immortal, she would have begun to suspect. His missing eye had almost completely regenerated.

He put the pedal to the metal and sped away, saying, "The rain will wash away her trail," his voice no longer heavy with desire.

The rain must have doused her scent. One point in her favor, at least.

Wet and shivering as fear frosted her lungs, she struggled to catch her breath. Did these guys know she'd joined the AW? They'd attributed her invisibility to Knox's shadows, so there was a good chance they hadn't yet guessed the truth. Also in her favor—no other combatant had ever absorbed another's memories or abilities. The idea shouldn't be on anyone's radar. Though Erik and Adonis had to wonder why they'd been so attracted to a complete stranger back in that motel room.

She doubted "I'm super hot, obviously," would put their minds at ease.

She did her best to look unaffected by the night's events, even bored. Her newest captors were warriors; they admired strength and courage. Or maybe her seeming lack of fear would infuriate them, and they would lash out.

Frick! Any way she played this, she was gonna get hurt. Why not launch an escape?

Very well. She would. But her options were limited. Did she try to leap over Adonis and jump out of the van? Or did she try to steal a weapon without getting caught and then slay both males?

No matter what, she couldn't rely on the pheromone to help. If a single whiff had turned these men into slavering horndogs, what would a deluge do?

No wonder Vale had felt uneasy when she'd first realized she'd inherited the woman's ability to seduce.

So. Back to her options. If she jumped, Adonis would probably catch her. And if he *didn't* catch her, he would definitely hunt her down.

She had to go for the weapon. Had to slay to keep trouble at bay.

A lump grew in her throat—*I'm just as bad as everyone else*—but she swallowed it back, allowing cold determination to overtake her. She would make two more kills. Only two, and only because they were necessary for her survival. *Then* she would find a way out of the war.

Could she purposely deliver a death blow, though? Even in self-defense?

Yes. Because she had to. There was no other way out of this.

Beneath slitted lids, she studied Adonis. Two daggers were anchored to the sheaths on the waistband of his leather pants. Getting one would be difficult but not impossible. First, she would have to create a distraction.

"Do you know who and what we are?" he asked.

To tell the truth or play dumb? *Like it's really playing, London.*

"Yes," she said, deciding to err on the side of caution, just in case she effed up and let a detail slip. "Knox enlightened me. You're part of an All War."

"Excellent. Saves us the trouble of explaining." Erik grinned at her from the rearview mirror. "You look better now than you did at my cabin."

His cabin? Shock punched her in the gut, freeing one of Celeste's memories. It swam up, up to break through the turbulent sea of panic in her mind. Erik stood outside the check-in point, Cannon's rod in hand, an army of Viking warriors flanking his sides, each one dressed in roughly hewn garments and crudely fashioned armor.

Erik had been human, and like her, he'd entered the war unwittingly. He'd loved his people; that had been obvious. He'd fought for his land. Now he fought for Earth—and he might actually have a shot at victory. He definitely had a better shot than Vale.

Knox hadn't known what happened when two people represented a single realm, and Vale wasn't going to ask these guys if they had a clue; whatever the answer, it wasn't a good enough reason to give away her ace.

Trust no one. Hide everything.

Besides, her chances might be *better* than Erik's. She could absorb powers, thank you very much; he couldn't.

"I'm the one who brought you snow gear, clothes and killed your guide," he said with an easy, breezy tone. "The male planned to hurt you and your friend."

He was the reason the guide had abandoned them? He'd *killed* the guide? A man who'd planned to, what, rape and murder her and Nola, if Erik was telling the truth? They'd had no idea.

"You could have returned our IDs and cash," she said. "You could have escorted us to civilization. So thanks—for nothing."

"Why would I return your IDs and cash when I'm the one who stole them?"

Well, okay then. Knox and Zion weren't the only ones who knew her name and where she lived.

"You'd stumbled upon my territory," he continued. "I had no idea who you were or what you wanted. Just be grateful you're alive. Everyone else who entered the area got buried in ice. And before you ask, I made an exception because you're sexy, and I'm shallow."

A very male explanation.

She sneered at him. "You saved us from a bad guy, then left us to starve or freeze to death. How very gentlemanly of you."

"I was busy preparing for the day the combatants escaped confinement. When I had time, I would have brought you food and firewood. But just in case I didn't have time, I left you with the means to hunt your own." A pause. "By the way, a warrior named Zion has your friend. Three others—Bane, Bold and Emberelle—are hot on their trail. You should have stayed at the cabin. I'm nice."

Adonis coughed in his hand.

"I'm *nicer*," Erik amended. "Sometimes."

She scoured Celeste's memories. Bane—he had a beast trapped within. Bold—he hailed from a realm of assassins. Emberelle— she was a mind reader, with pointed ears.

"Don't worry. They'll never catch Zion," Adonis said. "He's like Knox. A ghost. And speaking of Knox, I'm sure you'll be happy to know our beef is with him, not you. Be a good girl, and you'll make it out of this alive."

"Women *love* condescending men," she told him, batting her lashes. "Don't ever stop being you."

He chuckled, and she rejoiced. Nope, these guys didn't know she'd joined the AW, and they assumed Knox had killed Celeste—if they even knew Celeste was dead.

One day, they would find out the truth. Best to lay the groundwork for Nola's protection now. "FYI, I don't give a crap about the other girl. We work for the same company and traveled together as a stupid team building exercise." A lie steeped in truth, the hardest to detect. "So I'm a carrot for Knox, huh?" she asked before either male could probe for more information about her sister.

"If he survived the skirmish with Rush," Erik said with a nod. "Yes."

She gulped. *Had* Knox survived the skirmish with Rush?

Worry later. "Good luck with your carroting, gentlemen. Word of warning, though. Knox told me, oh, about a dozen times that I mean nothing to him. He values his life, and no other. He won't endanger himself for a search and rescue." He *might* endanger himself for a search and rescue. He'd promised to find her.

"He shielded you from one of Rush's arrows," Erik said. "You mean something."

Realization: They'd watched the other man's entrance. Had they watched the make-out session, too?

Gritting her teeth, she said, "How did you find us?"

"Mainly social media," Erik said. "I have hundreds of employees dedicated to searching the web every minute of every day."

Knew that would work! Whoa, back up. He had *hundreds* of employees? Frick! The man wasn't just prepared; he was smart.

"I've had centuries to prepare for this day," he added, "to find ways to defeat the men and women with awe-inspiring powers who dared invade my land."

He'd had unfettered access to the world and the ability to set countless traps, implementing contingency plan after contingency plan just in case something—anything—went wrong. *More dangerous than I realized.*

A clammy sweat broke out on Vale's brow. If there had to be a winner—besides her—she should root for the man who fought for Earth, not the man she had a crush on, who fought for his own freedom.

Adonis leaned toward her. In a stage whisper, he said, "Once, Erik considered us gods. As he should. We spawned many of today's myths and legends."

"Let me guess. You are the inspiration for your namesake, Adonis." She rolled her eyes. "Knox mentioned he was known as the god of darkness."

"Yes to both. Though Knox was supposedly the incarnation of Loki."

Why did that make him even sexier?

Erik drummed his fingers on the wheel. "The *gods* used to return to my territory once a month, killing any of my clansmen who neared. So, I killed one of their clansmen in turn. After interrogating him and learning all I could about the All War, of course. I had no idea I'd become an immortal until years later."

"What will happen to Earth if you win the war?" she asked softly.

Adonis shook his head, adamant. "I won't allow my queen to destroy this land the way she did my—" He pressed his lips together. "She won't win your world. I would rather remove my heart with a spoon. I will fight to keep *all* corrupt rulers from assuming ownership."

Corrupt...like Knox's king?

Erik had nothing to say on the subject, only nodded his agreement. A startling thought drifted through Vale's mind. *I could throw my hat into their ring.* Part of her kind of liked the cookies they were selling.

Deep in thought, Adonis fretted two fingers over his jaw. "Did Knox tell you anything about a woman named Celeste?"

"C-Celeste?" Vale stammered. Never mind. There'd be no hat throwing. As soon as these guys learned what Vale could do, they would consider her a danger they couldn't afford to keep around, guaranteed. And they'd be right.

"I bet he ended her in the motel room just before our arrival and hid the body," Erik said. "He has her sword, and wore her scent."

Yep, they blamed Knox. There was no reason to disabuse them of the notion, and a thousand reasons to play along. Right now, the two males were at ease with Vale, and unafraid. They didn't consider her a threat.

Now or never. With a faux screech of distress—all right, only *half*-faux—she pitched her body at the door, as if intending to leap to freedom. When Adonis grabbed her, she struggled against him, secretly clasping a dagger sheath. Bingo!

"Enough of that," he said, placing her in a choke hold.

Vision, going dark. No, no. She fought harder, fought with all her might, but darkness continued to encroach upon her mind, inch by dooming inch, extinguishing any hint of light.

Consciousness returned to Vale in gradual degrees.

Eyes burning, she blinked rapidly. Bright rays of sunlight combed through a canopy of trees…trees…she was outside? But why—

Memories surfaced, and she gasped. Erik and Adonis. The car ride. The choke hold.

Now her hands were tied with rope. As discreetly as possible, she rolled to her side to look herself over. Oh, thank the good Lord! She hadn't been divested of her T-shirt and shorts. While the clothes offered little protection against the cool breeze, her favorite parts were covered, so she called it a win.

Frick! The dagger she'd stolen was missing.

The bottoms of her feet no longer hurt; the cuts must have healed…because she was immortal. Had the guys noticed?

Silly question. If they'd noticed, she would be dead.

Tremors shook her, but at least the crisp, clean mountain air chased away any lingering head-fog. *Get free, and get going.*

The rope extended over her stomach and anchored to her ankles, making it difficult to sit up but not impossible. As soon as she succeeded, her temples throbbed. Deep breath in, out.

She scanned the area and jolted. The guys had dumped her in a valley, and left countless humans to guard her. The men and women appeared to be from every walk of life, some dressed in jeans and T-shirts, some in scrubs, others in suits or dresses. A few wore hard hats. No one spoke a word, and everyone stared straight ahead.

They were the ones from the article, she would bet. The people who'd disappeared in Colorado. But why were they here? What were they doing?

As if sensing she'd roused, Adonis shouldered past a cluster of men and locked gazes with Vale. "Our honored guest awakens at last."

Keep your cool. "My nightmare returns."

He grinned, his entire face lighting up, and okay, yes, the name Adonis fit him well. He was a beautiful man, with strong features and a total bad boy vibe. In the sunlight, his dark skin possessed a violet shimmer the same shade as his irises.

"Who are these people?" she asked, motioning to the crowd with a tilt of her chin.

"Meet my army." He patted the curved horn that hung around his neck. "I summoned anyone within a hundred-mile radius who is over the age of eighteen and had irrevocably harmed another mortal at some point in their lifetime. Apparently your realm is *filled* with such deviants."

Facts crystalized. The Horn of Summoning... With a single blow, he could turn large groups of people, animals or even the undead into mindless armies devoted to his will.

"Must admit, I expected Knox to come for you," he said, thoughtful. He closed the distance, held a canteen to her lips and helped her sip, delicious water sliding down her dry throat. "He promised he would."

The barb struck home, and she flinched. If Knox had wanted to find her, he would have succeeded already. Had he decided to wash his hands of her? Yeah. Probably. And she wasn't upset about it. Nope. Not even a little.

But dang it, why am I never good enough? "Told you," she replied softly. What was the big deal, anyway? *She* had planned to leave *Knox.* So he'd left her first? So what? Except...

His abandonment *was* a big freaking deal.

Tears stung her eyes. He'd kissed her as if he couldn't get

enough of her, as if they were part of a dirty fairy tale, and she was Sleeping Beauty, destined to wake with true love's kiss. He'd kissed her as if she meant something to him. As if he never wanted her to hurt, much less die.

This changes nothing.

I know.

She was stupid, so incredibly stupid. For her, the kiss had changed *everything.* She'd felt the vast depths of his inner pain, and something inside her had shifted.

Yes, she'd opted to ditch him in the motel room, but even then, even when she'd denied the depths of their connection, that kiss had scared the ever-loving crap out of her. He'd proved he had power over her, *sensual* power, and part of her had realized she could fall for her former captor. Oh, the horror. The cliché.

Clearly, Knox hadn't experienced the same earth-shattering realization. Like everyone else, he was too dim-witted to comprehend how special she was—how good she could be for him.

Fine, there was a slim chance she could be okay for him. *Good* might be a bit of an overreach.

Anyway. He didn't deserve to spend any more time with her.

This is for the best. Can't trust him.

"Are you going to send me on my merry way?" she asked, not daring to hope.

"Sorry, but you're staying with us, little mortal." Adonis gave her a half smile. "The bastard might decide you're worth a fight, after all."

Ouch. If he'd wanted to raise her hackles and scrape old wounds raw, he'd succeeded.

Her father wasn't the only one who'd walked away from her and never looked back. Nor were the boys she'd dated. Besides Nola, the foster sisters and brothers she'd bonded with hadn't cared to stay in touch.

I have so much love to give, but no one wants it. No one wants me.

Ugh. How many times was she going to whine about this?

Her worth wasn't based on the thoughts or actions of others. *I am Vale London, the only one there is, and I am priceless!*

I'm a treasure!

"What, no protests?" Adonis asked.

Never let them see you squirm. "You want a protest? Well, why didn't you say so? How's this?" She made a lewd hand gesture.

He burst out laughing, surprising her.

Trying to charm her? Too bad. She was going to blow this joint as soon as possible.

Celeste would unleash the pheromone, sending him into a sexual frenzy. He would cut her loose just so she could touch him. Barring that, she would become intangible if possible, grab his dagger, stab him and sneak off the mountain.

Giving away her secret and fake-seducing someone other than Knox would be *Operation Survive: No Other Choice.* She needed to think of something better—something even halfway decent.

"There's nothing. No tracks, no sightings." Erik joined the party, two rifles slung over his shoulder. His eye had completely regenerated. He glared at Adonis, snapping, "By the way, your army is creepy as hell."

Just how many people had congregated in these mountains, ready to obey the warrior's very command? "Creepy and useless," she said. "I've seen Knox fight. Your helpers are gonna go down like pins on bowling night."

"I'm sure I'd be intimidated if I knew what bowling was," Adonis said, all droll humor and sex appeal. "My translator is teeing up images of chicken wings, smashed cans of beer and rolling balls."

"Maybe if we hurt the girl, make her scream," Erik said, "Knox will hurry."

Considering she'd beheaded a woman, gotten stabbed, been captured and kissed by a murderer only to be kidnapped by *other* murderers, today's threats were just more of the same. Part of her new normal.

"Let me save you the trouble of exerting yourselves." Vale unleashed the scream of all screams, a sound fit for a horror movie. By the time she quieted, her companions were cringing. "Thoughts? Suggestions? Comments?"

Adonis gave her an admiring look while Erik regarded her with a pensive stare.

A wave of gunshots rang out, and she stilled, not even daring to breathe. One, two—*six* shots echoed through the mountains, followed by silence, followed by six more shots. As her heart kicked into a drunken race, mortals dropped around her, holes in their foreheads, brain matter and blood splattered over the ground.

In the motel room, she'd vomited at the sight of such violence. Now? She looked around, hopeful. Had Knox come for her?

"Surround the girl," Adonis called. He and Erik raced away, and the mortals rushed to her.

More gunshots echoed. The men closest to her got hit first, falling over dead one after the other.

"He's taking out anyone who nears her," someone—Rush?— shouted from somewhere in the distance. He'd survived. Had Knox?

He must. Who else would protect her like this?

More shots. More dead bodies.

Frantic, Vale looked for a rock, something, anything to aid her escape. Her captors had to be running through the trees, closing in on Knox. It would be three against one. She could better the odds. She owed him, after all. He'd taken an arrow for her.

Poppoppoppop! The next round of shots came so quickly, they bled together. There! A dead mortal with a tool belt.

Vale scooted across the dirt, dug through the tools. Hammer—no. Tape measure—waste of space. Screwdriver, pry bar, level—no, no, and no. Utility knife—yes!

She trapped the tool between her upraised knees and sawed at her bindings...

CHAPTER SEVENTEEN

Rage held Knox in an intractable grip, tension a powder keg inside him, set to blow at any second. He should be out there, hunting Ronan and Carrick, adding to his kills, collecting new weapons, taking strides to advance the war and remove his slave bands before Ansel ordered him to do something truly repugnant.

But here he was, chasing after Vale—an enemy—determined to lay the heads of her tormentors at her feet. Somehow, a single kiss had changed the very fabric of his being. The merciless Ivilandian with no ties wanted his woman back.

For too many centuries Knox had avoided kissing, and not just because of his trainer's warning. Having come upon other men trapped in the throes, he'd known, deep down, the power such a connection could wield. The devolving of your thoughts. The distraction, the world around you fading.

Knox never should have kissed Vale. His first suspicions had been correct. Learning the hope of what could be, the sweetness of her flavor, the softness of her lips, the heaven of her curves, the bliss of grinding his erection into her core—it had been lethal to his resolve. He'd been reduced to *this*, an addict who only wanted more, who was as much a fool as the soldiers who'd died guarding Celeste. A fear he'd had, and now lived.

But he understood the other males in a way he hadn't before. He'd glimpsed a future filled with satisfaction, contentment, peace and pleasure, so much pleasure, with no hint of battle, blood or vengeance, and he'd needed to make it a reality.

He wasn't sure how he'd existed so long without the hope Vale provided, but knew he wasn't going another night without her tucked safely at his side. If necessary, he would raze these mountains to reach her.

After a lifetime of war, she is my prize.

She hadn't feared his strength. No, she'd reveled in it. She hadn't winced when he'd squeezed too tight. No, she'd begged for more. *Demanded* more.

There was a problem. Her incredible scent had acted as an aphrodisiac to him *and* to the other males.

The truth had hit him as he'd tracked her through the rain, his head clearing of primal lust. It wasn't a perfume, as he'd first assumed, but a weapon taken from Celeste's arsenal. An innate supernatural ability Vale had absorbed, just as she'd absorbed the ability to become invisible—which she'd done seconds before Knox had urged her to run from the room.

He would find out more, just as soon as he had her in his possession.

Soon…

Positioned high in a tree, he had a full-circle view of the entire clearing. A golden sun glowed in a baby blue sky scattered with fluffy white clouds. A crowd of humans surrounded a campsite, while trees surrounded the crowd, forming a border. Wisps of white cotton danced on a warm breeze, like snow without the chill.

Vale crouched on a patch of grass, a knife held between her upraised knees, sawing at the thick rope that bound her wrists. As more humans hurried over to engulf her, Knox used the revolver to take down the ones closest to her; he commanded shadows to knock down the rest.

He would have enfolded Vale herself with shadows, but doing so would have blinded her.

{Get her back. Level of danger is increasing exponentially.}

Twigs snapped, signaling the approach of Adonis and Erik.

Shadows already enveloped Knox, allowing him to blend into the landscape. When the men burst past a line of bushes, clasping swords, they scanned the area, searching for him. His slave bands sizzled instantly, reminding him of Ansel's command to murder Adonis.

An opportunity had just presented itself, and the compulsion to obey was too strong to deny. Knox hammered at the trigger.

The male ducked and dodged before he and Erik charged forward, tracking the sound of the gun blasts. Knox enveloped the two with shadows—

They shed the darkness like a second skin.

Neat trick. *New* trick.

No matter. Knox emptied the cylinder of rounds, then jumped from the limb. Erik successfully dodged the missiles, but Adonis took one in the shoulder this time.

His landing was jarring, but Knox managed to remain upright. Both adversaries swung their swords, one going high, one going low. With a tornadic blast of shadows, he sent Adonis stumbling back without ever making contact. Erik was unaffected, and Knox had to jump back to avoid the blow. He exchanged the revolver for The Bloodthirsty.

The arrow zipped through the air, forcing the males to split up—following Adonis, chasing him through the trees.

Knox hooked the bow over his shoulder and palmed the short swords strapped to his back. Perfect timing. Erik engaged.

Whoosh. Clang. The sounds repeated again and again, intermixed with grunts and curses. One of Knox's blades sliced Erik's arm but blood never welled.

Interesting. His clothing blunted the blade, the material stronger than what Knox currently wore.

I want. I take.

He and Erik battled on the grass, hopped over fallen branches and leaped atop boulders. Adrenaline acted as both fuel and salve, urging him on while blunting the pain of each new injury. Gashes here, gashes there. Two broken ribs. Torn muscles. A fractured ankle. Goal unshakable, Knox fought on.

The viking's supernatural ability soon became clear, and it was as dangerous as Vale's. Erik could negate the supernatural abilities wielded by others. No wonder he'd shed the shadows so easily. No wonder Knox couldn't blow him away. No wonder The Bloodthirsty hadn't gone after him.

But why hadn't Erik negated Vale's scent? Why hadn't he prevented her from becoming invisible in the motel room, or stopped Knox from using shadows altogether?

Erik must have to purposely engage the ability, which required an extra step on his part. If he hadn't known the scent was an ability of Vale's, he wouldn't have known he needed to negate it. As for Knox, he could have hoped to test the boundaries of his skill, to learn what was possible and what wasn't.

"You won't win against me, murk," Erik said.

"You're at a disadvantage, viking. This is your world, your people. You have much to protect. Much to lose."

An army of footsteps caught Knox's attention. Multiple humans rushed past the bushes to swarm Erik. Adonis hadn't returned. Finally The Bloodthirsty got what it wanted and cut through a living body, then another and another. Anguished howls resounded.

"You know what to do," Adonis shouted from somewhere nearby. "Go!"

Men and women, young and old, struck at Knox, delaying him, and his frustration mounted. If the combatants fled, absconding with Vale…

A red haze fell over his vision. The mortals were obstacles in his way. Obstacles got mowed down.

When God made me, He was showing off.

I am the author of my own story. Today I'm writing myself a happy ending, and maybe possibly killing off the rest of the cast.

I am Vale Fricking London, and I've been through hell and back. I can overcome anything.

As Vale sawed through her bonds, she gave herself different pep talks. Finally. Success! Triumphant, free, she gripped the utility knife, grabbed the hammer she'd discarded earlier and lumbered to unsteady legs. Her heart thudding against her ribs, stomach pitching, she scanned the sea of bodies, blood and filth.

Vultures circled overhead, waiting for an opportunity to feast. Flies were too impatient to wait, and swarmed.

Outside the wall of death, living mortals stood guard. Too many to count.

Grimacing, gagging, Vale climbed over the disgusting blockade. Intending to sneak away, she took a single step to the right. A mere tiptoe. In unison, the mortals spun to face her, stretching out their arms like zombies. The super creepy synchronization sent chills down her spine. *Hive mind, anyone?*

Don't think, just act. The cry came from deep within her soul, and something inside her changed. Vale, the plucky girl with street cred and swagger who'd ended up hospitalized a time or twelve after ticking off the wrong people, morphed into a conduit of pure female aggression and an unwavering determination to survive.

"Let's do this." She glided forward and wreaked havoc. Never slowing, never hesitating. Anyone who reached out to snatch her got stabbed or jabbed.

Part of her remained cold and calculated. The other part of her screamed protests. *Murderer! Monster!*

The best way to help Knox right now—if he was out there—
was to lead the army away from him.

When Vale reached a row of cottonwoods, she paused to call
out, "Here I am. Come on, come and get me." Then she ran.

They followed.

Twigs sliced her feet, but she didn't care and quickened her
pace. Pain wasn't a factor in her do-or-die decision-making. She
darted around trees, boulders and mortals.

Think! Which way should she go? Which path would lead to
civilization? *Must avoid other people.* If anyone nonzombie-like
saw her covered in blood... She shuddered.

Taking a gamble, she veered left. Ragged breaths burned her
nostrils. Her lungs felt as if they'd been coated with acid. Despite
the afternoon chill, sweat trickled down her brow.

When the trees began to thin, revealing a road up ahead, she
threw a glance over her shoulder—dang it! When had she lost
the mortals? Had they backtracked, determined to reach Knox?

No help for it. She had to backtrack, too.

As she turned, a muscular man jumped into her path—Rush.

Her hand flew to her chest in an attempt to calm her riot-
ous heartbeat, and she skidded over the dirt. New facts flooded
her mind. In the beginning of the game, he'd targeted Celeste
specifically, hoping to interrogate her to learn how she'd won
a previous All War. But she'd used the pheromone against him,
and he'd altered his efforts, deciding to kiss and strip her instead. When she'd attempted a death blow, he'd snapped out of
the lust-induced haze, vowed to kill her and sprinted off.

He frowned at Vale. "You are a mortal, yet I sense a combatant. Or you *were* a mortal." His eyes widened, comprehension
dawning. "*You* killed Celeste."

Panic seized her in a vise-grip. The utility knife and hammer
would be useless against a skilled combatant like Rush.

He took a step forward.

"Don't do anything rash, okay." Her voice trembled with the same intensity as her body. "Let's talk about this."

"There's nothing to discuss. You entered the war. Therefore, you must die." He raised his crossbow, three arrows already nocked. But instead of firing on her, he stiffened and whirled around.

Gunfire exploded as armed men and women in uniform charged the street. Bullet after bullet peppered Rush's chest, blood soaking his shirt as he stumbled back and crashed into a tree.

"Stay down," an officer shouted.

"Ma'am, drop your weapons, put up your hands and get on your knees," someone else called. "Now."

Vale obeyed; Rush did not. He popped to his feet and dashed from the area, gone in a blink, leaving her alone with the cops… and no credible explanation for her condition or however many dead bodies waited only a mile or so away.

CHAPTER EIGHTEEN

Multiple people presented the same two questions to Vale, simply changing the wording. The gist: Who was she, and what had happened? Not knowing what else to do, she remained mute, never uttering a word.

Two officers drove her to the nearest hospital, where she was stripped, examined, poked, prodded, photographed, cleaned and given a pair of scrubs. The doctors and nurses asked her a thousand more questions she refused to answer.

Anytime she was left alone, she tried to become invisible and intangible to slip out of the room. But she hadn't developed control of the abilities, and figured her jacked up emotions blocked her.

Ultimately, cops hauled her to local PD headquarters and shepherded her into an interrogation room.

A kindly psychiatrist interviewed her first, using every trick in the book to learn the tiniest bit of information about her.

"Help me help you," he pleaded. "Unless you explain what happened, you're going to be blamed."

If she mentioned the All War, she'd end up in a mental hospital. Or worse.

You see, sir, aliens invaded our planet. They've turned our world into a gladiator arena. Winner gets everything, and all losers die.

No, thanks.

Eventually two police officers excused the doc and gave good cop/bad cop a chance. And she understood their reasoning, she really did. No one knew what to make of her, if she was a killer, or a victim or both. They didn't know if she'd wielded the knife and the hammer herself or stolen them from someone else.

Though she told herself what was done was done, and there was no rewinding the clock, or reviving the humans she'd slain, that she could only plow full steam ahead, her emotional numbness wore off. She wrapped her arms around her middle and sobbed.

The cops explained a hiker had spotted the army of missing people and called 9-1-1. Soon after authorities arrived, gunfire rang out.

"We've counted eighty-three dead bodies so far," Good Cop said. He was in his fifties, and was visibly shaken. "I expect the number to rise as more of the woods are examined."

Swallow back bile.

There was a silver lining, she supposed. In prison, she would be safe from other combatants. Unless someone paid another prisoner to end her, of course.

Although, there'd be no need. If Vale missed the next check-in, she would be disqualified, hunted by an Enforcer named Seven, tortured and killed.

Would she ever be safe again?

Knox had been right. *Big Brother* paranoid was the only way to live.

Maybe he would come for her again. Had he survived the last battle?

Miss him. Want him.

Need him.

She just sobbed harder. Had he defeated Erik and Adonis?

What about Rush? The rain of bullets had definitely weakened him, slowing him down. Had one of the other warriors swooped in to finish him off?

Not knowing what else to do, the cops locked her in a holding cell. Dejected and alone, she sat on the cot and drew her knees to her chest.

Today's slogan: *Reality* can *be worse than nightmare.*

So much to live for, so much at stake.

If Vale had any hope of salvaging her life, she needed to toughen up fast and face facts. Otherworld invaders were here, and they weren't going anywhere. She wasn't going to stop the All War. How many other players had tried and failed over the centuries? If a cease and desist were possible, someone would have done it by now.

Could she really stand by and do nothing while all of Earth was enslaved?

The planet might be a steaming trash factory, but it was *her* steaming trash factory. A lot of people sucked, yes. There was no denying that. But there were good people out there, too. And what about kids? The underprivileged? How bad would things get with new realm-lords?

Could she, a bona fide nobody, be the champion other earthlings so desperately needed? Could she purposely kill anyone who got in her way? Even Knox?

A clammy sweat sheened her forehead and the back of her neck, but she nodded. Yes. Yes, she could be Earth's champion.

She was going to do it, she decided. She was going to fight in the All War, all in, nothing held back. This nobody would fight for *everybody.*

Vale had no doubts she'd have to do reprehensible things to win. That she would cry before, during and after. But this was war, and she was a soldier, and she would never regret doing everything in her power to save an entire planet of people.

For better or worse, she wouldn't shy away from the tough stuff. *I'm in it to win it.*

A strange peace settled over her. And yeah, okay, the task ahead of her was monumental. She was plain ole ordinary Vale London, and the other combatants had tons more skill, but she had something they didn't. The ability to absorb the memories and powers of the combatants she took out.

The more heads she collected, the stronger she would become.

Knox—beautiful, sensual Knox—would be last on her kill list. The fact that he was on the list at all nearly broke her, but it had to be done. No matter how much she desired him, their feud was the real deal. They weren't pretendemies.

Once, he'd called himself a tool, used by his king. Ansel was a wretched, greedy man who obviously had no trouble doing terrible things to and with his tools, before discarding them. She couldn't let the tyrant rule this world.

She crafted a new POA. *Escape the cell by fair means or foul. If there are losses, there are losses. Find Knox, steal Celeste's Rifters and sword. Say goodbye. Take out the competition, win the war.*

The plan would remain fluid, as usual. If Knox wanted to make a final-two alliance with her, she would agree. Would he?

Could she trust him?

No, she decided. She couldn't. To him, freedom meant more than the girl he'd just met, and rightly so. But at the end of the day, he was still the best All War tutor on the market. She would have to be careful, weigh everything he said, and never drop her guard.

Her eyelids grew heavy, and her blood heated. What the—

A familiar, sweet scent saturated the air, fogging her head. The pheromone was seeping from her. Because she'd focused on Knox?

As she rejoiced, a male officer rounded the corner, sniff, sniff, sniffing. He licked his lips, his dark eyes glazing with lust.

When he caught sight of Vale, he quickened his pace, heading straight for her cell.

Nape prickling with trepidation, she vaulted to her feet.

The officer wrapped his fingers around the bars, and said, "I love you. Let me put a baby in you."

Oookay. *Today's stalker report: Bonery with a chance of ball removal.*

Channeling the seductive Celeste, Vale crooked her finger and beckoned her admirer closer. "Come, tell me everything you love about me. Leave nothing out."

He shook the bars and scowled, as if he couldn't understand what was keeping them apart.

Approaching him, she made sure to sway her hips. "Disengage the lock, silly. Let me out, and we'll talk." *Laying it on too thick?*

"Yessss." His pupils flared, spilling over his irises. "Disengage. Out. Talk."

"And hurry," she instructed. "Your love muffin has things to do."

Let the games begin.

Knox tracked Vale to a multistoried building with red brick walls and large windows.

He'd lost her trail a few times and had to backtrack. Once he'd been hit by a car. Soon after that he'd had a run-in with Domino that had ended with a broken spine. But through it all Knox had persevered, strengthened by the outcome he desired— rescuing Vale, carting her back to the bunker...and devoting *hours* to her pleasure.

He'd never tasted a woman's arousal, but oh, he'd wanted to. Anytime he'd tried, his lovers had tensed, so he'd changed course before ever reaching his goal. Vale would be the first... if she let him. Would she?

He craved the intimate act with her and her alone, and marveled that he had something to anticipate rather than dread.

Afterward, when he was no longer overrun with desire, he would figure out his next move.

Focus. Most of the mortals who entered and left the building were the police enforcers she'd told him about. Males and females in uniform, with guns strapped to their waistband.

Would they beat Vale bloody, lock her in a dungeon for a few days, then beat her all over again?

The *eyaer* hadn't yet decided if her necessity to him—saving her—was worth the risk to his life.

Didn't matter. Knox had already made up his mind. *Hurt my woman and die. No exceptions.*

One day soon, he would end Erik, Rush and Adonis. First he'd have to find them. Just before a horde of armed and uniformed mortals known as SWAT had come barreling into the clearing, the trio had vanished from the mountains.

Knox remembered Vale telling him SWAT meant Special Wingwoman And Therapist. Such an odd description for the gun-toting soldiers.

Chattering voices drew him out of his head, different people striding in and out of the police station. Since Knox had never seen inside the building, he couldn't enter through a rift. He'd have to go in the old-fashioned way.

Remaining hidden by shadows, he maneuvered to the front doors. No one paid him any heed. When the next human entered, Knox slipped in behind him to discover a large, crowded room. No telltale surge of power to signal a combatant lurked nearby. Not that he could relax. Any of these humans could be working for one.

Shiny floors reflected every movement around him. Small cubicles were partitioned from the main space by thick glass shields, and hallways were partially blocked by short, fat silver columns. Above, a second floor offered a viewing area of the space below—a parapet sheltered by a metal rail.

Different conversations fused together, but he mentally pried them apart to make sense of what he was hearing.

"—did he do this time?"

"—made a mistake, okay?"

"—we go now, please?"

Where is my woman?

No, not yours. The husband—

The husband meant nothing! A divorce was imminent, she'd said, saving the ex's life. Knox had never wanted a woman the way he wanted Vale, and he wouldn't share her with anyone. If the ex contested the divorce, Knox would make Vale a widow, as originally planned.

Determination impelled him onward.

"—Valerina London?" The declaration came from above.

Only two words, yet they acted as a verbal net. Attention snared, Knox commanded the shadows beneath his feet to spin faster and faster, lifting him higher and higher. Had he been visible, he would have appeared to stand atop a tornado, a master of the winds, unaffected by their violence.

"—was in the system," another male said. "Prints are a match. As a kid, she bounced between foster homes. One family alleged she attacked the dad with a kitchen knife, zero provocation but—" A long series of clicking and clacking. "He's since been convicted of sexually abusing one of his charges."

Someone had dared touch a young, vulnerable Vale? Bombs of rage exploded inside Knox.

"As a teen, Miss London had a few run-ins with the law," the man continued. "Petty theft, assault. Looks like she was quite the scrapper. Probably had to be. Once she was beaten so badly she had to be hospitalized."

Beaten? *My Vale?* Bits of shrapnel left by those rage bombs—they exploded, too.

"Do you think she killed all those people?" a woman asked.

The answer was drowned out as the back of Knox's neck prickled. A surge of power, a crackle of electricity…a combatant had just neared.

On the first floor, a crowd of mortals snaked around a corner, exiting the hallway. Vale occupied the center of the group, holding court.

Every muscle in Knox's body hardened. His hands flexed, as if they remembered holding her and *needed* to do so again. He was pleased to note she sported no visible injuries.

She wore a blue top and pants that bagged over her curves. The long length of her hair hung in black-and-white waves, the braids unraveled.

So beautiful. So mine. For a little while, at least.

The shadows beneath his feet slowed bit by bit, returning him to the floor. The mortals laughed at something Vale had said, and pride bubbled up inside him—she'd managed to overcome her circumstances.

Beneath the pride, however, was a tide of anger. He'd prepared to win a battle of legend on her behalf, and yet she had simply *flirted* her way out. She hadn't needed him. He'd wasted precious time.

The group of humans bypassed a row of those short silver columns, entering the lobby. Other humans grew dewy-eyed as they tracked her every movement, reminding him of puppies desperate to be petted.

Knox inhaled, catching a whiff of her powerful scent. An avalanche of lust rolled through him, destroying his common sense, overriding his *eyaer*—his everything. Only Vale mattered.

Must have her. Now!

Lust had caught her up, too. Her nipples were hard little points, her skin flushed by passion-fever.

If she wanted one of the mortals...

Knox growled.

At the front doors, Vale stopped. "All right, guys," she said, her voice huskier than usual. "This is where we go our separate ways."

Groans of disappointment. Protests. No one could bear the thought of losing her.

I know the feeling.

A few of the males grasped at her, inciting Knox's wrath further, but Vale sidestepped, avoiding contact—saving their lives.

Do not speak. Do not grab her and run. Do not kiss her. Not until she's safe in your bunker.

Maintain strict control. Wait. Follow her. What would she do next? Suspicions arose.

"You're going to miss me, I know," she said, and it was clear she hadn't realized a combatant stood mere feet away. "But you *must* stay here and let me go. Otherwise I'll be sad. You don't want me sad, do you?"

"No," they assured her in unison.

"No," Knox said, and another growl left him. As Vale's mastery of Celeste's abilities increased, so did his foolishness, apparently.

Amid a chorus of protests, the brazen wench blew everyone a merry kiss and strutted from the building.

CHAPTER NINETEEN

With the jailhouse in Vale's rearview, her fake smile vanished in a hurry. How long did she have before the effects of the pheromone ebbed, and the cops came after her, guns blazing? An hour? A few minutes?

Even the worst detective in the world would be able to unearth her location with little effort. Every time she turned a corner, she picked up a new stalker, until another crowd had formed. She was pretty sure she'd picked up a combatant, too.

Knox had told her she would feel a pulse of energy in the air, and she definitely detected a pulse. Had he tracked her? Or had another player found her?

If Knox were nearby, he would have revealed himself. Right? So, this *had* to be another player.

Decision time. Turn off the fumes to ditch her admirers, or let the pheromone continue to seep from her in order to ward off an attack?

"I love you," someone said.

Then, "I want to have your babies."

Still another said, "Marry me."

Off. Definitely off. A million flavors coated her tongue, leaving a foul taste in her mouth. Oh, how she missed Knox's whiskey and honey. Heck, she missed Knox, period.

Moving on. Celeste had exercised absolute control over her abilities. What she'd wanted, she'd willed. Focused, determined, Vale willed it off and…yes! The scent faded.

On alert, expecting the combatant to pop out at any second, she picked up speed. At first, the crowd trailed her. One by one they branched away, no longer enamored with her.

Relieved, she pondered the best way to contact Knox. The best way to get the sword and Rifters from him.

Someone bumped into her. As she stumbled, something small and hard slapped against her palm. Her fingers curled in reflex, holding on.

"Your sister says hi," rasped an unfamiliar voice.

Nola? Heart rate spiking, Vale spun, intending to race after the deliveryman. Dang. He'd already disappeared in the crowd.

Her heart rate spiked again when she realized she held a cell phone. Truly from Nola, or a combatant *pretending* to be Nola, hoping to track Vale through GPS?

Trust no one.

But she smiled when she caught sight of the screen; a message from SotY waited. Sister of the Years, Nola's moniker. No way anyone else could know that.

Paranoia disagreed. Zion could have tricked the information out of her, and Erik could have hacked a database to dredge up their message history.

Whimper. The message read: Sorry our convo got cut short. Do WHATEVER you need 2 do 2 survive, & don't worry about me, ok? I'm good as pie & gonna stay that way. Lady Carrie's girls 4ever! Oh, & don't believe Z. I repeat. Do NOT.

The vernacular fit Nola to a T. But what did she mean, "don't believe Z?" Z stood for Zion, obviously, but he'd never really spoken to Vale. Was he *going* to speak to her and tell her a lie?

Sounded ominous, but then, it was difficult to judge tone in a text.

With tears brimming in her eyes, Vale tossed the phone in a trash can without replying. Though she trusted Nola with her life, she wouldn't/couldn't/shouldn't trust Zion.

Okay. Next move. Finding Knox.

No, wait. First she had to gear-up. Vale walked to the nearest electronics store, certain the combatant tracked her. Though she remained on alert, he—or she—never made a move against her.

Though nervous, she used the pheromone to get a 100 percent off discount on two phones, a laptop and a top-of-the-line prepaid data plan. What she didn't feel? Guilt. The items would help her save the world.

Face it, she was basically a superhero.

Next she visited a clothing store to get new duds. Lastly, she stopped at a party supply shop to pick up a few surprises for Knox. Things they could use to celebrate their newfound partnership—the one she was going to pitch. He just had to say yes.

Still being tracked.

Her nervousness increased, invisible nails being drilled into her ribs, scraping her heart every time it beat. Unfortunately, she was also turned on. She wasn't immune to the pheromone's effects.

Concentrate. She needed to find a quiet spot to surf social media sites. Knox had picked up driving so easily. Why not internet surfing, as well? For all she knew, he was checking out her Twitter page right this very second. #KnoxOnWood #HardKnox.

Sacks filled with her purchases in hand, she headed to a nearby coffee shop. If she remained in a crowd, the combatant might not attack and—

"Hello, female."

Knox's voice came out of nowhere, deep and languid, sexy as heck, and she nearly launched out of her skin. On the plus side, the potent taste of whiskey and honey cleansed her mouth of the foul barrage.

Arousal redoubling, she whirled around and searched the sidewalks for him…the shadows… One blink, and he appeared directly in front of her. No one else seemed to notice or care.

Excitement coursed through her. Breathless, she said, "You're my stalker."

His eye sockets had darkened, his piercing blue gaze both chilling and smoldering. Rumpled black hair framed the gorgeous face that would forever haunt her fantasies.

He was shirtless, an eight-pack on magnificent display, but also smeared with dried blood. His leather pants were ripped. Had he come straight from battle, like a conqueror determined to claim his war prize?

Instant bliss-out. Her nipples hardened, and her stomach quivered. Hot need pooled between her thighs.

What is wrong *with me?*

The gloom cloaked his weapons—she knew he had weapons—but not the scabs and bruises that littered his torso.

He'd never looked better, or stronger or fiercer, and oh, frick, he turned her on more than the pheromone, just by standing there. He enthralled her.

Guard up!

He tilted his head to the side, giving her *the look*. Voice hoarse, he said, "Come with me."

Safety first. "Do you plan to murder me in private or engage in a little convo?"

"I could have killed you a thousand times today, and no one would have known. What do you think?"

Excellent point. "By all means, then, lead the way." As he strode down the sidewalk, she kept pace at his side. "So how'd you find me?"

"Easily," he replied, his tone lashing like a whip.

Well, well. Someone was in a mood. "Did you adios the terrible trio forever?"

"No." He ushered her into an abandoned alley, opened a shadowed rift and stood guard after they'd entered.

The rift closed, sealing them inside the bunker. Determined to clear the air before she lost her wits, Vale placed her bags on the floor and said, "Listen up, Knoxie. Things are going to be different between us this go-round."

"You're right." Rage pulsed from him. "I got a glimpse of a future with you, and I would rather die."

The unexpected rejection cut like a knife, the pain staggering. *Buck up. This means nothing. He* meant nothing.

She pasted on a sneer. "Oh, good. We're on the same page. Give me Celeste's sword and Rifters, and I'll be on my way." Screw an alliance.

He crossed his arms over his muscular chest. "Why don't you enslave me with your scent and *make* me do it?"

Gulp. He knew. At the very least, he suspected. Best she come clean. "Look. I'm not wearing perfume. It's a pheromone, and I'm producing it, just like Celeste. I think I'll call it Lust Potion Number 69—trademark pending. You were right. When I absorbed her memories, I also absorbed her abilities."

He pursed his lips. "I watched you. The pheromone superseded the will of others. An unforgivable offense."

How dare he judge? "You supersede the will of others every time you make a kill. Your victims want to live, but you want them dead. Who wins?" She lifted her chin. "I did what I did to survive, and I'm not sorry. If you don't like it, I'll get lost and you can get bent. *After* you give me the sword and Rifters. Don't think I've forgotten them."

Her unruffled response clearly threw him for a loop. Jaw clenched, he said, "Did Erik or Adonis touch you sexually?"

"What does that have to do with anything?"

"Tell me."

"Why, are you jealous?" Her cheeks reddened, and she wished she could snatch back the question. Giving him another opportunity to reject her—

"Jealousy *seethes* inside me," he hissed. His usual masculine arrogance was stripped away, nothing but a veneer, leaving only primitive possessiveness.

Shock hit her first, then delight...then disappointment. He knew a little about her abandonment issues, and could have easily unearthed her sweet spot: being wanted by another person. He could be playing her.

He'd warned her. Never trust him.

But part of her believed he'd told the truth. His muscles were bunched with strain, his color high. The way he was staring at her, as if she belonged to him and him alone...

"No, they didn't," she said, tremors slipping down her spine. "And I didn't want them to. They are mega old—like you. I prefer my dudes under a century."

He relaxed, only to tense again. "From now on, you prefer me, and only me."

Ugh. This Neanderthal routine was totally doing it for her, revving her motor. Why, why, why?

Move on! "By the way," she said, "I spotted Rush before the cops nabbed me. He escaped in a hail of gunfire. He knows I killed Celeste and hijacked her abilities."

Pensive, he fussed two fingers over the dark stubble on his chin. "That presents a problem."

"Yeah, it does. For me. Now, give me what I came for, or you'll get no more info out of me."

He sneered, saying, "Decided to embrace your destiny as a cold-blooded murderer, did you?"

Okay, that really chapped her hide. "Did I have any other choice? I'm not going to let your king waltz in and enslave my people."

He narrowed his eyes. "I'll give you the Rifters, but not the sword. I'll never willingly arm an enemy."

"As long as you aren't trying to kill me, I won't attack you." *Here goes nothing.* "In fact, despite your crappy attitude, I'd like to make a final-two alliance with you."

The condescending POS arched a brow, all *oh, you would, would you?* "You think I'll trust you to keep your word?"

"No." And she wouldn't trust him to keep his. "I expect you to fight me off if I'm dumb enough to attack. Or does the big bad wolf think he's too weak to fend off the little lamb?"

"You, a lamb? You are more like a piranha."

She fluffed her hair. "Thank you. Piranha eat wolves for breakfast." Probably. If given the chance.

"You want to gobble me down, then?"

Awareness crackled between them, stronger than before, sparks showering over her. His gaze raked over her once, fast, then a second time, slow, very slow.

"I'd let you," he rasped. Pupils expanding, chest rising and falling in quick succession, he took a step closer to her. "Would you let me return the favor?"

Breathe, just breathe. In, out. No, no. Mistake! The heady scent of his masculine musk, all those exotic spices, sent a thousand megawatts of heat through her, melting her bones. *Careful. Reveal nothing.*

"I'm going to make this real simple for you," she said. "I don't trust you, either, but I want you. If I'm going to risk everything to play nookie hookie with you, you're going to meet my conditions without protest."

"I'm the one who risks everything."

Galling! She continued, anyway. "You are *not* going to feed me a bull-crap line about keeping my weapon to protect me. I don't need a protector, Knox. I need my sword. If you refuse, we're parting ways right here, right now."

His hands fisted, as if he fought the urge to…what? Shake her? Grab her and kiss her?

Tell him everything. Clean the slate, start fresh. "In return," she said, "I will be a good ally to you. I'll never betray you. I won't make a play for your head until we're the last two players standing. And I'll be honest with you…from now on."

He flashed his straight white teeth, returning to his primitive animal-state. "You lied to me in the past?"

"Yes." This next part could go very right or very wrong. "I don't actually have a husband."

He relaxed. "This, I know. You are divorcing."

"No. I've never been married." Before he could comment, she added, "In my defense, I didn't know you, didn't like you and feared what you planned to do to me. By the time I realized a fictitious husband wasn't needed, you threatened to kill me if ever I lied to you."

Between one blink and the next, his expression blanked. "How was a fictitious husband supposed to save you?"

Good question. "I guess I thought it would prove someone cared about my well-being and humanize me. And, if you'd decided to ransom me, you wouldn't hurt the goods that were going to supply a big payday."

A pause. Then, "Is there anything else you need to confess?"

Dang it, what thoughts were rolling through his head? "Yes, there's something else. I think you're a terrible host. I had to dig past thousands of layers of cynicism and malice to realize your personality doesn't actually suck donkey balls."

"Stop. Your compliments are going straight to my head," he deadpanned. "Anything else?"

Her shoulders sagged. "That's it. And you're not going to punish me for the lie. You *are* going to teach me how to sword fight. Oh, and when it's time to part ways, we'll talk, not stab each other in the back."

A minute ticked by in silence, a muscle jumping in his jaw. He was a mystery. The unsolvable riddle. An enigma.

She decided to forge ahead, anyway. "Lastly," she said, "you will work with me to create a comprehensive plan of action."

"I *have* a plan of action."

"Let me rephrase. A good plan of action, with clear objectives." She was going to put her business degree to use, after all. "We need to get ahead of potential problems and *force* circumstances to conform to our goals, remaining fluid."

He arched a brow. "*Our* goals?"

"Well, yeah. Final two, remember?"

He stabbed his fingers through his hair, dark locks tumbling over his forehead. Locks she yearned to brush back. His mouth opened, closed, but no sound emerged.

Had she blundered? Was his desire for her strong enough to overshadow his objections?

In it to win it. She smoothed a shaky hand down her curves. "Say yes, and you can have all of this." *Please, say yes.* Despite the shimmer of distrust between them, desire had left her aching and agonized.

The blank mask fell away, revealing blazing eyes that seared her soul. Suddenly he looked at her as if he could devour her in one tasty bite. As if he'd never wanted anything more. As if he would die without her.

No one had ever looked at her like that.

"I agree to your terms, *valina*."

Shock and joy. Lust and anticipation. Nervousness. More emotion than she could handle.

"Wh-what does *valina* mean?" He'd used the term before, and at the moment, she could think of nothing else to say. "Because if you change one particular letter, you get a whole new word."

"Which letter?" He pursed his mouth. "Never mind. I've figured it out."

She almost—almost—snickered.

He hesitated, then admitted, "The sun that warms."

Great! Now she wanted to sigh dreamily. *I warm him?* Well, good. It was only fair. He melted her.

"Now," he said, all wicked seduction and secret fantasies, "you will agree to *my* terms."

What more could he possibly want?

More important, how could she resist?

Gaze hot on her, he languidly discarded his weapons. Swords, daggers. The revolver. More daggers. The bow and arrow. Throwing stars. Metal clanged to the floor, creating a macabre pile. Shivers of ever-intensifying need shook her.

He removed his belt, and she gasped. The tip of his erection extended above the waistband of his leathers, a bead of moisture glistening in the light.

Silent, he cupped the sides of her face. Mmm, his hands. Calloused and strong, so hot they burned through her scrubs.

He picked her up and carried her to the bed, then placed her on the mattress gently. She stretched out, their gazes tangled together. He came down on top of her, anchoring his hands beside her temples to hold up his upper body while the rest of them pressed together. An inferno of need blazed inside her, and she spread her legs in welcome.

The pheromone wafted from her, almost as thick as smoke, and she tried to will it off, like before, but failed. "I'm sorry... can't control..."

"Here are my terms," he said. "You won't be with another man while we're together. You won't use the pheromone out of bed. And lastly, we will not have sex—penetration—until I've developed an immunity to the pheromone."

What! "No penetration?" Great! Now she was a creep who whined when her crush wouldn't go all the way.

He shook his head. "I want to know my desire for you is real." He ran her bottom lip between his teeth. "Until then, we will do *other* things..."

CHAPTER TWENTY

Can't think. Need to think.

Great tides of desire submerged the *eyaer*. Knox had to build an immunity to Vale's pheromone, and soon; his survival depended on it. The more he scented her, the less he cared about the outcome of the war.

Perhaps he should leave the bunker. Just for a little while. Just until he'd regained control of his thoughts. He *had* to care about the outcome of the war.

Stay! Strip her naked. Suck on those puckered nipples. Sip between her legs.

Yes, oh yes. He would do all of that. Leaving wasn't really an option.

"Knox... I want you."

"Kiss me." Nearly crazed with lust, he fisted the hair at her nape and yanked her face toward his. A soft gasp parted her lips—lips he claimed in a frenzy of possessiveness, his tongue rolling against hers.

The nectar-sweetness of her only maddened him further.

With a moan, she wound her arms and legs around him, then gradually tightened her hold to pull him closer, as close as possible while they were still dressed. Her breasts pressed against his chest, her nipples harder by the second. Her heartbeat raced in time to his, creating an erotic symphony, a siren's song.

He slanted his lips over hers. The kiss quickly spun out of control, and he gloried in every nuance of her, of this. The contrast of male and female. The feel of her velvety skin, as soft as rose petals. The richness of her scent, sugar and spice, saturating every inch of him. The sounds she made, little mewls and purrs as she undulated her hips. The way she scored his back with her nails, leaving her mark.

With startling clarity, he realized he *wanted* to wear her mark. Wanted to leave *his* mark, too. But not like this, with blood smeared all over him.

The blood. How could he have forgotten it? Knox lifted his head, ending the kiss, surely the most difficult thing he'd ever done—made even more difficult when she urged him back down.

"I need a bath." Wanted to give her his absolute best, and *be* her best. He stood to unsteady legs and pulled her to her feet.

She pouted, saying, "But why? I like you dirty. Filthy, even."

How had he *ever* resisted her?

Knox scooped her in his arms and stalked to the pool, every step agony, his erection throbbing. After setting her on her feet, he yanked her shirt over her head.

A bounty of femininity stood before him. A thin white bra bound her breasts and kept her nipples from his view. *Those sweet little berries were made for my mouth.*

He wanted to see her. He wanted her out of the clothes someone else had given her.

He wanted her naked and begging for him.

Vale devoured him with a hungry gaze, like for like, making it clear she craved the man, not the combatant. A concept that was foreign to Knox.

She traced her fingers over the tree of life tattooed on his shoulder. "Exquisite."

As much as he hated the image, he also loved it. Until an Ivilandian slave won an All War, citizens regarded him with disdain, even considered him a lesser being. From an early age, Knox had learned to associate his self-worth with battle. One of the reasons he'd always fought so hard to achieve victory, no matter the cost.

"The rest," he said. "Off."

Vale removed her pants, revealing matching panties and mile-long legs. *She* was the exquisite one. Ecstasy and agony. Torment and bliss.

"The rest," he repeated with a croak.

"Ah, ah, ah." The pulse at the base of her neck hammered erratically. *Going to lick and suck her there.* "Your turn."

He kicked off his boots, shucked his pants and hissed as cool air kissed the heated flesh between his legs. She gripped his length and stroked up, up, and he hissed with more force.

"This is mine," she said and squeezed. "All mine."

About to erupt. He stepped back, determined to regain a modicum of control, and his shaft slipped from her perfect grip. *More.*

Not yet. Trembling like a lad, he entered the water, dunked once, twice, and though he was cleaned, his nerves remained on edge. He wanted. He *needed*. Desperately.

Knox pivoted to watch as Vale descended into the pool. Her undergarments remained in place, swiftly becoming translucent in the water. Was his woman shy?

Steam wafted around her, weaving her into the fabric of a dream—or his every fantasy.

"By the way." The fantastical illusion only deepened as she swooped a handful of water over her chest. No, not shy. "If you're the only man for me, then I had better be the only woman for you."

"You are." No one else compared.

She preened for him, radiant, and he stalked closer...closer...
Can't stay away. Gaze never leaving hers, he picked her up and
set her at the edge of the pool.

"Kiss me," he commanded.

She did, softly. He savored her sweetness, a divine contrast
to the hard lash of desire. But what began as a leisurely explo-
ration soon morphed into another frenzied claiming, their passion a wild thing.

By the time he lifted his head, they were both panting.

He fisted her hair, forcing her gaze to meet his. "Let me taste
you. All of you."

Her eyes widened, filled with eager delight. "Yes. Do it."

He lowered his head to lick a water droplet from her neck,
and her pulse leaped up to meet his tongue. Dainty hands settled
on his shoulders, sharp nails embedding in his flesh.

Nowhere in this realm or any other was there a female
like Vale. She teased him, amused him, riled him, spoke her
thoughts, and never made him guess where he stood with her.
Never backed down, either.

With a ragged groan, he traced another water droplet all the
way to her collarbone...to the valley between her breasts...

"More, Knox. Please."

Tightening his grip, he scooted her forward, then forced her
to spread her legs wider so that her body cradled his once again.
Anticipation razed him as he sucked one of her nipples through
the bra, then the other, going back and forth, back and forth,
getting drunk on her, burning up inside and out—*happy* to burn.

"Knox." This time, his name was a strangled cry on her kiss-
swollen lips. "How do you do this to me? How do you make
me want you so badly?"

"*Show* me how much you want me." Hand resting between
her breasts, he gave a gentle push. As soon as she lay on her back,
Knox slid her panties down her legs. He tossed the soaking gar-

ment aside, then placed her feet at the edge of the pool, keeping her legs spread before him...keeping her body vulnerable.

Goose bumps rose on her thighs. He started at her knee, chasing the little marks with his tongue, heading up, up, closing in on the source of his fascination. The closer he got, the stronger her pheromone became, the more his head clouded and his body ached...the more he liked it.

Resisting her? Impossible.

Why fight her allure? He only wanted more...and she'd so sweetly commanded he take it...

"Knox." She rocked against him, writhed and undulated her hips, seeking deeper contact.

"I've never done this," he admitted, currents of excitement speeding through him. To finally know the sweetness of a woman's desire...to know the sweetness of *this* woman's desire...so pink and wet...so lush and beautiful.

"Do you want to?" she asked, hesitant. "Because you don't have to if you—"

"*I want.*" More than he'd ever wanted anything. Overcome by agonizing need, Knox lowered his head.

Vale waited, tormented, every cell in her body set aflame. What if Knox didn't enjoy this? What if—

Liiick.

She screamed, her hips lurching up in reflex. The pleasure was *incredible.* Mind-scrambling! This was the epitome of rapture.

Releasing little noises of approval, he licked and sucked on her, and he had no finesse. He was a man starved for his woman, and the realization made her wetter. He'd lost all control. Because of her, Vale London. Because he couldn't get enough.

Being still was a feat she couldn't manage. Pleasure building inside her, building and building, she ground against his mouth. Her blood burned hotter, and her skin pulled taut. Her breasts ached, and her nipples pulsated with desire.

He reached up, ripped off her bra, cupped and kneaded her breast, pinched her nipple.

"Yes, yes," she praised him. "More. So good!"

"You are so sweet, so wet." He thrust a finger deep into her feminine sheath, and she screamed again, the pleasure too much, not enough. He pulled it out, pushed it back in, giving her a taste of relief, only a taste. Then the agony sharpened.

On the next inward glide, he inserted a second finger, stretching her, and she lost track of her thoughts. It had been so long since she'd experienced a man's attentions...*too* long. But never like this. Never this good. There was nothing better. In and out. In, out. Faster, faster.

Soon she would burst apart at the seams.

"I want you. Please," she begged. "Take me. Get inside me."

His moans and groans grew more ragged. As he worked his fingers even faster, she continued to beg, but her words were no longer coherent. The pleasure...still building...too much, too much...still not enough.

Then he began to scissor those plunging fingers.

"Yes!" Just like that. Satisfaction exploded inside her, sensitized nerve endings crying with relief. Vale screamed once again, louder than before, the sound broken at the edges. The muscles in her stomach contracted, her inner walls clenching and unclenching, trying to hold him inside. Her pulse points raced, her veins containing molten rivers of desire.

Knox removed those seeking fingers and gave her body a little push backward, making room, allowing him to climb onto the pool's ledge. Beautifully aggressive and utterly male, he crawled up and loomed above her just as he'd done on the bed. Their gazes locked. Strain darkened his features and thrummed from his body.

Never had he looked so fierce—or pained.

"*Valina,*" he croaked. "*My valina.*"

His. Yes. Touching him wasn't an option but a need. Hoping

to gift him with the same satisfaction he'd given her, she reached between their bodies to wrap her fingers around his shaft. Surprise overtook her—new tides of desire crashing into her. He was so wide, she couldn't close her fingers around him, and so hard he would wring moan after moan of pleasure from her as he hammered in and out of her, so long he would reach places no one else ever had.

"Does my warrior ache?" she asked, stroking, stroking. Up, down.

"More than anything." The words were somehow gravelly yet silken, and made her hungry, insatiable. He arched into her touch and braced his hands beside her temples, his biceps flexing.

Not hungry. Ravenous. "No penetration? You're sure?"

Looking agonized, his teeth gritted, he said, "No penetration. Sure. Make me come."

Up and down. Up, down. She pressed his length against *her* aching core, arched her hips and daubed her moisture all over his shaft. Up, down. Mmm, yes. *Delicious.* An easier glide. Up, down.

"That's the way." He grunted when she tightened her grip to keep his length pressed against her core, and moved against him. Stroked, moved. Stroked, moved. "I'm close."

The grinding motion had the same effect on her, arousing her all over again. Heaving, groaning and moaning, she said, "Going to have…my first two-for-one…climax."

"Yes. I want you to have this. You *will* have this."

He was so commanding, so fricking sexy. So strong and powerful but also putty in her hands.

"Faster, faster," she intoned. "You're making me…want it… *neeeed* it."

They moved together in dirty, filthy, delicious harmony. To Vale, nothing else mattered. Nothing but this man, this moment, her thoughts centered on her next climax. *Must have it. Must have it now!*

"The things you make me feel." He leaned down, nipped at her lips. "Never stop."

"Never." She squeezed his length, pressed with more force and lifted her hips. "There! Yes!" This second round of pleasure built on the first, and propelled her over the edge.

This time, Knox followed her over, throwing back his head and roaring with sublime ecstasy.

CHAPTER TWENTY-ONE

Even after Knox and Vale washed and dressed in clean clothes, after she mumbled something about needing a snack and retreated to the bed, leaving him by the pool, bereft without her, his mind refused to calm. What they'd done...

A foretaste of contentment unlike anything he'd ever known.

He'd never experienced anything so turbulent, wild or satisfying. The man known for being brutal, cold and calculated had *forgotten* about the war, betrayals and consequences. As feared, he'd lost track of everything but the warm, soft woman in his arms. A thousand armies could have stormed into his bunker, but he wouldn't have cared, as long as he'd gotten to finish what he and Vale had started.

He wanted to blame the pheromone. A drugging aroma still clung to the air, infusing every inch of his bunker, his body. But he hadn't slid inside her tight little channel, the way he'd so desperately craved. His resistance had been in shambles, but the pheromone *hadn't* dictated his actions, had merely heightened the emotions and sensations...the entire experience.

Even still, he wanted to be fully immune to it. Immovable, even. Therefore, he needed to train with it, again and again.

Hard work. Very hard.

Something else Knox had noticed about the pheromone. The more aroused Vale had become, the more the scent had sweetened. When she'd begged for his shaft—

His hands fisted, the urge to give her what they'd both so badly wanted almost too strong to deny, even now.

Resist. Immunity first, sex second.

He busied himself, storing his weapons in the bower and fortifying the shadows. He even spent a little time polishing Gunnar's sword. Vale had mentioned "liquefy" and "bond." Perhaps victims melted from the inside? But what bonded together?

Though Knox didn't like to use a weapon until he knew exactly what it would and wouldn't do, he decided to use the sword on his next foe and gauge the outcome.

When he exited the little room, he glanced in Vale's direction, the action unstoppable. He was drawn to her more powerfully than he'd ever been drawn to…anything, even the ice mountains at check-in.

Check-in. The thought caused a fine sweat to bead on the back of his neck. In a little less than two weeks, Vale would have to stand in a clearing, surrounded by combatants, trapped in the middle of a free-for-all. She'd defended herself against Adonis's mortal army, yes, but combatants were skilled killers, trained for centuries. Gods. Could Knox protect her while fighting others *and* safeguard himself?

It was a feat he'd never before attempted because, out in the wilds of a new realm, he'd never cared about any life but his own.

The odds were not in his favor. He needed to train Vale…another feat he'd never attempted, because he'd known anything he taught another could be used against him later.

Didn't matter. Had to be done. Vale wouldn't survive the Assembly of Combatants without tutelage.

Now, she perched on the edge of the bed, her bicolored hair

rumpled wantonly, just the way he liked it, her beautiful curves hidden by one of his shirts and a pair of his pants. The sight of her there, in his home, in his bed, wearing his clothes, made his chest clench harder than ever before.

She regarded him with a blank expression. Why?

He frowned. Though she'd come apart in his arms only half an hour ago, she'd already withdrawn from him mentally and emotionally? An intolerable development. Always before, *he* had been the one to withdraw from a lover, determined to avoid any kind of emotional tie, unwilling to give Ansel any kind of leverage.

Knox tried, tried so hard, but he couldn't withdraw from Vale. Every time he glanced at her, something akin to *affection* swelled inside him.

His *eyaer* wasn't pleased.

The Iviland king knew nothing about Vale, but he would find out. Soon. He had spies positioned in every realm, perhaps even this one. And as other combatants talked to their kings, word would spread.

If Ansel ordered Knox to hurt Vale… He'd feared it before, but now, the thought was like poison, breaking down his defenses.

Lips peeling back from his teeth, Knox fought the urge to punch a wall. *Hate the king! Will destroy him piece by piece. It's only a matter of time.*

Inhale, exhale. Good, that was good. When Knox worked with Vale on the best ways to defeat other combatants, he would also prepare her for a worst-case scenario—*his* attack.

The *eyaer* bristled, and he didn't have to wonder why. Teach someone how to destroy you, and you would be destroyed.

His pragmatic side agreed, and said, *Why bother teaching her anything? She has to die at some point.*

His optimistic side proved stronger than he'd ever realized, and savagely beat the pragmatism into dust, laughing with glee.

Knox wasn't ready to end his association with Vale. She'd asked for a final-two alliance, and when he'd agreed, he'd meant it. They could make this work.

Knox needed to rest and hopefully clear his head for the first time since Vale had been taken from him. Then he would begin her training. Afterward, he would hunt Ronan, acquire the spyglass, and turn his efforts to Carrick.

The sword is as good as mine.

"Are you having a mental breakdown now that you aren't kissing me, your concentration shot?" Vale asked conversationally.

Despite the sting of her words, her voice was like magic to him, soothing the ravages of his mind.

He stalked toward her and said, "Only minutes ago you looked upset but determined to hide it. Why?"

Temptation made flesh, she peered up at him, a half-eaten piece of fruit resting in her tattooed hand, a droplet of juice poised at the corner of her red, red mouth.

Will lap up the droplet and seize her lips in another fierce kiss.

No—not yet. *Resist. Can't get caught up again.*

Forget resting. *Will only dream of her.* They had played hard, so now they would train hard.

"Well," he prompted. "Tell me."

"You want to know? Fine. Here it is. You got what you wanted," she said, and threw the fruit at him. "But then, I clearly like 'em old, bold and paroled, so I should have been prepared for the brush-off."

Brush-off? "You got what you wanted, too." He spread his arms wide and wondered if he was the last sane person in all the realms—or even just this bunker.

"*Then* you went about your day," she added bitterly, "as if nothing had happened between us. Because you think I'm undeserving of cuddle time. And I know I sound ridiculous and pouty, but I thought it was important to show you every side of me. That's right. I just implied I'm doing this as a favor to you."

Cuddle time? Undeserving?

She'd been through so much in so little time, had probably felt on edge since all of this started. Then, while they'd pleasured each other, she'd found a way to block out the worst of her circumstances, most likely for the first time. *Then* he'd walked away, and the uncertainty had come crashing back.

The way her mind worked was both strangely adorable and utterly heart wrenching at the same time. Their insecurities were similar, and ran deep. Multiple rejections had left scars, and now she expected everyone to find her lacking in some way.

Vale, his tough-as-nails female, hurt in her heart, and Knox couldn't abide it.

"You want to cuddle," he said, "we cuddle."

She bristled, quickly donning her armor. "I wasn't saying *I* want to cuddle."

"Indulge me, then." In a lightning-fast move, he picked her up and tossed her to the other end of the mattress. As she bounced, he leaped on top of her and pinned her down.

Beautiful and enchanting, she laughed up at him. "Fine. I will do this. But only because I'm a giver."

"Obviously. Now, you should know I'm a cuddle-time virgin. You'll have to teach me how to do it. Afterward, I'll teach you how to sword fight."

"Agreed. Oh, and FYI, *pickles* is your cuddle-time safe word. If, at any time, you become afraid of your emotions, use your safe word, and I'll try to stop being amazing."

"Funny girl," he grumbled, and rolled her to her side to playfully smack her ass.

"Lesson one," she said, cupping his jaw and turning his head so that they were eye to eye. "You have to look at me like I'm the reason you breathe. Yeah, yeah. Just like that."

"I'm not—"

"Now wrap your arm around me, and fit me against the curve of your body. Hold on like you never ever want to let me go."

Easy. He *didn't* want to let her go.

He propped up on pillows and pivoted to his side, ensuring her head rested in the hollow of his neck as he draped his arm around her back and relaxed his hand against the underside of her plump breast. One of her legs brushed against his growing erection—he hooked his fingers on the underside of her knee to maintain contact.

"Fit you against me like this?" He hoped so, because it made *him* feel necessary to *her*.

"Like this." A sigh of contentment slipped from her as she drew a heart on his chest. "I'd consider this absolute perfection if not for your shirt. Why are you wearing one, anyway? You usually don't."

"Wear a shirt, clean a shirt. It's an endless cycle."

"You go shirtless to avoid laundry?" Her next laugh was music to his ears. "*Such* a guy thing."

"Your turn to answer a question." He lifted her lovely inked fingers to his mouth and kissed each knuckle. "What do your tattoos mean?"

"Honestly, there's no hidden meaning. I wanted to accessorize but couldn't afford diamonds."

One day he would buy her a big—

Nothing.

As she traced a fingertip around his nipple, she said, "Will you tell me about your daughter? About how she died?"

Always before, he'd denied such requests because he'd known the pain of his past could be used against him. But he *wanted* to share with Vale.

"She was two when the king—Ansel—forced me to attend my second All War. Though I fought, I couldn't stop the soldiers as she was marked for slavery in case I lost the battle. Then I had to leave her behind while she sobbed for me to come back."

Heartbreak and sympathy emanated from Vale. "Oh, Knox."

The rest of the story rushed from him; he knew if he paused, *he* would sob. "She was supposed to be protected. A valuable asset meant to ensure I eagerly obeyed my king. Instead, she was beaten, abused in horrendous ways and treated as less than nothing. She ran away a few months before I returned, and not even the best hunters could find her. But I did. She'd abandoned the underground tunnels to venture topside, where the hunters wouldn't go. The extreme climates and air toxins kept everyone but criminals and desperate citizens away. When I found her, she'd been... She was dead, had died only a short while ago, her battered body somewhat preserved by the elements."

His voice frayed at the edges. His eyes burned, seared by unshed tears, and his jaw ached as he gnashed his teeth.

"Oh, Knox," Vale repeated. She clung to him, *her* tears dripping onto his chest.

He knew she cried for all he'd lost, for all Minka had suffered. The woman who had refused to break down in front of him, who had lifted her chin time and time again to forge ahead despite the circumstances, had no defense against his pain.

I am gutted. He clung right back.

When she calmed, she said, "Did you punish the ones who'd hurt her?"

"They died screaming."

"I don't think I should be pleased about the suffering of others, but I am." She wiped her eyes and nose—on his shirt. "They deserved—"

"Let's put a pin in this conversation. Did you just use me as a *handkerchief*?"

"Yes." She blinked at him, all innocence. "Excuse me for being super high maintenance and all, needing a tissue you don't have."

He snickered, and then he barked out a strange sound that reminded him of laughter. This woman. Oh, this woman.

"Your situation was just as tough as Minka's," he said, brushing a damp lock of hair from her beautiful, precious face.

Her amusement died a quick death. So did his.

"Some of my foster parents were abusive, yes," she said. "One or two of the dads tried to get handsy. A handful of foster siblings ensured I understood that I didn't belong in their family. Trust me, I knew. Then I met Nola and a woman named Carrie, and they showed me the true meaning of love."

Aching for the girl she'd been, he cuddled her closer and did something new to him—he petted her. She'd never had a parent fight for her, never felt as if she belonged with a family, so she'd made her own.

He kissed her temple. They lay in bed, silent, fatigue soon catching up with him. Knox resisted the need for sleep. He wasn't ready to drift off, wasting precious time with Vale. And did he trust her in his bed, his bunker, unbound?

Yes. Yes, he did.

"I want to show you something." He reached back, opened the hidden panel in the headboard and pressed a series of buttons.

Above them, the ceiling transformed.

She gasped. "A night sky scattered with stars."

"Yes."

"Is this an illusion? Or are we really staring up at the sky?"

"Illusion. This is a standard amenity for luxury bunkers. Living underground, illusion keeps you sane."

"I'm awed."

The strange surge of affection returned and redoubled, and he peered at her, saying, "As am I."

Her gaze met his. Whatever she saw in his expression spooked her, because she hurried to change the subject. "So, um, we should probably get down to business. Erik mentioned he has spies everywhere, has tons of money, hired countless employees and set a million traps. A long-winded way of saying he's hindered everyone else."

He embraced the topic, not yet ready to face the emotions

blooming inside him. "Don't you mean *us*? He's hindered every one of *us*."

"Yeah, yeah, yeah. Since he's immortal, I'd bet he's switched identities a time or twenty. If we learn who he's been, we can figure out who he is and who he'll be, and steal his money. We can hinder *him*, using his advantages against him, taking away the things he's come to rely on."

A pause. Then, "You know this world better than I do. How do you suggest we proceed?"

Knox, changing my life one orgasm at a time.

He was changing her life one *look* at a time, too, and it was freaking Vale out a little because it was also thrilling her. Those looks made promises; they said he would kill for her...*die* for her.

An illusion, only an illusion, like the sky.

But frick a brick, a girl could get used to that, to him, to all of this.

They'd gotten together quickly, their entire relationship a whirlwind. With life-and-death stakes and a looming expiration date, she understood the need.

Just relax. Enjoy.

That, she could do. Practically purring with satisfaction, she snuggled deeper into his side. Now that she'd climaxed, eaten and bawled her eyes out, she had no defenses against him or exhaustion. A yawn cracked her jaw, and she struggled to remain awake.

She didn't want cuddle time to end. Knox's strength, warmth and lush sensuality surrounded her in a cocoon of bliss, making their different topics easier to handle. But the best part? He remained open with her. He'd even sought her advice about the war.

Pulling from spy movies, she said, "We could purposely feed him bad intel online, misdirect his efforts and lead him into a trap."

Thoughtful, he replied, "Erik is telling combatants to stop fighting each other to forever halt the All War. Adonis agrees it's possible. Rush pretends."

"Yeah, they hinted at this when they captured me."

"Rules state a war will rage as long as necessary, that there's no time limit. If a winner is never declared, no other realms can invade."

"But rules can be broken, right?"

"Exactly right."

Besides, she didn't like the idea of the AW suspended, the threat of invasion never completely eradicated.

Clearly uncomfortable, Knox rubbed the intricate tattoo banded around his neck. "What information did Celeste gather about me and my realm? I'm sure she kept a mental file on the combatants. Most of us do."

What did his mental file on his little *valina* say? "Let's see what else I can unearth," she said.

She closed her eyes and concentrated on Celeste's memories. Just as before, some of those memories were hazy, others crystal clear. *Knox, Knox—there!* His fight with Gunnar...*digging deeper*...taking charge when the Vikings attacked...*deeper still*...a shared glance with Celeste minutes before the attack...

Whoa! Celeste had *not* crushed on Knox. She'd feared him, his emotionless gaze leaving her cold and shaky.

Day one of the war, she'd witnessed his first kill.

Like a movie playing in Vale's mind, she watched as a man punched at Knox, who dodged and kicked out his leg, his booted foot snapping the other man's fibula. As he screamed in agony, Knox kicked again, shattering the bones in his ankle, hobbling him completely.

Another man sneaked up behind Knox, snaked one arm around his neck to choke him out and raised the other—a dagger with a brass-knuckled hilt glinted in the moonlight.

A dagger she'd seen Knox wield in real life.

All lethal grace and brute force, he grabbed the man's wrist and threw an elbow, bent down and swooped to the side, gliding free of the choke hold and using shadows to shove his opponent to the ground.

He leaped, grabbing the man's hair with one hand to lift his torso. With his other hand, he forced him to stab himself in the heart, again and again, hacking at the organ to remove it bit by bit.

Not once did Knox lose track of the fights raging around him. He was the personification of cold determination.

He was death walking.

Deeper still. Celeste stood in the center of a massive arena, shoulder to shoulder with other combatants while facing a cheering crowd. Robed Enforcers inspected weapons and Rifters, their hoods drawn forward to hide their faces. Her heart raced.

Fear had chilled Celeste's blood. She'd won one war, yes, but only because the warriors hadn't known about the pheromone—the best-kept secret of her realm. Now, with the High Council involved...what if the truth had spread?

As a distraction, she focused on her protect-and-kill-if-necessary list.

Malaki would be first. He owned armor with hidden spikes, and she would use him as a shield.

Hunter would be next. He had a small, thin wand capable of crafting illusions anywhere, anytime. While Celeste could hide herself for seconds, he could hide her for hours.

Ranger owned winged boots. If a situation got bad enough, he could whisk her to a new location. Plus, as old as he was, he might be strong enough to take out the fabled Knox of Iviland, who had no obvious weaknesses, had never trusted a partner and, according to rumor, would rather kill a woman than bed her.

Knox was a slave compelled to do his king's bidding, and once a command was given, nothing could stop him from obeying it. According to an Iviland soldier her sister had seduced and interrogated in the City of All, where the High Council resided and citizens from any realm could visit—where violence was prohibited—Knox had been forced to kill his friends as a child. So, even if Celeste did the impossible and convinced Knox to aid her, his king could override her hard work with a single demand.

Icy dread whisked Vale back to the present. She blinked rapidly, clearing her mind, and clutched her stomach to ward off a sudden ache. "I knew you were enslaved," she said, her voice trembling, "but I didn't know…"

He was rigid, emanating humiliation, frustration and rage. "Say it."

"Wh-whatever your king decrees, you are forced to do."

"Always. No exceptions."

She licked her lips. "If he tells you to lie to me, torture me or kill me…"

"I will lie to you, torture you or kill you. No exceptions," he repeated, his tone hollow.

Ouch. If she were smart, she'd gather her belongings and leave Knox in her dust. As long as he was bound to Ansel, he couldn't be trusted. He was an ambush waiting to happen. So why did she stay put?

"Since the moment of my birth," he said, "I've been bound by the whims of another, my life never my own. Ansel says he'll set me free if I win the Terran All War."

"And you believe him?" Trying not to hyperventilate, she sat up.

He stared up at her, bleak. "No. I want to believe, have told myself I have no other choice, but he must know he'd be better off killing me. Free, I would be of no use to him, would always pose a threat to his well-being."

"Did he explain *how* he'd set you free? Maybe we can duplicate—"

"No." Eyes like wounds, he toyed with the ends of her hair. "Centuries ago, I cut off hanks of skin and muscle to remove my tattoos. Slave bands. The marks grew back, the ink a taint in my blood, my cells."

Cut off... Wow. The pain he must have suffered. *Give me Ansel's head on a silver platter.*

"I want you to understand how grave our situation is," he said. "I had few friends as a child, but I killed them when Ansel gave the order. I couldn't stop myself. That is why I've never let myself grow attached to others, why I avoid alliances."

Until me.

That. That was why she didn't leave Knox in her dust. She meant something to him.

Vale ached for the boy he'd been and admired the man he'd become.

"With Ronan's spyglass," he said, "I can better hunt Carrick of Infernia. He has a dagger able to transform blood into lava. If I can burn away the ink's taint..."

He could gain his freedom. "It's too risky. If you accidentally burn to ash, you'll be dead. You can't recover from that."

"The very reason I won't allow him to stab me and simply be done with it. When the dagger is mine to control, I'll take every precaution, do the deed here in the bunker, while submerged in freezing water. No one will sneak up on me while I'm injured, so I'll have a better chance of mending." A bitter laugh. "Success or failure, it's a win for you. One less combatant to fight, yeah?"

Oh, that stung. "If you control Carrick's dagger, you'll be immune to its effects, right?"

"Wrong. The knife you wield cuts you just as easily as the knife your opponent wields. Same goes for a weapon's supernatural abilities."

The same was true for a *person's* supernatural abilities, she realized. Look at the pheromone, and the way it revved her motor. Still, she slapped his chest, saying, "I should be the one to kill Carrick, just to be safe."

"Or you like the thought of stabbing me."

"Yeah, that, too. To be honest, I'm hoping we can find another way to free you—"

"Pickles," Knox interjected, his tone soft.

She pressed her lips together, going quiet. The frustrating man had used what she'd meant in jest against her. Well, no matter. Vale London, superhero, was on the case. She would find a way to free him, independent of the war, without risking his life, and nothing would stop her. Not even Ansel. Which didn't bode well for her win-at-all-costs strategy.

Ugh. One task at a time.

CHAPTER TWENTY-TWO

Knox held Vale close as she drifted to sleep. He had passed tired a long while ago, reaching a state of pure exhaustion, yet he couldn't stop playing with his woman's hair, running his fingers through the silken locks. The contrasting colors mesmerized him. Black-and-white hair against his bronze skin.

He didn't know why, and wasn't going to analyze it, but he wanted to do something special for her, something that would mean more to her than the jewelry she'd once coveted. He knew of only one thing she wanted—her sister.

He'd convinced Vale to cut ties with Nola as a preventative measure. Had he made the right call? In the bunker, Nola would remain safe, protected. Outside the bunker, she was fair game.

If anything happened to her, Vale would be destroyed, would blame Knox and probably herself. After blame came hate.

Just then, he felt as if lava *already* charred his veins.

Weeks before the fifth month check-in, Knox had trailed Zion to an island filled with golden temples and statues, where they'd fought so fiercely they'd triggered an event that had sunk most of the land underwater. Zion wasn't a fool and wouldn't return…or he was a fool if he *didn't* return. What better safe house than the one other combatants believed you would avoid?

Knox untangled from Vale, stood and tucked the covers over her. Releasing a soft sigh, she buried her face in the pillow he now envied.

How badly the woman had scrambled his brain.

With a curse, he forced himself to weapon-up. He cast a final, lingering glance at the bed…

Want to return.

{*Remove Zion from the war. He grows in power.*}

Yes. Remove. Shadows acted as a shield, rising as Knox opened a rift to the other male's hideaway. Warm air fragranced with coconut and wildflowers drifted into the bunker, resplendent but in no way comparable to Vale's scent. *Nothing* compared.

Body hidden within the gloom, Knox stepped through the rift. Sunshine caressed a white sand beach. Waves lapped and birds called, all at peace.

Once the rift had closed, he trekked across the island. The only sign of human life? The footsteps he left behind.

The longer he was away, the more he missed Vale, until it wrecked his concentration. He imagined her in bed, warm and soft as she welcomed him back, her nipples like little pearls, her legs spread in invitation, her core wet and glistening for him and him alone.

{*Concentrate!*}

Teeth grinding, he left the beach to hike into the jungle, careful to avoid any traps that might be hidden in the dense, dewy ground cover or trees. Insects buzzed, snakes slithered and monkeys swung on vines. He found no evidence of shelters or traps, but kept his revolver aimed.

{*Someone nears. Prepare.*}

Knox paused. There was a sudden *swish* of branches. Zion jumped from a tree, landing directly in front of him.

Boom, boom, boom. He hammered at the gun's trigger.

Between each gunshot, he heard a ping of metal against metal as Zion deflected the bullets with his gloves. Birds squawked and flew away.

"I've been waiting for you, Knox." The warrior held up his hands, palms out in a gesture of innocence. "I don't want to fight you. I'm here to bargain."

Knox reloaded. "Funny. I have a bargain for you. Give me the girl, and I'll let you live…today. Don't, and your life ends in minutes."

"Forget the girl. She's of no concern to you. I know your Vale has joined our war, and there are two representatives for this realm. The same thing happened during my first All War."

It was a well-kept secret, then. Or a lie. "Save your stories for someone else." *Cannot rely on another combatant's word.* No matter how badly he craved the information.

Zion continued as if he hadn't spoken. "The High Council decided neither addition would be disqualified, that they would fight to the death just like the rest of us, since the prize—the right to rule the realm—was the same for everyone."

Made sense. A weight lifted from his shoulders, one he hadn't known he'd carried. Vale would not be eliminated for being the second Terran to join the war.

"If we hope to beat Erik," Zion said, "we must work together. His net is wide, his reach long."

"I will *never* work with another combatant." Vale was the sole exception, but even their alliance wouldn't last long.

"I had a similar reaction when Nola suggested it to me. Then I used my brain. You need someone to watch your back, and I need someone to watch mine. Think about it. My offer will expire when the next check-in ends." With an amused smile, Zion punched a tree, pulverizing the bark, sending the upper half crashing toward Knox.

Thorns snagged him, cutting, as he vaulted to freedom. By then, it was too late. The warrior had already rifted off the island.

Knox could have given chase and tracked the essence of shadows, but he'd been parted from Vale long enough.

A quick search ensured he was truly alone. He opened a rift, entered his home and waited. As soon as the doorway closed, he whirled around, frowned. The bunker had been decorated with colorful paper ribbons, a Congratulations banner hanging over the bed.

"What is this?" he demanded.

"Surprise!" Vale stepped toward him, grinned and spread her arms. "Welcome to our alliance celebration party."

A party. For him. That was a first. "Why would you do this?"

"Because foxy Knoxie deserves a party with his doxy. Translation—sometimes a boy's just gotta have fun."

"I…thank you." Rubbing his aching chest, he raked his gaze over her. She'd changed into the clothes she'd picked up after escaping authorities. A black shirt with a deep V neck and a pair of camo pants.

"You like what you see?" *Her* gaze roved over *him*, her lids growing heavy. "So do I. So where'd you go?" she asked.

"Hunting Zion." To tell her the rest or not?

Tell, he decided. There was no reason to keep it from her.

"I was going to bring back Nola, but I failed." The last word was snarled. Failure was unacceptable, always.

"Thank you for trying." Eyes wide, hand flattened over her heart, she whispered, "That means more than I can articulate."

"I *will* get her back for you."

His ferocity must have appealed to her. She shivered, awareness sizzling in her gaze. "Dude. I think we just discovered the secret to my seduction. Do. Something. Nice."

She stepped into him. He stepped into her. Then she leaped into his arms, coiling her arms and legs around him, and he held on tight to his prize.

Their lips and tongues collided, and a loud thud registered. The revolver. He realized he'd dropped it, and tensed.

Vale had hoped to distract and disarm him? Perhaps. And he wanted to care, he did, but she tasted too good, and he relaxed into her, kissing her back, his rock-hard shaft like a heat-seeking missile, finding the cradle between her legs. He'd craved this every second of his absence—had craved *her*. Now, he was swept up in a wave of blistering arousal, all sense eradicated.

They strained together, her nails cutting into his shoulders. The pheromone...

He jerked up his head, severing the kiss. "Why don't I scent the pheromone?"

"I'm controlling it...barely. Now kiss me. Don't stop. Don't ever stop."

His desire was kindling, and hers was the match. Burning up, inside and out, he obeyed, kissing her harder, faster. His most primal instincts insisted he push her past the edge of control and *drag* the pheromone from her. Keep it from him? No! One way or another, she could cede every fiber of her being to him. He would own her...as she owned him.

He waited for panic to cool his ardor. No way would he ever willingly submit to a woman's claim. One second, two. Nothing. Still waiting... Not even a blip. The fire raged on, undisturbed.

"More," he snarled.

"Please!"

Vale nipped and bit his lower lip as he stalked forward, fell onto the bed and pinned her beneath him. Animal sounds rumbled in his chest when he tunneled his hands underneath her shirt to knead and tease her breasts, and madden them both.

"Let me see these beauties," he said, and tore off her shirt and bra. "So pink and pretty."

She arched her back, offering her body in supplication, and no competitor's surrender had ever been so sweet. But she wasn't a competitor to him right now. She was a woman, he was a man. Nothing more, nothing less.

Frenzied, he yanked his shirt overhead and tossed the material aside. Skin met skin, and he drew in a reverent breath. *Sublime.*

He sucked one of her nipples and pinched the other, until both were pleasure-swollen. The uninhibited and fervent way she responded to him would be forever etched in his mind, the mental file titled Best Moments of My Life.

Sliding her hands down his sides, she said, "Let's make us both a little more comfortable."

She clasped the hilt of a dagger and again, he was too aroused to care. If she wanted to stab him, he'd let her, as long as she continued kissing and touching him. But she simply dragged the blade from the sheath at his waist and tossed it to the floor.

Soon she'd disarmed him and as a reward for his cooperation, she opened the fly of his pants and wrapped her fingers around his aching shaft.

A strangled sound left him. If this kept up, he would blow. He needed to slow things down, to savor. Then she squeezed, wrenching another strangled sound from him, and all thoughts of slowing down vanished.

"I want this," she said, her tone beseeching.

"And I want to give it to you." There was a reason he'd decided to wait to penetrate her, he had only to remember it. *Think, think.*

He recalled the pheromone…a desire for control…

Control was overrated.

She released his length—*No!*—and pushed him to his back. Though he'd never allowed a woman to top him, suspecting the position would leave him vulnerable, he was mesmerized by Vale's innate sexuality, and offered no protest. She rose over him and straddled his hips, her breasts bouncing, locks of her hair playing peekaboo with those pretty pink nipples.

"I hated waking up without you," she admitted. As he watched, enraptured, she traced her little tongue over her palm and each finger. "I was shocked by how much I missed you."

"I missed you, too." He'd never slept beside a woman, had never *wanted* to. Until Vale. She stirred all the wrong desires in him—or finally all the right ones. "Couldn't return to you fast enough."

Relish sparkled in her eyes and a salacious smile tilted one corner of her mouth. She wrapped that damp hand around his shaft a second time and squeezed harder.

The rest of his thoughts fled, his mind a blank slate. With a bestial roar, he tore open the waist of her pants, shoved his hand under her panties and thrust two fingers deep inside her—groaned. She was hotter than flame, tighter than a fist and so perfectly wet.

Crying out, she arched her hips, sending his fingers deeper; her inner walls clenched to hold him inside. Then. That moment. Her lush, erotic scent filled his nose and lungs and fogged his head.

"Sex?" she beseeched, riding his fingers, moving faster and faster, while pumping his erection up and down.

Pressure built in his body. Pleasure seared him. So close to the edge. How much better would it be with his shaft buried in her heat?

Too intense to survive, surely. *Must finish in her hand.* He shouldn't null and void such a monumental decision while lost in the throes.

"Your climax," he said. "I want it. Give it to me."

The second he circled his thumb around her clitoris and pressed down, she erupted, screaming his name, her inner walls constricting.

Though her body went lax, she tightened her grip on him. Between panting breaths, she said, "Now give me yours."

There was no denying her. *He* erupted, his testicles drawing up, his next roar one of pure, undiluted satisfaction.

When he'd emptied himself, his *valina* collapsed on top of him, not seeming to care about the mess they'd made. Their hearts raced in unison, a long while passing before either of them calmed.

She nuzzled the hollow of his neck. "Next time you go hunting for Z, I'd love to go with you."

"I'll take you. *If* you're ready." Or not. Parting with her, even for a moment, held no appeal.

She didn't miss a beat. "Then let's get me ready."

"Yes. Let's." His gaze slid over her, primitive male possessiveness overtaking him once again. "But first, we bathe."

CHAPTER TWENTY-THREE

Fresh and clean, newly satisfied and clothed in workout wear, Vale stretched in preparation of the upcoming combat lesson. Now that her sexual hunger had abated, her mind was able to motivate elsewhere, and replayed the dream she'd had while Knox pursued Nola.

In it, Celeste had sat before a crackling firepit, a shirtless Gunnar beside her, his chest littered with angry gashes, souvenirs from a battle with Ronan and Petra.

"Watch me," Gunnar had said, and held the sword hilt against his forehead, the metal extending over his torso.

Celeste had said, "Perhaps you shouldn't do this. The repercussions…"

"I've already paid the price," he'd replied. "Now I will reap the reward." The sword had begun to liquefy, silver droplets adhering to his skin.

He'd screamed in pain, and Vale had lurched upright, quaking, reaching for Knox—only to find the bed empty, the sheets cold. Her mind had become a hamster wheel, spinning, spinning. *What had pained Gunnar so horribly? What kind of reward was that? What were the repercussions Celeste had mentioned?*

Eventually, worry for Knox's safety had driven Vale out of bed. She'd decided to use the supplies she'd purchased at the party store to decorate the bunker for a surprise party. And thank goodness she had! For the rest of her life, she would remember the look he'd given her. One of shock and awe, soul-deep gratitude and agonized hope. A look she'd seen in her own reflection the first time Carrie had given her a hug.

"You ready?" Knox asked.

"Here's hoping." She shook the dream out of her head and faced off with him in the center of the bunker.

He held out Celeste's sword.

Vale's cheeks flushed with surprised pleasure. Humbled, she accepted the offering. The hilt fit her grip, as if made for her alone.

"Thank you, Knox." She angled her wrist and twirled the blade, entranced as the silver glinted. But the more she twirled, the more the sword's weight screwed with her balance and reflexes, until she nearly gutted her tutor. Oops. "Sorry, sorry."

His expression had blanked. "Do you have memories of Celeste's training?" His tone had changed, too, sharpening.

What the heck? "Some, but I'm not sure those lessons will translate to practical application."

"We'll find out."

He was going to make her sweat bullets, wasn't he?

They worked with the weapon, and though she tried, tried and tried again, she flunked poison activation.

"Dang it!" she said, and stomped her foot. "What am I doing wrong?"

"Nothing," he said. "Activation is supposed to be automatic. Your touch should be all that's needed."

Frick! "I get it. Other combatants absorb the power to activate their victim's weapon, not memories or innate abilities. I absorb memories and innate abilities, but not the power to activate my victim's weapons. I should have guessed. With synesthesia, there's always a catch."

He thought for a moment, nodded. "You might not be able to poison your opponents, but you can still remove their limbs. Let's continue your training."

For the next eternity, he pushed her harder than she'd ever been pushed. She'd expected hands-on training from a guy like him, but oh, wow, he had no mercy. Sweat bullets? How about grenades?

Somewhere between trying not to die from overexertion and *wanting* to die, she realized a disturbing truth. This was the way *Knox* had trained as a child, the poor darling.

Next he worked with her on hand-to-hand combat. How to make a proper fist. When to swing, when to block and when to dodge. How to use her lighter weight and smaller frame to her advantage, and what to do if someone grabbed her from behind or pinned her to a bed.

He was all business, never once making a pass at her. "You're weak," he said, taking her to the floor—again. His expression said *I'm disappointed in you.*

She thought she might prefer a dagger through the heart. "I don't require a reminder. What I need is a time-out," she said. Muscles she hadn't known she had ached.

"In battle, there are no time-outs."

"Too bad. If I don't get one, I won't be able to walk for a month." Or ever.

He pinched the bridge of his nose and heaved a sigh. "Look past your exhaustion."

Argh! "Give me a break, or I'm never making out with you again." A baseless threat. Probably.

"Attempting to control me with sex?"

"Yes!"

He blinked with a little amusement and a lot of amazement.

"You may rest for one hour, but you'll spend every minute crafting our plan of action, as promised."

Our, he'd said. Not *my*. "Agreed."

She lumbered to the table and plopped onto a chair, her limbs trembling with relief. She keyed up the laptop and, curious, did a news search on Colorado. The first article she read left her stomach churning.

"A car crashed into the coffee shop we visited," she said.

"And?"

"And witnesses say the truck came out of nowhere."

"Ah. A combatant opened a rift with the intention of injuring Ronan and Petra. More and more such incidents will occur in the coming months." He sat beside her and pressed his thigh against hers, as if he couldn't bear a lack of contact.

She understood. He was quickly becoming her favorite addiction.

Gotta do a better job of guarding against his allure, dummy! Their relationship wasn't a happily-ever-after in the making, and she had best remember that.

"I'd bet my savings Erik is responsible. He knows the world better than anyone else." The second article she teed up mentioned the dead bodies found in the Rockies, and how authorities were on the lookout for Valerina London, a person of interest. *Stomach cramp.* They'd included her picture.

She was officially a wanted woman. And not the way she'd always hoped.

"What's wrong?" He nudged her shoulder and almost… smiled? "Besides your lack of stamina, I mean."

"Ha-ha." *Do not to stare at him all dreamy-eyed.*

Okay, stop *staring at him all dreamy-eyed.* But how was she supposed to guard herself against this—a teasing Knox?

After she explained her dismay, he shrugged. Shrugged!

"Being hunted by authorities is a big deal," she told him.

"Not for you. In public, I'll conceal you with my shadows. No one will ever see you."

"That's great, wonderful. Except I can't be with you every second of every day." Or forever. "And I can't see when you use your shadows. I'm blinded."

"I'll help you kill Bane, then, and win his goggles. You'll be able to see through the shadows."

Go head-to-head with a real live Hulk? No, thanks. But someone had to do it sooner or later. "I can't activate weapons, remember?" What a bummer. "Maybe I'll cut and dye my hair to—"

"No," Knox bellowed. Then, more calmly, he grumbled, "You won't be changing anything about your appearance. Promise me. You are perfect just the way you are."

A secret part of her thrilled. *He likes me just the way I am.* Another part of her worried. "You wouldn't want me if I looked different?"

"I'll want you regardless of hair color or anything else. What I do not want is my inability to protect you to force a change."

All of her thrilled. "You told me to do whatever is necessary to survive. If I'm captured, I'll be locked away. I'll miss check-in and get axed by Seven."

"If you're captured, you can become intangible."

"I tried when I was imprisoned, but couldn't do it. Think about it. Celeste was an expert, but she couldn't ghost through ice. Which means the ability is limited—" The answer slammed into her. "Yes! Limited. Some things are impenetrable. Ice, metal. Vine. Rope." What else?

And dang it, maybe she should keep the torrent of info to herself.

He said, "You can use the Rifters to—"

"Let me stop you there. If Rifters were infallible, you guys would have gotten out of the ice a lot sooner. Plus, cops would've confiscated my Rifters before they'd locked me away."

A muscle jumped in his jaw. "By the time I'm finished with you," he said, his tone hard and uncompromising, "you'll be able to escape any situation." He motioned to the laptop with a tilt of his chin. "Teach me how to use this…whatever it is."

He was helping her, despite the danger to his game, so she would help him, despite the danger to hers.

Techy wasn't her favorite language, but she imparted what knowledge she could. "Erik has a team of people to monitor and even manipulate what's posted. At some point, everyone will acclimate to modern life, and he could use social media to lead players into an ambush." Unless he'd meant what he'd said, and hoped to stop the war in its tracks.

Trust no one.

As Knox played online, researching different types of weapons, watching movie clips on YouTube to "better understand how your people fight," she studied his maps of ancient Earth.

"I want Kevlar," he announced. "I think Erik wore a version of it when last we fought, and it's better than what I have. I also want a rocket-propelled grenade launcher. *Two* rocket-propelled grenade launchers."

Lord save me. "So acquiring weapons outside the war isn't against the rules?" Before she finished asking, Celeste's memories supplied the answer.

"Once we are on another realm, we can utilize any weapons we find."

"Military-grade gear will be tough to get."

"We need to find a way. Erik must have an incomparable arsenal by now."

"Yeah, he has a huge tactical advantage against all of us. Which makes killing him the ultimate coup." She tapped her fingers against her chin. "If I absorbed his memories, I could find out everything he's done and confiscate his stash. The rod would be rendered useless, though. Hey, speaking of, why didn't

Cannon freeze everyone? And what if Erik freezes us at the next Assembly of Combatants?"

Knox stiffened, confusing her—until an answer clicked. He didn't want her gaining any other abilities to use against him. *Ouch.*

"Mark my words," he said. "Erik will claim he let us go, but he'll be lying. That's what combatants do. I think the realm's atmosphere has heated considerably over the centuries, and the rod can no longer produce unmeltable ice. As for Cannon, I suspect he chose the rod for its ability to control weather anywhere, anytime. I also suspect the rod wasn't able to freeze us until Erik modified it somehow. But you're right about one thing. Erik must be eliminated, his resources utilized."

"How do we get to him?"

"I could open a rift directly into one of his properties, but he knows I can do it, probably *wants* me to so that he can execute an ambush."

She wiggled her brows. "It's not an ambush if you know about it." Amid Knox's protests, she claimed the laptop. "All right. Tell me everything you know about the players, every single one of them, and I'll tell you what I know. Then we'll come up with our plan."

At first, he was hesitant. The more he spoke, the more he got into it. She typed and typed and typed until she thought her hands would detach from her wrists. By the time she stopped, a 3D board had taken shape in her head, peppered with the names and abilities.

Closing her eyes to concentrate, she moved the warriors around, studied the trickle-down effect, whose death would impact whom, and which skills, powers and weapons had widespread impact.

"Him," she said with a nod. "Colt of Orfet. The ring that breaks apart to become hundreds of microbots. Is it his weapon or an innate ability? He controls the bots?" His own mini-army.

"Weapon. And yes. At the Orfetling's command, the metal bug-like devices burrow under skin and rip through organs."

Celeste's memories rose to fill in some of the gaps. "A rumor suggests the bots are spies and trackers."

Knox sat up straighter. "Where did you—or Celeste—hear such a rumor?"

"Ranger first, then Gunnar confirmed." And duuude. Suddenly she felt as if the little critters were crawling inside her mind, clocking her every thought. "If we control the bots, we can peg everyone at the next assembly, and do a little spying and tracking."

"Of course, but the bots could be used against us. As you said, an ambush isn't an ambush if you know about it. Someone could purposely lead us astray."

True. Which was probably the reason Colt hadn't spied. Ugh! Unless he *had*.

Knox's eyes narrowed. "Still. I want the ring. Colt is weaker than Ronan, and he'll be easier to take down. But he's a hider, and harder to stalk. He only reveals himself at assemblies."

"Not always. He met with Celeste once or twice. At the time, she was working with Ranger, and he wanted the ring, too. They planned to kill Colt together."

"Can you take me to their meeting spot?"

"I think so, yes."

He reached out, patted her hand. "Vale," he said, the cadence of his voice sexual, dazzling. "Your help has been invaluable. Thank you."

Praise from Knox? Ear porn! "You're welcome."

He leaned toward her, inch by agonizing inch; by the time they were only a whisper away, she was panting. So was he. His pupils expanded, a dark storm cloud listing across a morning sky.

"Here." He cleared his throat, straightened and held out a fist. His fingers opened to reveal a set of glittering Rifters. "These are yours."

Warm shivers, streams of excitement. "Thank you."

Silent, Knox slid one crystal after another over the proper fingers, and dang if it wasn't proposal-like...which kinda sucked because a part of her kinda sorta wished it was an *actual* proposal.

Marry a man she'd known less than a week? Hitch her forever-after wagon to her potential murderer? Hardly. But come on! She was already playing house with Knox.

Well, so what? They were part of a team, messing around, sharing secrets and pasts...maybe even falling for each other, even though they were doomed. The immortal version of Romeo and Juliet.

The more Vale liked him, the harder it would be to end him. And to save Earth, she had to end him.

"What's wrong?" he asked, caressing her cheek with two of his knuckles.

She'd made a mistake when she'd offered him an alliance, hadn't she? They needed to split up. *Soon.* In a day, maybe three. And no more making out.

She swallowed a whimper, pasted on a smile. "I've got my Rifters now. What could possibly be wrong?"

He frowned, radiating confusion, but let the subject drop. Standing, pulling her to her feet, he said, "Come. Rather than continuing today's training, we'll weapon-up and head to the location you mentioned."

Entering the real world for the first time as a wanted woman... actively hunting a man she hoped to kill... Vale shuddered. But she'd decided to go all in, so she would do both of those things and more.

As Knox strapped different weapons from neck to toe, she anchored Celeste's sword to her back and just breathed. In, out. In, out.

"Ready?" he asked.

"Ready."

He didn't open a rift, but peered at her expectantly. "Are you prepared to fight if it proves necessary?"

Nod. "I am."

"You're prepared to fight both immortals and mortals?"

"Yes." *One day, victory will be mine.*

Don't cry. Don't vomit.

"Are you prepared to *kill* an immortal?" he asked.

"I am. I won't think about it, I'll just act." The more combatants she killed, the more abilities she would acquire, and the more of an advantage they—*she* would have.

"When is the only acceptable time to strike at an opponent?" he asked.

"Wait. You're *quizzing* me about today's fighting lesson?"

"Just answer the question, Vale."

"You mean, answer the *trick* question. The only acceptable time to strike an opponent is *always*."

The corners of his lips twitched, enchanting her. Maybe she could stay with him a few weeks. "If you get into trouble...?"

"I'll shout for you?"

"Are you asking or telling me?"

"Telling," she said. Jeez.

"You'll shout for me unless...?"

"It's a matter of life and death. Then I'll run and hide, and wait for your signal to return."

He gifted her with a smile of approval, and it lit his entire face, leaving her dizzy. "Is kicking a man while he's down acceptable?"

Knox of Iviland smiled at me. Me! And it was glorious. "Kicking a man while he's down is *encouraged*," she replied. "Don't worry, I've got this."

"Very well. Open a rift."

"Me?"

"You." His eye sockets darkened as he summoned shadows to conceal them as well as the bunker. Darkness rose from the ground and tucked around their bodies, shielding everything but her eyes.

Oddly enough, the darkness comforted her.

Mimicking Celeste's memory, Vale pictured the location she wanted to visit and clinked the Rifters together. Vibrations. A surge of power. She reached out to swipe her fingers through the air.

The instant she'd completed the act, she had Rifters' remorse. "The article! What if I'm taking us to the middle of a highway and we're hit by a car?"

Knox shrugged. "We heal, and try again."

Roughly twenty feet away, the air ripped apart at an invisible seam, creating a rift that widened, bit by bit, as if two parts of a curtain were being pulled apart, revealing...more shadows.

The heavenly scent of lavender and—she sniffed—a hint of the pheromone drifted through the bunker, but it wasn't coming from her. And it was stronger than the one she usually produced.

Her cells seemed to catch fire, burning for Knox's. Leave him? No, never. She wanted him, *needed* him, all of him. Mouth... fingers...shaft. Yes, oh yes. Now!

"Valina?"

"It's not me," she said, her panties soaked. "What do you see?"

"A lavender field. Sunlight. No people."

Confused—and more aroused by the second—she unsheathed her sword and marched forward, keeping pace beside Knox.

Once she'd bypassed the shadows, she was greeted by the lavender. A lovely sight. Dappled sunlight paid tribute to purple petals, pollen dancing on a warm breeze.

On one side of the field was a stretch of dewy emerald trees. On the other side was a rolling hill that led to a quaint two-story cottage. Something about it prodded at her mind...what, what? Argh! The answer eluded her.

The gorgeous scenery offered nothing in terms of shelter or protection from other combatants. But then, Celeste and

Ranger had preferred to meet in the tunnel *beneath* the field, the combatants she'd brought here completely unaware of the other man's nearness.

Dang. How many players had she bagged and tagged?

"How did the field survive the passage of time without an immortal guard?" Vale asked.

"Celeste could have used the pheromone as a measure of protection. One whiff, and no one would want to harm these flowers."

Good point.

Head fogging…stripping away any fear for tomorrow, leaving only desire for today. This man enthralled her, causing arousal to boil her blood. His shoulders were so wide, the sinew in his torso a path for her tongue, his muscle mass bulging but also lean, his waist trim. In a word: delicious. She wanted to strip him and watch as sunbeams stroked his skin. Wanted him to strip her in turn and press her back against a soft bed of foliage… then plunge into her aching core as the sweet scent of lavender enveloped them.

Yes! *Give me.*

"Something's wrong. Very, very wrong. But also very, very right…" A single step brought her body flush against Knox, her breasts smashing into his chest. Every time she breathed, her nipples rasped against him. Mmm. She purposely breathed faster.

He fisted her hair to angle her face the way he liked it, and leaned down, only to pause just before contact. "*Eyaer*…danger." His eyes narrowed as he looked over the top of her head. Somehow he had enough strength to release her and step back.

She swallowed a groan of disappointment and spun away before she jumped him. Planting her weight on her heels, she analyzed the field once again. A memory unfurled…

When the ice cave came down, Celeste was stabbed in the ensuing fray. Ranger, a gorgeous male with hair the same baby blue as a morning sky and eyes as white as summer clouds, had scooped her up and brought her here, where she'd doctored the flowers with her pheromone at the start of the war. Long before she'd ever hooked up with Ranger or anyone else.

So, basically she'd roofied combatants.

Her blood, Vale realized. Celeste had doctored the flowers with her blood, letting it saturate the soil, absorb into the roots, in essence making the flowers immortal; they survived, no matter the weather, no matter the passage of time. And as Knox had said, no one had ever wanted to destroy them.

Once, Knox had mentioned mystical ink and its invasion of his cells. She suspected the pheromone had worked the same way, fusing with Celeste's cells, and now Vale's and the flowers.

As soon as Celeste had healed from her injuries, she'd left Ranger sleeping in bed and returned to the ice mountains to meet up with Gunnar, the man she truly loved—

Whoosh!

A large shadow swooped over the field, startling Vale from her thoughts. The blue-haired man from her memory flew closer. Ranger, who hailed from some kind of cloud realm, wore a white shirt, matching pants and boots with little wings on the heels. He stretched out his arm, as if reaching for her...and a stream of fireballs shot from his fingertips.

Those flames hit like bombs, exploding around them. The heat! Sweat poured as she backed away.

The smoke should have aided Knox's shadows, but instead chased them away, leaving both he and Vale out in the open. He nocked an arrow, the only one he carried, and released it.

The projectile soared after the other man, a happy whistle ringing out. Ranger dodged to avoid injury, arcing up, angling down, then spun to refocus on Knox.

The arrow returned.

"This is a life-and-death situation. Go," Knox shouted at her. And then he ran from her, putting distance between them.

Ignoring Vale, Ranger darted after him. Dodging, ducking,

avoiding the arrow. Had he learned about Celeste's death? Had he loved her? He must have.

He hurled a second stream of fire at Knox, who sidestepped. Yes! Except, the second inferno joined forces with the first, burning a trail straight toward her man. Oh, no. He wasn't getting hurt on her watch. They would part soon enough. Until then...

Vale stomped out the flames before they had a chance to lick off a layer of Knox's skin. To her horror, Ranger unleashed a third stream. Knox managed to evade it, too, and tossed a dagger, the blade whipping end over end.

Ranger crouched midair, executing a half turn. He would have avoided injury altogether if the blade hadn't passed him and boomeranged off the arrow, returning to slice through a wing on a boot. The arrow chased him as he fell, slicing through his chest and coming out his back.

Down, down, he tumbled. *Thud!* Upon impact, the ground shook. Was he alive? Dead? Surely multiple bones had shattered. New fires erupted around him, dark smoke curling through the air.

Sword in hand, Vale raced forward. She wished her reasons were 100 percent altruistic, but they weren't. She wanted to save Knox from another attack, yes, but she also wanted to hijack Ranger's ability. If she could find a way to combine the pheromone with the smoke...

I'll be unstoppable.

The arrow returned to Knox. He caught it as he raced toward the fallen man, just like Vale. He wanted the boots for himself. Boots Vale would not be able to use, ever. Maybe he also wanted to prevent her from strengthening, able to produce streams of fire from her fingertips. Something he would never be able to do.

Remember, hesitation can get you killed.

Ranger lumbered to his feet, blood pouring from his chest

wound. His blood was a darker blue than his hair and as lovely as it was obscene. Spotting Vale, he stretched out his arm. At the tips of his fingers, flames sparked.

Almost there...just a few more yards...

"No," Knox shouted. "Don't do it."

A demand for Ranger, who was in the process of drawing back his elbow, intending to hurl more flames? Or Vale?

Didn't matter. At the last second, Ranger turned and flung the flames at Knox. Contact. Knox bellowed with pain as he ripped off his flaming shirt.

Vale nearly tripped over her own foot.

Knox kept running, never slowing, and tossed another dagger at Ranger, cutting through the man's wrist as he turned and prepared to throw another fireball. This time, Vale would be the target.

So close...

"No, Vale. No," Knox shouted again.

There!

No time to ponder, or debate the wisdom of her actions. *Don't think, just act.* Vale swung her sword.

CHAPTER TWENTY-FOUR

Knox paced, frantic with worry. Vale was sprawled on the bed, thrashing as little fires flickered at the ends of her fingertips—fires he had to put out before she torched the entire bunker. If she wasn't mumbling incoherently, she was screaming in pain and terror.

At first, he'd been furious with her. She'd stolen a kill from him, taking the flying boots out of the war and gaining a new power to use against everyone, even him, *after* he had commanded her to stand down.

Then he'd thought, *Betrayed! She'll do anything to win.*

But it hadn't taken long for the truth to crystalize. He was a hypocrite. *He* would do anything to gain more power and win. How could he blame another combatant for doing the same?

And really, he couldn't have it both ways. He couldn't want Vale well able to protect herself, then strip her of power at every opportunity.

But as one day bled into another and she remained trapped in her mental hell, he wished he'd stopped her for another reason entirely. Ranger was one of the oldest combatants, and Vale was incredibly young. *Too* young to handle the psychological and emotional onslaught she'd absorbed.

Helplessness nearly suffocated Knox. He tried to occupy his mind by studying Gunnar's sword, but more than once Vale opened her eyes and commanded, "Kill me. Let me join them."

Them? Ranger's family?

Knox *needed* Vale to recover. Somehow, he'd grown to trust her more than he'd ever trusted another. He liked the way her mind worked, the way she considered the consequences and rewards of every action. She'd become a valuable asset, teaching him about her realm and helping him strategize ways to win the war.

They hadn't known each other long, but timing hardly mattered. All the greats in his life, good or bad, had happened in moments. The moment he'd created a baby. The moment he'd met his child for the first time. The moment he'd taken an arrow for a woman he was supposed to kill.

"No," she mumbled. The tips of her fingers crackled with flames again, and Knox lurched over to put them out, uncaring when multiple blisters popped up on his palms. "Nooooo."

Hate this!

"*Valina*. Sweetheart." He eased beside her, ensuring his hip pressed against hers as he gently traced his knuckles over her jawline. Contact with her wasn't just a want, but a need. "You must wake up. We've got to get you ready for the next check-in." He had so much to tell her, so much to teach her.

If he had to carry her to the assembly—which he would do if he had to—other combatants would view her as an easy mark.

Wouldn't they already?

And if not an easy one, a necessary one. When they learned Vale absorbed the memories and abilities of her victims—something no one else could do—they would stop at *nothing* to take her out.

She leaned into Knox's touch, her need for contact just as des-

perate as his. Such soft, luminous skin. Such a beautiful, brave
woman. How had he ever considered her of a lower class than
the "ladies" of Iviland? The circumstances of her birth meant
nothing. Rich or poor, princess or peasant, she possessed more
grace and honor than anyone he'd ever met.

"Hurts," she cried, and Knox jerked his hand away, hating
the thought of causing her pain. "Can't go on like this."

He wasn't to blame. So why wasn't he eased?

Her cries grew louder, more frantic, and he cupped her jaw
with more force. "I'm here, *valina*." The sun that warmed. She
had warmed him, hadn't she? For the first time in his life, his
mind was filled with something other than war. "I need you to
fight these memories."

"Nooooo," she screamed. "Come back to me."

Hate this. "Wake up for the girl, Nola. She'll suffer without
you, yes? You don't want that. Come back to her. Come back
to *me*. I'm your ally, and I'm right here." Waiting. Desperate.

"Hurts," she cried again.

{*Check-in nears. Wake her.*}

"I'm trying," he snarled. Deep breath in, out. He patted Vale's
soft, pale cheek. "I've had enough of this. You will fight Ranger's memories. Do you hear me? Fight!"

Fight!

Knox's ragged voice called to Vale, drifting on a cool breeze.
Despite the dark mire of her thoughts, she tasted the familiar
decadence of honeyed whiskey...smoke, so much smoke. She
got lost in it once again. And in the fires, so many fires, her
mind spiraling down a rabbit hole filled with memories she'd
never lived.

Jetha had been a peaceful paradise. Then armies from other-
realms had arrived. As battle after battle raged, Jetha was destroyed, just like Knox's Iviland. Resources were plundered,

cloud forests razed. Crystal clear oceans turned crimson as citizens and livestock were killed en masse.

More fires...

Ranger stood before the graves of his loved ones. A cherished wife, two beloved sons and a treasured daughter. He *yearned* for vengeance, to take what those other-realms valued most, and he believed he'd found a way. Something called the All War. As a combatant, he could prevent other realms from gaining new territories, and kill their best warriors in the process.

"Vale!"

Knox's voice again. More honeyed whiskey, with a dash of cream. Mmm. So good. She wanted more.

"Focus on me, *valina*. Fight to reach me."

Fight, yes. But even as she reached for him, an invisible chain shackled her ankles and dragged her back down, deeper into the hole. So much pain. So much determination.

Ranger had come to Terra for revenge. To his astonishment, he'd found a new reason to live. Celeste had awakened his deadened heart, and he'd *needed* her close, always and forever.

The feeling had faded whenever they'd parted, his sorrow returning, and he'd decided never to part from her again. He would do *anything* to bask in her, body and soul.

After breaking free of the ice, he'd saved her from certain death, whisking her to their special meeting spot, where he'd patched up her wounds and tucked her into bed, right next to him, where she belonged. Once again he'd experienced utter contentment...until he'd woken up and discovered she'd left.

Awaiting her return had been torture. But near the lavender field, he could smell her, lust for her, an endless fire in his blood.

Finally, another rift had opened. But the only thing he'd seen? A pair of hazel eyes that hadn't belonged to his beloved Celeste.

Who had dared invade his hideaway?

"Vale."

Knox's voice boomed inside her head. Yet again, she reached

for him. *Miss him so much. Our time together is limited. Can't waste another minute apart.*

"Vale!"

Louder this time. Reaching... A cool breeze returned, gusting through her, lifting her higher... The pit tried to suck her back down, but she continued rising.

"We have to leave," Knox snapped. "We have to leave *now*. We're due at the Assembly of Combatants. Now, Vale. Now!"

Higher still, the need to open her eyes, to stand up and walk, no sprint, no rift to the ice mountains too intense to deny.

Need to be on the mountains now, now—

NOW!

As if shocked with a defibrillator, Vale came awake in an instant. Ranger's memories receded to the back of her mind, realization settling in.

She was panting, drenched in sweat, but at least the intoxicating flavor in her mouth lingered. A clear film blurred her vision...blink, blink...a shadow took shape, looming above her. Blink, blink. Finally the film thinned, and she met the shadow's gaze.

Knox expelled a lengthy breath, his shoulders rolling in, and she frowned. What the heck had happened to him? Red rimmed his bloodshot eyes, bruises formed half-moons underneath them, and lines of tension framed them. He hadn't shaved in days, his beard stubble thicker and darker than usual. Welts covered his neck.

"Are you okay?" she asked, confused by the throatiness of her voice. Wait. Where was she? Definitely not the lavender field. A quick look around revealed she was inside Knox's bunker. And she was naked. "Did I faint after I killed Ranger? How long was I out?"

"I'm fine. And yes. You were out for almost two weeks. You're naked because you kept burning your clothes."

What! "Please tell me you're kidding about the timeline. And the clothes." She'd wanted the ability to shoot streams of fire, not the ability to turn her clothes to ash.

"I never learned how to kid. And now, we're out of time." He catapulted to his feet and rushed around the bunker, gathering clothing, strapping on weapons. "While you were out, I modified the six bullets in my revolver's cylinder. Upon impact, they'll produce spikes, causing more damage. When it reloads, the new bullets will be normal, so I'll have to put the spiked ones to good use. And I'll be taking Gunnar's sword, even though I haven't figured out what it can do."

He was babbling, probably to distract her from her weakened state, which was super cute, if macabre.

"Oh! I had a dream about his sword," she told him. "Gunnar and Celeste were alone. He was shirtless and wounded, and she said something about ramifications if he used the weapon on himself. He said he'd already paid the price, then pressed the hilt against his forehead and the blade against his chest. The sword just…melted, all on its own, and absorbed into his skin. He screamed in pain, and I woke up, so I don't know what happened next. I'm sorry."

Looking pensive, he said, "The metal liquefied, not the person. To heal him, perhaps? I've heard of other weapons with a similar trait… The ramifications…" His eyes widened and zoomed back to her. He peered at her with dawning horror.

"What's wrong?" she demanded.

"The *eyaer*…"

She waited for him to finish. His war instincts…what?

He took a step in her direction, stopped. Another step. His hands fisted. Then he leaped away as if she'd become toxic. "Doesn't matter," he croaked. "I won't be taking Gunnar's sword, after all."

"Why?" What was going on with him? If her head hadn't been swimming with dizziness, she was certain she could figure it out.

"I'll explain later. For now, we've got too many things to do."

"Right." Vale eased into a sitting position and inhaled, exhaled. As the dizziness ebbed at last, she caught sight of sheets littered with burn holes. Wait. "I did this?" she squeaked.

"Yes. You can create fire now. Up, up." He didn't wait for her to obey but tugged her to her feet. "We must join the assembly as soon as possible. Can't be late. Have less than an hour."

An hour? Dang.

Though she swayed, Knox dressed her. Bra. Panties. T-shirt over her head, arms through the sleeves. He bent down to yank a pair of pants up her legs. As he anchored her combat boots in place, she used his shoulders for balance.

Ugh. She felt like total crap.

"You have a choice," he said, holding up a coat. "Being warmish, or being cold and having better range of motion."

First assembly, first all-out brawl. The right outfit was imperative.

Vale remembered the crippling cold she'd experienced the last time she'd been in those mountains, but nervousness led her to croak, "Range of motion."

"Good choice." He tossed the coat aside and shoved a piece of fruit in her hand. "Eat fast."

All this rushing around made the nervousness worse. "I, um, need a moment," she said, and swallowed her first bite. The juice ran down her throat, mixing with the honey and whiskey, soothing irritated tissues.

"You've got half a moment." He kissed her forehead and gave her a little push toward the bathroom.

On the walk, she devoured the fruit, pleased when strength returned to her limbs. After brushing her teeth and splashing cold water on her face, she caught sight of her reflection and flinched. Tangled hair, tired eyes, chapped lips.

But a girl didn't need to look pretty to kick butt.

Reaching up to wipe a water droplet from her lashes, she noticed the tips of her fingers had turned black, and nodded with dread and satisfaction. Ranger's ability to create streams of fire—an ability Knox hadn't wanted her to have—now belonged to her. But there were plenty of complications.

I can do this. "You're not going to the assembly to make friends," she said aloud. "The other kids on the playground are bullies. They don't have to like you. They just have to die."

"Vale," Knox called. "If you are worried...just know that I'll do everything in my power to keep you safe."

What was she going to do with that man? He hadn't wanted her to gain a new ability, but he'd also saved her when she couldn't save herself, and he hadn't offed her when he'd had the chance. He would protect her, despite everything.

He was a hero and a villain rolled into one. But so was she.

"We must go," he said.

"Coming, I'm coming," she called back. One final glance at her reflection. *No mercy.*

When she emerged, Knox wasted no time, strapping Celeste's sword to her back.

"Thank you. For everything," she said. She owed him big-time. "Did you happen to grab Ranger's clothes or boots?" Even though she couldn't activate the boots, she felt drawn to them, just as she'd been drawn to the sword. And the clothes might be fireproof, considering they hadn't burned.

"They are in the alcove, but the boots are damaged, unusable. The clothes won't fit you, or conform to your body. Listen. I'd hoped to prepare you for what's to come but—" Dark curses spilled from him.

What *was* to come? Ranger's memories rushed to the surface, Celeste's hot on their trail. The two clashed, the battle sending sharp pains through Vale's head.

Knox grazed her cheeks with his thumbs, the action soft and tender, so at odds with the hardened man standing before her. For a moment, she wondered if *he* had absorbed some of Ranger's

fire-making skill, as well. He sparked little flames of desire inside
her. With a little stoking, each one could blaze into an inferno.

As her heart raced, he leaned down to brush the tip of his
nose against hers. When she clasped onto his shirt, clinging to
him, his eyelids turned heavy, and he dipped his hands to her
ass to pull her against his erection. If only those hands would
delve under the waist of her pants, slide forward and cup the
liquid heat now pooling between her legs...

Would he always arouse her so easily, so quickly?

"Focus on me, *valina*," he said. Blistering desire had turned
the words to sensual smoke.

"Yes. You." Beneath her hand, his heartbeat raced in time to
hers. Knox became the center of her world...

Knox, the man she craved but planned to leave.

She bit her tongue. *Is ditching him really what's best?*

She suspected...yes. Not today, maybe not tomorrow, but
soon. Soonish. He'd won four All Wars without a partner, for
good reason. Partners turned on you.

While she trusted Knox with her life—for now—that could
change in a blink, a breath, a second. Better to get out of this
before her desire for him developed fangs and a tail and morphed
into a beast she couldn't tame. Whatever *this* was.

First, they had to survive tonight's assembly.

Frick! Breath wheezed from her. What if they died tonight?
Not ready to die. Not ready to watch Knox *die.*

Moaning, Vale rose to her tiptoes and fed him a passionate
kiss. She gave him everything she had, but took from him, too.
And he let her do it, because he gave and took right back, kissing her with untamed ferocity, his tongue thrusting against hers.

He fisted strands of her hair, those calloused hands angling
her head. A habit he'd developed. One she loved. Helpless to do
otherwise, she surrendered her body utterly, fully.

With a growl, he tore his mouth from hers. Panting, he said,
"We must go."

Dismay prickled at the back of her neck. *Not yet, not yet.* "We're going to the ice mountains where we first met?" The pull hadn't lessened.

He gave a curt nod. "We'll rift nearby so they see us arrive together, then make our way to the prison rubble. For one hour, we'll be trapped inside a small clearing, surrounded by invisible walls, our powers and weapons deactivated while the Enforcer—Seven—communicates with the High Council."

One hour. Got it.

But he wasn't done. "Remember everything I told you about the other combatants, and guard your thoughts. Emberelle and Saxon can read your mind, and stop a blow before you deliver it."

Well. At least she wouldn't have to worry about freezing to death.

Wow. What a silver lining.

She could finally talk to Zion about Nola—

False. One, she couldn't trust him to impart truth. And two, she didn't want to confirm Nola's importance to her, encouraging others to use the girl as bait.

"Do not engage Bane unless he challenges you," Knox said. "But if you can, stab him. Maybe there's enough poison dried on your sword to stop him from transforming into a beast and shredding us like paper."

"If he's so strong in beast mode, why doesn't he just transform and kill us all?"

"He can't wear his goggles in beast form, and without them, he's vulnerable to light and easily blinded. I also suspect he has a secret agenda, that he wants this war to continue for an unknown reason. During the first four assemblies, he sat on the sidelines, yawning as others fought, daring someone to attack him. The three who accepted the invitation died badly."

"Peachy."

"In former wars, I killed the Adwaewethians last, because

they are excellent trackers, and they can slay multiple combatants at once, hurrying the war along."

She frowned. "A risky move. The more combatants they kill, the more their arsenals grow."

"Yes, but in my second war, I was anxious to return to Minka. For the others, I was anxious to win my freedom. This time, I'd hoped Zion would challenge Bane, and Bane would rip off his gloved hands. With you added to the equation, I think it's time to remedy the situation." He stroked his chin. "High emotion can trigger Bane's transformation, whether he wants to beast-out or not. But whatever you do, do not—I repeat—do *not* kill him. If you were to absorb the beast…"

Her blood flash-froze, her limbs quaking. "I can't overstate this enough, but I absolutely, positively do *not* want to morph into a dragon on steroids. Like, ever."

"For that matter," Knox added, "try not to kill anyone. You can't afford to drown in a new flood of memories."

She gulped. Fight, but don't kill. Stab Bane, but don't get mauled or eaten. There was too much room for error. "If I use Celeste's invisibility or intangibility, most people will blame your shadows, like Erik and Adonis did. Ranger's streams of fire are a different story. They'll realize I can absorb their abilities."

"They will." No sugarcoating. Not with Foxy Knoxie.

"I'll be target number one, won't I? More wanted than Erik."

He nodded, expression grim. "Until the assembly ends, no one will strike at us. But we won't be able to strike at others, either, no matter how badly they taunt us, or we'll be disqualified. And we don't want to be disqualified. Also, when the battle begins, don't think you have to fight everyone at once. The herd will thin. Some combatants will run off, and others will pursue. The ones who stay in the clearing are determined to take a head or two."

Was she ready for this? No. Did she have a choice? No, again. But that was life. "If Colt runs, we'll follow?"

"No. We're running, period. If an opportunity presents it-self on the way out of the clearing, I'll kill Colt. Or Carrick. Or both. But our objective is simple—fight our way out of the circle as quickly as possible. I'll hide you with my shadows as best I can. If you need to use your abilities in order to survive, use them, don't hesitate, and we'll deal with the fallout later."

"*If* I can use them while I'm jacked with adrenaline." The unpredictability of her skills sucked.

"If it's a matter of life and death, you can and you will because you must. Understand? Once we're far enough away from the combatants, I'll open a rift to an island hideaway. From there, we'll return to the bunker, recover from whatever injuries we received, *then* go after Colt."

"Have you ever run from an after-assembly party before?"

A muscle jumped under his eye. "No."

"And have you ever found Colt or Carrick outside of an as-sembly?"

Another grated, "No."

"Then you're not running tonight unless we're chasing Colt. Okay? All right? We're playing the long game here. To get Car-rick's dagger, you need Colt's ring."

Knox of Iviland would not die a slave.

Don't want him to die, ever.

"If we're not moving forward," she added, "we're falling be-hind."

Knox thought for a moment, nodded. "Very well. We'll chase Colt. You need only to survive—without making a kill—until we're home. I'll do the rest."

She leaned into him and pressed her forehead to his chest. "You're sexy when you go full he-man, you know that?" A flippant response tinged with hysteria, and a perfect display of the overinflated arrogance she'd cultivated as a teen, a protec-tive measure to safeguard her heart whenever she was forcibly ejected from a foster home.

He kissed the top of her head before sliding his knuckles along her jawline and lifting her head. Gaze earnest, he said, "Whatever happens, I will do everything in my power to protect you, *valina*. You will not die today."

She believed him. He was many things, but he wasn't a liar. "Thank you. I've got your back, too."

He hugged her close, currents of electricity bouncing between them, fueled by uncertainty and urgency.

It was time.

Tense and silent, he drew back, took her hand and opened a shadowy rift. Instantly, icy winds blustered into the bunker, making Vale's teeth chatter.

Head high, she marched through the doorway, side by side with Knox. The second they bypassed the curtain of shadows, mountains came into view. Her personal hell. Shards of ice danced on the wind. The sun was setting, golden rays illuminating an endless sea of white.

The rift closed, and Knox led her to the edge of a cliff, where they stood, surveying the war zone.

The last time she'd been here, she'd worn a coat and thermals, and hypothermia had almost killed her, anyway. Now she wore only a T-shirt and pants, but the cold wasn't nearly as biting. Immortality had its perks, she supposed.

But then, immortality also had its drawbacks. Soon she would be face-to-face with the people she was supposed to kill—the people determined to kill her. Vale looked down...down...and there they were. The other combatants. Mostly men, a few women. One black-robed Enforcer.

Everyone stood side by side, forming a circle, staring at each other and probably trash-talking. The last vestiges of the prison had been removed, the fractures Zion had caused with his gloves filled.

"Four combatants are missing," Knox said.

"Fingers crossed they're dead," she muttered, hating the cold-hearted person she was becoming.

Today's slogan: *I'm screaming on the inside.*

"When the battle begins, part of you will want to open a rift to evade the action. Don't," he instructed. "Others will follow you through it. You shouldn't open one until you're at least a mile away."

"Noted."

"Last piece of advice," he said, peering down at her. "I will remain beside you in the clearing, but I will be emotionally distant. I don't want Erik, Adonis and Rush—or anyone—to know what you've come to—" He pressed his lips together, and her heart threatened to burst from her chest.

He'd stopped himself from saying she meant something to him, hadn't he?

What do I mean to him?

She cleared her throat. "Don't worry. I'll give you the emotional stinky boot, too. For the good of our cause, of course. I'm sweet like that."

He lifted her hand to kiss her knuckles and her wrist, and she had to lock her knees to stop them from buckling.

"I've always liked your armor," he said.

A mere five words, and yet they meant more to her than any compliment about beauty or smarts. Those words told her Knox understood her in a way few others ever had. When times got tough, Vale London got snarky. A defense mechanism to help her cope. And he liked it.

"Knox," she said.

"Yes, *valina.*"

She patted his chest. "I like your armor, too."

A flare of joy illuminated his cobalt eyes, only to be extinguished by alarm. With a final kiss, this one on her lips, he let her go.

"I'm going to head down now," he said. "Follow directly behind me. Stay close."

"Wait. Shouldn't I delay my arrival? I don't want to show up right on your heels."

"One of the missing warriors could be out here, planning an ambush. I want you within range of me at all times."

Okay, then. *Right behind him it is.*

And oh, crap, soon she would be smack-dab in the middle of a Temple-of-Doom-type situation. This was real. This was happening.

Never let them see you sweat. Fake it till you make it.

He began his descent down the side of the mountain, and the fact that he trusted her at his back a true miracle.

Vale maintained a sickly distance. That was a thing, right? A healthy distance meant far away. Therefore a sickly distance meant close up, and dang it! Panic was making her stupid.

She tried not to let her mind wander to other inane details…

Her mind wandered.

Maybe Erik and his boys would think Knox broke up with her, maybe not. The odds were 50/50. Or 40/60. She was now a combatant, and Knox's distrust and disdain for his foes was notorious.

Potential problem: she couldn't hide the fact that she had the hots for Knox. Anytime she caught sight of him, her heart seemed to tap-dance to the beat of *hubba hubba*. And she couldn't cast blame. The guy exuded primal aggression, his muscles rippling with every movement.

No man had ever looked so dangerously delicious. Forget Lucky Charms. He was Lethal Charms.

Closing in on the warriors… Her limbs started quaking again.

One by one, her enemies turned to eye her up and down, and take her measure. Judging by their expressions, they found her lacking.

So what? Jerks! She would—

Electric pulses raced from the top of her head to the soles of her feet, startling her. At the same time, the ends of her fingers cooled, as if a switch had been flipped inside her. From ON to OFF. She'd just passed the invisible wall, hadn't she?

Now she was well and truly trapped.

Don't you dare freak out.

A tall, blond man with a wealth of tattoos smiled at Knox, his violet eyes glimmering with wicked humor.

She recognized him. This was the infamous Carrick.

He spoke in a language she didn't understand, but Knox clearly did. He turned as rigid as stone.

"How about you share with the rest of the class," she said, batting her lashes.

Carrick answered in kind, saying, "I told the murk I didn't realize this was bring your whore to work day."

"What makes you think we're sleeping together?" she asked with an easy tone. "And guess what, *whore* isn't exactly an insult to my way of thinking. You just implied I like sex and money. Big deal. I do." What did *murk* mean, though? "Oh, and good news. This whore is trolling for customers. Tonight is the grand opening of Vale's Little House of Slays, and you're all invited. I give good beheadings. Free of charge."

Snickers only egged her on, and she decided to take this opportunity to introduce herself properly. With an overconfident wave, she said, "Happy to be here and super-duper excited to get to know everyone a little better...before I kill you. Oh! BTW, Celeste and Ranger send their regards."

Gasps of disbelief abounded, and Knox gave her the look. Oops. Was she supposed to keep those details quiet? Had she just made herself an even bigger target?

Well, what other choice had she had? Predators preyed on the weak, and she had to appear strong.

Voices called out. "No way, no how."

"This little princess did *not* kill Ranger. There's just no way."

Yes, keep underestimating me. Please.

The one she recognized as Bane said, "I'm guessing Knox teed up the bodies and let the lil miss deliver the final blow."

She flipped him off and scanned the crowd, searching for the black-haired Zion. Dang, he was one of the missing. If he'd gotten killed, Nola could have gotten killed, too, and—

No! Vale wouldn't think that way or she'd break down.

Erik winked at her. Adonis and Rush eyed her with curiosity, and maybe a little regret that they hadn't taken her out while they'd had the chance.

Screw you, gentlemen.

A man with a whip entered the circle. Three missing.

Next came a man with green hair. Him—Colt, the one with the microbots. Their target. He kept his gaze on the ground, his expression blank.

Good guy? Bad guy?

Don't go there. She had a job to do.

A third male entered the circle, and conversations momentarily ceased. Zion. Finally. She stared hard, trying to read him, but his dark gaze purposely avoided her.

"You're the one who ran off with the other human, isn't that right, Zion?" The tall blond flashed another wicked grin. "Didn't you get the memo? You were supposed to bring her here for our enjoyment."

Zion crossed his arms over his chest. "Sorry I couldn't oblige. I killed her when I was done with her."

CHAPTER TWENTY-FIVE

Zion's announcement sent a shock wave through Knox. He wasn't sure how he found the strength to plant his feet and remain rooted in place, not committing cold-blooded murder.

{*Harness your rage. The girl's death doesn't matter.*}

The *eyaer*—Knox ground his teeth. Earlier, when Vale had told him about Gunnar's sword, his survival instinct had pretty much sighed with relief. The time had come. She'd outlived her usefulness, and she was no longer necessary.

The *eyaer* had demanded Knox kill her.

The instinct had wanted a way to sever ties with Ansel, and she had provided one. When she'd explained the healing properties of Gunnar's sword, Knox had realized how valuable and dangerous the weapon was, and how it could help him. That was why he'd left it in the bunker.

The *eyaer* operated on a subconscious level, picking up cues his mind missed. After predicting the likelihood of Vale joining the war, his instinct must have sensed her memory-stealing ability and guessed she would supply information that wasn't available any other way.

Information he hadn't yet unpacked to his satisfaction.

The ramifications she'd mentioned… They presented a whole new set of problems. Using Gunnar's sword to heal a wound, any wound, would bind Knox to the metal. If that bond proved stronger than the taint of slave ink, Ansel would no longer have power over him, but still Knox would be enslaved. Whoever owned the sword would control his actions.

Maintaining ownership of the sword would be imperative. If someone stole it from him, he might long for the days he'd served Ansel.

Can't risk it.

{Kill Vale. Soon. The danger of her ability outweighs the aid she offers.}

To the *eyaer*, nothing mattered more than Knox's survival. He just couldn't bring himself to hurt Vale.

He studied her. She had paled, horror seeping from every pore. Needing to comfort her, he reached behind her, under her shirt, and curled his hand on the waist of her pants. Holding on to her had the added bonus of preventing an attack against Zion.

When tears streamed down her cheeks, *he* took a menacing step toward the male. Very little had the power to break his *valina*, but the Taverian had found her weak spot.

Why had Zion killed a sick, innocent girl? And why had Bane fallen to his knees, thrown back his head, and roared up at the night sky, as if he mourned the girl's loss?

"Ohhhh. Z decided to play nasty." Emberelle grinned with chilling calculation. "It's about time."

Thorn said, "He's lying. I'd bet my soul on it."

"Brag about offing a mortal?" Bold of Mörder shook his head. "That isn't exactly something to lie about. There's no upside."

Lying. Yes. Zion had to be lying. He'd won three All Wars without slaying a female. Why start now?

"She told me not to believe Z, so I won't believe Z," Vale whispered, rocking back and forth on her heels.

Ignore your curiosity.

Impossible. Who was *she*?

Mind whirling, he watched the sun disappear behind a mountaintop. Above, green and purple lights flickered to life in the sky. Seven glided to the center of the circle and lodged his scythe in the ice, sparks spraying from the metal.

Check-in had officially begun.

Glowering at everyone, Knox took stock. One warrior was still missing. Union of Kerris, who possessed an ability to manipulate reality with illusions. He'd owned a belt that doubled the wearer's strength. Good riddance.

Now, only nineteen combatants stood between Knox and victory. Eighteen enemies, and a single ally.

Vale went quiet, lifting her chin and squaring her shoulders, displaying nothing but determination. Knox had never been so proud.

Bane breathed with great heaves, projecting dark rage at Zion.

"Who killed Union?" Emberelle asked.

Wind whistled, but no one spoke up. And no one wore the belt, which would have given the killer a major advantage.

"If he's trapped somewhere," Bold said, "he's disqualified. Seven will get the kill, the belt no longer up for grabs."

"Who killed Orion on Liberation Day?" Ryder of Belusova patted the motorized axes that hung from hooks at his waist. "Oh, yeah. I did."

"Forget the dead," Carrick said. "What are we going to do about our Terran challengers?"

Frost glinting in his beard, Erik glided forward, Cannon's rod clutched in his hand. Though Knox's translator told him that he'd spoken ancient Norse all those centuries ago, today the man used Vale's language, modern English. "This is your chance, your only chance, to join me. While you were trapped, I used my freedom to my advantage. The measures I've taken to ensure victory are vast. I've done things you can't imagine. Things you can't protect yourself against."

"And yet, we're still alive," Thorn said, spreading his arms wide.

Some warriors cheered. Others peered at the viking with interest. Fools. How could they not see the truth? Erik would gain their trust, then kill them when they least expected it. He had no king to command him, no reason to stop the war before a victor was declared.

With a humorless smile, Erik said, "If you want to live here the rest of your days, if you hate your realm for forcing you to fight and threatening your loved ones, you will cease killing and ensure a winner is never declared. If you want to win the war so your realm can enslave mine, I will come for you, and I will defeat you."

Most of these warriors had family members awaiting their return. Like Knox, those warriors would stop at nothing to emerge victorious.

"You know nothing about the High Council." Ronan's scathing tone mimicked the one inside Knox's head. "Frozen, we were unable to communicate with our rulers. An unprecedented event. After five hundred years, the council sent a whole new crop of combatants here. *Their* All War hasn't ended, either."

What!

Vale's small, delicate hand settled between his shoulder blades as questions assaulted him. Where were the other warriors now? Who had survived? Another Iviland slave might be here, alive and well, even now.

When and where did the second group assemble? What powers and weapons did the survivors possess? How could Knox guard Vale from a threat he couldn't identify?

Would the High Council decide to combine the two All Wars, or opt to wait until both wars had a victor, then pit the two against each other?

"You lie," Saxon of Lassistan spat. When his ability to read minds was deactivated, he was more suspicious than most. "A favorite pastime of your race."

"No," Luca of Graeland said. "He doesn't lie about this. I was told the same. Currently there are nine survivors of the second war."

"Who? Give us names," Petra demanded.

"I only know a new realm was added to the Alliance sometime before the second Terran war kicked off. It's called Llura, and their representative is more dangerous than any of us." He added, "But the entire group went silent years ago, along with their Enforcer."

A small, smug smile lifted the corners of Erik's lips. "They went silent because I imprisoned them. And the Llurian is just as dangerous as claimed." Amid gasps of shock, he said, "When I heard rumors about warriors who mysteriously appeared in the west part of the North Atlantic Ocean—"

"The Bermuda Triangle?" Vale gasped out.

"—I captured and interrogated one," he said. "As soon as I learned about the second All War, I apprehended the rest in ways only I can." His smile held a thousand secrets. "They won't escape unless I free them. Their war won't interfere with ours."

Some soldiers paced, each lost in their own thoughts. Minutes ticked by, one after the other, each soldier lost in their own thoughts. The only thing that was certain? The coming bloodbath.

Vale masked her trepidation, frustration and rage. She wanted Zion splayed out on the ground, her boot compressing his throat, the tip of her sword resting between his legs.

She would demand answers about Nola, and he would provide them, or he would hurt.

Who was she kidding? She would hurt him regardless.

He was still standing only because she suspected he'd lied to protect the sick Nola. Her sister had warned her. *Do not believe Z.* Finally the text made sense. But Vale *needed* confirmation, and soon, before her nerves razed her.

Waiting for the melee to start had to be worse than the actual melee.

Vale clashed gazes with Pike of La Fer. He stared, which was creepy enough. Then he blinked. Had a milky film just slid over his irises?

He was tall, muscled, golden from head to toe, and absolutely stunning, but he radiated pure hate. For all she knew, he'd lusted for Celeste like so many others.

Knock, knock.

Who's there?

Celeste's lovers.

Celeste's lovers who?

Celeste's lovers want you dead.

Knox stepped in front of Vale, claiming Pike's attention. A single action, and yet he'd completely undone their efforts to appear unattached.

Who was she kidding? No one had bought the pretense.

Head a little higher, Vale faced Colt of Orfet. He was shirtless, and she noticed an iridescent tint on his shoulders and arms. Scales? On his right hand, he wore the ring he used to communicate with his ruler. On his left, the ring comprised of microbots. It was silver with a bulbous center.

"Fifteen minutes till showdown," Knox whispered.

How could he tell? Her trepidation worsened, her knees quivering. *So much at stake.*

"Time is running out," Adonis announced, and she tasted cinnamon and cloves. "I have joined Erik's roster. You would be wise to do the same."

Two warriors agreed. Bold, who possessed a hammer capable of shattering bones with a single strike, and Ryder, the one who'd killed Orion.

Vale knew Ryder had a nifty device he could use to be in two places at once, fighting up close *and* at a distance.

"No others?" Erik asked, and the flavor of salted caramel over-shadowed the cinnamon and cloves. "I admit, I expected more."

"We are not fools," Bane said, his tone deceptively casual. *He* tasted like butterscotch with bite.

Soon, she was going to have to stab him.

Erik looked at Vale, one black brow arched in question, and she shook her head no. If he was telling the truth, he intended to push a pause button, nothing more. What would happen if the High Council got sick of waiting and kicked off a third AW, or sent their Enforcers to invade? Better to have a definite outcome than an uncertain future.

He shrugged, all *Your loss, sugar tits.*

"You'll never halt the war. But I'll help you take out the murk and his female, your greatest opposition." Emberelle's voice reminded Vale of frosted strawberries, until one tang mixed with the others. She cringed.

The pale beauty had secured a pair of wrist cuffs from the one named Lennox, and Vale really, really wanted them. Because she couldn't activate them, Knox was the better choice. If they could reverse time in short bursts, as suspected...

They could right any wrong they inadvertently committed.

"You'll have to get in line." Rush directed a patronizingly sweet smile at the fairylike woman. "I'm going to rip off the murk's head and display it on a spike as a lawn ornament."

Petra batted her lashes at the pair. "I'll let you stab the murk after I decapitate him."

"Wow," Vale mumbled to Knox. "Your antifan club is super passionate."

He shrugged, unconcerned. "It's a gift."

Was he even a little nervous, or just an expert at hiding it? "What does *murk* mean?"

Now he stiffened. "It's a derogatory term used for those who control shadows, derived from the word *murky.*"

"Dude. Immortals are *so* mature," she said with enough volume to catch the attention of everyone around her. "What?" she demanded. "You want a piece? Come and get it."

The taunt left her mouth before she could stop it.

Thankfully, no one took her up on the offer—yet.

"Ten minutes." A whisper, Knox's honeyed whiskey obscuring the other flavors.

How the heck was he keeping time? Her mind was too busy whirling with questions, fears, hopes, ideas and everything in between.

"I feel so *Lord of the Flies*." Her heart raced. *Remember, a good business owner adheres to a plan. A great business owner adapts to change.*

Be the coffee bean.

"You will give me your attention." Seven's husky timbre boomed through the mountains, eerie and reminiscent of sex, gravelly, like music, but also like screams. "The High Council has decided."

Shivers rushed down Vale's spine. Iced vanilla vodka invaded her mouth.

A bomb could have exploded in the clearing, but she doubted the players would have budged. They watched the Enforcer with dread.

"Your war will continue as is," Seven said. "If combatants from the second war are found before a winner is crowned, they'll join you. Representatives who hail from the same realm will compete against each other, just like everyone else. If combatants from the second war are found *after* a winner is crowned, it will not change the outcome. Those warriors will be returned to their realms."

Silence, a whistle of wind.

"Five minutes," Knox said softly.

Steady. Control your reaction. Other warriors began to prepare, unsheathing their weapons. There was a coil of whip, and different size swords. Daggers. Guns of every caliber. A stun gun of some sort. Metal gloves different from Zion's, with links that ran the length of the wearer's fingers, and ended in claws.

Smiling with anticipation, Domino lifted a shield and banged his fist against the center.

Vale unsheathed Celeste's sword, the tips of her fingers burning. Knox kept his hands free, his attention laser-focused on Emberelle. Yes, the woman had threatened him, but come on! They had another target in mind.

Unless he found her attractive?

Fairy-girl is going down.

"In addition," Seven said, and groans abounded. "When the second group of combatants disappeared, the High Council sent a third to a place called Antarctica. They are still active, and their war will join yours at the next assembly."

More men and women to fight. Great!

Erik's brows drew together with confusion, as if he couldn't compute what he'd heard. "How many warriors are left?"

"You will discover the answer at the next assembly," Seven replied.

"Four minutes," Knox intoned, unfazed by everything he'd learned.

Different slogans began rolling through Vale's mind.

Blood is the new black.

All War: You're going to lose your head.

My boots are made for stomping—your butt.

How many players would converge on her? On Knox? At least three immortals had stated their desire to end her man first. What if Vale inadvertently distracted him?

Can't let myself distract him.

"Three," Knox said.

Okay. Vomiting wasn't a possibility, but a probability. *Keep it together.* Tremors rocketed in intensity and collected in her joints. Though she wanted to appear strong and confident, she might have to settle for *conscious.*

Would this be her last day on earth? A day of blood, pain and failure?

"Two minutes."

Deep breath in, out. No matter what, she would give this her everything. She wouldn't curl into a ball and cry until it was all over, and she wouldn't hesitate to do what needed doing.

She studied the placement of each player, mentally plotting a course to Colt, a 3-D map forming in her head. Four steps ahead, dodge left, three more steps, shift right, four more steps, contact.

And Bane… She couldn't go after Bane *and* Colt, just like Knox couldn't go after Carrick and Colt. And just like Knox, she had to make a choice. Colt won. She wasn't sure her sword would work on the beast-man, anyway. Next time, though, she would make sure she was standing next to Bane during roll call. And she would pre-poison her blade with earth-made toxins.

Gulp. First, she had to survive.

Knox popped the bones in his neck. "One minute."

She began to wheeze.

"Fifty-nine seconds. Fifty-eight. Fifty-seven."

As he quietly counted down, her tremors upped in intensity.

"Forty-three. Forty-two."

The best pep talk she could currently manage: *Don't die.*

"Twenty-nine. Twenty-eight."

The Enforcer lifted his scythe and, like a ghost, seemed to float away from the combatants. He stood off to the side. Vale's knees knocked together. Her lungs constricted, making breathing more difficult.

"Twelve. Eleven. Ten."

Run! Flee! Before it's too late.

No. You must go after Colt.

"Three. Two."

One.

"Happy warring," Seven said.

Whoosh. G-force gales charged with raw aggression blustered through the clearing, but none of her adversaries reacted.

This was the calm before the storm.

Then, with his gaze locked on Emberelle, Knox palmed his revolver and—

Whoa! At the last second, he'd repositioned and shot Erik six times. A savage act. Merciless. Knox went for the eyes, nose and throat, then put two in the Viking's heart. The only other earthling collapsed, out for the count, but not dead.

Ding, ding. Suddenly war cries pierced the night. Footsteps stomped, bodies slammed together and metal clinked against metal.

Happy warring indeed.

CHAPTER TWENTY-SIX

Pained grunts, groans and bellows of rage. Chaos all around. Skin and muscle split. Blood spurted, and not all of it was red. Different species meant different body compositions.

Adonis laughed as he hacked through the crowd.

Knox fought the compulsion to follow him and win the Horn of Summoning, as Ansel had ordered him to do, should the opportunity present itself. This wasn't the right "opportunity," which was the only reason he was able to focus elsewhere.

Playing the long game.

"Gremlins just got watered," Vale said when Knox punched a man who was trying to get to her.

Whatever that meant. He homed in on Colt, who had gotten pinned in, unable to leave the clearing.

{*Kill the girl, go after the bots.*}

Ignoring his *eyaer*, Knox cloaked himself and Vale in shadows, making sure the darkness never blocked her sight line. If she'd had the power to activate Shiloh's lenses, he could have hidden her completely. But she didn't, so he couldn't.

Fear for her incited a riot in his chest, torching his wits. His thoughts devolved, the urge to punish the warriors who threatened her well-being nigh overwhelming.

Keeping an eye on Bane and Zion, lest they come after his woman, Knox moved forward. Vale kept her back pressed to his, moving with him, guarding him as he guarded her. He wished he'd had more time to train her, wished she'd learned how to control her abilities without thought or effort. Mostly, he wished he could whisk her to safety and return to fight alone.

Gunshots from behind…in the mountains? He spun, putting his body in front of Vale's, just in case. Good thing. A bullet slicked through his chest, burning like fire.

"Knox!" She pressed a hand to the exit wound, stemming the flow of blood. "Maybe we should go."

Ignore the pain. "I'm fine." On the move again, Vale at his heels, he replaced his gun with a sword he'd won from a viking centuries ago, and a hooked dagger.

Colt had inched closer to Rush and Adonis, who stood guard over the fallen Terran. Erik had yet to heal from the spiked bullets.

"If you can," he said, "chop off Erik's feet." They had a minute, maybe two, before they lost their tactical advantage.

"That's gonna have to wait. Petra and Ronan are on our six." Vale gasped. "His sword…"

"Look away." Knox glanced over his shoulder to find the Solorian's sword lit up. Shiloh's lenses saved him from temporary blindness, but Vale wouldn't be so lucky.

Ronan had to be stopped. Otherwise he could strike while Knox and Vale were distracted by Colt.

Very well. Knox switched gears, preparing to—

Zion appeared, punching into Ronan's chest, his fist coming out the other side. The Solorian dropped, sword dulling.

With a scream of shock, Petra slammed her weapon into the ice, and a tower sprouted directly in front of Ronan. Zion's next punch shattered the obstruction into thousands of tiny pieces.

{Take him out.}

"You're welcome," Zion snapped at him, before leaping at Bane, who'd decided not to sit on the sidelines for once.

A surprised groan had him spinning, tensing. Vale grappled with Pike, the two caught up in a lethal ballet. She landed more blows than the experienced warrior, winking in and out of focus, her motions as fluid as water.

Knox's shadows tracked her, trying to stay with her, but they failed. But Pike couldn't track her, either. Had Ranger's memories surfaced?

When other warriors joined the fray, Knox pushed them away with a whirlwind of shadows. He did the same to Pike, who stumbled backward. Vale struck the bastard next, gouging his torso and twisting the blade. It was clear the poison had been washed away when Pike dropped his weapon, but remained standing.

Huffing and puffing, she raised her sword. Knox recognized the maniacal gleam in her eyes. She'd been ensnared by bloodlust, a deep seeded need to save herself from future attacks.

{Let her proceed. When the influx of memories immobilizes her, end her.}

Knox's lips drew back from his teeth. Dagger sheathed, revolver in hand, he shot Pike in the knees. Vale's sword cut air, buying him a little time.

Snarling, she followed the male to the ground.

"No!" Knox dove for her. Too late. The blade—

Stopped midair, blocked by Bold's hammer. Screaming in agony, Vale collapsed. Vibrations from the hammer had just shattered every bone in her body.

With a savage roar, Knox fired a succession of bullets at Bold. Two clipped his shoulder, sending him careening into Emberelle.

Movement at his other side. He turned. A glowing whip lashed around his wrist, electric pulses frying him inside and out in seconds. Muscles contracted until he lost control of his limbs, but he did his best to shoot Thorn, the whip's wielder.

His best wasn't good enough, his aim off. Thorn avoided the onslaught. The only good news? Emberelle took a bullet to the thigh, and Svaney of Frostland took one to the gut. He'd take down *anyone* who threatened Vale.

Clink, clink. Out of bullets.

Knox needed to reholster the revolver. *Come on. Move!* Though he struggled with all his might, he remained in the same position: hunched over and teeth gritted, volts of electricity streaming through him.

Smug, Thorn closed in. Then he stopped and shouted as flames engulfed his boots.

Knox followed the line of fire with his gaze, and found Vale at the other end. She was still prone, still in pain, with one arm outstretched.

Unless her life was in jeopardy, she wasn't supposed to reveal her ability to create fire. Yet, here she was, revealing, putting herself at a disadvantage in order to save Knox.

This woman...she was a true ally, just as Shiloh had been. Knox wouldn't make the same mistake with her, wouldn't punish her for a good deed.

At last the glowing whip uncoiled from his wrist, ending Knox's electrocution. Thorn was too busy battling the inferno to care.

Pop, pop, pop. Another round of gunfire sounded.

Pain exploded in his shoulder, a large caliber bullet tearing through muscle and bone.

He wasn't the only one to get hit. Bane and Zion fell, blood gushing from new wounds.

Knox pushed through, holstering the revolver and grabbing his bow. He glanced up, up, and was stunned to find countless men crouched at the top of the mountains, long-range rifles in hand. An army summoned by Adonis? Or Erik's threat made flesh?

Perhaps both.

Knox created a tornadic vortex of shadows around Vale, then himself, preventing anyone from approaching them as he readied The Bloodthirsty. Then he killed the winds and unleashed the arrow. The first victim plunged over the cliff, others quickly following.

Shouts arose. Men ran this way and that.

Letting the arrow do its work, Knox took a step toward Vale, then halted, horrified. Carrick stood behind her, a sword lifted, and she had no idea.

Certain the male's force field would knock him back at first contact, Knox slung the bow over his shoulder and dove atop Vale instead, rolling her out of the way. Miracle of miracles, Carrick's sword missed them both. They lumbered to their feet.

As Carrick regrouped, Halo of Forêt swooped from the sky, metal wings flapping, and yanked the Infernian into the air.

My target. Mine!

Each wing resembled a raven in flight, and each wing had the power to detach from Halo's back and aid him in battle. Vale would look good with those wings.

Knox trailed the pair on land—*will kill Carrick and offer Halo to Vale.* Stars winked through his vision, and he slowed. His lungs flattened, inhaling a chore. He glanced down. A jagged piece of ice had pierced his side.

Vale noticed and didn't hesitate to wrench the protrusion free. After he shouted an obscenity, he thanked her.

"Tell me you're all right," she said.

"I will be," he replied.

More gunfire from above, more warriors falling.

Ping. Dom's shield deflected a bullet.

Want that shield.

No, no. Focus on the plan. Knox searched the area. Carrick was nowhere in sight. Halo remained in the air, firing a semi-automatic at the men in the mountains. There was a swamp to the left and multiple towers of ice at the right, each one created by Petra.

Colt had sneaked from the clearing. He was running away, soon to vanish for another month.

"This way." Knox gave chase, Vale keeping pace.

But in seconds, an icy tower sprouted between them, separating them. He knew who to blame.

"Petra!" He shouted her name like the vile curse it was. Through the haze of the tower, he watched as she attacked Vale.

He dove, using his body as a jackhammer to blast through the ice… *Not going to reach her in time, hurry, hurry.* As ice chips rained, Bane appeared out of nowhere, raking claws over Knox's side. Skin and muscle split, exposing his ribs.

Incredible pain, hazing vision. Blood pouring from the gashes. He hit the ground, and was pretty sure his spleen ruptured.

Vale rocketed around the tower, coming up behind Bane before he could render another blow, and plunging the tip of her sword through his spine. A quick in and out. He dropped, temporarily paralyzed.

"Thank you." Inhale, exhale. Knox staggered to his feet, his own sword in hand.

"Anytime. Now do us both a favor and kill Beast-man."

"With pleasure."

But Zion had other plans. He launched into Bane, and the two men rolled a safe distance away before standing and bailing.

Working together now? Frustration mounted.

Pop, pop, pop. Another bullet shredded Knox's shoulder, and another curse left him.

No more distractions.

Breathing through the newest flood of agony, he scouted Colt's location—there. The male had collapsed a good distance away, a crimson pool surrounding him. Dead?

Halo fell from the sky, one of his metal wings bent at an odd angle.

Both Adonis and Rush had an arm wrapped around Erik, acting as crutches as they dragged him away. Someone had heeded Knox's advice and chopped off one of the viking's feet. Until the appendage regrew, Erik would be vulnerable.

Anyone who trailed the trio got shot by the men on the cliff. There were no ice towers outside the combat zone, which meant there was no place to hide.

Upon reaching Colt, Adonis released Erik and hauled the other combatant to his feet. Why not kill him while he had the chance? The Orfetling hadn't joined their cause.

Unless they'd come to terms before the battle, and had hoped to keep it secret? Perhaps they'd noticed Knox's interest in the male.

Perhaps Erik had told the truth about his intentions.

"Go get our man, and come back for me," Vale said, laboring for breath. "I've got this."

Clank, clank. She had just engaged Svaney.

"Yes, Knox," Svaney said, ice daggers growing from her nailbeds. Growing, growing like vines. The perfect foil for Vale's fire. Her crown had grown into a crystal skull and now masked her entire face, a phenomenon that happened—he didn't know why. "Leave the big girls here to play."

Known as the Ice Queen, she hailed from a realm covered in hoarfrost and flourished in these mountains. Proof: she'd frozen his shadows, preventing them from nearing her, and stopping them from protecting Vale.

More ice daggers, more streams of fire, the two clashing. The daggers melted, the skull following suit, even though the flames never reached Svaney's face. Thick wafts of black smoke sent her into a coughing fit, but didn't slow her.

Knox had a choice. Leave Vale behind, no longer remaining able to shield her, or let their target escape.

{*Go, go!*}

A flare of raw desperation. When it came to Vale, his *eyaer* couldn't be trusted. But he was going to do it, he decided, was going to leave her behind. The number of warriors had thinned significantly, and she displayed skills he hadn't expected. She would prevail.

She had *better* prevail. The thought of losing her...

He drew the revolver once again, aimed for Svaney, and hammered at the trigger. As she dropped, he charged after the fleeing warriors. Zion and Dom also barreled after the fleeing warriors, Dom's shield doing its job, expanding to deflect bullets.

Pop...pop.

At least the gunfire came less frequently, The Bloodthirsty doing its job, forcing the shooters to run while discharging another round.

Knox pumped his arms and legs faster, picking up speed before hitting his knees. He skidded across the ice and purposely plowed into Zion then Dom, cutting one after the other with a sword he'd won from Xander of Aouette—the wounds it caused took longer to heal.

As soon as Knox had bypassed the roaring pair, he somersaulted, rolling to his feet, running once again.

The only thing he hated more than an enemy at his back was *two* enemies at his back. No help for it. He tucked his shadows tighter, preventing either male from locking on him, aimed the revolver and fired.

Rush slowed.

Adonis tripped, but jumped up with Colt's help.

Closing in... If he could take out Colt *and* Erik... no, he had to leave Erik to Vale so she could absorb his memories.

She would also absorb the power to negate Knox's shadows, and place him at a disadvantage.

He swallowed whatever emotion bubbled up. Fury, or acceptance, he wasn't sure which.

Erik and Rush veered left while Adonis and Colt veered right, dividing their forces. Knox had to choose. The long game with a partner or the immediate satisfaction of ending Erik?

The ground shook, nearly toppling him. Zion had just punched the ice, no doubt about it, a crack spreading, arcing between Knox's feet. He dove to the side, barely avoiding a plummet into an abyss.

While being dragged away, Erik stretched out his arm, raising the rod. Thunder boomed, and lightning flashed in the sky. Dark storm clouds trundled over, obscuring the luminous streaks of green and purple. Rain poured, fist-sized hail pelting the terrain.

Knox took the hits and headed straight for Colt. Decision made. The long game.

Rush sprinted through the rain, firing off his three arrows. One embedded in each of Knox's shoulder, plus his sternum. The agony of movement…ripping muscle, cracking bone… Though he stumbled and slowed, he didn't stop. Closer—

They crashed together and wheeled over the ground in a tangle of limbs. Impact thrust the arrows deeper, then finally pushed them out.

Punches and elbows were thrown. Legs kicked out. Daggers slashed. Shots rang out.

Knox's brain rattled against his skull, and air gushed from his lungs. The hail grew to cinder block–size and a piece smashed into his ankle, already fractured bones reduced to powder.

A lesser man would have been hobbled. He fought on, holstering the revolver to refill the cylinder.

Flat on his back, Knox kicked Rush in the chest with his good leg and fired. The male hurled backward, his heart shredded with six bullets.

Revolver, sheathed. Head swimming with dizziness, stomach heaving. *Can't stop.* To make an official kill, he had to remove Rush's head or heart.

Hurry, hurry. The other man was reviving. Knox prepared to hack through the vulnerable column of his neck.

Eyes popping open, Rush blocked.

More gunshots. Dom dropped. One of Knox's kneecaps exploded. The agony! But he'd trained for times like this, whistled and lifted his free hand. The Bloodthirsty returned to him. He caught the shaft, nocked the arrow and took aim. Biggest threat at the moment? Rush.

{*Danger approaches from behind.*}

Too late. A final wave of gunfire wailed, burning pain erupting in his nape, the rest of his body going numb. A bullet had just severed his spinal cord.

Losing control of his limbs, Knox face-planted on the ice. He fought, but remained prone. He tried to breathe, but couldn't. Darkness encroached, and for the first time, he couldn't use it to his advantage.

He struggled to remain conscious. If he drifted off, he would die.

The great Knox of Iviland, helpless on a battlefield? Never!

Colt fell a few feet away. Zion, too, though he had control of his actions. The Taverian punched into the other man's throat, tearing out his trachea like the war prize it was.

Knox drifted off at last, one thought remaining at the forefront of his mind. *I'm going to miss Vale.*

CHAPTER TWENTY-SEVEN

Exhaustion settled over Vale, her muscles quaking. Sweat beaded on her skin and froze. Fatigue dogged her. Drawing on a well of strength she hadn't known she possessed, she pushed through the weakness, her determination unyielding, and fought full throttle, nothing held back. *Disregard the blood and intestines.*

Thanks to cohosts Celeste and Ranger, she'd managed to thrive amid the most savage battle of her life. Every time someone had challenged her, instinct had kicked in and Vale had known just what to do. And she couldn't forget the times Knox had stepped in to help.

The way he'd fought… Vicious, utterly without mercy. He'd gone for eyes and vital organs, the screams of others only emboldening him.

Before Vale had joined the AW, such a gruesome sight would have frightened her. Heck, mere weeks ago the sight *had* frightened her. Today? She'd felt strangely comforted.

Then the worst had happened. Her powerful, seemingly invincible warrior had toppled, and he had yet to rise.

"No!" Rival forgotten, Vale rushed forward, frantic to reach her man.

Emberelle moved in front of her. Parry. Thrust.

Argh! Vale needed to speed this fight along so she could guard Knox. Before, adrenaline had turned her blood to fuel, creating streams of fire. This time, the ends of her fingers...cooled. Was her lighter on the fritz? Or had she burned through every drop of the fuel?

In no mood for this, Vale finessed her way to the woman's left, and slammed an elbow into her high cheekbone. The beauty with gorgeous snow-white hair tottered to her knees but quickly jumped up and drew her sword for another dangerous swipe.

"He'll betray you," Emberelle grated. "Helping him is foolish."

Disregard her words, as well. Again she parried and thrust.

A glowing whip snaked around Vale's wrist, electric pulses tearing through her arm, stopping her cold. A scream lodged in her throat, the muscles in her jaw locking. Her vision wavered, but not before she caught sight of the whip's owner. Thorn, the striking man littered with scars.

"Sorry, sweetheart," he said. "This isn't personal."

Felt personal. The pulses only strengthened, leaving her unable to respond. Another layer of sweat frosted her skin, making her movements more difficult. *Tin Man needs oil.*

Grinning, twirling her sword, Emberelle edged closer to Vale. "It was nice knowing you. Or not." The metal arched toward her—

A staff sliced through Vale's back and exited her chest, stopping Emberelle's sword. Before and after impact, waves of agonizing pain consumed Vale.

The impaling had saved her life, but also made her wish she'd died. Blood gurgled from the corners of her mouth.

The culprit—Pike. The one who could blink a film over his eyes. Great! Now she had three immortals to defeat at once.

Her survival depended on her ability to go invisible and intangible. The cat was already out of the bag, her talents revealed.

And she could do it. She wasn't in a tomb of ice, surrounded by metal or bound by vine or rope. Only a whip, and a piece of wood. Would they stop her?

She flipped the switch...waiting... Nothing.

Thorn released her to catch Pike, who had yanked out the staff.

Vale collapsed. Stars winked before her eyes. Vale had a second, maybe two, before someone else got the drop on her. Again, she flipped the switch...still waiting...again nothing. Dang it, what was the holdup? The electric pulses had ceased. She should be good to go.

Stand—good. Step forward—excellent. She picked up the pace, soon dashing off, zero grace, her muscles in a jellylike state. When she tripped *through* a player, she realized she had succeeded, after all. Go intangibility go! But the second she came upon one of Petra's ice towers, she ricocheted backward, overtaken by tangibility.

Back on her feet. Running. Faster. The hailstorm ended, leaving a fine mist of rain. She leaped over a swampy pit.

Incoming! A volley of arrows headed her way. She dove, finally exiting the clearing. Was she already too late? There was no sign of Erik, Adonis or Rush. Colt lay on the ground, his head a few feet away.

Who had made the kill?

Zion stood over Knox, his bloody hands clenched.

"Stop!" she shouted. "Don't do it. *Please.*"

The big guy looked up, but stared over her shoulder. He glowered. Was she being chased?

A quick glance behind her. Yes. A determined Pike dogged her.

Zion bent down to heft Knox over his shoulder. Planning to take him to a secondary location?

Without a break in her stride, Vale picked up the weapons

Knox had dropped. Finally, she caught up with Zion. She struggled to control her breathing.

"Don't make a play against me." He wasn't even winded. "Your sister isn't dead, and I mean Knox no harm. Not today."

Truth? Lie? "Prove she's alive. Prove you mean Knox no harm. Take us to your safe house."

"Endanger your sister? Endanger *myself*? Never."

Yeah, it had been a total long shot. As they rushed around boulders, slipped down slopes, she asked, "Why would you help Knox?"

"I think Erik can and will do everything he claimed. I think we are the only ones capable of besting him. *If* we work together."

Heavy footfalls echoed behind her. She cast another glance over her shoulder and screeched with irritation. Pike closed in.

She wasn't sure she trusted Zion, but right now she had no other lifeline. "I'll think about your offer. *After* we get Knox to safety." He'd saved her life, and she would return the favor.

"Done," Zion said. "Where do you want to take him?"

Yeah. Where? If she opened a rift into his bunker, potentially leading others there, he would never forgive her. *Think, think.* The lavender field was out of the question, too. The tunnel underneath was *her* safe house. Only Ranger had known about it, and he was dead.

More than that, Celeste and Ranger had set some sort of trap there. Something other than the pheromone. But what?

The only other spot she remembered was a cave in the Amazon jungle. A go-to meeting spot with Gunnar. Had it been razed?

"I'm going to open a rift," she said. "You're going to toss Knox through it and take care of Pike. If you come after us, I'll burn you alive. That's a Valerina of Terra guarantee."

He flicked her a loaded glance. "When combatants make a kill, they inherit the ability to activate the victim's weapon, nothing more. Creating fire was an innate ability Ranger possessed, not a weapon, and yet you can do the same. An interesting development, no?"

"I will neither confirm it nor deny it." Staring roughly fifty yards ahead, she clinked her Rifters and waved her hand.

The landscape split, two layers peeling away from each other, revealing rocky walls. No sign of people or animals. Perfect.

Zion chucked Knox as if he were a baseball and said, "We'll chat again."

Knox flew through the rift, skidded over a dirt floor and slammed into a rocky wall. Vale followed him inside. Sword ready, she spun lest someone dared to enter.

Zion had already changed directions. He clashed with Pike, who gave as good as he got. Someone was going to die bloody—

The rift closed, the scene vanishing, and relief buckled Vale's knees. The weapon fell from her trembling hand. But concern overshadowed relief as she crawled to Knox. What injuries had he sustained? Why wasn't he waking up?

Vale gently patted his cheek. "Wake up for me, baby. Let me see those ocean blues."

No response. She looked him over. His clothing was torn and soaked with blood. Tremors intensifying, she felt for a pulse, whimpered. His heartbeat was slow and reedy, but it was there. A good sign, right?

Or not.

One hour trickled into another, and Knox remained as still as a corpse. Dang it, she had to help him. But how? Gunnar's sword had healing properties, but came with consequences she knew nothing about. What if she did more harm?

Another hour ticked by. Knox's pulse grew weaker rather than stronger, and she decided she had no other choice. She had to act, regardless of her ignorance.

After double checking to make sure no one hid nearby, she

opened a rift into his bunker, collected the sword, and raced back into the cave. Perfect timing. The doorway closed.

She placed the sword over Knox's chest, mimicking what she'd seen in her dream. One second passed, a seeming eternity.

Nothing happened.

Knox must have to do something to activate its power, since he was the one who'd won it. Which meant she couldn't help him.

Another hour ticked by with no improvement on his part, but she didn't freak. Instead, an eerie calm descended over her. Or maybe shock. She felt like she'd just watched an F-5 tornado rip up trees by the root and demolish houses brick by brick. It had been horrible to live through, but amazing to survive. But now that the storm had passed, and the debris had been cleared, she could see the world with fresh eyes.

The All War was awful, and provided irrefutable evidence that there were forces beyond her control—forces Earth wasn't prepared to face. The High Council. Enforcers. Portals and rifts. Other realms. Alien technology.

Whatever the cost, Vale had to win this thing. It was time to get her butt in gear. Not as a sidekick, but as the superhero she'd professed to be.

Her gaze returned to the unconscious Knox, shivers of regret stealing through her. She owed him, so she would guard him while he healed. And he had better heal. As soon as he was better, she'd give herself a night with him, make a memory to last the ages...and then she would say goodbye.

Knox came awake with a jolt, jerking upright, his body teeming with aggression. *Kill!*

Reaching for his daggers, he leaped to his feet. A sweep of his gaze revealed a spacious cavern, with colorful deposits of iron ore.

How had he gotten here? Better question: Why wasn't he dead?

The hot, humid breeze contained a metallic bite but lacked any kind of electrical charge. No other combatant lurked nearby, and yet he scented Vale's pheromone.

Realization—*she saved my life*. On the battlefield, she'd aided him, true, but this was different. She must have opened a rift and lugged him through. Which would have taken energy and time, putting her own life at risk.

Had she died because of it…because of him?

Red flashed through his vision. If someone had hurt her, that someone would die.

The fine hairs on the back of his neck lifted in warning as he sprang toward the exit. A combatant approached…

{*Dangerous. Slay without mercy.*}

Vale whizzed into the cavern, igniting a storm of relief and desire. She was alive and well.

{*Slay her. Now.*}

Defiant, Knox sheathed the daggers. The *eyaer* had one purpose, and one purpose only: to save his life. Trusting anyone else, even the woman who had risked her life for his, would get him killed. Maybe not today, maybe not tomorrow, but soon.

He didn't care.

He drank her in, the beautiful temptress who'd upended his world. She looked delicate but tough in a black tank top, ripped blue pants and steel-toed combat boots.

Just like that, he shot to full arousal. He wanted this woman more than…anything.

The realization was startling, but true. There, in that moment, he recognized her for what she was—a prize worth dying for.

He would have to be careful, have to remain guarded, but he would not give her up.

"Knox!" She squealed with happiness. A first for him. Most people screamed his name in fear or cursed it with hostility. Throwing herself into his open arms, she said, "My sleeping beau awakens."

He held her tight, one hand on her nape, the other on her ass. Lust was a living entity inside him, filling him up, reaching all the hidden nooks and crannies.

Control shredded, he crashed his lips against hers and thrust his tongue into her mouth. He devoured her hard and fast. Shaking. Burning up. *Slow down. Savor.*

He had a choice. Take her here, in this cave, endangering her life, or pause and whisk her back to his bunker, where they could continue in peace.

No contest. With a moan, he wrenched his face from hers. "How long was I out?"

"Forever." She toyed with the ends of his hair, her heated green-gold gaze glued to his lips. "Fine, fine. Only a few days. Let's celebrate with another kiss."

Days? "What is this place?"

"A cave in the Amazon jungle. I had to leave you here to run errands, but before I left, I smeared my blood on you to coat you with my scent. Smart, huh? I remembered how Celeste turned the lavender field into a total beat-off zone. If a combatant found you, they would've jumped your bones rather than take your head. You're welcome. And check it! I went back to the ice mountains, hoping to get a look at our slain shooters, but their bodies were long gone."

He stiffened. "You must take more care. What if someone had set an ambush?"

"I would have kicked butt." She patted his cheek, all *aren't you adorable*, and chattered on. "I filched these clothes from a log cabin Erik owns. The place I stayed before I stumbled upon your prison. I'd hoped I'd catch him while he's weakened from his foot amputation, but no such luck. I came back here and scouted the area, just in case someone had sneaked in while I was gone. They hadn't. But, uh, can we chat about the rest later?" The flush in her cheeks deepened. "In case I haven't been clear, I want to sex you up *immediately.*"

He grew *harder*. They had a thousand things to do, to discuss, to decide, and momentary pleasure would never be more important than the war. But he wasn't going to deny their bodies any longer.

One of them could have died during the assembly. Time was limited and precious. He was done putting his happiness on hold. Especially now, with Vale peering at him with such yearning, as if he wasn't just good enough, but good, period.

"I want to be with you, *valina*. I accept your invitation to sex up." He would have her, finally, the pheromone be damned. "But not here. And not until after our bath. For our first time, I'm not going to be covered in battle grime."

He set her on her feet, surely the most difficult task he'd ever done, and opened a shadowed rift into the bunker. Amid the snarling protests of his *eyaer*, he tugged Vale inside.

Waiting for the doorway to close, he realized *this* was more difficult. He had his woman where he wanted her, but he was still unable to act.

The second they were sealed inside, he picked her up, carried her over and tossed her in the pool. She came up laughing, but quieted when he stripped, amusement no match for the ravages of their desires.

Ruined shirt, gone. Belt buckle, dropped. Boots, off. Pants, shucked. She watched his every action, as though mesmerized. When he gripped his rigid length, shivers cascaded through her, sending ripples dancing over the water.

"You're conditioning me to become aroused anytime I even *think* about taking a bath," she told him, a glimmer of her luscious scent wafting through the air.

"What can I say, *valina*? I like you wet."

Holding his gaze, she removed her sodden shirt and tossed it aside. Her pants—jeans, according to his translator—received the same treatment, then the undergarments, leaving her wonderfully bare.

Slowly, he walked into the water. Her purrs of pleasure caressed his ears, a siren's song. Compared to the sizzling temperature of his skin, the liquid was like ice. He dunked once, twice, washing away the evidence of war before moving to the makeshift waterfall, where he tilted back his head and drank, cleansing his mouth.

"Your control of the pheromone has improved," he said, impressed.

"My control is nearly shredded," she admitted, "but I'm definitely getting better. Celeste's ability—"

"*Your* ability, not Celeste's."

"Mine," she said with a nod. "I'll keep the scent on a tight leash as long as I can, so you won't have to worry."

"I'm not sure I care where the desire comes from anymore."

A *hint* of her luscious scent gave way to an irresistible deluge. He inhaled deeply, couldn't stop himself, and savored the fragrance. He'd missed it.

Jasmine and dark spices infused his cells, so that he wasn't just Knox of Iviland anymore. He was Knox, Vale's man, and glad for it.

New tides of pleasure sensitized him. Suddenly he could feel every droplet of water that sluiced every ridge of muscle, could feel the stroke of oxygen against his pores, could hear the raggedness of Vale's inhalations.

Need ruled him. Need to have her in his bed, to kiss and taste every inch of her, to plunge inside her, to become one being with one purpose—climax.

Need for *her*.

He used his shadows to lift her out of the water.

"I'm floating!" The darkness whisked her through the bunker, drawing little gasps of delight from her. "Knox, this is incredible."

She was incredible, and he wasn't going to keep his hands off her a moment longer. He climbed out of the water and stalked his prey...

The shadows eased her upon the mattress and whisked away.

Vale's hair spilled over the pillows, white twining with black to create a glorious merging of light and shadow.

He devoured the rest of her with his gaze. Her pink nipples tightened for him. The flat plane of her stomach quivered. When he caught sight of the small thatch of curls between her long, trim legs, he nearly started drooling.

He placed a knee on the bed, then the other, and crawled up her perfect body. She welcomed him, as eager and tantalizing as ever, creating an erotic cradle for him. Hot, wet skin pressed against hot, wet skin. Male against female. He groaned. She gasped.

Soft and pliant against him, she twined her arms around his neck, as if she feared he would leave. As if he was strong enough for such a feat.

"You feel so good," she said, her breaths becoming more hectic. "I need more."

"More. Yes." To him, she felt like...life. Like everything he'd ever wanted or needed. As if she was made just for him. A prize to be savored, a treasure to be enjoyed. "There's no woman lovelier than you. No one I've ever wanted so desperately."

Eyes framed by the thickest, blackest lashes he'd ever seen widened. Expression ravenous, she cupped his jaw, glided her thumbs over his beard stubble and rubbed her knees up the sides of his body, the heels of her feet gliding along his calves.

"I'm in love with those words," she said, and turned her attention to his lips, tracing her finger around the edges, "but I want you to stop talking and start kissing again. Always finish what you start."

Defeated, Knox drew her face closer to his slowly, unbearably slow, allowing anticipation to build and burn in them both, burn so hot. His grip on her was too tight, he knew it, knew he needed to relax his hold before he bruised her tender flesh. But she moaned a ragged sound that dripped with pleasure, and he exalted, gripping her tighter.

Their lips met, electricity arcing between them, powerful and undeniable. A dark primal urge to possess her assailed him. Then. That second. Knox realized another startling truth. If he had to train with Ansel five hundred more years, if he had to win a thousand more All Wars, if he had to kill a million more warriors simply to be here with Vale and experience more moments like this, he would.

"Don't stop," she gasped out. "Whatever you do, don't stop."

"I'll *never* stop."

CHAPTER TWENTY-EIGHT

Connection. Something Vale had longed to share with a man, but never had. She'd craved adoration, too. Amusement and comfort. A partner to share the good, the bad and even the ugly. Acceptance. Had yearned for a companion willing to stick by her, no matter what. Knox was a bigger flight risk than most, but here, now, he made her feel everything she'd ever wanted, and more.

With increasing intensity, he teased her with sweeping flicks and forays of his tongue. Soon she was frenzied, drunk on honeyed whiskey. Then he sucked harder, nipped, nibbled and bit, and she burned hotter, ached so fiercely.

Her scent fused with his, the way the pheromone had fused with the lavender, becoming *their* scent. Sweet and wicked, deliciously heady.

Once, twice, he lifted his head to peer down at her, his yearning palpable, as if he needed to assure himself she was here, and she was real and she was his. That look was more addictive than any drug.

He was addictive. Vale craved every inch him...the muscle stacked upon muscle, the dark smattering of hair on his broad chest. The darker line that led to his navel, and even below it, providing a path to his erection. A real prizewinner, it checked all of her boxes, and then some.

Physically, no other man compared.

Before the night ended, she would have that shaft in her mouth. *Knox—he's what's for dinner.*

But her desire for him wasn't just based on appearance and all that masculine perfection. She valued his cunning mind, delighted in his wit and sharp sense of humor—something he'd shared with her and only her. When he wanted something, he fought for it. Nothing swayed him.

Desperate for him, she petted his chiseled jaw with one hand and grabbed a fistful of his hair with the other, sinking her nails into his scalp. His every shallow, raspy inhalation drove her wild, and his every exhalation warmed her skin, making her crazed.

He kissed her jaw and nibbled on the lobe of her ear, and goose bumps popped up all over her. Goose bumps he chased with his tongue. When she was writhing against him, he turned his attention to her breasts.

He suckled one nipple and pinched the other, and the dual sensations—one worshipful, one wild—maddened her.

"Knox," she said, his name an entreaty from deep within her soul. "Please."

"Does my *valina* need more?" He rose to his knees and maneuvered her so that her ass rested on his thighs. Biceps bulging, he settled his hands on her knees to push them farther apart.

Vale sucked in a breath as cool air met heated flesh. "Yes, yes. More."

His gaze gobbled her up one bite at a time. Only fair. Her gaze devoured him. His dark hair was still damp from the bath and stuck out in sexy spikes. Tension etched every line of his face, a testament to his raging desire. *For me, only me.*

"This," he said, curling his fingers around the base of his shaft and stroking once, twice, "is all yours." A bead of moisture wet the head.

"I want it, give it to me." She imagined sucking on it, just the way she craved, and drew her lower lip between her teeth. Soon! But first things first. She had to get him inside her before he changed his mind. "Condom," she said. "We need a condom *now*."

"No need. Immortals are immune to disease, and I can't get you pregnant."

Wait. "Ever?" she blurted, then cringed. A casual lay shouldn't care about starting a family in the future. Knox hadn't offered her a commitment—he couldn't. And she couldn't offer him one, either.

Ugh! She didn't know what they were, or what they would be, only knew she craved him. Time was short, and not just because of the war. She would be leaving him, but for now, she was done resisting the pull between them. They were together in this moment, and that was enough.

She cleared her throat. "Let me rephrase. How can you prevent pregnancy without a condom?"

He teased her inner thighs with his fingertips, wrenching a ragged groan from her. Those fingertips traced the wet heat between her legs, then stopped to circle her navel as if—no, surely not. But...maybe? As if he imagined her big with his child... and he liked it.

"During my third All War, I won a magical realm. While there, I bought a potion. Until I take an antidote, I cannot get you or anyone pregnant."

So, one day, after this newest war had ended, they could—

Nope. They couldn't have each other *and* victory. *Don't go there. You'll only ruin the moment.*

"How do you know your king hasn't given you an antidote already?" she asked.

"Magic becomes a part of you, like desire. You *feel* it."

"Like the magic between us?"

In an increasingly roughened voice, he said, "*You* are magic. Look at you. Nipples swollen with need. And here..." Irises blazing blue infernos, nostrils flared and jaw clenched, he traced those naughty fingertips along her core, grazing her little bundle of nerves. "So pretty and pink. So wet for your man."

Her back bowed, the only sound she was capable of making a mewl of bliss. "My man. Yes." He was, for now. She undulated her hips, impatient and desperate for some kind of relief from the pressure building inside her. "Touch me."

"Like this?" Slowly, torturously, he sank a finger deep into her sheath.

Coming undone. "Get inside me."

"Not yet. I'm going to savor this."

What if he changed his mind?

"I won't," he told her, and she realized she'd spoken the thought aloud. "We're going to be together. Nothing will stop us." He moved that magnificent finger in and out. In and out. "I love the way you welcome me inside, all hot and wet, so tight it's like you want to hold on and never let me go."

She almost didn't recognize his voice. The low, husky tone *smoldered* with possessiveness.

On his next inward glide, he added a second finger, stretching her—thrilling her. As she clutched at the sheets, writhing in pleasure, warmth collected in her fingertips just as it had done on the battlefield.

When Knox circled his thumb around the epicenter of her need, tiny flames sparked above her nails. No, no, no. She had to control the ability. If she torched his bunker, the lovemaking would stop.

If she hurt him, she would never forgive herself.

"Too much?" he asked. He didn't wait for her response. The merciless man fed her a third finger.

The flames flickered higher... "Ranger's power—"

"*Your* power. Never forget. You earned it on the battlefield." His eyes deepened to a stunning cobalt, passion and pride banked in their depths. "Why fear it?"

He was right. Ranger had attacked them, and she'd taken his head. The fire-starting ability belonged to her. If she set something on fire, she set something on fire.

"I won't fear it anymore. Infernos can be doused," she said.

Leaning down, he brushed his nose against hers and said, "Except the one raging inside of me."

A smile bloomed, something clicking in her heart, the flames at the ends of her fingers dying. No longer did she have to fight for control; she simply *had* it.

"That's my beautiful girl." Knox studied her again, as if he'd never seen anything so fine. Ragged breaths sawed in and out. "Now I will reward you. Tell me what you want, and I'll do it. Nothing is taboo."

"I want…" One desire was more vivid than the others. The one she'd wanted forever, it seemed. The one she could have without fear of missing what came next. He'd promised. "I want to taste every inch of you."

His eyes widened, and his pupils flared. *Blink.* Lightning fast, he flipped their positions, putting her on top of him.

"So eager for me." Feminine power filled her, and it was delicious. As strong as he was, as fearsome, she was stronger, at least in this. He was putty in her hands.

As she kissed her way down his muscular chest, he groaned.

"*Desperate* for you," he croaked. Hands tangled in her hair, he rolled his hips, again and again, rubbing his erection against her belly, stoking her need higher.

She flicked her tongue over one nipple, then the other. Licked a path of fire to his navel.

He groaned. "Your reward is my dream come true. Never had this…always wanted it."

She would be the first to pleasure him this way? Down she moved, relishing his gritty praise when she nipped an outline around his shaft.

Down... Finally, she reached the object of her fascination. He stilled, as if he didn't dare breathe, lest *she* change her mind.

"Do it," he pleaded. "*Need* you to."

Yes, yes. Will have him screaming my name.

Nearly drunk with that heady mix of desire, power and triumph, she licked the tip of his erection like a lollipop.

He fisted the sheets this time. He arched his back, and cried out with bliss. And yet, *she* neared orgasm. *The way he responds to my every touch...*

Vale opened her mouth wide to feed his length down her throat. "Mmm." So big! He stretched her jaw until she saw stars.

"Give me your finger," he commanded roughly.

Up and down. She reached up. He croaked, "No. Touch yourself first."

Oh. *Oh.* She fingered herself for a moment, loving the sensation of Knox in her mouth and fullness down below.

"Give it to me, *valina*. Now."

Moaning, she offered her finger to her man. She felt empty, until he licked the digit, laved and sucked it, pleasure battering and barraging every inch of her body.

Mouth sliding up and down, pace quickening. She took him deeper. Deeper still. Oh, the sounds he made. Grunts and groans. The uninhibited way he rasped her name, unafraid to reveal just how much he liked what she was doing.

"I'm going to... Vale, if you don't stop, I'm going to..." He radiated strain.

She didn't stop. No, she sucked faster, working her hand with her mouth, squeezing him tighter, unwilling to relinquish her prize.

"Vale!" He came, rearing up, lifting his hips, and digging his heels into the bed.

When she'd emptied him out, he sagged onto the bed. His eyes were closed, his breathing heavy, but he was already hardening again, readying to possess her.

Every inch of her burning with desire, she crawled up his

body… *More, need more.* "I hope I didn't exhaust you," she purred. "There's still work to do."

His eyelids popped open, blazing blue irises peering at her as if she had created the world—or had just become the center of his. So incredibly gentle, he traced her jaw as he'd done so many times in the past. But there was something different about the action tonight. Something almost…reverent.

Then, in a rush of movement, he clasped her hips to switch their positions and loomed over her, one of his hands delving between her legs. She moaned as he thrust two fingers inside her, without preamble, pleasure leaving her dazed.

"You liked sucking on me," he said, his tone awed. "You're soaked."

"Soaked and *aching.*"

A layer of his calm got stripped away, his expression raw and primal, lush and sensual. "That was… *Valina,* I don't have the words to express the depths of my satisfaction."

Desperate now, she wrapped her arms around his neck and whispered, "Show me, then."

"I will. I'll show you so good."

"Show me *hard,*" she said. *Please.* "I want to feel you tomorrow." And every day after.

Levered over her, he ran her lower lip between his teeth, a mimic of what she'd done to him, except he wasn't gentle about it. Good.

She lifted her head to snag his lips in a fierce kiss. He met her tongue with a thrust of his own, taking, taking more, taking everything, before wrenching free.

Panting, he hooked his arms behind her knees. Every movement heightened her pleasure. "I'm going to fill you now," he rasped. The cords in his neck were strained. "Are you ready?"

"I—"

His hips jerked, just a little, and his erection breached her inner walls, just an inch. Just enough to tempt and tease and torment her.

"Yes," she rushed out. "Yes, yes, a thousand times yes."

But he didn't slide in the rest of the way. "I want to keep you...like this...always," he rasped.

A man wanted to keep her around. Her. Vale London. And not just any man, but her favorite one. "Yes. Always. Pleeease."

Still he remained poised at her entrance. A bead of sweat trickled from his temple. She watched it, her thoughts derailing, the pleasure and pressure too much. If she didn't climax, she would die.

"We cannot go back, *valina*. Do you understand?"

"I think so." *Concentrate.* "Now give me what I want. What I need. I'm in *agony*, Knox."

"I don't want my female agonized." In one long, pounding stroke, he filled and stretched her.

She came instantly, a scream of satisfaction bursting from her, her world beginning and ending with Knox of Iviland. As her inner walls clenched and unclenched on his length, he plunged in and out, in and out, prolonging her orgasm.

"I can *feel* you, *valina*. The way you're squeezing me..."

In, out. In, out. Faster. Harder. She writhed, clawing at his back, already desperate for another climax. This was better than anything she'd ever experienced, better than anything she could have ever imagined. This man... He owned every cell in her body, because this...this wasn't sex. This was transformation, and Vale would never be the same.

A second orgasm sneaked up on her, and she combusted. Knox's name fled her lips, her mind suddenly soaring with the stars.

Back bowing, he lifted his head and roared, creating a symphony within her. Then he was shuddering—giving her everything.

Becoming her everything.

CHAPTER TWENTY-NINE

What Knox felt for Vale was wild and frenzied. And still foolish, considering their circumstances. But nothing could have stopped him from cuddling her close and luxuriating in contentment. For the first time in centuries, he felt balanced on the brink of...happiness.

He started making plans. No more putting his life on hold. He would explore the world with Vale at his side, and discover what excited her most. He would delight in her preferences—mountains, beaches, rain, sunshine—and learn his own.

Earlier, she'd said they needed to talk. Though his brain had been fried by rapture, he was eager to hear what she wanted to say. He thought he knew. She hoped to find a way to be together, despite the war. To *stay* together and never part.

"Knox," she breathed, rolling to her side.

"Yes, Vale." He would tell her that there wasn't a way, not long-term, but that they could remain together until the very end of the war. They would help each other, guard each other—save each other.

"I think we should split up."

What? He shouted a violent, savage denial, and the bunker walls shook.

"I want to win," she said, "and so do you. Where does that leave us?"

{*Kill her. Do it.*}

"That leaves us working together until we're the last two standing, just as *you* requested." He flicked his tongue over an incisor. How many potential partners had he denied over the years? Now he fought to keep one. "Give me another month—two—five—a year." A mere snap of time for an immortal. "We're better together. The assembly proved it."

"So we make love one day and behead each other the next? And what about afterward? Let's say I do it, I kill you. I'm pretty sure I'll kill the last shred of my humanity, too. Unlike the other players, I know and admire you."

Before he'd met her, he'd avoided making friends because of this very dilemma. But he couldn't give her up. Not yet. The damage was already done. He admired her, too. Why not enjoy the perks?

"Where will you stay?" he asked.

"Somewhere secret."

"So you don't know. Here, at least, you're safe."

"Am I?" She pinched the bridge of her nose. "Until you've ditched the slave bands, you can't be trusted, and even then it's iffy. Also, you don't want me killing combatants and gaining new powers. Admit it."

"You need me to stand guard when you *do* make a kill. Admit *that*."

They lapsed into silence, both of them breathing more heavily. Anger had him in a choke hold, but so did desire. He felt a sudden and intense need to brand her irrevocably, before he lost her. He felt a lash of urgency to lock her down and cement their alliance. He felt a driving possessiveness, an urge to fetch the chains hidden in his closet and secure her to the bed—a more reliable method than the vines.

But he did none of those things. Over the centuries, he'd cultivated a well of patience. A well he'd flouted since meeting her. He drew from it now and waited.

"All right," she finally grumbled. "And don't you dare comment about how easily I caved. We'll continue helping each other, but in the end, victory matters most. If you make a move against me, I'm gone."

"Agreed." The anger loosened its grip, leaving the desire... and every wicked impulse. First things first. "Tell me how I got into your cave."

She stiffened and said, "You'll be mad."

"Tell me, anyway."

"Sure." She grabbed his testicles before he realized her intent. "For quality assurance, you should know I'm recording this conversation in my brain. Oh, and I plan to rip these babies off if you yell at me, insult me or utter a complaint."

When had his little *valina* become so vicious?

When had he begun to like it?

"Fair enough," he said, "but we both know you like those babies right where they are."

"You're right." With a mock growl, she shook her free hand at the ceiling. "Dang my insatiable lusts. They've foiled the perfect punishment."

He barked out a laugh, sobered and frowned. Laughter? From him?

She scrambled upright to peer down at him, her hazel eyes wide but also luminous. "Duuuude. You are *gorgeous* when you laugh. Seriously. You just gave me goose bumps."

"I will investigate these bumps. *After* you explain what happened."

"And after I've taught you how to text. If we're going to have a true partnership, not just my one-sided illusion—"

"Not *going to* have. We do. We have."

"—then we've got to have a way to communicate when we're separated."

"Agreed again. But you're stalling."

"Fine." She squared her shoulders, then launched into an explanation about what had happened.

The more she spoke, the more irritated Knox became. But he didn't yell, issue insults or complain, and not because of her threat. He understood why she'd accepted Zion's help. His problem began and ended with the other man's intentions.

The warrior had proved himself trustworthy—most likely because he'd planned a long con. Make the girl believe he was innocent in order to lead her into an ambush later. Knox had seen it happen again and again in other competitions.

Now Vale would be inclined to rely on Zion, and believe his claims of innocence, helping him get ahead.

"Zion killed Colt," Knox said. "He controls the bots."

"And that's bad, I know. But not as bad as someone else getting the bots."

See. Already she saw the warrior as an ally.

Knox decided to change the subject before he ruined their brand-new, tenuous truce. "Tell me what you like most about me." What better way to *fortify* the truce? Whatever you focused on, you magnified.

"Someone fishing for compliments?" She fastened a lock of white hair behind her ear before resettling beside him and kissing his pectoral. "I happen to be crushing hard on your strength. Somehow, I almost always feel safe with you. I like that you are kind—to me. Your intensity is off-the-charts sublime. You give your all to everything you do. I dig your protective nature, enjoy the way your eyes light up every time you look at me. And I am head over heels for…your body."

He was so used to others fearing and reviling him. Her simple praise went straight to his head in a dizzying rush. Woe to anyone who tried to take her—take *this*—away from him.

"Well?" she prompted.

"Well, what?"

"What do you like most about me, dummy?"

Ah. "I'm awed by your courage. No matter the situation, you rise up and overcome. I enjoy your honesty. Even when you dread my reaction, you tell me true, or nothing. Do you know how rare that is? Your sensuality, the way you take what you want, is ecstasy. I'm humbled by your loyalty to your sister. Another rarity." He wanted that loyalty directed at him. "I'm fascinated by the way your mind works, how you study every angle of a situation. And," he said, helping her straddle his waist, "I'm also head over heels for every inch of your incredible body."

Exquisite pink nipples puckered before his gaze. As he reached out to cup and knead her breasts, vibrations raced along his ring finger, and he issued a dark curse. King Ansel wished to speak with him.

"My king has requested a meeting." He all but tossed her aside. "I can't not speak with him."

She groaned but said, "So speak with him, but try to hurry. I've got a better use for your mouth."

"You will stay in the closet, hidden from his view." He leaped to his feet, pulling Vale up with him, then rushed her to the closet and gathered clothing.

The vibrations intensified. His slave bands heated, soon blistering his skin. He yanked on a pair of pants, stalked toward the table and held up his hand. With a swipe of his thumb, light glowed above the center of the ring, and Ansel's scowling face appeared.

The king wasted no time. "Kneel. You know I prefer you on your knees."

Compulsion drove him to the floor, humiliation stinging his cheeks, his hands fisting. Vale valued his strength, yet here he was, revealing his greatest weakness.

"Better." Ansel waved away someone near him, someone Knox couldn't see. "Give me a progress report."

Knox gave a detailed accounting, omitting details about Vale. "According to Seven, the third round of competitors will be joining our war at the next assembly."

"There's been no word from the survivors of the second competition?"

"Erik of Terra has them hidden somewhere."

"If possible, find them. During last check-in," Ansel said, "my representative was alive. I want him freed, my chance of success doubled."

He didn't bother to ask which of the slaves Ansel had sent, because it didn't matter. One was the same as any other.

"Now, the reason for our chat." Ansel grinned with relish. "I've heard rumors about your companion. A Terran who killed the Occisor and Jetha combatants."

Knox swallowed a shout of pure, unadulterated rage; Ansel planned to use Vale as leverage. He'd known it would happen, but he'd expected more time.

He had one recourse. Bluff. "And?" he asked, a brow arched.

"Where is she? Tell me."

Though he fought it, the words rushed past clenched teeth. "She's here. With me. In my bunker."

"As I suspected." Ansel's grin widened. "I want to see her. Show her to me."

Careful. If Vale insulted the male...if Ansel ordered Knox to harm her... He chastised himself for a lack of preparation.

A fierce need to protect her arose, but still he was compelled to call, "Vale."

"Yo." She peeked out of the closet, a vision of incomparable loveliness.

He waved her over, the motion clipped. "Come here." Wait. If she hadn't dressed—

Relief. Wearing her black tank and ripped jeans, she sauntered over and eased beside him. On her knees. The wrongness of it... Vale had no business kneeling before a man like Ansel.

"Hey." Looking bored, she checked her cuticles. "Nice to meet you, I guess."

Ansel scanned her leisurely, as if he had days to complete the task. By the time he finished, casual interest turned to masculine appreciation. "Very nice. I see why you've acted out of character, allowing her to live."

He covets what belongs to me. He dies.

{Blank your mind, mask your face. Reveal nothing.}

Again, Knox drew from the well of patience, reviving the illusion of calm and cobbling together a new mask.

"If you want to survive the war," Ansel told her, "you'll give yourself the Mark of Disgrace. Then, after Knox wins, the two of you may live in my new realm, free and at peace."

Up went Vale's chin. "I'm not exiting the war for any reason."

Panic minced the hard-won calm in seconds, until it could be tossed like confetti. If Ansel ordered him to punish Vale for her insolence...

"Slave." Ansel unveiled a chilling smile. "I'm in the mood for a show. Gut yourself."

A horrified Vale latched onto his wrist, trying to stop him as he unsheathed a dagger, but he was too strong for her, the compulsion to obey was too strong for *him.*

He sank the blade deep into his gut.

Warm blood poured from the wound, soaking his pants. He glanced at her, just as horrified, but also eaten up with shame.

The king smirked. "I can see you care for him. As he must care for you, considering he put himself at risk to do so. But worry not for him. He'll heal. Worry for yourself. If I order him to kill you, he will kill you. You will not talk him out of it."

"I need her," Knox rushed out. "The *eyaer* told me she's necessary for victory." Truth. He simply left out the part about her usefulness running out.

Ansel hiked up a single shoulder in a casual shrug. "What is necessary today can be expendable tomorrow. You can have everything or lose it. Your choice. Remember that, slave."

Curt nod. What else could he do? But all the while he seethed. Anyone who dared threatened his woman would pay the ultimate price. And the fact that Ansel had threatened her with the ultimate weapon—Knox himself—meant Ansel had to pay double.

"Are you any closer to collecting the Horn of Summoning?" the king asked, unaware—or uncaring—about the beast he'd roused.

"No."

A hiss of disappointment before Ansel snapped, "Get closer. My sources say the horn will decide the war's victor." He concluded the meeting then, the light above the ring dying.

Sources. Oracles from the magical realm Knox had acquired?

Knox struggled to control his breathing, his heartbeat thundering in his ears.

Vale rushed around the bunker, gathering supplies. When she returned to his side, she cleaned and bandaged his wound. "He's a total tool, isn't he?"

"Tool. Like a hammer?"

"Like a jerk or a prick. There's no way I'm taking the Mark of Disgrace. I'll understand if you're compelled to give me the hard sell, but don't get mad when I refuse. After getting up close and personal with your monster of a king, I'm more determined to win the war."

"As long as I'm bound to him, I can't go against him. I *must* get free." Perhaps he would risk using Gunnar's sword, after all.

But the ramifications hadn't changed. Even as a free man, he would remain Ansel's representative, since he'd entered on his king's behalf. On the flip side, as a free man he could kill Ansel the next time they were together, before the king ever sat upon the Terran throne.

Problem was, Vale would be dead by then.

{*Yes. Kill the girl. Her power will only grow.*}

He didn't care. He couldn't, wouldn't harm her.

Unless ordered.

Inhale, exhale. With the truth at her disposal, she might decide to forgo their partnership and strike at him, forcing him to defend himself. But even then, he doubted he would strike back. He needed more of the ecstasy he'd found only in her arms.

"I'm going to kill Ansel," he admitted. "I will ensure he never enjoys the spoils of my victory."

"Your victory?" She shook her head. "You and I both know there's only one sure way to guarantee Ansel loses."

Yes. Knox had to die. But they weren't at that point yet. "We need to figure out an alternative. My death would save your realm, but no others."

Raring for contact, he pulled her against him. He was shaking as he wrapped his arms around her, shaking worse as he tightened his hold and rested his chin on the crown of her head.

She was shaking, too, and holding on just as tightly.

"If I live," he said, "you die. If you live, I die." With her, he was doomed. But without her, he wasn't sure life would be worth living. The impossibility of the conundrum left him ragged.

"If we're going to stay together, we can't lose our heads over each other. Figuratively. Or literally. What?" she said when he cursed. "Too soon for decapitation jokes?"

"Forever is too soon."

"Yeah." She sighed. "So what's our next move? I owe Zion, and I won't fight him for the bots. Do we go after Ronan and his spyglass, then? Or straight to Erik, the source of our problems?"

"Any other time I would say Ronan. While appendages are tougher to regenerate than organs, Erik won't be out of commission for long. Just a few more days, possibly a week." And in turn, they could take out Adonis, appeasing the compulsion to acquire the Horn of Summoning. "You will kill him, and I'll protect you while you recover. You were right. His memories will aid us."

As for Gunnar's sword, Knox hadn't yet decided. Take the risk, or not?

Vale leaned back, staring up at him, her shock evident. "Thank you for trusting me with Erik's mojo." She kissed his stubbly cheek. "All right, let's think this through. You have the ability to open a rift into one of his homes. And I know you expect an ambush. Why don't I just toss a grenade?"

"He will have taken precautions against such a move. And what if he has innocent mortals stashed in the house?" At one time, collateral damage wouldn't have bothered Knox, but these were Vale's people, and he didn't want to harm them unnecessarily. "We would be better served drawing Erik's allies into an ambush of our own. With their memories, you can lead us straight to his door."

"Where could— Never mind. The cottage near the lavender field." She gasped. "Ranger killed the owners, burned their bodies and set up shop. *He* had begun planning an ambush. The good news is we can piggyback on his work. But we'll need help. This is currently a numbers game. The other team has numbers, we don't. If we enlist Zion, he can—"

"Stab us in the back," he interjected. "No matter how good he's been to you, you cannot trust him. Never forget a single mistake can cost you your life."

"But—"

"No buts. If you won't take my word as a man, take my word as a four-time champion."

She pursed her lips, but nodded. "We'll go it alone."

Another reason he liked her. She didn't argue for the sake of arguing, and she gave as much as she took. "Tell me more about Ranger's ambush."

"The details are fuzzy, but I'm certain I'll remember more clearly when I'm there."

"Then to the cottage we go."

CHAPTER THIRTY

The sun slowly set on the horizon, painting the sky in a dazzling array of gold, pink and purple. Vale stood on the outside edge of the lavender field, scanning the cottage and surrounding area. Nothing seemed out of place.

Never had she seen such a tranquil environment...or been plagued by such sharp foreboding. She was looking at a past and future battle zone.

At least she'd grown semi-immune to the effects of the pheromone. Though the scent was thicker than molasses here, she remained in strict control of her thoughts. However, she wasn't quite immune to *Knox*. Being near him made her want...everything.

Dang it! She was falling for him. Actually, she'd been falling for a while, she just hadn't wanted to admit it. Then she'd met his king and gotten a firsthand look at the torture Knox had endured most of his life, and she'd started falling *faster*. *Then* he'd admitted he wanted to help their cause by strengthening her. Her, not him. He'd put her first, something no man had ever done for her, and she'd started falling *harder*.

The way he looked at her, held her, pleasured her...he might be falling for her, too. He definitely hated the thought of parting with her, just as she hated the thought of parting with him.

She wanted to give him what he craved most—freedom. And she would. Already, ideas brewed. But everything else she wanted conflicted. She wanted to live, but wanted him to live, as well. Wanted to win the war herself, but wanted Knox to win, too. Wanted to live together in peace, happily-ever-after.

And yes, okay, a cold-blooded assassin seemed like an odd choice for her lifelong companion. But Knox was *her* cold-blooded assassin. The man had taken arrows and bullets on her behalf. She would have him, and no other.

Never had a romance been more doomed.

So many obstacles stood in their way. How was she supposed to be the coffee bean in a situation like this?

"My instincts are on edge," he said, and she savored the familiar taste of honeyed whiskey, "yet I detect no foul play." He towered at her side, strong and aggressive, with a duffel bag strap draped over his shoulder. Stuffed inside were cameras, tools, traps and weapons. He had a wealth of weapons strapped on his body, as well, while Vale carried a single sword.

When you had the ability to shoot fire from your fingertips, daggers and guns were superfluous.

Once again they wore matching uniforms: black shirt, black pants, combat boots, everything taken from his closet. Go Team Valox!

"Let's go inside," she said. "I don't like you being out in the open."

On alert, he took her hand to lead her to the cottage. For a moment, one silly, necessary moment, she pretended they were on a date, headed to dinner and a movie. If he played his cards right, she would kiss him at the door and invite him in for a nightcap.

If only they lived in one of her favorite paranormal romance books. After they'd had incredible sex, their world would come crashing down, sure, but good would conquer evil and all would be well in the end.

Real life sucked. Was she setting herself up for failure? Yes, definitely. From the beginning, she'd known she couldn't have Knox *and* victory. The two were mutually exclusive. If there'd been an alternative, someone would have discovered it by now.

As for the Mark of Disgrace… She risked the destruction of her world. If Knox took it, he would be returned to his king for punishment and probably killed. Plus, there was a good chance Ansel had forbidden it, and Knox wouldn't be able to take the mark, anyway.

They ascended the wraparound porch, the steps creaking. There was a rocking chair and swing, two normal objects that caused a very abnormal reaction for her. Longing so visceral, she whimpered.

Knox squeezed her hand. "I'll go in first," he said, and tested the doorknob. Locked. He shouldered his way in, hinges splitting under pressure. "Wait here and keep watch."

"For you, anything." Despite the gravity of the situation, she loved watching him in action. He was all coiled strength and preternatural grace. Unshakable. Unflappable.

He winked before disappearing inside. *Be still my heart.*

Sword in hand, she scrutinized the stretch of land littered with scorched trees, thanks to Ranger.

"The Jethaling was definitely living here," Knox said when he returned, "but I don't think anyone has visited since his death."

Steps tentative, she entered the two-story abode. As she marveled at the charming interior, her steps were more certain. Stone walls complemented floral-print furniture, and a wooden mantel topped an elaborate marble fireplace. On the floor, faux fur rugs stretched over aged panels. Homey, yet extravagant. The kind of place she'd dreamed of having as a foster kid.

"He planned to draw people to the field, where they would

become lusty animals," she said, details crystalizing. "He was going to pick them off. We can do the same."

"We just need to get our targets here."

"You can go into the nearest town, and do something worth mentioning online. If you're covered in blood, they might post pictures. If you break things, throw a fit, steal something, they might post video. Erik will notice and want to investigate."

"Leave you?"

"I hate the idea of parting, too. But we'll do anything for the cause, right?" She kissed him, her longing for him almost more powerful than resolve. "Go, before I decide to surgically attach myself to your side."

He dropped the bag at her feet, gripped her hips and tugged her against him, then pressed his forehead against hers. "Do it. Attach to my side. Come with me."

"I need to stay here and figure out what else Ranger did," she said, toying with the ends of his hair. "Just think. If the enemy gets slayed today, you get laid tonight."

His beautiful blues twinkled with merriment, the rare sight nearly bringing tears to her eyes. "There is no better motivation." This time, *he* kissed *her*, and he wasn't swift about it. He claimed her lips, dominating her mouth, setting her aflame. In a millisecond, she went from zero to the speed of light.

By the time he lifted his head, she was panting, clinging to him, her fingers curled in his shirt. Letting go struck her as foolhardy.

He rubbed the tip of his nose against hers and croaked, "I'm glad I met you."

"I'm glad, too," she said, her voice growing thick. No matter what happened next, she couldn't regret the time they'd spent together. "You have your phone?"

He patted his pants pocket. "I do."

"Text me updates, okay?"

"I will. And you'll do the same for me if anything is amiss. Anything."

She nodded. "I will. Promise."

"If something goes wrong," he said, taking her by the fore-arms and shaking her, "you do whatever is required to survive. Swear it."

Her throat quivered and seemed to swell, but she whispered, "I swear."

One more kiss, and then he was stalking outside.

Oh, that man. He lit her body on fire.

As she wandered through the house, taking stock, she saw the home through two sets of eyes: her present and Ranger's past. She observed Memory Ranger—MR—as he paced. His booted feet stomped over dark floor tiles, his impatience for Celeste's return driving him faster and faster.

Vale followed MR past a small china hutch to the kitchen. Open shelves displayed dishes. A table with a lace cloth perched directly in front of a bay window. MR kept going, entering a pantry where he cut a hole in the floor and dug. Finally, he reached the tunnel he and Celeste had dug before their imprison-ment in the ice cavern. An escape route that stretched for about a mile in one direction and half a mile in the other.

My tunnel. Mine!

Vale followed Ranger's memory up the stairs, into a bathroom the size of her closet at home, where a claw-foot tub took her breath away. They entered a bedroom. Quick scan. A queen-size bed with a brass frame and colorful quilt. A crystal chande-lier hung above it, and a rug with pink roses draped the wood floor. A porcelain side table. A windowed alcove looked down upon the lavender field.

MR stood, peering out, waiting. There! He noticed move-ment in the field. Celeste? Or someone who'd tracked him, de-termined to slay him?

Spying a pair of hazel eyes through a crack in the darkness, he reached for the remote he'd hidden behind a loose beam in the wall. That remote controlled the land mines buried in the lavender field.

Land mines that had been made here on Earth—land mines Vale and Knox could activate!

She smiled, feeling as though she'd come full circle. *Be a lady, unless you have to be a land mine.*

The time to explode some crap had come.

If Ranger hadn't sensed Celeste the day Vale and Knox had visited, he would have blown them both to smithereens. How close they'd come to death, and they'd had no idea. *Could have lost everything in a mere blink of time.*

She whipped out her phone and texted Knox, telling him about the land mines. Every time he responded, she smiled.

"Hello, Vale."

Tasting citrus, she dropped her phone and spun. Her heartbeat careened out of rhythm as she lifted her sword. Her gaze landed on the big, dark-haired warrior with equally dark eyes, and a cold sweat broke out over her skin.

"Zion. What are you doing here?"

"He's with me."

Vale encountered the beloved flavor of warm brown butter. "Nola?"

A sickly Nola stepped out from behind the warrior, offered her a wobbly smile and collapsed.

Eleven minutes earlier

Knox raced along a lavish countryside filled with wide-open spaces, beautiful trees and grazing herds, closing in on the nearest town while creating a trail to the cottage. When his pocket vibrated, he frowned. Then he remembered the cell phone Vale had given him.

He checked the screen.

Vale: Land mines are hidden in the lavender field, controlled by a remote I CAN activate. Anyone can. Be careful on your return, okay? XOXO

He typed: Qhat dies XOXP meab.

His fingers were too big for the keyboard, and he misspelled everything, yet the phone automatically corrected two of the words, attempting a guess about his meaning. What dies XOXP mean?

Incorrect, but he pressed Send, anyway, certain he'd mess up worse if he tried to fix it. He hoped Vale understood.

Her response appeared on the screen mere seconds later.

Kisses and hugs ☺ ☺ ☺

He almost smiled.

Throughout his life, Knox had hungered for freedom and vengeance the way other men hungered for riches. Then he'd met Vale, and she'd somehow upended his world. The man who had once forsaken romantic ties couldn't abide the idea of being without his woman, even for a few hours.

{*Must take her out. Cannot allow such a dangerous combatant to live.*}

Understand me, eyaer. I will not be taking her out right now. I'm not sure I will ever be able to take her out. The need to protect her was too strong—and only growing stronger—practically programmed into his DNA.

Knox would instruct Vale to chain him up if Ansel ever followed through with his threat. While he'd never had the power to disobey a direct order, he'd resisted for a minute or two. Just enough time for her to disarm and bind him.

Willingly submit to captivity? Yes. For the first time, yes. For Vale, he thought he would do anything. The same way she would do anything for him.

Hurry. Finish this, and return to her. The countryside tapered into a cityscape, fields replaced by paved streets. Two-and three-story structures loomed on each side, few gaps and alleyways between them.

Hidden in shadows, Knox slowed and, following Vale's instructions, ran a dagger across his palm. As blood welled, he smeared it across his face and neck.

The stage was set.

Shifting his shadows so that only his weapons were concealed, he made sure to stumble around, bumping into people. Some asked if he was all right, but he offered no response.

A necklace glittered in a store window, beckoning Knox. How lovely the piece would look on Vale. Twelve stones, each a different color. One was green, one gold, a perfect match for her eyes.

Had a male ever given her such a present, or would Knox be the first? He imagined her face lighting up... fantasized about making love to her while she wore the gemstones, a smile and nothing else...

I want. I take.

No! She'd told him to steal something, yet the most primitive part of him demanded he buy this for her. *I want. I...earn.* Sometimes, a gift that cost you nothing meant nothing. The more he spent, the more she might understand her value to him.

He delivered a single punch to the window, using all of his might. Bones cracked and skin tore. *Worth it.* Glass shattered. An alarm screeched to life as broken shards rained over his boots.

Oh, yes. Erik would hear of this.

Hand bloody, Knox reached through the jagged opening and grabbed the necklace, then tossed one of his prized daggers into the store. Payment rendered.

Vale's value—priceless.

The *eyaer* screamed in protest, louder than the alarm, but he ignored it.

People congregated around him. Time to go. Knox took off

in a sprint, summoning more and more shadows around him, soon vanishing from view.

He dropped the necklace in his pocket, and withdrew the phone, then typed as he ran. Like before, his mistakes were corrected.

My work is done. Heading your way.

He waited, but no response came in. The foreboding he'd experienced earlier surged anew, and he fired off another text.

Talk to me. Tell me all is well.

Waiting...

Still no response.

{*Trouble lurks. Proceed with caution.*}

Caution was no longer part of his skill set. Knox quickened his pace. Should he rift directly into the cottage?

No. He didn't want to lead anyone else directly inside it.

What about the lavender field?

No, again. He'd have to wait for the rift to close. He could reach her faster on foot. The cottage came into view. Curtains were drawn over the windows, preventing him from peering inside.

If something had happened to Vale...

Keep your wits. An outcome had never been so important. He palmed the revolver and a dagger, his grip unsteady, and inspected the field. Nothing appeared amiss, but he skirted the edge, anyway, just to be safe.

He couldn't lose Vale. He just...couldn't.

She'd brought him back to life one smile, taunt and caress at a time. For centuries, he'd clung to his solitary existence, enveloped by his shadows, unable, no, unwilling to fight his way out of the darkness. Then she'd shown him the beauty of light, and forever changed the course of his life.

He wasn't Knox of Iviland; he was Knox, Vale's man. He couldn't—wouldn't—lose her.

He blazed up the porch, burst through the door… and ground to a halt. Though his feet had stopped moving, his heart continued to race. Confusion muddled his thoughts as he struggled to make sense of what he was seeing.

In the living room, Vale sat on a couch—next to her sister. Nola was pale, thin and shaky, nothing like the upbeat girl he'd seen in the ice cavern. The sisters were holding hands and talking in hushed voices, giddy.

The reunion had a single flaw. Zion stood a few feet away, aiming a rifle at Knox's chest.

The warrior grinned without humor. "Glad you could join us, Knox. We have much to discuss."

Vale had…betrayed him? Had consorted with the enemy behind his back, choosing to work with Zion, and ambush *Knox*?

He knew her, knew she wouldn't do this. But the evidence stood mere feet away.

Feeling as if he'd just been flayed alive, Knox stumbled backward. This wasn't…this couldn't… A roar burst from him, the pain too much to hold inside.

CHAPTER THIRTY-ONE

How quickly life could change, for better or worse.

One moment Vale was immersed in an emotional cocoon, concerned about Nola's declining health, but over the moon happy to be together again, savoring the taste of warm brown butter. The next she was positioning herself between two rabid beasts, feeling like the only rib eye at a discounted all-you-can-eat buffet.

"Guys. Please," she said, holding out her arms, as if such a puny action could stop either one of these hulks. "Talk first, kill later. If we're all alive, we've got options."

Dried blood smeared Knox's face, the crimson stark against his now-ashen features. So badly she wanted to wrap her arms around him and explain the situation, but she held her tongue. Harsh betrayal gleamed in his eyes. He might not believe her. Plus, he was a god of war with a god of war's pride. The odds of her saying something she shouldn't in front of witnesses were pretty high.

Nola trudged to her feet and clasped Zion's arm. She was in the middle of a flare *and* opioid withdrawals, her body racked with pain. Lack of sleep had left bruises under her eyes, and her cheeks had hollowed from days of vomiting.

Vale had no idea how to help her sister, and it sucked. If Nola entered the All War, she would become immortal, just like Vale, and her pain and suffering would end...but she would be hunted and forced to kill others. *No good options.*

Already the AW had screwed with Nola's life. Apparently Bane had kidnapped her from Zion multiple times—who'd ultimately kidnapped her right back. Beast-man believed he and Nola "belonged together."

Nola might agree. She'd blushed while she'd talked about it.

Vale had a trillion unanswered questions. The highlights? What happened the night the ice prison collapsed? Where, exactly, had Nola been all this time? Besides getting kidnapped, what had she been doing? Was she attracted to Zion, too? How badly was she attracted to Bane? Had anyone hurt her, and how viciously did she want Vale to hurt them back?

Scowling at Zion with the ferocity of a bear cub, the weakened Nola said, "If you hurt my sister's boyfriend, I will be supremely displeased."

"For once, I'm willing to risk it." Zion turned his attention to Knox. "Whatever you cut me with after the assembly left a wound on my leg that hasn't healed. I am *not* amused."

Still, the big bad male lowered the gun, leaving Vale flabbergasted. She'd watched him punch through another man's chest, and now little Nola Lee's temper intimidated him?

"Sit, mortal, and do not get up again." Zion gave Nola a gentle push toward the couch. "And if you ever approach an angry combatant again, or get in the middle of an impending fight, I will... I'll..."

Nola blew him a kiss with bite and resettled on the couch.

Earlier, Zion had limped to the kitchen to fetch her a glass of water—the wound Knox had given him truly *hadn't* healed. Vale had asked her sister straight up, "Are you guys sleeping together?"

"No," Nola had replied. "He's like my adopted brother. Which I could really get into, maybe, probably, but he's afraid he'll break me, and that's a hard limit for me."

Vale shared Zion's fear. He could break the fragile girl with a twist of his wrist.

In the present, Knox glared at Zion—*his* pistol remained aimed and ready. "Did you contact him, Vale?"

Oh, how galling! He thought so little of her integrity, so little of her loyalty that he automatically assumed the worst. "Hey, remember when you didn't die at check-in? Yeah, that was because of me and Zion."

He refused to bend. "Remember when *you* didn't die at check-in? That was because of *me*."

"I didn't contact him," she said, pushing the words through gnashing teeth. "He tagged me with one of Colt's bots." She'd found the bugger under her skin, in one of the places she'd been stabbed during the battle. It must have burrowed through the gash and stayed put when she'd healed. "I would never betray you."

A slight softening around his eyes, but it didn't last. "Through you, he has learned the location of my bunker."

"But he didn't take advantage," she said in a small voice.

"What's worse," he continued, "you didn't text me to alert me of another combatant's presence, as you swore you would. Nor did you run, as ordered."

An-n-nd her indignation was back. "First, I'm not your slave, and I don't do as I'm told," she snapped, causing him to blanch. "Second, I was only supposed to run if I was about to die. Third, I didn't text you because I got caught up in the moment. Nola fainted and needed me. They've only been here a few minutes. Just…give Zion a chance. Please. For me. For *us*. He's here to help with our Erik problem. Help we desperately need."

Knox didn't say a word, but the rigidness of his posture screamed all kinds of obscenities at her.

"Give Zion a chance," she repeated.

"My instinct tells me trouble brews. I can't—I *won't* work with him." He glared. "You won't, either."

She understood his reasoning, but resented his demand. Hackles raised, she said, "How about you stop telling me what I can and can't do? And maybe trust your girlfriend more than your stupid instinct."

"That stupid instinct has never failed me."

"And I have?"

The glare intensified. "I only want to protect you, *valina*."

Her already-fragile calm shattered. This set a terrible precedent. Knox right, Vale wrong. Knox strong, Vale weak. Knox head, Vale tail.

"Look," she said, "you want to protect me because I'm necessary for your victory. I get it. But—"

"You aren't necessary," he interjected. "Not to the *eyaer*, not anymore. Not since the hour before the assembly."

"Um, what's that now?" She'd stopped being necessary, and he'd stayed with her, anyway? *Another plot twist.* "Never mind. We'll discuss it later. Just...stand down and trust me. I won't do anything to risk your life, or my sister's or my chance at victory. Or even *your* chance at victory. And I realize how contradictory I'm being, but I want us all to survive this."

"Wait." Nola flattened her hands over her stomach. "You're a soldier in their war? How can that be?"

Okay, so she hadn't yet dropped that particular bombshell, hadn't wanted her sister worried. And it was clear Zion hadn't, either.

"I am, yes," she said, remaining fixated on Knox, the love of her life.

Oh, frick. Vale wasn't just falling for the man. She'd already hit the ground and splattered on the sidewalk.

She loved him deeply, madly, wholly, nothing held back. Tim-

ing didn't matter to emotion. The swiftness of the relationship
didn't matter. He had her heart, and she had a no-return policy.

There had to be a way to have it all, the alternative too
wretched. She refused to settle for anything less than happily-
ever-after.

"Please, trust me," she pleaded. "I want us to be together, as
a family, not just surviving, but thriving."

He flinched at the word *family*, as if sucker punched by a startling realization. He softened completely, his anger just...gone.
As he looked between her and Nola, he was suddenly stripped
of his civility.

He nodded as if he'd just made a life-altering decision that
devastated him, his features heartbreaking and heartbroken all
at once. Dread shivered down her spine.

Tone gentle, he said, "My truce with you stands, Valerina of
Earth. Now and always. But I won't be fighting at your side.
Today, we part ways, and I take out combatants from the shad-
ows, where I belong."

Part ways? Gutted by the thought, she gave an adamant shake
of her head. "Are you trying to make me choose between you
and Nola?" Her eyes burned with tears she refused to shed, and
her chin trembled. Losing sight of the others—who watched the
exchange with budding trepidation—she swallowed the lump
in her throat; it settled in her stomach, fizzing, agonizing her
further. "Please, don't do this. We can succeed, together. Remember?"

"I don't want you to choose," he said, still so gentle. "Earlier, you believed we'd be better off apart, but I convinced you
otherwise. I was wrong to do so."

"No! You were right. We *save* each other." She wanted to
shout, *I love you, and love conquers all, even evil. Love is everything.*
Love is worth fighting for. I am worth fighting for. Love never fails—
but you are going to fail our love if you walk away.

She pressed her tongue to the roof of her mouth and remained silent. No way she would use her feelings to manipulate or pressure him. And yeah, okay, she realized she had no right to censure him, either. She'd wanted to ditch him before, and not because of the game but because she'd hoped to avoid *this*. The moment he realized he was better off without her.

Always be the leaver.

For once, she hadn't wanted to be the leaver. No wonder he'd convinced her to stay so easily; she'd latched on to any excuse. In her heart of hearts, she knew he was brave and strong, nothing like her selfish father.

"I expected better from you," she whispered. *Do not sob.* "You're a coward."

"I'm a man, doing the best I can in a hopeless situation. Because we *can't* save each other," he said, destroying her world piece by piece. He breathed deep, exhaled with force, lowered his gun and faced Zion. "I'm going to ensure Vale reaches the final two. As long as you're guarding her, I won't target you. If you try to stop me, or hurt her in any way, I will make your death a cautionary tale, and even Seven will shudder with revulsion."

"Agreed," Zion said.

"Stop this." *Do. Not. Sob.* "No one's leaving anyone. What is it about *stronger together* that you don't understand? A twofold cord cannot be broken."

Knox bowed his head. "I'm sorry, Vale."

"No," she repeated, vision blurring as she blinked back those stupid, stupid tears. "If you walk out the door, we're done. I won't take you back, even if you crawl."

But he wouldn't come back. They never did.

"I know you won't." Knox took two steps back, spun on his heel and fled. Before he vanished around the corner, she caught a final glimpse at his expression.

Never had a man exuded such wretchedness.

Then he was gone, and she thought he might have left his own shredded heart behind.

★ ★ ★

Encompassed by shadows, Knox marched along the perimeter of the lavender field, avoiding the land mines while dodging trees. He kept the cottage in sight, straying just far enough to detect if a combatant neared.

Leaving Vale with Zion had been the most difficult thing he'd ever done. But *difficult* didn't mean *wrong*. He knew he'd made the right decision. For her. For them both. Still. His grip tightened on his daggers as the dreadful ache in his chest amplified.

Vale hadn't betrayed him, and he never should have doubted her. She was loyal to Nola, yes, but she was also loyal to him. Or rather, she had been. He'd destroyed whatever feeling she'd had for him.

He couldn't get his last image of her out of his head…the shock and horror that had glinted in her hazel eyes, fury, too, perhaps even hatred, all magnified by unshed tears. She'd been pale and unsteady, so hopeful about their future. He'd thought he'd spied a shimmer of *love* in her eyes, had suspected she would willingly risk her life for his…had feared she would be forced to give up her dreams for his.

He couldn't let her do it. He just… He couldn't. She'd lost too much already.

From now on, Knox would spend his days taking out every obstacle in her path. He would be her first line of defense.

And she would hate him forever.

He drilled a fist into his temple. He'd hurt her, and he deserved a lifetime of misery for it—which was exactly what he was going to get.

One day, she might look back and thank him for this. Never would she have to choose between her lover and her sister. Her lover and her world. Her lover's life and her own.

My sweet valina, lost to me forever. She'd brought his dreams to life, and he'd done the same for her worst nightmares. He'd walked away, just like her father.

I expected better from you, she'd said. *You're a coward.*

He *was* a coward. Maybe he *hadn't* done the right thing.

He'd won multiple wars, and he couldn't find a better way to aid the woman he loved?

Loved. Yes, he realized, stopped cold. He loved Vale London. The knowledge glowed, bright and undeniable, as if Valtorro—the sun that lit—had dawned inside him.

Like Minka, Vale had brought his deadened heart back to life. He'd failed his daughter but he wouldn't fail Vale. He would do *anything*, give up *everything* to secure a better future for her.

Only now, in this moment, did he understand and accept that he'd lost the war the second they'd met. The All War, yes, but also the war within himself, and even his private war with Ansel. In order to grab hold of Vale and keep her safe, Knox had to let go of his vengeance.

He chose her. He would *always* choose her. After he'd laid her enemies at her feet, he would present himself to Seven and cut out his own heart. War over.

Live by the sword, die by the sword.

Only one thing stood in his way. Ansel's compulsion to win, whatever the cost. Which meant Knox would have to take the risk and bind himself to Gunnar's sword. Maybe it would work, maybe it wouldn't. He'd worry about a backup plan if it failed.

{*Danger comes.*}

A combatant? Dagger and revolver at the ready, he scanned—

{*Too late. Rift!*}

Leave Vale to face the danger? No. He clinked the Rifters, intending to enter the cottage.

Boom!

A white-hot blast flung him across the field, into a tree. Gnarled limbs stabbed through his torso, impact cracking various bones. He lost his breath and his hold on the shadows.

Half the skin on his face had melted off, and a hank of muscle hung from his jaw. Shiloh's lenses protected his eyes and corrected his vision without missing a beat—

What he saw utterly wrecked him. The cottage...it...it was... *ruined.* Only rubble remained.

Blood roared in Knox's ears. He struggled to make sense of what had happened. The land mines hadn't exploded. The field was intact.

Vale had been inside the cottage, and it had just blown up.

Didn't matter, didn't matter. Even if each of her limbs had been amputated, she would recover. She would hurt, but she would recover.

The fire wouldn't kill her, either, since she'd absorbed Ranger's ability. If her heart had been ripped out, or her head had been blown off—

"Vale!" He screamed her name and reached toward the cottage.

Just outside the field's boundary, bushes shook and tree branches slapped together. Erik stepped into sight. His foot had regrown, and he looked to be in peak health. A rocket launcher was slung over his shoulder.

Adonis and Rush flanked his sides, an army of mortals spread out behind them.

The roar in Knox's ears faded just in time to hear Erik say, "Told you."

Rage like he'd never known unfurled. This man...this bastard...had just bombed Vale's house. Had just... He'd... Knox threw back his head and shouted curses at the smoke-infused sky, the sound broken and animalistic. *Like me.*

I will slaughter this man and all he holds dear.

"Let me hip you to a few truths," Erik said when he quieted. "I'm the reason the ice prison fell. Me. As soon as I was ready, I used the Rod of Clima to warm up the cavern, bit by bit."

"You lie!"

"Global warming helped speed up the process, so I wasn't

where I was supposed to be when the columns cracked. But I'm here now, and I will postpone this war."

"You cannot defeat the High Council." *You'll be too busy being dead.*

Erik waved the statement away. "I had centuries to find and prepare traps in different safe houses. Those I couldn't find, I made arrangements to hunt, putting cameras in the mountains, recording combatants as they rifted away. Modern technology had been my best friend."

Enough! "I. Will. Kill. You."

"You are one of the only males I couldn't track," Erik continued, "even after you invaded Shiloh's camp. But I'd hoped you and Vale would return here to the cottage. Then, suddenly, I got my wish." He smiled, but quickly frowned. He sniffed the air.

Vale's pheromone fused with smoke, drifting past. The viking didn't deserve to smell her—*I will stop him.*

With a snarl, Knox yanked his body free of the tree limbs.

Erik flicked a glance to Adonis and Rush. "Shall we have a contest of our own, boys? The one who kills Knox of Iviland wins his weapons, of course, but also wins the day."

CHAPTER THIRTY-TWO

Four minutes earlier

"Oh, Vale. I'm beyond sorry," Nola said, hauling her close for a hug.

For the first time in Vale's life, tasting warm brown butter failed to comfort her. She wanted whiskey and honey.

No. No, she didn't. She hated whiskey and honey. The owner of that whiskey and honey voice considered her disposable.

Buck up. She'd been broken before and survived. She would survive this, too.

Would she?

Hurts so bad.

"Nothing to be sorry about," she said. "Good riddance, right?" If a man didn't want to stay with her, if he wasn't willing to fight for their relationship, he wasn't worth another thought.

But why wasn't she ever good enough? Why was she so easy to abandon?

"If I hadn't seen with my own eyes, I never would have believed it," Zion said. "That man loves you."

Hope soared, then crashed, hard. She'd told Knox she wouldn't take him back, and he'd left, anyway. He hadn't looked back. Love her? Not even close.

"I don't agree. But even if you were right, it wouldn't matter. Sometimes love isn't enough." Her deadened voice lacked any hint of emotion. "You don't convince your love to stay, letting her pin her hopes and dreams on you, then forsake her a few hours later." Oops. Not so deadened, after all. "Anyway. No more chatter about Knox. Did you happen to tag any other players with a bot?"

"There wasn't opportunity." Zion took Nola's hand and helped her to her feet. "If Knox created a footpath to the cottage, other competitors will arrive. Soon. Let's stash Nola somewhere safe."

Nola rested her head on his shoulder, unable to stand on her own. The sight of their easy camaraderie roused the darkest, ugliest thread of jealousy, and a bucket of guilt. Nola deserved every happiness, every moment of peace and connection. What was more, her sister's good fortune didn't preclude her own.

Brave face!

She wondered if Nola had been this at ease with Bane, wondered if she missed him, and what she would do if—when—he was taken out of the game.

A beast with his destructive tendencies *had* to be taken out of the game, and soon. He could tear this planet apart at the seams. The fact that he hadn't already done so was a miracle.

"Where can I go?" Nola asked Zion. "Your safe houses are compromised."

Vale could take her sister to the cave in the Amazon but... if something happened to her today, Nola would be stuck out there, helpless. Better to leave her near civilization.

"There's a tunnel beneath the house," she said. "It runs a mile and a half. Ranger and Celeste dug it before they were frozen. Then, when he was freed, Ranger discovered the cottage was built over it, killed the homeowners to ensure he had privacy and dug a new entryway."

Nola placed a hand over her heart. "Those poor people."

"I know." But she couldn't let sadness pull her strings. "Come on."

She marched into the kitchen, her guests not far behind. In the pantry closet, she kicked away a dirt-stained rug to reveal the secret hatch. Ranger had done amazing work in a very short time.

Zion was the first to descend the wooden ladder, wincing when he put weight on his injured leg. Nola was second, and Vale took up the rear, not bothering to close the door since she would be returning in a moment.

Darkness enveloped them, making her miss Knox like crazy. He flourished in this kind of environment. Well, screw him. She would flourish without him.

With a simple mental command, flames ignited at the ends of her fingers. Flickering light scared the shadows away. *Take that!*

"Oh. My. *Gosh*," Nola said. "You do realize you are the coolest person I know, right? How is this even possible?"

"I'll explain later." Vale kissed her cheek and strode over to pick up a lantern Ranger had left. After the wick caught fire, she blew on her fingers.

Zion reached out to claim the lantern's handle. "I'll be back as soon as I can. Nola has your new number. She'll contact you if we spot any combatants in the area."

"Thank—"

Boom!

The ground shook with so much force, both Vale and Nola toppled. Because Vale was directly underneath the hatch, she got hit with the worst of the blaze, an inferno licking over her, burning holes in her clothes but not her skin. What *did* injure her? Planks of wood and pieces of kitchen appliances rained upon her, crushing and slicing with abandon.

Already pinned down, she couldn't dodge when a concrete block slammed atop her leg.

As she screeched with pain, Zion limped over, heaved the block off her and helped her stand.

"What happened?" Nola said between coughing fits. Dust and smoke seemed to clot the air, and soot streaked her face.

"Bomb blast," Vale said. Her best guess. "Are you okay?"

Her sister's dark eyes flittered with the beginnings of hysteria. "I—I'm fine. You?"

"Fine." Vale shared a worried look with Zion.

"This is Erik's doing, I know it," he grated.

Oh, yes. Most definitely. Had Knox remained nearby, intending to kill Erik on his own, or had he returned to his bunker?

Knowing Knox, he'd remained. Was he hurt?

What if *he* had bombed the house?

She sucked in a breath, suffused by horror. He wouldn't do such a thing...would he? He'd promised to stay with her until the very end, but he'd lied about that. Plotting to destroy her wasn't too far outside the realm of possibility.

Despite her aches and pains, she said, "Let's not wait around for the culprit's next trick. Let's go."

"Once we're aboveground, you'll stay with Nola and I'll double back for Erik." He swept Nola into his strong arms and sprinted for the exit, and it was clear he was ignoring his pain, too.

"Strategy isn't your thing, hot stuff." Vale kept pace at his side, the sword bouncing on her back. "Nola will stay in the tunnel, and you and I will head out together to fight side by side, guarding each other's back." *Do it. Tell him everything.* They were allies—for now—and there were things he deserved to know. "I have to be the one to kill the combatants. I can absorb their abilities, as you suspected. What you didn't know? I can also absorb their memories and learn their plans."

"Memories? Truly?" Though his brow knit and his mouth

floundered open and closed, making him look like he wanted to settle in for a lengthy Q and A, he said, "Very well. You will make the kills."

When they reached the exit, Zion said, "You know our deal, Nola."

What deal? Nope, she wasn't going to ask. Mission first, personal curiosity second.

Zion set Nola on her feet. She was trembling, quaking really.

"You're going to be all right." Vale enfolded her sister in a quick hug. "I love you."

"I'm not worried about me," Nola said. "Just…come back alive."

"I will. I'm a superhero. Intangy Girl. Trademark pending. And baby girl, I pity our opponents."

Though she loathed leaving Nola behind, she followed Zion up the second ladder. Up top, he labored to dislodge whatever blocked the hatch.

A boulder, she discovered as they exited. A boulder he rolled back into place, sealing Nola inside the tunnel.

Vale peered at her sister until the last possible second, trying not to crumple when a lone tear slid down Nola's soot-streaked cheek.

Head in the game. If Knox had taught her anything, it was the danger of distraction. And that men sucked worse than she'd realized. And trusting people would only ever lead to heartbreak.

She took stock. A wealth of trees. Air tinged with smoke. No homes in sight. No animals—they'd flown the coop.

With Zion blocking the signal, there was no way to tell if a combatant lurked nearby.

"Come on," he said.

They backtracked, heading to the lavender field. Homes came into view. People stood on their porches, peering into the distance, chattering about what could have happened to the cottage.

"By the way," she said between panting breaths as they entered a thicket. "Ranger planted land mines in the field. The remote probably got destroyed when the house blew."

"I'll be careful."

They cleared the bushes, and Vale stopped, aghast. Knox had stayed, as she'd suspected. The places he wasn't bloody, he was bruised, his skin molted and swollen. Pieces of flesh and muscle were missing. One of his ribs stuck out of his chest.

No way he had set off the bomb. From the looks of it, he might have been the main target.

Adonis and Rush hustled in the opposite direction—why? Couldn't take the heat, or planning an ambush? Where was Erik?

Knox purged an army of mortal soldiers, despite his injuries. He was the most lethal and aggressive male she'd ever beheld, leaving a trail of broken bodies in his wake. He had no mercy, only seething ferocity, and a mighty grudge. He looked at each of his victims as if they'd stolen his most prized possession, whatever that possession happened to be.

Though Vale was furious with him, hurting over his desertion, she couldn't help but bask in his skill and rejoice when his enemies fell. But for every man he took out, three others swarmed him. There were simply too many, and not even the savage Knox could destroy them all.

Or maybe he could. The mortals never went for a kill shot. They tried to…kiss him?

Her eyes went wide. The pheromone was doing its job, twining with the smoke, drifting on the breeze and causing widespread sexual hunger.

"If you feel like making out with the guys you're fighting," Vale told Zion, "just go with it. I can use their distraction to my advantage."

"I feel like killing," he said, but he didn't sound entirely sure. Color suffused his cheeks. "If I'm injured, or things go badly, I'm returning for Nola. I suggest you do the same." He launched

into the fray, concentrating his efforts on the mortals, punching
holes in their chests and proving just how dangerous he could be.

A handful of mortals broke rank, lurching toward her. *My cue.*
She launched into the fray, too. Invisible, she ghosted through
one man, spun, rematerialized, and struck. A single swipe of
her sword ended his life. Rinse, repeat.

Other mortals sensed her, and rushed her way. *Bring it.*

As she fought, she kept Knox in her periphery. He hadn't yet
noticed her or Zion, his single-minded focus awe-inspiring.

She took a peek at Zion to gauge his progress. He paused to
shake his head, as if to dislodge an unwanted thought.

An animalistic roar echoed, Bane shooting through a rift.
Bane, and yet *not* Bane. Vale recoiled.

He was bigger than ever before, like, Hulk big, his muscles
bulging around his torn clothing. He had *predator* eyes, malice
and death glowing within their red depths. His hair had grown
longer, giving him a thick lion's mane, and he had fangs. Or
maybe they were *tusks.* Or dragon sabers? Whatever they were,
they caused serious damage. A small, razor-sharp horn pro-
truded from different places on his body. Black claws tipped his
fingers and his toes.

Had he come for the other combatants...or Nola?

Mustn't let him near the fragile girl. Ever.

Bane tossed lusty mortals through the rift, three at a time,
until it closed. He mowed through the others, blood spraying,
spurting and gushing, turning the field into a macabre water
park. What if he turned his sights to her allies?

An arm flew through the air, minus its body. And there went
a head. Vale...had no reaction. After the assembly, she was only
growing increasingly immune to such brutality.

It was kill or be killed. Today, she would prove that making
a move against her or her associates came with a death sentence.

Two bodies flew past her. Bane—

Was helping Knox and Zion thin the herd, she realized. But what if he turned on the immortals?

"Girl," Bane shouted, his beastly timbre unrecognizable. Before, she'd tasted butterscotch whenever he spoke. Now she tasted mint and lemons. "Give. Her. To. Me."

Zion abandoned ship, hurrying away. No doubt he was going back for Nola, as planned, intending to whisk her away before Bane tracked her. A plan Vale wholeheartedly supported. *Unless things go badly* barely scratched the surface of tonight's events.

What should she do?

Knox blocked a swipe of Bane's claws. As feared, the beast was turning on her allies.

Revolver in hand, Knox plugged his opponent with bullets.

Seemingly irritated, Bane picked up any mortals standing between him and his foe—with his teeth— biting off their heads as if they were made of paper.

Uncaring about the risk, Vale called, "Hey, beasty-boy. Look over here. Look at me." No luck. "Yo, Bane. You want to talk about Nola? You've got to deal with me."

Success! He faced Vale, and roared.

She didn't let herself stare at Knox, who had faced her, as well, and didn't let herself think about how shocked he looked as he reached for her, as if *she* were the prized possession he'd lost.

"Come get me, Bane." She crooked her finger. "This way. Yes, that's it. I've got the one you want."

Uh-oh. Mortals charged her, their lust undeniable. Vale backed away, Bane moving with her. Good, something in her favor.

She pivoted and kicked into a sprint. A glance over her shoulder. Mortals and Bane followed, as hoped. If Knox stayed behind, he would have a reprieve, time to heal. He would be saved...

But she might be killed. She had no idea where to lead her pursuers *without* being ripped to pieces.

CHAPTER THIRTY-THREE

Vale lived!

The realization shook Knox to the core and changed him irrevocably. He'd told himself he'd left her because he'd wanted to save her from having to choose between him and her sister, or him and her world. An unintentional lie. The truth was so clear now. In a secret part of his mind, he'd feared she *wouldn't* choose him.

His decision to sacrifice his life for hers should have been a last resort rather than a first response. He should have exhausted every option in a search for ways to stay together, ways she could win and he could live, while also saving her home. *Their* home. And he would. He would search until desire became reality.

My woman and goal are in sight—go get them. Feeling as if he had wings, Knox chased after her, closing in fast. He had to reach her before Bane, and had to bypass the male without engaging in battle.

{*Outnumbered. Danger level rising. Rift away.*}

Knox would do *nothing* without Vale. His world began and ended with her.

He braced. Behind Bane…beside…finally beyond. No incident. Pleased, he took in everything. Erik, Adonis and Rush had vanished when the beast arrived. They'd known they couldn't beat him. Were they hiding nearby to spring a trap? *I'm ready.* There was no trace of their new allies, Bold and Ryder, and he had to wonder if the males had lost their heads already.

Movement in the trees. Knox homed in… Rush crouched on a limb, three arrows aimed at Vale.

"No!" he shouted, but the warning came too late.

The arrows found a new home in her chest. Crying out, she tripped over a branch and toppled, landing on her side.

Frothing with rage, Knox exchanged his gun for a sword.

Rush leaped from the tree and, though Vale batted away his hands, he easily scooped her up. He glared at Knox with an air of challenge.

No one takes my woman from me.

Knox drew closer…closer still…

"You will come with me, Knox of Iviland." Rush backed away, using Vale's weakened body as a shield. "Or I will—"

"Vale, go lax. Now!" Without pause, he slashed through the other man's neck, savagely severing his head.

Vale had obeyed. Still, the blade had skimmed over a small section of her forehead, filleting a layer of skin. Her next cry of pain filleted *him.*

Rush's body dropped. Knox caught Vale before she hit the ground, clutched her against his chest and ran. She maintained a firm grip on the slain male's crossbow, bringing it with her.

"Let me go," she said, the words slightly slurred. If she'd had the strength, she would have fought him; he had no doubt.

"Never again," he vowed. Running, running.

Bane was gaining on him. Knox had to take action.

"I'm sorry," he said—and yanked out an arrow.

As she screamed, agonized, he spun in a circle, hurling the arrow like a spear. The missile sliced through Bane's eye, and he stumbled.

"I'm sorry," Knox repeated, yanking out a second arrow to repeat the entire process. Spinning. Hurling. The second missile sliced through the beast's other eye, blinding him.

"You…bastard," Vale accused, laboring for breath.

Maneuvering around trees, he reached for the remaining arrow.

"Now wait just a second," she said, latching onto his wrist. "Don't do it. Just…give me a minute to breathe, okay? I just need a minute, maybe an hour to—"

Ruthless because she needed him to be, he yanked out the final barb, allowing her to begin to heal.

"Bastard," she repeated, her voice weaker. He wished he could kill Rush all over again. "No heart…dead inside."

"I *was* dead inside, but you brought me back to life." He glanced over his shoulder. No trace of Bane. No mortals, either. He'd lost them?

What about Erik and his cameras?

Knox ran another mile, just to be safe, before opening a shadowed rift into his bunker. As soon as he had Vale inside, he chucked her on the bed, apologized, then waited, poised to fight dirty.

As soon as the rift closed, he raced around to gather medical supplies.

"I don't want to stay here," she said.

He nudged Rush's bow away and sat at her side. Color dotted her cheeks, her strength returning.

"We can go wherever you want. After." He cut away her shirt, cleaned the wounds to speed up regeneration.

Though she offered no resistance physically, she was detached emotionally and mentally. "Soon as you're done, I'm leaving. Alone. Don't try to stop me."

"I won't. But wherever you go, I will follow." Now and always.

She humphed. "Don't act as if you care about my well-being." As she spoke, torn flesh wove back together.

Pleased, he smoothed a lock of hair from her damp brow and hooked the strand behind her ear. She flinched, avoiding further contact. The rejection hurt, but he tendered no rebuke. He deserved this, and more.

"I do care, *valina*."

"You don't. You can't." She looked away from him. "You didn't trust me."

"Only for a moment."

"You left me behind."

"I did, yes, and it is a decision I will forever regret. It was also the most difficult thing I've ever done, even though I thought I was doing the right thing, even though I thought I was making things better, easier for you. Then we were bombed and... I thought you'd died. I was inconsolable."

"And that's supposed to make things right between us?"

"No. Nothing can. But in time, I will prove I'm here to stay. I won't be parted from you for any reason."

She studied his expression, her own hardening. "*I* don't care, then. You knew how I'd suffered after my father's abandonment and left, anyway. You hurt me."

The heavy weight of dejection settled on his shoulders, but still he persisted. "You'll never know how sorry I am."

"Sorry doesn't make it right, either," she said, her chin trembling.

Again, he felt his heart being ripped from his chest and stomped on. "I would do anything to go back, to stand by you when you needed me."

"I don't care!" A whirlwind of hurt and fury, she erupted, hitting his chest with tight fists. "You react badly to threats, remember? Well, here I am, threatening you, and I have no plans to stop. You had better leave before I push you past the point of no return."

"I'm not going anywhere. Hit me all you want, all you need. I can take it."

Tears streamed down her cheeks as she took him up on the
offer, hitting him until her newfound energy was depleted.
With a sigh, she sagged against him, resting her cheek upon
his shoulder.

"Did I hurt you?" she asked softly.

"No. I'm fine." Better than fine, now that he had her wrapped
up in his arms. Soon she would learn just how far he was willing to go to keep her there.

"That's a shame."

The corners of his mouth twitched.

"Maybe you did the right thing," she said, and sniffled. "A
relationship between us was never going to work. We are blood-
born enemies."

No! "I will *never* be your enemy, Vale. You can trust me in
all ways, at all times."

"Not if your king—"

"I have a plan," he interjected, sensing there might be a chink
in her armor. "I will use Gunnar's sword."

Lifting her head, she searched his face with red, puffy eyes.
"You figured out the ramifications?"

"Yes. I pondered it during our last cuddle time," he said, and
she blushed. "There are specific indentations on the hilt. If I
position my hand correctly, I believe the metal will liquefy, absorb into my body and heal me of any wounds before seeping
out to reform into the sword."

"Great in theory, but mystical ink isn't a wound."

Combing his fingers through her silken hair, he said, "The
metal should also cleanse my blood and filter out the ink."

"And the downside?"

"Even if Ansel's compulsion isn't filtered out, I will bond
to the sword. That bond should override the ink, but it means
whoever holds the sword will hold my future. They'll have the
power to control me."

She frowned. "So you'll trade one master for another. Where's the upside?"

"Ansel won't be able to compel me to hurt you or chase certain combatants. I can do what's best for us, rather than the Iviland ruler." He could search for a way to free himself from the sword.

"What if you're wrong, and you're bound to the sword *and* Ansel?"

"We will have a contingency plan in place." He would rather die than put Vale's life in peril.

"I think you're missing a few steps. I mean, the pheromone is in my blood the same way the ink is in yours. You should drain yourself as much as possible first, drill holes in a bone or two to get to your marrow, *then* absorb the metal so that it goes straight to the source." She pursed her lips, as if irritated by how much she'd shared, and stood. "Anyway. This conversation is over. I'm leaving."

He dropped to his knees directly in front of her. "I don't deserve mercy, I know, but I'm begging for it. Stay. Please. You're safe here."

She was unmoved—no, there were definitely cracks in her armor. Her features were cold and hard, but her hands were wringing together.

Might as well tell her everything.

"I'm not going to win this war, Vale. Victory will be yours, one way or another. And I *will* find a way to survive your triumph. Not even death will keep me from you." He'd meant what he'd said. Nothing would part them. He just needed time. "I know I've made mistakes with you, but you are the first and only woman I've wanted specifically, the first person I've trusted. From birth, I experienced betrayal at every turn. During war, I *expected* betrayal or I died, and to me, survival mattered most. Survival, vengeance and freedom. Until you. *You* matter most, and if you tell me how to fix this, I will. I'll do anything."

Her hands fisted. Voice hoarse, she said, "I told you I wouldn't take you back, even if you crawled."

A tinge of panic. "You're allowed to change your mind. Please, change your mind."

"I just... I can't risk going through this again. My motto? Always be the leavee. You confirmed my fears were well-founded. The same day you convinced me to trust you, you bailed."

"I'm a fool, but even fools can learn the error of their ways."

She scrubbed a hand down her face. "You said you'd do anything to fix this. Well, I'm asking for space to think, okay?"

This was going to hurt. Bad. "I will give you space." Knox straightened. He strode to the foot of the bed, where he removed the swords and daggers strapped to his body. Even The Bloodthirsty. He placed each weapon on the mattress. Then he stalked to the alcove and closet to gather the weapons stored there.

At the bed once again, he unloaded his bounty. Vale watched with an air of confusion and wariness.

Shoulders back, he told her, "My bunker and my arsenal are yours to do with as you please. And this—this is yours, too." He rooted in his pocket and withdrew the necklace he'd bought for her. "I saw it and thought of you."

Her mouth floundered open and closed.

"May I?" he asked. When she nodded, he glided behind her to anchor the jewelry around her neck. The different stones looked magnificent on her, better than he'd imagined.

"I want... I want...argh!" A tear streamed down her cheek as she traced the sapphire, and the sight nearly undid him. "Right now, I want to take a bath and wash off the battle grime. You can stay, but you can't join me. Got it?" She stomped off.

Before the temptation to hide in shadows and watch over her overwhelmed him, he sat and gripped his knees. His love for her was a raw and ferocious thing. The softness in his heart. No, it *was* his heart. The organ beat for Vale alone. He had no life apart from her.

His ears twitched. Clothing rustled and water splashed. Fantasies wove through his head. He imagined water droplets sluicing along Vale's naked curves, her skin flushing with heat. Cool air kissing her puckered nipples. Her belly quivering, and her inner walls slick and aching to be filled.

He would lay her upon the bed, and she would spread her legs in welcome.

He hardened swiftly, throbbing for her.

"I can almost *hear* your thoughts," she called. "Stop."

"Impossible. Let me worship at the altar of your beauty."

"You can look, but you can't touch." When she emerged, she paraded past him, unabashed, head high. She wore water droplets and the necklace, and his gaze remained riveted on her until she disappeared inside the closet.

By the time she exited, he was quivering like a randy school lad. She had dressed in one of his shirts and a pair of his pants, the material cinched to her body.

"I'm going to take a nap," she announced without glancing in his direction. "It's been a long, hard day. I mean *tough*! It's been a *tough* day. I'm going to sleep on the bed. Try to join me, and I'll cut off your testicles."

Long. Hard. Had she, perhaps, looked his way, after all? "The loss would be worth the prize, but I'll respect your wishes. Always. I love you, Vale, and if you'll give me a chance, I *will* find a way to prove it."

She blinked rapidly while shaking her head, mouth opening and closing again. "You don't love me. You can't."

"I can, and I do. You mean *everything* to me." Giving her the space she required, he trekked to the pool.

After programming the water to arctic, he jumped in. And it was odd. For the first time in centuries, he had no weapon nearby. He wasn't cloaked in shadows, or clocking a companion's every move.

If Vale wanted his head, she could have it. *I'm hers for the taking.*

He soaked for over an hour, determined to get his body under strict control...failing. Giving up, he climbed out of the pool, draped a towel around his waist and headed for the closet. He would dress, and—

Die of happiness. Vale wasn't napping. She stood at the foot of the bed, the weapons he'd given her scattered across the floor. Panting, she ate him alive with her gaze.

He shot harder, his erection jutting under the towel. She was still desirous of him? "Vale?"

"I need a favor," she said, the words a wicked incantation.

He was instantly bespelled. "Anything. Forever and always, your wish is my command."

Vale craved Knox with the passion of a thousand suns. Honeyed whiskey in her mouth, need in her blood. She'd fought to remain detached, but in war, there were always causalities. Her common sense was the first to die.

Her resistance had just gotten hit with an H-bomb.

In this case, H = horny.

The universe seemed to be aiding his cause. While Knox had bathed, Vale had gotten a text from Nola, letting her know all was well. Relief had quickly eroded her defenses, and she'd thought, *No one is guaranteed a tomorrow, not even an immortal.*

Then the floodgates had opened, and she'd thought, *Everyone makes mistakes. Knox didn't trust me, and I didn't trust him. I considered leaving him, too, I just didn't have the lady balls to pull the trigger. Now we're even. Why not go back to our original deal? Enjoy each other while we work to get to the final two.*

Also, Knox's stunning proclamation had played on constant repeat inside her head. *I love you.* Three little words, yet they'd torched the rest of her anger.

And really, the man had given her his home and his weapons. What had she ever given him? Besides a mix of grief and pleasure. He'd bowed before her, as if she were his sovereign queen, and entrusted her with his future. Could she do the same for him?

Her heart still smarted, but forgiveness had become a certainty rather than an impossibility.

"Zion and Bane are with my sister," she said. Business first. "The trio is alive and well and working together."

"I suspected as much during the assembly."

"Yeah. Bane's reaction to Nola's supposed death threw me. Apparently, he kidnapped her from Zion multiple times. He's smitten, and as long as he cages the rage, he's the best protector she could have. The problem is, Erik turned safe houses into hazard zones, so Team Zanola has no place to stay."

He grimaced, as if he'd just been kicked in the honeypots, but said, "The bunker is yours. If you want them here, they are welcome."

She'd offered the bunker to Nola, and Nola alone, but her sister had refused to part with the guys. "Let's be real. You can't play nice with the other kids on the playground. And that's okay. I trust Bane with Nola's life, but not ours. While I do trust Zion, I could change my mind." Better safe than sorry. "You once mentioned a backup crib."

His eyes brightened. "Yes. Erik didn't find it. I doubt anyone did. Shadows are stationed there." He rushed to the table, swiped up a map and brought it to show her. "It's here, under a temple."

A temple that was hidden in the jungles of Guatemala, and probably in ruins. Mayan? Maybe visited by tourists, and oh, wow, Knox smelled good. Growing dizzy with desire, she hastened on. "I'm meeting with the group in about an hour."

The map floated to the floor as he studied her face. Those crystalline irises projected reverence, hope and a passion so vibrant its glow would shine inside her for years to come.

In a gravelly voice, he said, "What should we do while we wait?"

Easy. "Each other." Why fight her attraction to him? What

good would it do? "I'm not saying everything's perfect between us, but I want you. That hasn't changed."

She reached out. With a flick of her wrist, she removed his towel. Suddenly he was gloriously bare, all that muscle-cut bronzed skin on display.

He'd been irresistible before. Despite everything that had happened—heck, *because* of everything that had happened—he was necessary now.

"The hunger in your eyes humbles me." He traced her lips with a single fingertip.

"These markings," she said. The tattoos she longed to trace with her tongue. "They're like scars. A testament to everything you've overcome—everything you *will* overcome."

He trembled beneath her gaze.

She peered at his erection. How could she not? It was pointing directly at her, the tip glistening with moisture, just the way she liked.

"See what you do to me." He gripped the base and stroked up, and her inner walls clenched. "This is for you, *valina*. Only, ever, for you."

"Then give it to me. I want it."

He exuded male satisfaction as he shucked off her shirt. When he realized she wasn't wearing a bra, he groaned, as if in pain, then ripped at the waist of her pants.

The second she was naked, except for the gorgeous necklace she never wanted to take off, he wiped a hand over his mouth.

"I will *never* tire of looking at you, *valina*."

And she would never tire of *the way* he looked at her, as if she were a miracle come to startling life. The object of his fascination and obsession. That look did something to her, acting as a soothing balm, beginning to heal the hurt in her heart. Combined with his willingness to give a safe house to an enemy, just because she'd asked…yeah, she was a goner.

With a curse, he crashed his lips into hers, plunged his tongue into her mouth, and demanded total surrender.

She gave it, feeding his passion with her own.

The kiss was wild right from the start, untamed and unstoppable, a prelude to every delicious thing to come. Helpless to do otherwise, she clung to him.

There had been times he'd made her blood seem like a fine wine or smooth single malt. Today it was hard liquor, one hundred proof, and she got drunk fast.

Her knees weakened. He held on tight and leaned forward, urging her onto the mattress as the pheromone enveloped them in a rapturous haze. There was no stopping it. But it didn't change the tone of the kiss—the sizzling chemistry between her and Knox was all their own.

His muscular weight settled over her, pinning her. The width of his hips forced her legs to spread and make a place for him. Naked flesh met naked flesh. Heat met heat, male met female. She sank her nails into his tree of life tattoo, leaving *her* mark.

He ground his erection against her slick femininity, which only made her greedy for more. As his big, calloused hands alternated between kneading her breasts, strumming her nipples and stroking her stomach and inner thighs, she licked the bands around his neck, just as she'd fantasized.

He stiffened. When she purred her approval, he relaxed, angling his head to give her better access.

"You want to come?" he demanded.

To silence a plea, she bit the cord that ran along his shoulder. The words escaped, anyway. "Pleeeease, Knox. Yes. Get inside me. Let me come."

"What do you want inside you?" He slid a finger into her aching core. "This?"

Her thoughts were fragmenting. *Dizzy with need, too much, not enough.* "Need this..." When she wrapped her fingers around the base of his shaft and attempted to draw toward her entrance, he shifted his hips, denying her.

"Ah, ah, ah." He tsk-tsked. "I'm showing you how much I love you. A process that takes time and attention."

He'd become a hedonist, torturer, and everything she'd ever desired. Slowly, almost lazily, he sucked on her nipples, then tongued her navel, her body his personal playground of sensual delights.

The heat...the pressure... Streams of pleasure drove her to the brink again and again, and yet the diabolical man somehow circumvented her climax every time.

He slid his finger out of her to circle the heart of her need.

"Knox!" Need screamed inside her.

"Do you want me to finger you deeper, sweet *valina*?"

"Yes, yes! Deeper." Eager, she spread her legs wider, expecting him to give it to her, plus interest. He would stretch and prepare her for penetration but...

He drew tantalizing circles around her clitoris, again and again, never quite making contact. She shifted her position, trying to lead him where she wanted him, but he merely shifted with her.

Circle, circle.

Breathless with longing, she praised him. She cursed him. She begged and bargained. She commanded. Through it all, he remained steadfast in his determination—but he did not remain unaffected. Sweat trickled from his temples, tremors rocked him and his inhalations shallowed.

He kissed her jaw...ran her earlobe between his teeth. "I was born and bred to kill. You were born into this war and given the ability to seduce. Physically, I am stronger, but it is you who wields the power. You bring me to my knees."

Circle, circle. "Knox. Please."

"I plan to strip you of sanity, love. I want my devotion to you branded inside and out. Want every part of you to crave every part of me."

She beat at his shoulders, crying, "Every part of me craves you, I swear. And I know you love me. I do. Now get inside me!"

"But do you know *how much* I love you?" He flicked his tongue against the pulse that tripped at the base of her neck and finally, wildly, wantonly thrust two fingers into her feminine sheath.

"Knox!" She arched her hips, chasing those fingers as he drew them out. "Make me come."

"Do you know how much I love you?" he repeated. Another inward thrust. Another hated exit. In. Out.

Need became madness, pleasure soon tinged with pain. A girl had to give as good as she got. Vale reached between their bodies, and this time he couldn't move away fast enough—or maybe he hadn't tried. She squeezed his erection, earning a groan from him, and said, "If this is my measuring stick, then you want me more than *anything*."

"That's right. More than anything."

She stroked him. Then she let go. Cruel to be kind.

He lifted his head to meet her gaze, and if she'd been standing, her knees would have buckled. His irises were alive with longing, burning, burning, no longer cold, calculating pits of malevolence. She saw every ounce of love he professed to have for her, adoration and affection, too. Everything she'd ever wanted to see from a man.

Beneath it, she saw regret for the way he'd treated her, determination and lust, so much lust.

This warrior would die for her without a moment's hesitation. He wouldn't leave her again, she knew it, felt it. The knowledge cauterized the last vestiges of hurt in her heart.

Vale flattened her hands on the muscle and sinew decorating his chest. Pushing him back, rising to straddle his waist, she said, "All right, baby. It's my turn to show you just how much *I* love *you*."

CHAPTER THIRTY-FOUR

Primal need had reduced Knox to his most animalistic self. Arousal heated his skin, hotter and hotter. Vale's slick core pressed against his shaft, drenching every inch, daring him to thrust inside.

He'd never experienced anything like this, an all-consuming need to possess and be possessed, to own and be owned, to surrender everything but take everything, too.

His ferocity on the battlefield couldn't compare to his ferocity here, in this bed, with this woman. *His* woman. He planned to spend the rest of his life—however long or short—attending to her every whim.

Then her words registered, and he lost the ability to breathe. She loved him?

"Tell me again, *valina*."

"I love you, Knox. Your strength and courage are without equal. No one has ever protected me the way you do. And the way you make me feel…as if I'm something special, and you can't live without me… I'll never get enough."

"You are. I can't," he said, framing her radiant face with his hands. "You are everything I ever wanted, everything I ever needed. A prize among prizes. The greatest treasure in this realm or any other."

She was poised above him, the length of her bicolored hair streaming over the pillow, her features soft and her nipples hard, the necklace glittering around her neck. Need for her strengthened him in ways he'd never expected.

Having loved ones wasn't a liability, he decided, but a privilege. This exquisite woman had given him a reason to fight. Not just to live, but for a better life.

Love conquers all, she'd said. And she was right. Love was a far more stalwart motivator than hate.

"I had no cause to laugh. Until you," he said. "I didn't look forward to anything but the possibility of freedom. Until you. I never experienced true pleasure. Until you. My life begins and ends with you."

The smile she gifted to him would fuel a thousand fantasies. "As my life begins and ends with *you*. You are mine, my man, and I'm never letting you go."

Knox marveled. She did love him. Despite the past and the complications, this brave, beautiful woman loved him. "We'll find a way to overcome. Nothing will separate us again."

"Nothing," she agreed.

{*Protect her, no matter the cost.*}

The command surprised him. The *eyaer* understood now. He'd had nothing until she'd become his everything. With her happiness, he'd found his own, her life the reason he woke in the morning, and dreamed at night.

"I love you, so much. There's no one more beautiful. No one smarter, wilier..." He traced a fingertip down, down, between her breasts, along the flat plane of her stomach, then circled the little bundle of nerves between her legs with more force, making her cry out.

Her eyelids fluttered as he brought the finger to his mouth and licked away her wetness.

"There's no one more delicious," he said.

Moaning, she leaned down to claim his mouth in a searing kiss. Her breasts smashed into his chest, her nipples hard little points that rubbed against him, sparking friction between their bodies.

Lost in her and hoping never to be found, he met each thrust of her tongue with one of his own. He made promises with that kiss. An eternity of love and dedication. To find a way to be together forever. His life given for hers, if necessary.

He wound his arms around her, one draping her nape, the other resting on her lower back, both holding on to the most precious part of his heart. Tongues dueling. Moans rising. She rolled her hips, moving her feminine heat over his erection.

He nearly came apart at the seams. "Again, *valina*."

She understood. "I love you, Knox."

As a reward, he delved his hand between the beautiful globes of her ass, angled his wrist to find her feminine sheath—the center of his world—and thrust three fingers deep inside her. Scalding hot, soaking wet, tight as a glove. He moved those fingers in and out, in and out, propelling her toward the brink.

"Yes," she cried. "Yes, yes, yes."

Mimicking sex, still thrusting those fingers in and out of her, he planted his feet on the bed and lifted his hips to grind his erection into her clitoris. Her next cry broke at the edges, and her inner walls quivered.

She would have climaxed if he hadn't withdrawn his fingers. Somehow found the strength to croak, "Not yet, love."

"Knox!" She nipped at his bottom lip. "Put those fingers back inside me right this second or pay the price!"

He maneuvered her to her back and loomed over her. "Going to give you something else to come upon. Something bigger, harder."

"Yes." She nodded, eager, and wrapped her legs around his waist. "That. Give me that."

"But since you complained…" He slid a single finger inside her, bent his head and sucked her nipples with enough force to leave a mark.

Teasing her was both a delight and a torment.

Her head thrashed. "How about this," she said between gasping breaths. "You give me what I want, what I need, and I won't kill you."

"You need it, then? You're desperate for it?" *For me.* He gripped the base of his erection and dipped the plump head into her tightness. "Like this?"

"Yes!" Her back arched, and she tossed her arms overhead to grip a vine. "More."

"How much more?"

"All of it, baby," she said, her voice thicker, throatier than ever before. "Please."

Baby again. An endearment. She was the first to ever use one with him.

Just like that, his iron control snapped.

"Yes. I will give it to you. All of it." Frantic, Knox thrust his hips and plunged deep into his woman, filling her, giving her every throbbing inch of his shaft.

She screamed. He roared, the pleasure almost too much. He willed himself to last. This would not end until she'd come apart in his arms.

Gritting his teeth, he moved in her, sliding out, then in. Ah! Had anything ever felt so right? Her body had been made for his. She gloved him tighter than a fist. Was so hot and wet. Perfect.

In, out. He tried to go slow, tried to savor. Tried to make love gently, tenderly. Tension coiled inside him, ecstasy and agony.

"Harder! Faster," she commanded, clawing at his back. Tension coiled inside her, too. Never had she looked so anguished.

Knox quickened his tempo. Soon, he was slamming inside her, rattling the entire bed. The potted trees that acted as bedposts shook, leaves falling from limbs.

On his next inward glide, he rotated his hips in a circular motion, gyrating, hitting Vale deeper, harder. Hips a piston, he pounded into her, nothing held back, his testicles slapping against her ass. Not once did he temper his strength. Tomorrow, she would feel him every time she moved and breathed.

He hooked his arms under her knees, lifting her legs, and another scream burst from her. Her inner walls squeezed his length, again and again, demanding more of him—demanding *all* of him.

Resistance was futile.

Succumbing to bliss, Knox threw back his head and bellowed with satisfaction.

After Knox cleaned their bodies, he cozied up beside Vale for cuddle time, and it thrilled her.

Breathing in the sweetness of their mingled scents, she enjoyed the paradise known as aftermath.

Vale had never experienced such mind-blowing pleasure. Knox had upended her entire world. The planet could have imploded, and she wouldn't have cared.

Knox traced the ridges of her spine. "BTW. Earth men are idiots."

She snorted at his adorable use of the acronym. "How so?"

"No one snatched you up while they had the chance. Now they'll die if they attempt it."

"Well, like you said, I'm beautiful, smart and wily, which means I'm *way* overqualified for the job of girlfriend."

He chuckled and kissed her temple. "This is true."

Despite the moment of amusement, familiar worries spread like a virus. Diagnosis: terminal.

"What are we going to do?" she asked softly. "The war rages on. Only one winner can be crowned. Until you're free of the slave bands, your king has unmitigated power over you. He can command you to betray me, and you'll be forced to obey."

To stop himself from hurting her, Knox might try to off himself. Might? Ha! He would, definitely. He'd already threatened it. Face it, the man was gaga over her. As stalwartly as he'd always fought on the battlefield, he now fought for Vale.

Could she do any less for him?

For the first time in her life, she had a man who loved her unconditionally, who put her first, who loved her, yes, but liked her, too. He'd learned from his mistakes and would never again abandon her. She was keeping him, now and always. Final answer.

"We are going to love each other," he said. "We are going to be honest and open with each other. Help each other. Trust each other. Fight side by side. Fight for each other and Earth. No other realm will rule this land, we'll make sure of it. But we'll prepare for invasion, just in case. And after we escort your sister and her guardians to the temple, we'll return here, drain me of blood and bind me to Gunnar's sword."

The risk unnerved her. What if the sword failed? They'd never put it to the test. What if he *died*? "Maybe we should wait. A day or two won't make a difference, right?" She'd just gotten him back, and she wasn't ready to lose him again. Or ever. "We can research the sword. Maybe Celeste knows more, and I just haven't tapped into the right memories." But in her heart of hearts Vale knew there were no more recollections about the sword.

"I don't want to wait. Ansel will contact me soon. After he threatened you..." He shook his head. "No."

He'd been a slave so long. He must feel like a kid at Christmas, only ten million times more anticipatory, since this particular wish had been on his list for centuries.

Only a monster would ask him to wait.

She'd rather embrace her inner monster than lose him. "I just want to make sure we're taking every precaution. Give me one

day. Just one. I can scour the internet, check out different my-
thologies and see if there's something based on Gunnar's sword."

He kissed her temple, and though it cost him dearly, he said,
"One day, then. For you, anything."

"Thank you, baby. Truly."

They lounged in bed, but all too soon the clock zeroed out.
They dressed, donned their swords and rifted to the spot she
and Nola had agreed to meet—somewhere they'd sworn never
to go, and probably the worst place on Earth. The football stadium of their high school rival, Blueberry Hill High. Under the
bleachers, to be exact.

Night had fallen, and the stadium was currently empty. Vale
used her cell phone as a flashlight, determined to memorize her
surroundings in case she and Knox had to make a hasty getaway, and immediately regretted it. Trash was scattered about,
as expected, but hidden among the empty candy bar wrappers
and plastic cups were used condoms.

A Where's Waldo of discarded peen sleeves.

At one with the darkness, Knox performed a perimeter check
before taking a post at her side. Perfect timing. A rift opened a
few feet away, giving Vale a peek into a well-lit…motel room?
Must be. The small space had modern furnishings, with a decorating style she'd call cheap chic.

A scowling Zion marched through first, then Nola, with Bane
in the rear. Suddenly three aggressive males—centuries-old enemies—were in close quarters, and unlike the assemblies, their
powers remained activated.

Before a situation could develop, Vale got the ball rolling,
hugging her sister, who had a little more color in her cheeks
and a little less shake in her stance. "You should know," she said,
"I'm going to find a way to make you immortal *without* joining this war. Considering all the supernatural weapons floating
around, there's got to be a way."

"The boys are on the case, too," she replied.

Good. Three heads were better than one. Speaking of "the boys." "You sure you want to stay with Zion and Bane?" she asked loud enough for everyone to hear. "You're my innocent little sis, and they—"

Both men snorted.

Bane arched a brow. "Innocent?" he asked, his voice pure butterscotch. "That's like calling a dragon a bird."

Nola elbowed him in the stomach. "I'm not that bad."

"You're right. You're worse."

The heat sizzling between those two...

"She's sure," Zion snapped, and Vale tasted citrus.

"Watch your tone," Knox snapped back. "You speak to Vale with respect, or you don't speak to her at all."

That's my man. Pride puffed up her chest. "Yeah," she said. "Respect."

Nola looked like she had to stifle a grin.

"If everyone walks away from this expedition with only minor injuries," Vale said, "I'll consider it a win. Who am I kidding? If everyone *crawls* away, it'll be a win."

"Is it my turn to speak now?" Nola asked Zion, then rolled her eyes when he offered a royal wave. "Yes, I'm sure I want to stay with these nutjobs. I like having strapping immortals at my beck and call."

"Those immortals better like being at your beck and call, because you are the only reason *my* immortal offered up his guest home." Vale flicked Knox a *just go with it* look. "In return, they'll owe us. Big-time."

He did more than go with it; he ran at full speed. "You will help us end Erik and Adonis—but you will stand down for the kill. Vale renders the final blow, and that is nonnegotiable."

Zion popped his jaw but gave a curt nod. He'd agreed before. Why so reluctant now?

Bane gritted out, "Very well."

"So, we're doing this, then?" Vale asked. "We're forming a

kick-A alliance? You don't harm us, we don't harm you, and we all work together with a common goal?"

"I...would like that," Knox said. His chin was up, his shoulders back, pride in every inch of his bearing. "I've never had true allies before."

"Shiloh," Bane began.

"I never gave Shiloh my word. In fact, I warned him not to trust me." Knox looked to Vale, heartbreak in his eyes. "My king allied with his, and I was supposed to work with him. But Shiloh didn't know Ansel had also given me a command to kill him if it would help advance my cause. So I did it. I killed a good man."

She kissed his cheek, offering support rather than censure. What he'd done had torn him up inside, that much was obvious. Ansel had to be stopped.

Was Gunnar's sword truly the only way?

"If you keep your word," Knox told the others, "I'll keep mine. I will fight to save you rather than destroy you. When Erik and Adonis have been taken out, we can reevaluate our alliance. With the warriors from the other wars joining ours, we might need to band together longer than anticipated."

"I'll stand with you," Zion said.

Bane peered at Nola, silent, then nodded. "I'll stand with you, as well."

"Let's get you ensconced in your new safe house, then." Knox opened a rift, not bothering to cover it with shadows, and motioned the others to enter.

Zion stepped through first, then Nola, then Bane. The males didn't like having people behind them, especially enemies, and repeatedly glanced over their shoulders, as if expecting an attack. Knox and Vale took up the rear, side by side.

With Bane and Zion at his side acting as lookouts, Knox guarded the rift until it closed. Vale studied the most luxurious cave in history. A limestone bedrock had collapsed, forming a gorgeous cenote, the water so clear she could observe the little fish swimming below the surface. Crystals twinkled from the ceiling, almost as dazzling as stars, and though the air had a faint musty scent, there was no hint of rot or decay.

"Careful," Knox said to the others. "The tunnels are vast. I haven't been down here since before our imprisonment, so I have no idea what's happened to them. Above you is a temple. Around the temple is a jungle. There are no physical exits down here. You'll have to rift in and out."

"Thank you," Nola said. "We appreciate this." She nudged one man, then the other.

"Thank you," Zion and Bane muttered in unison.

Knox went rigid, his dread palpable as he glanced at his ring.

"What's wrong?" Vale asked. But she knew.

"Ansel is requesting a meeting."

So soon? "Can you ignore him?"

He brought her hand to his lips, kissed her knuckles, his gaze telling her everything. No, he couldn't; if speaking with the king wouldn't place his life in danger, he was compelled to answer.

"We must return home," he said, and she knew the pull of the summons was only growing stronger.

She winked at Nola, and Nola winked back, the small action assuring Vale that all would be well. Then Knox dragged her into another antechamber, out of sight. As black branched around his eyes, he opened a shadowed rift into the bunker.

By the time the doorway closed, sealing them inside, he was shaking...couldn't stop himself from brushing his thumb over the ring. A screen of light appeared, Ansel's image taking shape in the center. Vale stood behind him—it—so he couldn't see her.

"Kneel," the purple-haired male ordered unceremoniously. His tone was hard, and it filled her with dread of her own.

A scowling Knox dropped to his knees. The ends of her fingers heated, her body gearing for a fight.

"Is the Terran girl with you?" the POS asked.

Knox offered no response. At first. Compulsion proved irresistible and he soon gave a clipped nod.

She expected Ansel's next question, yet it resurrected her ire in a hurry. "Has she taken the Mark of Disgrace?"

"No," he said.

"Very well." The king performed a royal motion with his hand. "Confiscate her Rifters. If she protests, hurt her. Break something."

What was Ansel's endgame here?

Before Knox could obey, she marched to his side and removed the crystal-metal hybrids, unwilling to put him through a physical altercation.

He accepted, his narrowed eyes projecting sorrow and rage. Trembling, he shoved the bands into his pants pocket.

"Kneel," Ansel told her.

"Nah. I'm going to stand." Last time, she'd knelt in a show of solidarity with Knox. Now she knew Ansel a little better and would rather die than encourage his god complex. "You aren't my king."

"Not yet, but soon." Ansel raised his chin. "This is your last chance to take the mark, female."

The sorrow and rage intensified, Knox's sense of helplessness probably fueling the flames. *Must win his freedom.* Convincing him to wait even a day had been a huge mistake.

"I see your *last chance* and raise you two fingers." She flipped the king a double-bird salute.

He had no idea what the gesture meant, but he did understand her intent. "Very well. You have brought this on yourself." He offered Knox a cold smile. "You will keep the girl's Rifters. Do not give them back for any reason."

Knox breathed in, out. Silent. His trembling worsened.

"The second All War combatants have been found," Ansel said. "They are alive, and like the third group, they will be joining your war at the next assembly. My son, Prince Rorick, is one of the survivors."

Knox glanced at Vale with dawning horror, and she figured Prince Rorick was just as evil as Ansel.

"I know what you're planning," Knox rushed out. "Do not do this. After everything I've won for you, I ask this, and only this. Do not—"

"You will kill every combatant in the war, excluding Rorick," the ruthless Ansel interjected. "You will start with the girl, Vale of Terra. Kill her. Stop at nothing to get the deed done. Then, when all the others are dead, you will kneel and offer your heart to Prince Rorick."

CHAPTER THIRTY-FIVE

Kill her. Stop at nothing.

The command resounded inside Knox's mind as the king's image faded. Slave bands burning, blistering, he sprang to his feet.

Vale stood before him and backed away, her beautiful face pale, sickly. "Let's talk about this, Knox."

"Pick up your sword and behead me," he commanded. He had to force the words past the overwhelming compulsion to end her life, hatred for Ansel seething inside him. Fury, too. Fury and frustration and pain. "Do not wait. Do it. Do it now."

Kill the woman he loved? He would rather die. And so he would. He would die.

"No. I'm not going to hurt you, and you're not going to hurt me." She gave a violent shake of her head, long hair slapping at her cheeks. *Tangled* hair. Because she'd thrashed against the pillow only an hour ago, screaming with the pleasure he'd given her. "We'll drain you and use Gunnar's sword, just like you wanted. We'll break the compulsion."

The *eyaer*...wept. Because it knew the truth—he was dead either way.

"I'll resist the process now," he said. There was no other way. "Do it! Kill me," he said, his hand unwittingly unsheathing Gunnar's sword.

She stepped back, but she also unsheathed Celeste's sword.

He closed the distance, but she made no move against him. Shaking, he gripped the hilt of his weapon so tightly his knuckles almost ripped through his skin.

Tears trickled down her cheeks, leaving little pink tracks. "Please, Knox. Fight this."

"I'm trying, but..." *Failing.* Only a matter of minutes until he succumbed. "You must kill me. There's no other way you'll walk away from this."

"Just...give me the Rifters. Or I'll steal them from you. Then I'll leave. We'll stay away from each other until you're able to use Gunnar's sword on yourself."

"Can't bring myself to do it...will only hunt you down...run you to ground like an animal and take your head," he choked out, his voice wet, thick. "Kill me before I kill you. Please." Before he snuffed out her warmth and her light. Before he destroyed his sun. "Don't let me do this to you, *valina.* I'm dead, anyway. You heard the king."

"No. No! Don't you see? I'm dead if I kill you. I can't live knowing I took your life."

Still, he stalked closer... "Vale. We're running out of time... not sure how much longer I can resist."

"Knox," she breathed.

The moment he was within range, he swiped out his arm, unable to halt the action. No, no, no! Fear wrung a cry from deep in his soul—

She skidded back, the blade missing her throat by less than an inch. Relief flowed through him, but it faded as quickly as it had erupted. She might be able to hold him off for a little while, but in the end he *would* overpower her. He had too much experience, and with the shadows, she would never see him coming.

"Vale, *please*. I beseech you. Kill me."

Backing away... The weapons that were scattered across the floor tripped her, and she stumbled, fell, landing beside the chains he'd once considered using to bind her. As she leaped to her feet, he felt his body lunge, his arm slashing through the air.

Memories guided her, as they'd done at the assembly. She rolled out of the way, and he'd never been so grateful that another warrior had the skills needed to evade and use against him.

"Because of you, I had a good life, Vale. I have no regrets. Not anymore. Kill me and win the war. Help me see my Minka again. Send me to her. Save your realm. Save your *sister*."

More tears. A sob. "Stop!" she shouted. "Just stop."

"What if Ansel tells me to kill Nola next? What then? *Save her!*"

"I—I can't. I love you."

"It's almost too late, Vale. Please."

And then it *was* too late. Knox pursued Vale through the bunker, over furniture, again and again their weapons clanging together as he thrust and she parried.

Sweat dampened his skin, his muscles shaking from exertion as he tried, tried so hard, to oppose Ansel's command.

"Don't let the king win," she pleaded. "Fight *him*."

"Want to so bad." Even when Vale's sweet, luscious pheromone electrified his senses, rousing his desires, the compulsion remained unshaken. He twisted, struck at her. "Can't."

She dodged, but not quickly enough. The tip of his blade sliced her shoulder. With a yelp, she dropped her sword. He twisted again, struck again, and she dove backward, rolling to her feet with his bow in hand, The Bloodthirsty aimed at his chest.

A crimson river poured down her arm, and the sight destroyed him.

"The arrow won't chase me." He stalked around her. She followed his motions, never dropping her position. "For you, the arrow is simply an arrow. It won't even slow me. You should have picked up the revolver." She could use it, if there were bullets in the chamber. She just couldn't reload it. "A shot between the eyes will buy you a little time." *Listen! Heed my words. Slow me!*

"Focus on me. On our love, on our relationship and our future. Focus on what can be, if only we survive this." Tears pouring down her cheeks. Her arms began to shake.

Hot tears poured down *his* cheeks. *Can't do this. Can't hurt her.* His slave bands said, *You must.*

The *eyaer* disagreed. {*Her death heralds your own. Save her, and you will save yourself.*}

Vale did nothing as he kicked the bow out of her hands. Did nothing as he backed her up against a wall.

"Why aren't you fighting me?" he shouted.

"You showed me how much you love me," she shouted back. "Now I'm showing you the same."

Inside his head raged the bloodiest war of his life. He loved this woman. How could he harm her? She meant more to him than anything else in this world. More than victory. More than vengeance. More than freedom. More than a vow or a compulsion. *How could he harm her?*

Then. That moment. He found the strength to step back. He was panting, his nerve endings razed. "This is your chance. If you love me, you'll take me out before my control cracks." Any second... He picked up her sword, tossed the weapon in her direction hilt-first.

She caught it.

As she neared him, he said, "Hurry."

When she lunged at him, she twirled her weapon so that she gripped the hilt and the blade faced away from him. She planned to knock him out. The slave bands *sizzled*, his body moving of its own volition to block the blow.

His heart thudded against his ribs as— No! Compulsion forced him to swipe up two daggers, no longer a matching set since he'd left one at the jewelry store—*Vale...priceless.* He swung, aiming for her throat.

Clink. When she blocked, he moved automatically, swinging his other arm. She realized his intent a little too late. Though she kicked, her strength was no match for his, and the second dagger sank deep in her chest.

An agonized gasp split her lips. Horror nearly felled him as he ripped out the weapon, taking bits of bone and heart with him. Blood gurgled from the corners of her mouth.

No! Hate Ansel. Hate myself! Grunting from exertion, he tried to stop his next actions but...again, he swung his arms. Target: her neck. This time, the daggers would act as scissors, cutting through flesh, muscle and bone. She would die.

Stop! Don't do this!

She feigned left, darted right, but pain and blood loss had slowed her momentum. At least she'd managed to avoid decapitation. This time.

To his surprise—and gratification—she pivoted at the last second to slice a line across his throat. For a moment, he couldn't breathe.

Out for the count?

No. He cursed. His head was still attached to his body.

Stop at nothing. Ansel's words reverberated inside his mind.

Struggling to breathe, he summoned shadows. In seconds, darkness filled the bunker, blinding Vale, while his view remained unobstructed.

He studied her, this woman he so adored—his next victim. She stood, head up, shoulders back, sword raised, legs braced apart. A warrior's stance. His ally until the end, willing to fight for him, even if she had to pay a terrible price.

With a roar, Knox dove on her. They landed on the bed and bounced on the mattress, Vale absorbing the bulk of the impact. Air gusted from her, his heavy weight crushing her. The wound he'd given her gaped open, a river of blood pouring out.

He ripped the sword from her grip and rose to his knees. She whimpered. Did she try to stop him? No. Did she try to flee from him? No again.

She surrendered to him, accepting his inability to defeat the compulsion.

Though she couldn't see, she tendered a sad, watery smile up at him. "It's okay, baby. I understand. If you're going to die later, I'm happy to die now. I'll be waiting for you on the other side. I'm excited to meet Minka. I'll tell her all about the wonderful man you've become. It's okay, baby," she repeated, reaching up to pet his chest and offer comfort. "It's okay. Do it. Do what you must. I love you, and I forgive you. It's okay."

Baby. She'd called him baby once again. He choked back a ragged howl and raised his blood-soaked daggers. His arms shook uncontrollably.

About to end her life...

And she was going to let him do it. Because she couldn't bring herself to hurt him. Because she loved him more than she loved her own life.

She was going to tell his daughter good things.

Wonderful man...not even close.

As Vale peered up at him, love shining in her eyes, he dropped one of the daggers. Only one. *Come on, come on.* The hand with the weapon shook. Sweat ran down his brow in rivulets now. Muscles strained, some on his side, others on Ansel's.

"Help...me," he pleaded, dismissing the shadows. "Knock me out before—"

Between one blink and the next, she swiped up the discarded dagger and rammed the hilt into his temple, once, twice, a third time.

"Harder." The blade inched toward her neck...toward the

pulse hammering with life. A place he'd kissed and licked and wanted to kiss and lick again.

The bones in his shoulder fractured as he resisted. Inching down...

Love her so much.

"Please," he croaked. His breaths grew more labored. So did hers.

If he ended her, he would have to watch her eyes dull and her body go limp.

Another inch.

Another.

Accepting her inability to knock him out, Vale stopped hitting him...and stabbed him in the neck.

The blade exited with a piece of his throat. He welcomed the sting, rejoiced over the burn in his lungs, thrilled as warm blood jetted from the wound...smiled when he sagged forward, his world going dark.

Even as Vale's heart shattered like glass, she got to work, wiggling out from under him. She was soaked with blood, a mix of hers and Knox's.

If they were mortal, they'd already be dead.

"He's going to live, and he's going to live free," she said, giving herself a pep talk. They were superheroes, and superheroes got happy endings.

Plagued by urgency, she rushed around the bunker, performing necessary tasks one at a time, trying not to think or worry— trying to just *do*.

Get the chains. Lock one of his wrists to the foot of the bed so that he couldn't chase her around. Dig her Rifters out of his pocket, just in case. Cut off the remains of his T-shirt. Pick up Gunnar's sword.

She examined the hilt, searching for the indentations he'd mentioned...yes, okay. They were slight, but they were there.

Shaking, she forced Knox's free arm to lift and his fingers to curl around the hilt, the metal resting against his chest as she'd seen in her dream. But just like in the Amazonian cave, the sword remained intact, and Knox continued to bleed. The gaping wound in his throat had begun to close at least. He was healing on his own.

Frick! It was too soon.

Was he resisting the bond to the sword? Did he need to be conscious for it? Had she placed his fingers on the proper indentions?

She readjusted his grip, only to pause. Maybe she should drain him of more blood first? Should she cut off the tattoos, too? Drill holes in his bones, as she'd suggested before? Maybe, maybe not, but she was going to complete every task just to be safe, because she couldn't go through this again.

Hating herself, she set the sword aside and used one of the daggers to flay the tattoos from his flesh. Around his neck, his wrists and ankles. More blood poured from him.

"Lack of blood won't kill him," she told herself. Her hand shook a thousand times worse as she labored, sometimes cutting out too much muscle, or severing an artery or vein. Tears streamed down her cheeks as she rolled him to his side to remove the marks on his spine.

Time for another pep talk. "Only beheading, the removal of his heart or burning him to ash will kill him. He'll recover from anything else."

Twice she lost the battle with nausea and had to step away to vomit, but always she went back, sitting on her haunches, cutting, cutting. When she finished with the marks, she tried to use the daggers to drill into his bones, but ended up causing compound fractures instead.

She posed him with the sword once again. Adjusted the hilt. Readjusting. Readjusting—

Knox's entire body jolted.

Bingo! She fell back, strength beyond her as she watched the metal liquefy and absorb into his skin. He lay there, as still as death, his wounds closing, skin weaving together...the tattoos growing back, too.

A shriek of frustration left her. What had she done wrong? Unless the tattoos had returned simply because they were part of his immortal makeup, and now lacked power? Beneath the cold lash of fear, hope was like a warm fire.

When would he awaken?

As if he'd read her mind and hoped to reassure her, he opened his eyes and bolted upright.

"Knox!"

He turned his head, his gaze finding her. She gasped. His eyes were not blue, but silver, the same shade as the sword.

"Put. Hilt. Back," he commanded, his voice low and raspy as she tasted her beloved honeyed whiskey.

She tossed the hilt in his direction. He caught it, held it against his forehead...the silver cleared from his irises, the melted metal bubbling up from his skin, forming into a sword and hardening.

His arm fell to his side, the weapon tumbling from his grip. Their gazes met once again, and she waited, tense and hopeful...

"The compulsion to obey Ansel," he said, sounding amazed. "It's gone." With a single tug, he busted free of the chains and wrapped his arms around her.

What he didn't do? Try to kill her.

As she sagged against him, she laughed and cried at once. "If I'd known you could break through chains so easily, I wouldn't have bothered with them."

Really? Those were the first words out of her mouth?

"They kept me from you. Nothing keeps me from you." He kissed her neck, her racing pulse. "I'm so sorry, *valina*. I'm so sorry I hurt you."

"I understand, and I'm good." She nestled closer, all but burrowing into him. "And let's not forget I hurt you, too."

"I will be forever grateful that you did. You stopped me from destroying what I treasure most. You…my sun. You warm me, light my path and guide me, and I would rather die a thousand deaths than harm you."

Oh, this man of mine. There was none better. "What will Ansel do when he learns the truth?"

"I don't know. I only know he has no more power over me. I'm free of him." He laughed with unadulterated joy. "Vale, I'm truly free of him!"

Not to be a total downer, but… "Are you bound to the sword, as feared?"

"Let's find out. Hold it, and command me to do something I don't want to do."

Though she hated letting go of him, even for a second, she did it. After picking up the sword, she gave her lips a nervous swipe with her tongue, she said, "Knox, I command you to… smack my butt."

She waited with bated breath. When disappointment flared in his eyes, she knew. Yes, he was bound to the sword.

He lightly smacked her butt.

"Oh, Knox." Stomach sinking, she dropped the sword. "I'm so sorry."

"No, don't be sorry." He gathered her close. "We've done the impossible. I'm free of Ansel, the power of the slave bands nullified. Now, we will guard the sword. No one will take it from us. We will fight this war on our terms while searching for a way to break the weapon's power over me."

"And a way to win the war, the two of us, together, and save Earth," she said, her voice soft now. "If we have to, we'll defeat the High Council, too. We'll earn our happily-ever-after one way or another."

"I'm living my happily-ever-after already," he replied, and she smiled. "In shadow, you are my light."

With their foreheads pressed together, she responded in kind. "In ice, you are my warmth."

"In life and in death, your love guides me home." He kissed her. "In war, you are my prize. In darkness, you are my sun."

She laughed with relish. "Sap!" Then she sighed dreamily. "In this world and any other, you are my forever."

"Eternity with my Vale. Where do I sign?"

Knox relaxed in the warmth of the pool. Vale's back was pressed against the ledge while *his* back was pressed against her chest. Her legs were wrapped around his waist as she ran a cloth over him. Despite the uncertainty of the future, he'd never been happier.

Not only was he free of the vile Ansel, he'd received a pledge of unwavering love and devotion from his woman.

Would they have smooth sailing for the rest of their lives? No, absolutely not. She was still wanted by the Earth police for the things that had happened in Colorado. The All War promised to be more savage than ever; they were fighting a completely different battle now.

Everything had changed.

Earlier Vale had said, "In the words of Gandalf, the battle for Helm's Deep is over. The battle for Middle Earth is about to begin." Knox had understood the gist. They had so much more to do.

Now, the stakes were higher. He had a sword and woman to guard with his life when two other groups of warriors entered the fray.

Maybe the original combatants would band together to take out the newcomers. Maybe each set of combatants would team up with other representatives from their home-realm. Time would tell. Either way, Knox was glad to have a team in place. Vale, Zion and Bane. His allies.

He'd never had true allies before, other soldiers willing to put their lives at risk for him, just as he would put his life at risk for them. To his surprise, a strange, beautiful peace accompanied the knowledge.

Who were these new warriors? What powers did they possess? What weapons did they wield? What was so bad about the representatives of Llura?

And what if the war *could* be stopped? What if the remaining combatants could live here, always, a winner never officially declared? Both Vale and Knox would be saved. The warriors would have to turn their sights to the High Council instead of each other.

Not a bad idea. The High Council had to be dealt with, and soon. Knox would broach the idea to his allies, get their take on the matter. He actually looked forward to it.

Once the All War and High Council were neutralized, he would return to Iviland with Vale at his side and kill Ansel, as planned—as needed. Until then, Knox would console himself with the death of Ansel's son. The prince would be the first to taste death in this new war, for Knox could never allow the greedy bastard a chance to rule.

Now, at least, Knox had time to figure out the best way to achieve each of his goals.

Vale rested her chin on his shoulder. "Your life was a whole lot less complicated before I stumbled upon your frozen body, huh?"

"That is true. My life was also a whole lot less exciting."

"You aren't wrong. But let's be real. Without me, you could have gone farther in the war by now."

"I would have remained a slave to Ansel, dead inside. He never would have kept his word, and I would have been forced to fight in another war, and another, until I died." Knox reached back to comb his damp fingers through her hair and angle her face toward his. "If you think I would change anything that happened, you are sorely mistaken. Adversity brought us together, made us stronger—strong enough to do what needs doing. We wouldn't be ready otherwise."

He kissed her, hard and thoroughly, stealing her breath and destroying rational thought. By the time he lifted his head, they were both panting.

"Winning your hand in marriage," he said, gently tracing a finger along her jaw, "will be the greatest victory of my life."

She grinned at him. "You want to marry me?"

"I want to tie your life to mine in as many ways as possible. I want to be yours, in a way I've never been another's. I want us both to have the family we've always craved."

"Married…a family of my own…yes, yes, a thousand times yes. I accept your proposal, and promise to love, honor and cherish you all the days of my life." She glided her hands down his stomach and wrapped her fingers around his erection, squeezed. "So, do you know anything about earthly honeymoons?"

Air hissed between his teeth. "No."

"Then it will be my pleasure to show you, baby. Hang on and enjoy the ride."

★ ★ ★ ★ ★

*Gena Showalter's thrilling
Gods of War saga continues with
the story of Bane and Nola,
coming soon… Don't miss it!*

List of Combatants,
as dictated by Knox of Iviland
and Vale of Terra

Adonis of Callum. Male, with a multicolored mohawk and symbols shaved into the sides of his head. (Why? What do they mean?) Wields the Horn of Summoning, which is able to raise an army of animals, men and women, living or dead. Allied with Erik.

Ammarie of Evain. Female, comes from a smoke realm. Uses a mystical bow and arrow known as The Bloodthirsty, which shoots with 100 percent accuracy. The arrow must taste blood before it will fall; if the arrow *continues* to taste blood, it will remain active, and has the potential to defeat an entire army.

Bane of Adwaeweth. Male with a beast trapped within. When the creature breaks free of its inner leash, it can level mountains. Comes from a shadow realm; his greatest weakness is light. Weapon is a pair of goggles that allows him to see through any obstacle. Despised by most other realms, like all citizens of Adwaeweth. Has won two other All Wars.

Bold "Bo" of Mörder. Male, from a realm of assassins. Wields a hammer able to shatter every bone in an immortal body with a single strike. Allied with Erik.

Cannon of Dellize. Male, from an ice realm. Wields the Rod of Clima, able to control weather.

Carrick of Infernia. Male, well-known prince from a fire realm who obeys the dictates of no one. Has strange markings tattooed on his face and body. Those markings pulse with magic and create a temporary force field around him and anyone he touches. Owns a dagger capable of turning blood into lava, burning a victim from the inside out.

Celeste of Occisor. Female, from somewhere known as a "flowering" realm. Has the ability to temporarily vanish from sight, becoming intangible, and wields a sword that leaks poison capable of nullifying innate abilities. Also produces a seduction pheromone. Has won a single All War.

Colt of Orfet. Male, with a ring that contains hundreds of tiny bots. Those bots can burrow under a person's skin and shred their organs; they also act as trackers and spies.

Domino "Dom" of Rhagan. Male, from a fire realm. Has a metal shield able to surround him completely; it can appear in a blink and vanish just as quickly or remain in place for hours, and it is the only thing capable of withstanding Zion's metal gloves and Ronan's sword.

Emberelle of Loandria. Female. Has a metal band that drapes over her forehead and allows her to read the minds of anyone around her.

Erik of Terra. Male, former mortal viking. Acquired the Rod of Clima. Claims to desire peace with the combatants. Has built a massive arsenal.

Gunnar of Trodaire. Male, able to move objects with his mind. Possesses a healing sword. Lover of Celeste.

Halo of Forêt. Male, with mechanical wings that allow him to fly. Each wing resembles a raven and has the ability to detach and fly on their own. He can walk through walls.

Hunter of Klioway. Male. Has a small, thin wooden wand—capable of remaking the landscape?

Jagger of Leiddiad. Male with fangs that liken him to a vampire. Owns a revolver able to mystically reload.

Kellen of Villám. Male. Has a sickle with unknown power.

Knox of Iviland. Has won four All Wars, and is about to win his fifth.

Legend of Honoria. Male, with a matching set of daggers. Hooks at the ends of the blades, brass knuckles for handles.

Lennox of Winslet. Male with wrist cuffs that may or may not have the power to reverse time.

Luca of Graeland. Male, with a long-range rifle—able to shoot at great distances.

Major of Etheran. Male, with a spyglass that can glimpse into the lives of others, wherever they are.

Malaki of Highgard. Male. Wears armor with hidden spikes.

Orion of Sieg. Male, from a swamp realm. Wields motorized axes. Can create tar pits.

Petra of Etalind. Female, from a heavily treed mountain realm.

Can make barbicans grow in any location. Allies with Ronan of Soloria. Are the two lovers?

Pike of La Fer. Male. Sometimes when he blinks, a white film settles over his eyes. What the film does—currently unknown. Wields a staff known as the Soul Harvest. Must learn more about it.

Raine of Baptiste. Male, with the ability to turn into mist. Wields a sword with unknown abilities.

Ranger of Jetha. Male, from an air kingdom. Can create fireballs with his hands. Weapon—a pair of combat boots with small wings on the heels, giving him the ability to fly. Loyal to Celeste.

Ronan of Soloria. Male, from a desert realm. Wields the Sword of Light, a weapon capable of temporarily blinding an opponent.

Rush of Nolita. Male, from a swamp realm. Has a crossbow capable of shooting three arrows at once, in three different directions.

Ryder of Belusova. Male, from a cavernous realm. Has a device that allows him to be in two places at once, fighting up close *and* at a distance.

Saxon of Lassistan. Male, able to read minds. Wields a staff with unknown power.

Shiloh of Asnanthaleigh. Male, from a heavily forested realm. Has eye lenses that allow him to see through anything, anytime. Good with swords and daggers. Avoids battle if there are innocents nearby.

Slade of Undlan. Male, from an underwater realm. Has a trident that creates floods of water and causes tsunamis. Can also cause water to surge up from the ground.

Svaney of Frostland. Female, from an ice realm. Can create and throw ice daggers. Has a crown that allows her to see the past, present and future of anyone nearby, and somehow morphs into a crystal skull. Why the change?

Thorn of D'Elia. Male with scars on his face. Wields a glowing whip that can electrocute an opponent.

Union of Kerris. Male, with the ability to manipulate reality, casting illusions for short bursts of time. Has a belt that causes the wearer's strength to double. Having missed an assembly, he is disqualified—unless he was killed before the assembly. If so, who did the deed?

Vale of Terra. Gorgeous female, with the ability to absorb the memories and intrinsic powers of her victims, though she cannot activate their weapons, like everyone else. She is not to be harmed, ever. (And she's probably definitely the coolest person ever to live. PS: SHE is the next All War winner, thank you very much.)

Valor of Liisi. Male, with a mystic sword. Wounds caused by this sword cannot heal. Also, the sword is able to communicate with its user.

Wilder of Titanious. Male, with the Mind Scrambler—a scepter with the power to render both immortals and mortals temporarily insane.

Xander of Aouette. Male. Injuries caused by his sword take longer to heal.

Zion of Tavery. Male, from an aggressive race, where warriors are always foaming-at-the-mouth eager for battle, and yet he has an aversion to harming females. Has won three All Wars. Wears metal gloves able to punch through anything. Embedded in his skin are jewels set in specific patterns—why?

Warning—spoilers ahead!

103rd All War Kill Tally.

Bane.
Malaki of Highgard.
Raine of Baptiste.
Valor of Liisi.

Emberelle.
Lennox of Winslet.

Erik.
Cannon of Dellize.

Knox.
Gunnar of Trodaire.
Jagger of Leiddiad.
Legend of Honoria.
Rush of Nolita.
Shiloh of Asnanthaleigh.
Xander of Aouette.

Petra.
Luca of Graeland.

Ronan.
Major of Etheran.
Saxon of Lassistan.

Ryder.
Orion of Sieg.

Shiloh.
Ammarie of Evain.

Vale.
Celeste of Occisor.
Ranger of Jetha.

Zion.
Colt of Orfet.
Hunter of Klioway.
Kellen of Villám.
Wilder of Titanious.

Unknown.
Union of Kerris.